AMERICAN SAINT

BY SEAN GANDERT

American Saint
Lost in Arcadia

AMERICAN SAINT

SEAN GANDERT

What is the difference between the magical, the miraculous, and the maniacal?

In this visionary novel framed as a hagiography, the ruminative, subjective memories of Gabriel's witnesses— spiritual, familial, romantic, and political—converge to make sense of the man's confounding works and message. As they do, a surprising portrait develops . . . not only of the deepening mystery of Gabriel Romero himself but also of a country in conflict and the faith it takes to fight the suspicion and fear that divide us.

"What I'm going to tell you is a love story, because those are the only stories worth telling. What I'm going to tell you is also a tragedy, because the story is true. Believe me, if I could tell you anything else, if I had the heart to change the ending or even some of the details along the way, then I would. But I'm tired now, and those parts of the past that I used to lie about, even to Gabriel, even to myself, I don't have the energy to twist anymore. I know who I am and what I've done, and all that matters to me now is that the story is told right."

American Saint
August 20, 2019 | Literary Fiction | 47North
Hardcover | $24.95 | ISBN 978-1542044059
Kindle eBook | $4.99 | ASIN B072BYZJDR

PRAISE FOR SEAN GANDERT'S *LOST IN ARCADIA*

"*Lost in Arcadia* is such a rich, immersive experience, the virtual reality of the novel used to great effect. At its heart this is a tender family drama but it's wrapped in a shell of computer simulations, online addiction, and societal collapse. Sean Gandert plays on the line between these poles with a sure hand. This is the debut of an author to watch."

—Victor LaValle, author of *The Changeling*

"*Lost in Arcadia* is a fascinating and ambitious first novel by a very talented writer. Its fast-moving narrative centers around the father, Juan Diego, who creates a game that compensates players according to the treasures they find and skill levels they achieve. When Juan Diego disappears, his family begins to disintegrate. *Lost in Arcadia* suggests that our technology hastens the breakdown of relationships and the fabric of society. This important and revealing theme makes the novel an indispensable read ... By 2037 will we be masters of cyber-technology, or will we remain lost in Arcadia?"

—Rudolfo Anaya, author of *Bless Me, Ultima*

"This novel is like if *Sword Art Online* and *Stranger Things* had a child, just so it could tell you a story about the future. This brilliant novel is about how what we love about games can become what we fear about the world, without our noticing, until it is done. Prescient, funny, smart, a story to disappear into and come out the other side."

—Alexander Chee, author of *The Queen of the Night*

"Sean Gandert has written an impressive first novel. It has a rare combination of vision and heart—not to mention a funny, scary dystopia that is both impressively imagined and dismayingly plausible."

—Tom Bissell, author of *Extra Lives: Why Video Games Matter*

"Sean Gandert's new book is a must read, a gotta read book, a go out and buy the damn thing. Once you buy it, share it, carry it in your backpack, and tell your friends about it, you're not going to get this kind of book in school, this is way ahead of school books, it dips into real life, it dives into the underworld of our feelings and holds you there, until you discover the pearls."

—Jimmy Santiago Baca, author of *A Place to Stand*

"*Lost in Arcadia* is futuristic in its vision but wonderfully old-fashioned in its sprawling, complex plot and its fundamental commitment to character. This is a novel of real scope and ambition."

—Chris Bachelder, author of *The Throwback Special* (National Book Award finalist)

AMERICAN SAINT

A Hagiography

SEAN GANDERT

Text copyright © 2019 by Sean Gandert

Published by 47North, Seattle

www.apub.com

Amazon, the Amazon logo, and 47North are trademarks of Amazon.com, Inc., or its affiliates.

ISBN-13: 9781542044059 (hardcover)
ISBN-10: 1542044057 (hardcover)

ISBN-13: 9781542048965 (paperback)
ISBN-10: 1542048966 (paperback)

Cover design by Isaac Tobin

Printed in the United States of America

First edition

For José and Lillian

HAGIOGRAPHY

noun
ha·gi·og·ra·phy | \ ha-gē-ä-grə-fē
Definition of hagiography:

1.   : the biography of a saint
2.   : a pejorative term, used to describe a biography that stretches the truth to idealize its subject

ISABEL ROMERO

I don't care what you heard, my mother was not a witch. She was a curandera, a healer and a mystic, but sometimes people misunderstand what that means. Regardless, she was definitely not a bruja. A curandera and a bruja are like day and night, life and death. Only idiots think that all magic is the same—Jesucristo was a healer too, after all. Let me ask you this: Would a witch trudge to church every week of her life, struggling through the snow to make it to communion, or quiz her daughter on passages from the Bible? Would a witch die with her old brass and turquoise rosary clutched in her hand, its crucifix smoothed down from years of devotion? She kept the faith—of that there can be no doubt.

Yes, my mother was a healer, performed miracles. Faith and magic are not incompatible, you know. That's just how Protestants like to pretend the world works, and I couldn't care less what one of them thinks about her anyhow.

Healing wasn't how she paid the bills—that was by doing laundry at Presbyterian Hospital, a job she held from before I was born until the day she died, pero it was what everyone in the neighborhood knew her for. Curanderismo filled our lives and our house. I grew up in a brown adobe square of a building, two bedrooms and a combination kitchen–living room overflowing with clutter. Velas on every surface, some burning and some burned out, and some only to be burned on the most sacred occasions. Paintings of santos on every wall, carvings of santos on every flat surface. Bundles of dry, brittle herbs and vegetables hanging from the house's vigas. Yerba buena tea and powders ground from her metate y mano on the counter, prayer books and a black-and-white television always murmuring in the living room. The sound of chickens in the backyard coop, the smell of tortillas and beans mixing with incense in every room of the house. This was where I grew up.

Even though it was packed with the evidence of Mamá's calling, our house was just as noteworthy for what it lacked. There was no heating or cooling system aside from the fireplace and windows. There was no man in the house. Even our cats were mujeres, and my male friends made any excuse they could think of to avoid entering the front door, its borders painted turquoise to ward off evil spirits. Jesucristo and some of the santos were male, but they were already dead, and Mamá always preferred la Virgen anyhow. More than anything else, though, the house was missing one key element: money.

This never seemed to bother Mamá. She didn't have to be seen at school wearing home-sewn dresses while all the other girls wore Jordache jeans and GUESS blouses. Mamá wouldn't pay for me to own jewelry or makeup. Even during senior year, I walked to school because she wouldn't buy me a car. And at home it was the same foods, huevos and beans and pans full of green chile enchiladas made to last an entire week. But really it was the clothing that bothered me the most, the way you could tell just from looking at me that I got my lunches free from the district. Being poor is bad enough, pero having everyone else *know* you're poor? That might as well be hell.

Even though it put me in debt, I moved into the dorms for college. I wanted to blend in, you know. I took out extra loans and went over to Thrift Town and purchased a whole new wardrobe. I bleached and dyed my hair while everyone else was at orientation, going punk not because I liked the music or even the look but because it was cheaper than anything else—wearing safety pins for earrings meant I was "edgy" and wearing the same ripped clothes every day meant I was "making a statement." Mamá hated it, but by then that only made me happier. During the first week of school, I made up for all the rebellion I'd missed earlier in life, ditching classes, getting drunk with my roommate Bella, and sleeping with men just because I could.

I didn't completely transform during college or forget where I came from, even though most of the time I wanted to. Growing up, I hated going to San Ignacio with Mamá every Sunday, but I still attended Mass during college, spiked hair and all. I prayed to la Virgen y los santos for everything from grades to boys. I don't know what I really believed back then, maybe none of it, maybe all of it, but the traditions weren't easy to drop.

During sophomore year, I was taking one of those large history lectures with Bella. We liked to get there early because the air conditioners were all in the front of the hall and the walls at the back got so hot from the sun that you'd have to sweat through the whole hour. We'd sit there and watch the other students pile in, whispering about anyone who looked particularly funny or weird or, most important, cute.

This was how we spent a lot of our time together, and because we fundamentally disagreed about what made a guy attractive, we could argue at length. Bella was into machismo. The men she dated had wifebeaters and tattoos beneath their leather jackets. They were in a band or in a gang or on parole. Her relationships never lasted long, because as sexy as she thought those guys were, she didn't like their violence and mood swings. She was a chica who wanted to tame her man, and we bonded over her series of failures. She always needed a shoulder to cry on until she found her next crush, and I was more than willing to supply that shoulder so long as she kept me updated on all the juicy details.

No lie, I barely cared what they looked like, at least in the traditional sense. Or what they did for fun, what they liked to talk about, whether they were más o menos listos, any of that crap. I knew that the one way to get out of Martineztown for good was to find a mancon mucha plata, and at UNM those weren't as easy to come by as you might think. A lot of guys liked to act preppy, popping the collars of their polo shirts and walking to class as if they owned the place, then driving back home in a beat-up Camaro, just like the boys I grew up with. So I scouted for signs of real wealth. Expensive watches were key, but also haircuts and even backpacks. It was easy to know what clothes to buy, pero there was a certain smugness to the truly wealthy, a way they seemed to colonize the area around them, that I learned to pick up on.

Early in the semester, I noticed a boy in a bright-red Lacoste shirt and khaki pants strolling down the stairs. A girl was at his side, a Barbie clone whose expression looked as molded as the doll's. Two friends accompanied them, seemingly tethered to him by invisible strings. The light glinted off his gold Rolex and onto his carefully tousled bangs, and I knew what I wanted.

I nudged Bella.

"I see him," she said. "But you know his girl's right there."

"Not now," I said. "Just wait." I didn't have a plan then, but I've always been patient, and I knew something would come to me.

Two days later, at the next history lecture, we sat closer to him. And even closer the one after that. Bella seemed amused, and since this was the first guy I'd seriously gone after since losing interest in meaningless sex early freshman year, she did everything she could to encourage my infatuation. I tried to explain to her that it wasn't an infatuation, it was a matter of appraising an investment, but she just laughed at me.

I tried wearing low-cut shirts and tighter jeans. I dropped the whole punk thing and dyed my hair back to black, brushed it sleek and shiny. I borrowed Bella's perfume and makeup, tried to catch his eye all through class and bump into him afterward. Nothing worked. He just sat there listening through the world's longest and most boring lectures, his arm around a different but identical bimbo every couple weeks. As we neared the end of the semester and I still didn't even know his name, I became desperate.

Like I said, Mamá was not a witch. She didn't use magic for evil, would never condone it, pero that doesn't mean she didn't cast spells or brew potions. And growing up the only daughter of a curandera, you learn things, even if you're not particularly interested. Mamá had occasional apprentices she trained, and I simply watched and learned. Her remedios were a part of our day-to-day life. We didn't have Neosporin for infections, we had ailé. Oshá for flus and chalahuite for an upset stomach, mariola for lung and liver problems and altamisa de la sierra for high blood pressure. But my mom wasn't just una yerbera, era una sobadora y una partera and, most importantly, una espiritualista.

One of Mamá's clients had been a young wife whose husband was already cheating. Mamá advised her to leave him. She was young and beautiful, you know, with no children to tie her down. Why stay with such a man when she could find ten more in a day who would treat her como una princesa? This woman, though, she cried and tried to explain that despite his infidelity, she still loved him. So Mamá made her a potion and told her to pray the rosary every day, and a month later, when she came by the house to thank Mamá for her services, the woman explained that her husband had become a new man. He'd stopped sleeping around, was devoted to her, and she felt it was all because of Mamá's potion.

Mamá said it was nothing. She was careful to never promise that her remedios would work, said that even los santos knew that the only one who could predict these things, could control whether they worked or not, was Dios himself ... or maybe la Virgen.

So as the end of the semester approached, I snuck into my mother's backyard while she was working at the hospital. There I found her prized datura in full bloom, a white flower with hints of lavender deep in its petals. I carefully dug around it, then pulled off the end of one of its roots. I mixed this with a pinch of chile powder, some cornmeal, a half cup of milk, some mashed worms, and finally—and most importantly—a drop of my own urine. I stirred this mixture, clockwise, over the stove for half an hour while saying prayers to Santa Therese de Lisieux, Santa Teresa Urrea, San Nicholas, San Valentine, and every other remotely relevant santo I could think of. I knew that datura could be poisonous, but it was also the most powerful herb Mamá had, and I was using only a tiny cut of its root, not a seed or petal.

The next day before class, I told Bella about the love potion. I just needed to find a way to slip it into the Coke he always brought with him. Even a drop of it would be enough. Bella laughed at me, but I could tell she was a bit spooked. And excited.

I sat next to him, and all through class, I couldn't concentrate. My heart pounded, not because of his presence— boys never made me nervous—pero ... because I'd never tried making this potion on my own before. What if he caught me? What if even that small bit of datura proved poisonous? What if I'd said the wrong prayers?

The professor paced to the side of the classroom, and my target's gaze followed him. I leaned over the table and squeezed an eyedropper of my mixture into his soda. A minute later, I watched him take a big swallow. Nothing happened, and relief washed over me. The potion was puro mentira, like all Mamá's beliefs. Of course it was.

Class ended, and I felt depressed. As we were leaving the auditorium, Bella asked if I'd done it, and I said no, because I didn't want her to find out that it hadn't worked. That I was a failure, a sap who thought some psychosomatic bullshit was real. I was so distracted that I stumbled on the stairs, dropping my textbooks and falling.

"¡Maldita sea!" I said—my apologies for the cursing— my knees scraped and stinging. I sat there for a few seconds, not caring that I was holding up everyone behind me.

Then, a voice I recognized asked, "Are you ok?" He lifted me up, then picked my books off the ground.

"I'm fine," I said.

"I'm John," he said. He was staring straight at me, like we were the only ones in the room, the city, the universe. He stared at me so hard, and with such desire, I barely caught what he said.

"Sorry about what happened there. That looks real bad." He pointed at my knee, and I was so surprised I didn't know what to say, so I just kind of grunted.

"Hey, so would you like to get coffee?" he asked.

JOSHUA WHITEHURST

What I'm going to tell you is a love story, because those are the only stories worth telling. What I'm going to tell you is also a tragedy, because the story is true. Believe me, if I could tell you anything else, if I had the heart to change the ending or even some of the details along the way, then I would. But I'm tired now, and those parts of the past that I used to lie about, even to Gabriel, even to myself, I don't have the energy to twist anymore. I know who I am and what I've done, and all that matters to me now is that the story is told right.

I wouldn't meet Gabriel until college, but I need to go back further than that if you're going to understand me. The best way I can think of to explain how things were is with our old photo albums. Picture this: a mother and father. Twenty-four and twenty-six, respectively, both with golden-blond hair, wide smiles showing straight teeth. One pair of blue eyes and one of brown, but both with the same happy glint. Their faces look tired, especially hers, but nestled between them is a perfect baby boy, with wisps of the same hair and a hint of the same smile, though with green eyes from parts unknown. This is the earliest photograph of me, taken by a nurse sometime after I was born. An almost too-happy couple, the sweat on their faces and circles under their eyes the only things not quite advertisement perfect.

The next photograph: me again, but now standing at six or so years old. Beside me my younger sister, Grace, sunlight shining on our two heads. I'm wearing an all-white suit with a cornflower-blue shirt. Grace wears a matching dress and headband, her hair whipping behind us in the wind. We're posed directly in front of a two-story, all-white house with a pitched roof—the only one in the neighborhood, though you couldn't tell from the photo. Behind us, a green lawn and a red door that pops against our clothing. Completing this world of straight lines and symmetry, we stare directly at the camera lens. Behind it, my mother is taking our picture while we wait for my dad to come out of the house so we can head to my aunt Debby's wedding. From the look of things, you'd think we lived in the Midwest in the fifties and not a desert in the nineties, but all that is outside the frame, and my mother was careful to keep us tightly inside its four perfect edges.

One last image for you: thirty kids sit in three rows in front of a blank gray background, and a black felt sign with slotted letters says Mrs. Romo's 4th-5th grade class at Double Eagle Elementary School. I'm seated in the second row, third to the right. I'm older now, though still a kid. Prepubescent, and my hair is combed and held down with gel so it looks solid and smooth like a helmet. Most of us are white, though there are a few light-skinned students in the third and first rows who look like they might be Hispanic. Back then I didn't really think about those things, so I couldn't tell you whether they were. It's the last photo we have where I'm smiling that same smile as in the first two, but if you look for more than a second, you'll probably notice that I'm putting bunny ears behind the head of the boy next to me. I can still name maybe half these students if I tried, but the only one who really matters is Samuel Stiles, the boy with the bunny ears and the brown collared shirt, a cautious look on his face halfway between excited and afraid.

Sam was not my best friend at the end of elementary school or in middle school—a designation that seemed to have the utmost importance back then—but we were part of the same group of guys from Double Eagle who hung out before school, during lunch, and whenever we could meet up after the final bell rang. By seventh grade, these groups were practically codified, who the skaters were or the cholos or the drama geeks. My group's thing was that we were all from well-off families and played in either the school orchestra or the band.

Right before winter break there was the big holiday concert, where all the school's music groups played together in one squeaky, warbly display of uneven tuning in the gym. Sound bounced off the high roof and cinder-block walls in a way that made it difficult to make out what songs even the advanced groups were playing, let alone their time signatures, but it was still a big event that everyone's parents attended in suits and jewelry as if we were in Carnegie Hall. It was a gala, decorated with paper cutouts and disjointed lighting, reserved seats and social hierarchies. I didn't give a crap about any of it, except that afterward all my friends, Sam included, would be staying over at my house for a sleepover.

We lived in that same house I asked you to picture earlier, well kept by weekly visits from a lawn service and maid. Both my parents worked full-time and didn't have the energy for that sort of thing, but they still knew what they liked: clean, airy spaces, white paint that showed the slightest smudge, and toys placed neatly into their boxes at the end of every day. While I'd been to many sleepovers, this was the first time I was allowed to have anyone over at our house, to interrupt that quiet and sanitary haven with my friends' bombastic energy for more than a few hours. Mom and Dad didn't mind entertaining adult guests, but they disliked any children who weren't their own. Sam and the three other boys who were staying over that night had all been vetted. My mom knew them, knew their parents, their GPAs. They were all "nice boys" and gave her no reason to suspect they would trash the house.

I went to so many sleepovers when I was young, from elementary school on through high school, that they mesh together in my brain, a thousand and one nights of staying up until sunrise, of worn pajamas and crumb-scattered rugs and acquaintances sharing their deepest, most intimate selves until the morning, when all would be forgotten. I couldn't tell you what video games we spent the evening playing, or what we ate, or even precisely who was there. But that's because none of that really matters. What does is what happened after the lights went out.

Outside, snow coated the ground like a down comforter. Inside, the heater roared. Everyone except me had lined up their sleeping bags in my bedroom so that their heads were as close together as the room's furniture and geometry allowed. This made it easier to whisper, even though our discussions would inevitably rise in volume as the evening continued. We lay there in the dark, waiting the requisite dozen or so minutes that it would take to feel safe, each of us feigning sleep in case my parents checked on us. Listening for the telltale signs of their door closing, and soon afterward, the toilet flushing, signaling they were down for the evening.

Metallic clangs from the overhead vents interrupted our ritual. This continued for several minutes, and we could hear my dad stomping around, yelling something rendered unintelligible by the door's muffling. Hot air stopped blowing altogether, and five minutes later I heard a light knocking.

"Guys, sorry to wake you," said my mom, cracking open the door. I remember feeling embarrassed that she was wearing an ill-fitting white bathrobe atop her oversize pajamas, her hair up in rollers. "But the heater's gone out for the night, so it might get cold. Josh, if you want to show everyone where the linen cabinet is, so they can get blankets out, that would be fine."

I thanked her but waited until she was gone before I asked whether anyone wanted to take her up on this. Although it was still toasty, we pulled a pile of blankets from the closet, but since my sister and parents had apparently already grabbed what they could, there were only four older and frankly uglier blankets for us to choose from. Sam said it was fine, he didn't need one, so we made do and marched back to my bedroom.

The night took its usual turn as we talked about girls, games, classes. Drinking, drugs, rumors that Marcia the piccolo player had gotten pregnant. Worries about death, the afterlife, and whether any of that even mattered. Completely exhausted, and with only the moonlight seeping through the shades keeping the room from complete darkness, we could say anything without fear. There was laughter and ridicule, sure, but the normal rules about what was up for discussion disappeared into this strange liminal space. Eventually we drifted off to sleep, not because we had to but because of a consensus that there was nothing else to be said.

At this point, it still seemed like a normal sleepover. But then I woke up to a hand against my shoulder. The room was still dark, the only sound someone snoring lightly. I opened my eyes, and standing above me, shivering, was Sam. He wore a pair of plaid boxers that did little to hide a long, scrawny body that had suddenly grown since the beginning of the semester. He looked frightened, unsure. Confused, even. He looked beautiful.

"I'm cold," he said in a whisper so light I might have imagined it. "Can I...?" He pointed at my bed, and it took me a moment to respond. Was he really asking for this? I nodded and did my best to remain impassive.

Sam slipped beneath the covers and lay behind me. I didn't know why he was doing any of this and began sweating with worry about what might happen if someone else in the room woke up and looked over. I wanted him to leave, to disappear altogether, but also for him to stay and wrap his arms around me. He did neither, but his left arm rested on my side, and I could feel his warm breath brushing past my ear. If I could have turned around and kissed him, I would've, but I thought any slight provocation might ruin this, either sending him back to his bed or disrupting the silence enough to wake our friends. So I did nothing.

As we lay there perfectly still, time seemed to stop. He smelled sour and almost smoky at the same time, and because I couldn't turn around to look at him, that's my main memory of that evening. His smell enveloped me, overwhelmed me, and I wanted to become part of it, to take a swim in a pond filled with that curious perfume. I've never found a man since who smelled quite the same as Sam did that evening, though Lord knows I've tried.

I don't recall falling asleep again, but I remember waking up in a panic. Beams of light flooded from the borders of the shades, and I could see my friends still asleep in roughly the same positions as before, with one exception—Sam was on the floor again, as if he'd never left his sleeping bag.

The rest of the morning played out as usual. So did the following day, then the following week at school. Whenever I tried to make even a veiled reference to that evening, when I knew we were alone, Sam ignored me. Gaslighted me. Pretended it had never happened. I got so frustrated that I nearly asked him about it directly, point-blank ... but I could never get up the guts.

Eventually Sam ignored me entirely, left the school band, and took up shop. Then he went to high school at the Academy instead of La Cueva like the rest of us, at least that's what I heard, and I never saw him again. I had many more sleepovers after that, and in each one I waited for another Sam to join me, planned and hoped and prayed that someone else might lay with me while the soft moonlight caressed our heads. Rest his hand on my side without squeezing, without moving further than I was comfortable with, all the way until dawn. Smell sour and smoky in just the right combination. But it never happened.

ISABEL ROMERO

The rules for being a good girlfriend are simple. Laugh at his jokes. Smile at his friends. Agree with his opinions on politics, sports, the economy. Don't ask questions when he shows up late or cancels altogether to hang con sus pinche cabrones. Have sex regularly but only on your terms and not all the time—you need to keep him wanting more. I could go on, but the most important thing to remember is that so long as you keep telling him he's right, even when he's dead wrong, he will stay with you. That's how you become the girl of his dreams.

There are men out there looking for something more from a woman, I'm sure of it. A friend. A soul mate. But I'm also pretty sure that those men aren't rich and white. When the disciples didn't believe him, Jesucristo himself had to repeat how difficult it was for a rich man to get into heaven. And you know that's coming from a guy who was all about forgiveness.

I was with John for less than two years, but I still remember it well, the same way that Broadway actors remember their lines long after their show's closed. No one could play the role of his girlfriend better than I could, no matter how much the understudies tried to push their way onstage. It took me time to learn my lines, weeks where I misread the cues about when he wanted me to agree and when he wanted me to stay silent. There were rough patches and icy glares when I got his favorite sports teams wrong, and the contortions required to say something positive about Ronald Reagan were like a graduate-level exam on doublethink, but eventually all this became natural. And when it did, I became a star.

I wasn't just his girlfriend—I was the platonic ideal of a girlfriend, and with me on his arm, we lit up every party we attended, every Lobos game we suffered through in the snow. It wasn't all bad either. I liked being admired, you know, wearing beautiful clothes and jewelry, being seen on the arm of a man other women blushed to pass by. Don't think I wasn't aware it was shallow, but the world is, at its heart, shallow. Pretending that material rewards aren't rewards is beyond stupid, and they can make you happy—anyone who says otherwise has never been poor. And at heart, it was a successful relationship, a mutually beneficial exchange. He got the novia he wanted, and in return I received money, security, and status. I don't know whether he knew the rules of the game we were playing, but I certainly did.

At the end of the following year, John proposed to me. Bella pleaded with me to stay in college, finish my degree, but I left anyhow. Didn't have the heart to tell her I'd never even declared a major or that all my grades were garbage. Everyone went to college for the same reason, to improve themselves, but I was one of the few people there who was honest about what it actually took to achieve that. Once my goals there had been met, there was no reason to waste my time being scolded by TAs for missing class.

I moved out of the dorms and into a small house with John near UNM. He paid for it. I worked a little bit at a bar downtown, but John was jealous and didn't like me "being leered at," so he began paying me an allowance to stay home instead. Not long afterward, I feigned surprise when all the marriage proposal clichés unveiled themselves like a straight-to-video rom-com: him on one knee in a restaurant, a string quartet playing while he slipped a huge diamond ring on my finger, the room applauding as the waiter popped a bottle of champagne. I even cried real tears—everything was as grand and elegant as I could have hoped.

A week before the wedding, Mamá asked me to come by for dinner and told me not to go through with it. "I don't see what you like about that man," she said. She'd always hated John. From the first time he met her, he couldn't help but smirk at her messy bun, flare his nostrils at the stink of incense forever caught in her clothing. I couldn't blame her.

"There's nothing to see," I told her. "He doesn't mean anything."

"Entonces, ¿por qué casarse con él?"

"I want to get out of this," I said, gesturing toward her old, decaying house. Pero I didn't mean only that—I also meant the cracked Martineztown streets that surrounded it, maybe even the city. "This might be enough for you, but that's because you're perfectly fine with your bullshit religion and your even sillier superstitions." What can I say—I was young and angry.

"Out! ¡Fuera!" she yelled, and I left, intending to never see that house again.

Mamá showed up at the wedding, and we pretended none of that had happened. I wore a designer bridal gown, new shoes, and a veil that swept out six feet behind me. We held our reception on the rooftop of one of the tallest

buildings in Albuquerque, and the party lasted until the
sun peeked over the Sandias. When John carried me over
the threshold of our hotel suite, tossed me onto our large
bed, and said he wanted to—pardon the vulgarity, he was
a vulgar man—fuck me like he'd never fucked anyone
before, I may have truly loved him, if only for a moment.

Maybe I believed in the magic of the potion. Maybe
I believed that my particular husband wasn't going to be
the pendejo that everyone else's was. I was naive. Less
than a month passed between that rapturous evening and
when he first returned home after a night out "with his
friends" with some other woman's perfume on his neck.
You couldn't even say that the honeymoon was over,
because we hadn't gone on ours yet—a planned trip to
Paris and Rome to see the sights and taste all the delicious
food. We never would.

I could have told him to eff off. Could have punched
him en sus huevos and tried to kick his pinche culo to
the curb. But that would have been the end of it, and I
would have been back where I started. He had the money,
and who was I? Just some poor Chicana he'd met in
college—what's worse, some poor Chicana he'd already
lost interest in. I told him to shower and made us both
eggs for breakfast. I pretended nothing had happened,
that he was my sweetheart, my true love … then I went
to Mamá and asked her to help me conceive.

Perhaps because of all the drama the last time we'd
spoken more than a few words to each other, Mamá asked
no questions. She made me drink a bunch of strange con-
coctions, gave me a massage, and told me she was excited
about my wish for a child. I didn't tell her why I wanted
one, and she didn't ask. Two months later, I confirmed
I was pregnant, and soon we learned he would be a boy.

We chose the name Gabriel, because I'd taken to calling him our little angel.

You wonder, I can tell, what I thought this little one would do for me? The fact is, I did want a child, no lie. However, I admit that I hadn't fully thought things through. I knew what the prenup meant when I signed it, and I also knew what his rich white lawyers would do if I tried to fight it. But what if a child were involved? I realize it wasn't completely rational, but I was angry and searching for any direction forward that didn't involve losing the life I'd built. ¿Tonta? Perhaps. Pero maybe I had a bit of hope that the child could change things. Maybe I thought that the problem wasn't my cheating husband's wandering eyes but that we didn't love each other. Gabriel might fix that, or at least make living through a loveless marriage worth it.

I told John I was pregnant, and I could see something change in his eyes. He didn't dote on me, that was never our relationship, but he was kinder. He stayed in more frequently, or at least came home around midnight. He tried cooking dinner for us a few times before ultimately deciding it was easier to grab takeout or order pizza, and he decluttered some of his junk around the house, though real cleaning was still left to me. For a little while, I thought we could make it work, you know?

But then, for no reason that I could pick up on, it ended. I was six months pregnant and at that stage where you ache so much that you start fantasizing about somehow just floating wherever you needed to go. It was early morning, he'd been out all night, and I was exhausted and couldn't hold myself back. I said something snippy, something maybe slightly over the line, though probably I just said something like, "Why were you out so late?" I don't remember. I could have said that he should shut his maldita boca and die, and it wouldn't've mattered. Whatever I said, it was just words, while he chose to speak with action.

I don't remember it well, probably because he went for my head first, hitting it and then slamming it against the wall. He screamed that I did not tell him what to do, that I was not his boss, or his mom, or his anything. This went on, for how long I don't know. It seemed endless. I put up my arms, and he hit them too, repeatedly, and as I started to run, he pulled me down so that my knees smashed into the wooden floor. He dragged me across the room, and I curled into a ball as he kicked me. All I can recall from that moment is the fear, a great wall of fear so vast and dark and overwhelming that it was all I could see.

When he stopped, I lay there on the ground, crying. I heard him slam the bedroom door behind him, and through the pain all I could think was that he wasn't even drunk, at least not that drunk. During the whole beating, he'd been careful to avoid my stomach, to destroy my body without injuring Gabriel's—as if Gabriel weren't a part of me and I him, and my pain his, and my fear all I could imagine him seeing, even with undeveloped eyes.

Things changed. I was John's wife but no longer su esposa. Una esposa es una compañera, y su esposo su compañero. But a wife is chattel, something you trade for, make deals for, the other party to a legally binding state document, the additional name on the tax form. Being a wife was that part of the prenup that said there were no circumstances where I could leave John and still offer Gabriel the lifestyle he deserved—at least, none that meant I'd stay a part of it too.

* * *

Let me say it again, my mother was not a witch. But she was a specialist in removing curses and had some knowledge of brujería, though she was more of una sanadora espiritual. For some reason, many curanderas were suspicious of her skill removing una maldición, so Mamá was not as popular as other curanderas from the area, had to spend her days doing laundry at the hospital when she should've been upstairs performing the healings that even los médicos, with all their fancy degrees and expensive machines, couldn't manage. No one removed el mal de ojo like she did or had a better understanding of how to banish un demonio who'd possessed a house. But to break black magic, you have to know its secrets.

I watched my mother destroy maldiciones my whole childhood. We didn't have any money to pay for a babysitter, so I'd tow along with her. I saw the methodology, knew which curses were the strongest and deadliest.

I'm not going to tell you the specifics of how you make the clay. I hope that will die with me, be lost and forgotten for good. You mold it into a little figure, a model, an effigy. You must shape it with your own two hands, and although it will be too small and crude to carve any details, you'll still be able to conjure your victim's face on it. The link between the figure and your victim—if you've made it right, said the correct words, and heated the clay in a fire at midnight—will be visible. You're dabbling in the Lord's craft, and as Isaiah said, "We are the clay, and You our potter; And all of us are the work of Your hand." Now the Lord's clay will be in your hand, and even if they're as small as mine, you can close your fist around the figure without difficulty.

None of this is on the police report, though, or in the newspaper's tiny mention of John the following week.

And I wouldn't have dared mention it to Mamá. I don't care anymore whether it's out, though, and no one except her would've believed me, even then.

The police report also won't tell you that at the same time as the accident that was no accident, I was alone in a taxi headed for the hospital. It won't say how Mamá was headed to the hospital to help with the delivery, praying that Gabriel would be alright and that the médicos she didn't trust further than she could spit wouldn't mess things up. It doesn't mention that I had torn off the head of that model and buried it in the backyard earlier that morning or that, as I rode toward the building and was taken upstairs, I prayed over and over again for Dios to kill John, who had beaten me again just days earlier when we both knew Gabriel could be born at any time. I prayed, and I told Dios that if he answered me, I would raise Gabriel to be the good Catholic I never was. I prayed to Dios y los santos y la Virgen, and I didn't believe any of it, but I prayed with all my heart that John's head would be bashed in, heart stopped, air ripped from his lungs, blood stilled in his veins.

What the report did say was that the accident wasn't his fault. That the truck, unremarkable and never identified despite so many bystanders and witnesses, ran him off the road and into that block of concrete right by the overpass at San Mateo. It said that he seemed to have died instantly, perhaps painlessly. The report was shorter than you might expect, shorter even than I might have hoped, with one man's fate summed up by a couple pages of cheap paper in an almost unreadable handwriting.

I wouldn't find out any of this until later, after Gabriel was born, completely healthy. Where there had been darkness, now there was my beautiful angel, with pink skin almost as light as his dad's and a wisp of black hair and two clear, already-knowing eyes darting around the hospital room as if following something invisible to the rest of us. When I finally learned what happened to John, with Mamá whispering the words to me as I lay aching and exhausted in my hospital bed, I understood. Dios had kept his half of the bargain. I would have to keep mine as well.

JOSHUA WHITEHURST

I would be lying if I said that Sam made me understand myself, my sexuality. But while I knew that I wanted to re-create that evening with him, to take it even further and see what lay at the end of that winding trail, those were only my thoughts while alone at night. I only allowed those swirling, beautiful thoughts that excited and frightened me in equal measures when my bedroom door was shut and locked, the moments before I drifted to sleep with no energy left for analysis or shame. They were definitively not thoughts for school. La Cueva was like one of those countries that claims to have no gay people. There, I was just one of the guys, passing for straight less because I wanted to than because there was no other option available.

One thing I have never been able to figure out is which is in control: our minds or our bodies. What I've come to accept is the idea that the two of them are in constant flux, though maybe it would be more accurate to say competition, and that what we call our identity can change from one moment to the next, depending on which is ascendant. During high school, when so many of my friends seemed to be letting their bodies make their decisions, I was just the opposite. My brain told my body to shut up, and I tried to appreciate the girls at school for what they offered on a purely intellectual level. Which makes absolutely no sense, when I think about it now, but at the time it was the only way for me to get through day-to-day life.

Not that I feel I need to make excuses, but there's another reason why I dated Cassandra, beyond a simple desire to fit in: I was curious.

During all four years of high school, my elective was chorus. La Cueva's chorus program was revitalized by Mr. Ferris, a charismatic black man with a lovely baritone and a smile that never faltered—even when yelling at us for not practicing. I signed up as a freshman because it sounded easier than even band and didn't require marching around football fields for the pleasure of jocks' families, but from the day Mr. Ferris first tested my vocal range, I fell in love with singing.

When I arrived home later that day, doing my best to warble some current pop song, I remember my sister, Grace, asking me what I was doing. I explained to her, with absolutely no humility, that I was going to be a famous singer. I already knew, after less than two hours with him, that Mr. Ferris was the most talented vocal coach in the city, the state, perhaps the country, and with his help I was destined for stardom.

Grace laughed. "You sound like someone ran over a canary."

"Fine, you don't get to come on my world tour," I said, then continued singing. Through all of high school and college, she actively hated my new hobby, but our parents were supportive. I'd never played sports, didn't have any particular interest in drawing or painting or any other sort of pastime that kids were supposed to take up, and had been increasingly moody over the past couple years. Singing made me visibly happy, and if putting up with my cacophonous, dead-bird yelps was the price they had to pay for a newly cheerful son, then so be it.

Cassandra and I had gone to middle school together, but we'd barely spoken and never had a class together. She was a year older than me. My sophomore year, we were both in show choir, a before-school program that Mr. Ferris recommended I try out. Much to my disappointment, I was not the strongest singer in my class. But I was the most dedicated, the only one who took the class as seriously as Mr. Ferris did. To be honest, I was a bit of a teacher's pet and felt no shame in this. There was a magic to singing, to creating ephemeral beauty that shot from our mouths and disappeared only moments later, and Mr. Ferris was the sorcerer who introduced me to it.

Cassandra had short, curly brown hair that bounced as she traipsed around the rehearsal studio, effortlessly showering us with clear soprano vocals. She took show choir because her elective was orchestra, where she played first-chair violin with a nonchalant gusto that both amazed and exasperated the teacher, who didn't know what to do with her combination of extreme talent and fuck-you attitude. Music came to her with a naturalness that was unnerving, inhabiting everything from the way she walked to the way she laughed. I wasn't attracted to her sexually, but I wanted to be with her as much as possible. Or maybe just be her.

Cassandra smoked, both cigarettes and weed, and was at every party I ever heard about, usually wasted by the time I arrived. She was immoderate in all things, a dervish with no compunction about sex, grades, or morality. I was timid then, always afraid of my feelings, my body, but I liked being around people without these neuroses. If I was near

Cassandra, I could witness her whirlwind of brilliance and depravity, her stunning solos and the moments afterward when she hurried offstage to smoke outside.

I wouldn't have had it in me to pursue a girl, and certainly not one like her, but with Cassandra that hardly mattered. After the Spring Gala concert, one of the other show choir girls hosted a small party at her house. By this time, I'd begun drinking, though only at these sorts of events, where I felt safe. Two beers and maybe a shot or so was my limit. I was scared of losing control, of what I might do with my filters turned off, but knew that drinking nothing would be noted. The one singer who refused to drink entirely was, after the first party of the year, never invited again—better to risk drunk driving than being judged a buzzkill.

There were only fifteen or so of us there, girls far outnumbering boys. Radio-friendly pop-punk played loudly on the stereo as we lounged around the living room, occasionally making trips to the kitchen for more beers or mixers poured one-to-one with vodka. I was still on my second beer, but a couple kids had already left, and the party was starting to die down. It was past midnight on a Thursday, and we still had school the next day, though fortunately morning rehearsal had been canceled. Cassandra announced she was ready to leave, and I took that as my cue to head out too.

"You going with her?" someone joked, and I smiled but didn't say anything, only shrugged.

"Of course he is," said Cassandra, looping her arm into mine and walking me out the front door to the sound of laughter from everyone still inside.

The spring air smelled crisp and alive, mixing with the cigarette smoke wafting from her curls. While she glided, I practically stumbled along the unlit cobblestone path, unsure what to do or what she had planned. Her arm felt awkward and strange against mine, uncomfortable. It didn't fit. Once we reached her car, she told me how well I'd sung at the concert and gave me a kiss goodbye, on the mouth and far from chaste. I could see eyes peering from the window and knew that this performance would be all anyone talked about the rest of the night.

As I walked home, two miles in the dark through the Sandia's lower hills, her whiskey-and-cigarette breath wouldn't leave my mouth. I'd hoped that in kissing a girl, I would feel nothing. That I could adjust to these physical sensations robotically, use my brain to identify the "objective" beauty of the woman kissing me, and enjoy it as a sensation every movie, every story and song I'd ever known, had told me would be fulfilling and joyous. Instead, I was repulsed.

If Sam taught me to wonder, Cassandra confirmed my suspicions.

I had no choice but to ask her out, not that the phrase meant much. We would kiss sometimes during lunch or before rehearsal, if there was time, and she made intimations of more to come. Without alcohol in me, in the cold light of day, it was easier to keep my emotions in check. But after a few weeks, she dumped me for someone else, complaining that I was stiff and "the worst kisser she'd ever met." Even when this last part became public knowledge, I felt only relief.

Cassandra took the pressure off. No one seemed to suspect me of being gay, since I'd been with one of the most beautiful girls at school, and given Cassandra's reputation, possibly unfounded, I no longer had to answer questions about my virginity. Now I could make excuses, say that I was waiting for another girl as hot as she was, unwilling to settle for less. That level of arrogance wasn't uncommon from other insecure guys at school, so I faded into the pack, my cover secure.

By the end of high school, I felt isolated. There was no one I could even talk to about my sexuality, let alone pursue in any sort of nonfarcical relationship. As a result, I spent more time singing—even becoming an aide for Mr. Ferris senior year—and at home. I only saw my friends at school, stopped going to parties, and largely opted out of any nonchoral social activities.

When we were younger, Grace and I hadn't gotten along terribly well, but by my senior year, we were doing much better. She was studious in a way I never was—she would later be her class's valedictorian—and stayed home as much as I did. We spent a lot of time hanging out, my head propped up on the arm of our overstuffed couch, eyes closed or staring at the wall, Grace staring down at her SAT prep book. After school, our parents wouldn't be home for hours, and between her math problems, we'd talk sporadically about politics or art or whatever else. I thought I could tell her anything. I thought wrong.

I don't know what we'd been chatting about that after-noon, maybe nothing. I just remember the words coming out, automatic and unbidden. "I don't know, what if I don't like girls?" I spoke casually but immediately knew the gravity of what I'd said. I turned my head and looked at Grace. She seemed stiff, concerned.

"You're just joking, right?"

"Ha, yeah," I said. "You know, just one of my hypo-theticals. Didn't know you'd get so pissy about this one."

She kept staring at me, though, and I kept looking at her, wishing she'd go back to studying. I thought about going to my room, slamming the door, and blasting Sondheim on my headphones but knew that would only make things worse.

Eventually, she spoke again, her voice just above a whisper. "You know that's a sin, right? You know Pastor Kurt talked about that last month."

Of course I knew—that was one of Pastor Kurt's pet causes. He seemed to have the entire Bible section about Sodomites memorized, had at one point given a twenty-minute sermon on two antigay verses from Leviticus. We went to Hoffmantown Church every Sunday, had for as long as I'd been alive, and while I used to zone out during services, by this time I'd come to dread them. Pastor Kurt didn't speak every week, and none of the other pastors seemed particularly concerned about homosexuality, but when he did, it was excruciating.

"I was just joking, alright? Sorry you can't take a god-damn joke." I made a point of staring at the wall again. I could feel her eyes still on me, but I ignored them. I didn't change the subject, just stayed there on the couch until dinner, pretending nothing had happened.

I assume Grace never mentioned this to our parents, though I can't know for sure. But for years after that, whenever I considered coming out, images of Grace's look of disgust, her unfeeling, unsympathetic gaze that told me I was worse than nothing, that I was no longer her brother, haunted me. That was the look I'd imagined and feared, the one that had kept me with Cassandra, and to see it in reality ... I can't even tell you what it felt like.

Overall, though, we were not a terribly religious family. To me, Jesus was just a small annoyance on Sundays, one I planned on being done with once I graduated and went to college, which by then I knew would be UNM because my grades weren't good enough for anywhere else. I would become a Chreaster, showing up with my family on Christmas and Easter and forgetting about everything the rest of the year.

Obviously I didn't follow through with that plan, and it was because of Mr. Ferris. Every Sunday he sang the eleven o'clock Mass at UNM's Newman Center. When he found out I was headed to UNM, he asked if I was interested in joining the choir. I was slightly nervous, but I was also more than a little curious. The place was so different from the megachurch I'd grown up in. Mr. Ferris never asked if I was Catholic, and I never really considered how strange and perhaps sacrilegious it was to sing with them, despite not believing for a second in their mystical mumbo jumbo, as Pastor Henry at Hoffmantown used to put it. I just knew that I wanted to keep singing and that I could perform regularly. I said yes, that sounded delightful, and joined him at rehearsal the following week.

ISABEL ROMERO

I kept my promise and raised him Catholic. And ok, I admit that probably would've happened regardless—I doubt Mamá would've let me raise him any other way, and I didn't have the time or energy to go back to rebelling against her. I needed her. Not just during those first few years, when it became clear that John's family cared less about his child than about stealing back his money, but also when Gabriel was older. Mamá's patience extended past his whining and crying, his diarrhea and his refusal to keep food in his mouth—it extended to me and my exhausted frustration with the whole damn world.

When Gabriel was two years old, I realized that I'd need to start working again. After I began waitressing at Kelly's Brew Pub, I'd come home sore and greasy, with a headache from the loud music and louder customers. Mamá kept our lives from collapsing. Gabriel's Batman pajamas—which he wore everywhere, from the front yard to the grocery store—would be in the washing machine while he slept, Mamá reading her Bible next to him. She'd kiss me on her way out, headed to another night shift at the hospital. For some reason, I could never tell her how much all of this helped, that without her I wouldn't have been able to make it. But I'm sure that she knew.

Pero I'm getting ahead of myself, aren't I? All of that came later. First, I mourned John's death, unsure whether I had anything to do with it or not. Logically, I knew that the car accident was in every sense the opposite de un milagro, but still ... you have to wonder, right? And maybe it was a perverse attempt at self-justification that made me stupidly mention John's abuse to his family. It was this, more than anything else, that turned them against me.

"That you would speak ill of the dead, of your own husband. It's absolutely disgraceful!"

I remember his mother screaming this from the far side of the family's oak dinner table. To that point, his relatives had been ... well no, not generous, but at least accepting of the idea that the money in John's trust fund should go to his widow. That perhaps I, his son's mother, might be the person to raise John's child. Pero after I mentioned his violence, there were the pinche lawyers. There were accusations of lying and an attempt at stealing custody away from me. My quote, unquote "claims" to my husband's money showed my unfitness as a parent, my insanity. Sweat stains on my clothes after a day at work showed I was slovenly and kept an untidy home. Gabriel crying during a deposition—Mamá couldn't watch him that day—showed I kept no discipline. I started thinking of all lawyers as vampires, and whenever I noticed any at Kelly's, I'd spit in their drinks and let their food sit until it was good and cold. In the end, the crosses Mamá nailed above every entrance to our home warded them off, as she told me they would—that type of magic is very powerful. So Gabriel grew up without his father's family, but I don't think that did him a bit of harm. Most of the Fishers were lawyers, you know.

We moved into our own house just three blocks from Mamá's. The place was both cheap and convenient, though it meant I was back in Martineztown. Gabriel, my angelito, was a large baby, fat I guess you could say. He smiled a lot and giggled. He was smart, probably because Mamá read to him every day. Usually she read from the Bible or the *Lives of the Saints*, some days in English, some in Spanish. Maybe that's why he didn't speak for a long time—at least that's my theory, that all those words for the same things confused him, though you could see in his eyes that he was taking it in. Me, I read him children's books, because *The Very Hungry Caterpillar* seemed like a much better story for a baby. It was Mamá's business if she wanted him to believe, so I didn't interfere, but I also didn't particularly encourage her. My promise to Dios meant that I would lead my lovely little horse to water, but it was Mamá who wouldn't be content until she saw him take the biggest gulp he could manage.

I had him baptized with the name Gabriel José Romero. My college roommate, Bella, and her boyfriend that year held him in his white gown as Padre Gonzales anointed his little head with oil and poured holy water three times onto his wisps of black hair. I think it might have been the happiest I ever saw Mamá, who cried tears of joy for so long that I was embarrassed.

From a very young age, he followed Mamá on her rounds as she healed our vecinos, asking her question after question about what in her rituals caused estas curaciones tan milagrosas. Was it the prayers, or the herbs, or the incense? Mamá's patients respected and honored her, but Gabriel came to idolize her, and he might've worshipped Mamá como una santa herself if she hadn't put a stop to it. I remember his first communion, when he threw a tantrum before confession because he couldn't think of anything to confess, which supplied him with exactly what he needed. Later, when he was an altar boy, he was always the serious one, you know, standing alongside the priest with a look of concentration and piety despite his youth.

But all of that's just a small part of a little boy's life. And I know, you're interested in hearing about his faith. Faith this, faith that. But you know, what really astonished me more about him as a child was how good Gabito was at everything he tried. He played fútbol really well, and basketball. Later on, he even skateboarded. He was in the middle school chess club, the best player by far according to the club sponsor, and after Mamá bought him a little child-size easel, he started painting and drawing regularly, mostly portraits de su familia but also some of his favorite characters from the Bible or books I read to him, Narnia and Oz and stuff like that. And then, after he saw David Copperfield on television in second or third grade, he started practicing magic tricks.

"Mom, how is David Copperfield flying?" he asked. He'd scooted so close to the TV in our living room that I could barely see past his face to catch glimpses of the special.

"I don't know," I told him. "Probably wires. Or magnets or something."

He turned to me, completely deflated. "So it's not real?"

"Well … I don't know." I felt like I'd ended his childhood. "Do you see any wires? I mean, if everyone thinks it's real, then that's just as good, right? If no one can prove that it's not, then who can say?"

He didn't respond for a little while, but he was back to staring at the screen again, so I felt like I'd done the right thing. After that performance, he asked me to take him to

Rob's Magic and Joke Store on Central, where he made me wait in the car so I wouldn't learn any secrets. From then on, his interest in magic occasionally waned, but it always returned, and he'd head back to that magic store to spend money on a new card trick or a floating silver ball or whatever else. When Mamá found him reading a book of magic tricks he'd checked out from the library, she was shocked and doused it with holy water. Gabito had to show her that what he was doing was simply illusions, sleights of hand. When he performed a trick for her, he'd show her how it was done so she could make sure the devil had nothing to do with it. After a few years, Mamá ended up approving of how his trucos took advantage of the weak-minded. She even took him to Rob's herself, because she liked the way the store conflated magic with jokes, and she watched with glee whenever Gabriel amazed someone with a trick she already knew.

But more important to him than anything else was music. One of Mamá's uncles used to play the guitarrón—badly, I might add—but that was the only sign of musical aptitude I ever heard about on either side of his family, so I don't know where it came from. Maybe I can take some credit for it, since I bought him his first keyboard for his sixth birthday, a little Casio that was more of a toy than an instrument. He spent the next week messing around with it, driving us crazy until we got him a pair of headphones. Mamá secured lessons for him in lieu of payment for healing a bad back, and once a week he would walk over to his teacher's house and come back an hour later with new sheet music in hand.

There was something Gabriel seemed to get out of the music that I never did and that I never knew how to ask about. One day I arrived home from work, and he was lying on his side with his right ear pressed against our scratched and uneven wood floor, playing a chord on the keyboard with his left hand. I asked him what he was doing, and Gabriel only shrugged.

He asked me, "Do you think that sounds out of tune?"

"How would it get out of tune?" I answered. "It's a machine."

He shrugged again and said, "I don't know, it just doesn't sound right. It doesn't sound like it should."

I didn't know what to say, so I just told him to move his head off the floor or he'd get sick from dust, but years later he explained to me that he heard it all, the notes or tones or whatever you want to call them, in his head. There was a sort of divinity he felt when all the notes he heard were "right," especially when he was the one playing them. I know all of this sounds ridículo, but that's what he told me, and he was so earnest about everything that I never had any reason to doubt him. Though he was an extremely happy child, Gabriel rarely made jokes, and he definitely wouldn't have joked about something like that.

In fifth grade, the middle school orchestra teacher visited his elementary school and showed off the string instruments in order to recruit prospective students. That evening, Gabito told me that he'd fallen in love with the cello. He was so cute, talking as fast as he could about how cool the instrument was—the first time I'd ever heard a classical instrument called *cool*—and that he was going to start playing.

Why not the violin, I asked him, and he told me that not only did the cello sound the prettiest of the orchestral instruments, it was the one that sounded closest to the human voice.

"What does that mean?"

"Mrs. Foley said that the range is like if you were singing," Gabriel said.

"Wouldn't you want to try that instead, then?" I asked, mostly because I knew how much those instruments cost.

He looked at me with a mixture of scorn and confusion, and soon enough I gave in.

I've spoken with other parents whose children were musicians, and something that always comes up is practice. How they forced their child into practicing. How they bribed them, tricked them, deprived them in the name of spending just a few hours a week with their instrument. I never had to do anything like that, and neither did Mamá. If Gabito didn't want to practice, he didn't have to practice. He did anyhow. Maybe because, for all his talent and activities, he never seemed to have any close friends. He got all A's, was more knowledgeable about his Bible than the teacher by the time he started confirmation classes, but he rarely went to friends' houses after school or met up for parties.

What he did instead was practice and perform. When he hit high school, the orchestra teacher offered to give him weekly private lessons for free. By the time he graduated, Gabito was arranging pieces for his string quartet and even composing short pieces. He'd stopped seriously pursuing piano but still subbed in whenever the church's regular pianist couldn't make it.

That was my Gabito. Quiet, except with an instrument in his hand, and, at least from what I saw, uninterested in a lot of typical adolescent behavior. He never went to prom, or dated girls, or came home at one a.m. and passed out drunk on the couch. I thought he was headed for Juilliard or some other conservatory, and I think he would've continued in that direction had it not been for Mamá.

During his junior year of high school, Mamá had her first stroke. It didn't come as a huge shock to me. After all, she was old, and her life hadn't been easy. But for Gabriel, who never seemed to notice Mamá's hair going from dark brown when he was little to a mixture of white and gray by the time he hit high school, it came as a shock. He started spending a lot of time at her house, doting on Mamá the way she had with him only a decade earlier. After months spent treating herself and consulting with a curandera friend rather than dealing los médicos that she didn't trust, Mamá improved. She returned to work, and while parts of her face now sagged, her mischievous smile returned.

A year later, the second stroke hit, and she never walked on her own again. Gabriel moved into her house, cooking her meals, managing her bills. At her request, every night he prayed el rosario with her. In the dim candlelight of her bedroom, he would speak the words loud and clear, while she muttered them, her back and head propped up by a pile of pillows. Her room still smelled of herbs and incense, but now these mixed with the fouler smells of urine and excrement. When I was there, I didn't have the patience to sit through the whole ordeal, as it could last more than an hour, with specific prayers to various santos whose intercession might help.

Usually, when Gabito closed the door behind him at the end of a prayer session, he looked, if not happy, certainly content. Not optimistic but wearing a similar face to the one he made at the end of a successful concerto performance. I think there was a sense of having achieved something, or at least having provided a valuable service. They would watch Mass on television together on Sundays, and Gabriel would bring home a blessed wafer from San Ignacio for her to eat alongside a tiny plastic container of wine the priest poured just for her. She said her eyes hurt when she tried to read the Bible, so Gabito brought her tapes from the library, and she would listen to them with her eyes closed while he washed the dishes, vacuumed the floors, or practiced his cello as quietly as he could in the other room.

All of this became normal with remarkable speed. His grades suffered a bit, but he didn't care and didn't apply to college anywhere besides UNM because he wanted to stay close to us. I helped too, whenever Gabriel was busy ... but to be honest, he was closer to Mamá than I was by that point. You know, he seemed to like helping her, pero I did it only out of duty and guilt—and Mamá raised me with guilt about everything, so I'd learned to ignore that long before he was born. Maybe I should've done more. At the time, all I knew was that I was tired and happy to see him taking over.

Several months after Gabito moved in with her, I came home and was surprised to find him in his bedroom. Most of his clothing, alongside his cello, keyboard, computer, and school supplies, had long since moved to Mamá's house, so the room felt bare, even though posters of Bach and Tchaikovsky still hung from his walls, and his dresser remained covered in the clutter of santos, sheet music, and CDs gathering dust. He was lying on an old quilt, staring at the ceiling with his eyes open. He took no notice of me as I entered. I stomped my feet as I walked toward him so he'd know I was there, and when he didn't react, I got scared.

I asked him what was wrong, and he still didn't say anything. "Gabito, you have to answer me. I'm your mother."

"She told me not to pray for her to heal," he said. "I started praying to todos los santos y la Virgen and … and she told me to stop."

I didn't know what to say, so I sat down on his bed and waited. After a couple minutes, he started crying, and between his small, quiet sobs, he told me that the two of them prayed for her soul instead. They had never done that before, and he still wasn't sure why it was even necessary.

"I understand why sinners and criminals and atheists and … but I don't get … I mean, we've always known Mamá would go to heaven," he said. "But she made me pray the rosary for San Pedro to let her pass."

He cried for a minute while I thought about how to answer him. I mean, who could say why Mamá did anything? Certainly not me, but I did the best I could.

"Mijo, we both know that, but Mamá knows we're all sinners. She knows that no one gets into heaven sin la gracia de Dios, and maybe she wants you to remember that. If she didn't worry, that would mean she didn't have faith."

Gradually, Gabriel calmed down. We ate a dinner of reheated rice and beans in silence, just the two of us, for the first time in a long while. I asked if he needed to return soon, and he responded by asking me to stay with her for the night instead. I said of course. The next day, he was back to normal, taking care of her and praying with her as if nothing had happened, only now they prayed not for her body but for her soul.

Mamá died less than a week later. I wasn't there to see it. He'd slept in late because it was a Saturday, and when he woke up, Mamá was dead, su rosario en su mano. After I rushed over to the house, Gabriel told me that he'd dreamed of Mamá. He saw a pair of angels come down through the roof to lift her from the bed by her arms. Mamá looked strong and healthy, younger than he'd ever seen her. She laughed and kicked her legs in the air like she was treading water as they flew together into Albuquerque's rose-colored dawn sky, clouds parting for them as they rose higher and higher until disappearing into a beam of endless light.

He cried. We both cried. Pero Gabito didn't seem as devastated as he had before. He said that their prayers had worked, that there was no reason to be sad. I agreed and said that Mamá would want us to rejoice that she was in heaven.

Later, I learned that she'd died in her sleep from an even worse series of strokes, not in the early morning but in the evening, probably soon after she fell asleep, while Gabito was practicing cello in the other room. Not that I ever told him, because I mean, what good would that have done?

JOSHUA WHITEHURST

Obviously, I have a lot of time to myself now. I spend some of it reading. Some writing. Even working out, mostly just for the variety. But between all that, I do a lot of remembering. Maybe it's because I used to think so little about the past that now it seems so important, or maybe it's that I have nothing better to do. Whatever the case, I enjoy it. Lying on my bed at night, with its rough sheets and useless pillow, memories keep me warmer than my blanket, give me the will to wake up each day and look forward to another sunrise.

But how do our memories work? I've read books about it, the way our brains forge new connections, electrical synapses that bind together our versions of the past. And although I don't really know what that means biologically speaking, it rings true. The past is not a long road that winds out behind us, letting us trace the precise route that led from who we used to be to who we are. The past is those random bundles of synapses, the key moments and events that stick with us, not the filler in between. We skip from rock to rock, milestone to milestone, and the rest? The rest we simply make up later to fit the narrative we like best—usually the one that makes us out to be the hero.

Those few memories that I latch on to, they've only become clearer, even as the edges around them grow foggier. I keep coming back to the first time I saw Gabriel, even though it was patently unspectacular. I was still a freshman, but I'd already been singing with the small chorus at the Newman Center for half a year, and by then I knew not only the songs we sang but the entire rigmarole of a Catholic church service. The first time I sang for Mass, I was weirded out by how many times everyone had to sit, stand, or kneel during an otherwise monotonous hour of talking and repetitive songs. My favorite singers were divas, whether women or men, people who didn't just hit the notes, they also put on one hell of a show. Catholic singing was about as far from diva-hood as you could get, but still, it was a performance, and Mr. Ferris remained an excellent leader for our merry group of five to eight singers.

The chapel's design was counterintuitive. At some point, they'd renovated and made the pews all face the center, where they'd set up an altar. We sang from where a traditional altar would've been, on a raised stage, and so anyone who was actually near enough to see us, to watch our faces as we belted out mediocre praise songs, never actually looked in our direction. As I said, it was kind of a diva's nightmare, but according to Mr. Ferris, this made it a perfect place to work on your skills: a real room filled with real people but no one paying enough attention that they'd notice a few missed notes.

Gabriel, though, was the exception. Every time we started singing, he turned so that he was staring straight at us, paying rapt attention as we did our best with lyrics that consisted, literally, of the word *holy* repeated ad nauseam. He wasn't the first person to watch, or the last, but when he stared at us with those big brown eyes of his, it startled me so much I completely lost my place.

This is what he looked like at the time: dark black hair, long and slightly unruly but in a way that looked sculpted. Bushy eyebrows, full lips, and a bit of stubble that made him seem too cool to talk to, especially paired with his black jeans and white V-neck shirt beneath a blazer. He stared at us as if that were normal, and although I thought he was half smirking at something, I later found out that this was simply his resting face. With every song, he turned and looked at us, and I felt like he wanted to say something about the song or our singing or the musicians, something.

I expected to see him after Mass, meandering in the lobby, maybe grabbing a doughnut and meeting with other students, but by the time I made it out there, he was gone. The next few weeks, I didn't see him, and I assumed that he'd switched to one of the other services—we only performed at the eleven o'clock Mass—or even another church. His presence would have been a blip had he not soon reappeared at a house party.

It was early November and warm, so warm that every window was open and fans were blowing full blast, and even so, I remember sweating through my chinos. But I didn't particularly care because I was drinking, and back then when I'd had a few, I honestly thought that my sweat smelled pretty good, manly and robust. At least it would to men, and that was all I cared about. Before, I barely drank, but after a couple nights in the dorms, that changed. In college, the consequences for losing control didn't seem so major anymore. Grace and my parents wouldn't find out what I was up to, so fuck it, I was free to do as I pleased ... though I needed a little alcoholic assistance before actually turning this theory into praxis.

By the time I saw him, I'd pregamed a couple shots of Wild Turkey back in the dorms with some guys I barely knew, plus half a dozen beers from a keg. He stood at the far side of the room, nearby fans giving his hair and faded polo shirt a dreamy windblown effect like he was in a movie. I felt myself practically float over to him, my body making the decision all on its own. There were two women with him, students I probably got to know later, but I don't remember who. It's a haze now, but I think it was also a haze then. What I do remember is that I never properly introduced myself. Instead I just joined the conversation, and when, some time later, we headed to a dance floor forming on the other side of the house, it all felt smooth and liquid, the night having its way with us.

He danced wildly, his hips and head always in motion. I … well, I'd only really danced at parties since arriving at college, so it's safe to assume that I danced badly. It didn't matter, as none of it was about me, it was all about him. Gabriel danced with me, and he danced with those girls we'd been talking to, and he danced with everyone in the room. There were probably twenty of us, but all eyes were on him. I wouldn't even say he was a *good* dancer, but he was excited and uninhibited. He was the center of the room we all gravitated toward, a mesmeric presence who everyone wanted to pair with for at least a few moments so that they could feel the white-hot spotlight of his attention. Toward the end of the night, he took off his shirt, and sweat poured down his shoulders while he moved, and I wanted to fuck him so badly it hurt.

Even in such an important memory, parts are missing. I forget how we ended up at the Frontier later that night, first with a group and then, as the evening wound down, just the two of us sitting at a booth by the back door.

What did we talk about? There were so many conversations that picking out any one, even that first night, is a struggle. What I do remember is trying to fill the air with my voice so that he would think I was smart and his easy laugh at some of my jokes. But eventually there was an awkward silence, because there always is.

He pulled out a cigarette and held it in his right hand. He grinned at me, then waved his left hand in front of the cigarette, and suddenly it glowed red at the end. He took a puff on it and breathed it out across the table.

"What the fuck—you're going to set off the smoke detector and get us kicked out," I said.

"You're no fun."

"Fuck you, the security guard's headed over here," I said, though that wasn't true. I just wanted him to stop.

"Fine," he said without looking up. He waved his left hand in front of his right, this time in the opposite direction, and suddenly the cigarette was not only out, it was unlit, untouched. The only evidence of what had happened was the smoke dissipating above us.

"Alright, it's been fun," he said. "But I've gotta get going."

"Don't leave," I said. It just came out, the thoughts I would've hidden if I could. I reached my hand across the table, past long-finished plates of greasy food and empty paper cups, and he placed his lightly on top of mine. He rubbed my fingertips, just barely, offered up the tiniest smile, and said he really did need to get some sleep. He disappeared out the back door, and then it was just me and an old man mopping the floors.

It wasn't difficult for me to find him. I searched Facebook for Gabriel, and he came up immediately, a profile pic of him staring directly into the camera like he didn't quite trust it. I sent him a friend request but did nothing else all week. The following Friday afternoon, I sent him a message asking what he was up to, and he responded a few hours later, saying that he and some friends planned on heading to a frat party. And that I was free to join them if I wanted to. At the bottom was his phone number. Later that night, I texted him saying, **Hey man I'm headed over to Sigma Chi.**

He responded, **cool c u there.**

Here's where my memories get spotty again. All our days and weeks and months of parties and late nights morphed into one, the endless party that was freshman year. We went out in big groups, laughing and joking and drinking and smoking from party to party, migratory birds searching for the next place to settle on our journey to ... well, something, certainly. Thursday night kicked off the weekend, and from there it was always a question of where next, where do they still have drinks, where do they have better music, where do they have cuter guys or girls, fewer gringos or cholos or douchebags or punks, more drugs or less drugs or just somewhere that could make us feel more free, more happy, more alive.

There were nights when we tried to tamp down on the excess. We'd consciously plan an evening in, watching some dumb flick and throwing popcorn at the screen while we drank from cans of High Life every time Nicolas Cage punched someone. But then we'd go out, because at a certain blood alcohol level, staying still was no longer an option. There were other nights that began as ragers and ended as three-hour philosophical discussions around the pool tables down at Anodyne. No two were the same because the search had no end, no final destination in mind. At least, for the rest of our gang there was no end.

For me, well, I was there to be with Gabriel, but I'd be lying if I said I wasn't happy with the rest of the ride.

Maybe I'm misrepresenting things a little bit, because if I had to put my finger on what we were all looking for, it was sex. And most of them were getting some too, at least on occasion. Relationships formed and dissolved at random. Friends cheated and were cheated on. Not me, though. And not Gabriel, so far as anyone knew. At least, not during that first crazy year.

To be honest, for a little while I thought I'd made up that first night altogether. I'd been drunk when Gabriel touched me across that table, so gently, so sweetly. It wasn't like he ignored me after that; we saw each other nearly every day by the end of the second semester. But he never acknowledged that any of it had happened, which meant I couldn't either—Sam Stiles all over again. Even if it was just the two of us—lounging across the futon in my dorm room while listening to opera, because no one else we knew liked it, or drinking and playing *Halo* at Jesse and Erik's house during the afternoon when they were out—that first night was tacitly off-limits. Nor, as time went on, would we discuss evenings spent dancing together or the way, when he was really wasted, Gabriel would start leaning against me while we walked down the side streets off Central. We would never talk about the way he put his arm around me for support and slurred into my ear how glad he was that I was the one helping him home.

Here's the thing: I wasn't really in the closet anymore, but I wasn't out either. During that first year of college, I simply pretended not to be a sexual being, even when that was all I could think about. If someone had asked me, directly, whether I was attracted to men or simply to

Gabriel, I wouldn't have known how to answer. But no one was asking, I guess because we weren't that type of group. We were friends because we partied together, not because we gave a shit what anyone actually said or felt.

It wasn't until summer, when the cycle of coffee and alcohol and bleary classes and five a.m. nights came to an end, that things moved forward. That was a weird time for me. After all that craziness, suddenly I was back on the far side of town, back in the closet with my goody-two-shoes sister and dull-as-dirt parents and nothing much to do. I didn't want to work, mostly because I didn't have to and knew that staying at home without a job would drive my family crazy—even my sister had a position volunteering for the local RNC. A lot of my friends from college were working, and the ones who weren't were busy traveling the world or whatever. I spent a lot of time driving around, hiking in the foothills, playing pool. I practiced singing and spent some time studying music theory because the required courses at UNM were killer. But for the most part, my hours seemed to disappear, a cruel magic trick performed by no one but myself.

All that time alone meant I could finally recover from the semester and try to make sense of it. One thing I realized was that while it had been fun, I didn't want to repeat it. I'd promised myself that in college I would be more honest about who I was, what I wanted, yet I'd spent the semester with someone I was desperate for and done nothing about it. Toward the end of the summer, I woke up sometime after noon one day, music still playing in my headphones. The scent of my unwashed body, beneath a blanket and sheets I hadn't changed in months, filled me with a sinking feeling. Something had to change.

It took me a couple more hours in bed, listening to some of my favorite pump-up songs, but finally I managed to do it. I texted Gabriel to ask if he was free for dinner anytime soon, and a few minutes later he sent back, **Of course.**

I hadn't asked him out in any official capacity, but it still felt different. I got a haircut, purchased a new shirt, and rehearsed a few lines in front of my mirror. Mostly, I prepared myself for disappointment. Ways the evening could go wrong seemed almost infinite, and in my isolation I imagined dozens of uniquely embarrassing and devastating rejection scenarios. But it didn't matter. I had to do this, or I might as well never get out of bed again.

I arrived at Seasons in Old Town five minutes early, but Gabriel was already waiting outside the front door. He seemed disconcertingly stiff, wearing the same blazer and V-neck combination as that first time I'd seen him in church. When he greeted me with a hug, he smelled like vanilla, a scent I came to both love and hate. He'd also had a haircut recently, and although he was as warm and friendly as ever, he seemed less wild than usual. It was only later that I realized this was one of the first times we'd seen each other completely sober.

After they seated us in the back and took our orders, I asked Gabriel what he'd been up to during the intervening months.

"I've been, umm, volunteering. For the church…" His reluctance was impossible to miss, though why exactly, I had no idea.

"That's great," I said. I asked him more, but when he mumbled a vague response, I changed the subject. We talked about classes we planned on taking the next semester, and I learned that he'd decided to move off campus and already lived in a house with a couple of friends. We probably talked about a lot of other things too, things that I no longer remember—I don't want to make anything up, so I'm not going to pretend I have a photographic memory here. What I know for sure is that we ordered several rounds of drinks, and that when the check finally arrived, it seemed far too soon.

The sun was still up, so we drove to the downtown multiplex and watched something loud and dumb. I barely noticed what was on the screen. What mattered was the way his arm pressed against mine on the strip of plastic between us. I leaned close, and he leaned close, and I decided not to wait any longer. I turned my head to him and we kissed, and even though I didn't know what I was doing, I can tell you that it was the greatest kiss that has ever been, the most grand and electric and sensual kiss, a kiss that defied the idea of hyperbole, though it lasted only a few moments. And the one after that was even better.

FR. PATRICK CONKLIN

I moved to Albuquerque when I was eight years old. My father had just finished his PhD in mechanical engineering and found work at Sandia National Laboratories, over in the Kirtland Air Force Base. What I remember best is the size of our new house, with six bedrooms and a basement that my siblings and I used as an extra playroom. I am the middle of five children, so our place was overflowing with noise and toys, food and friends and the bric-a-brac of family. My mother did not work, which was a blessing, because taking care of us was more than a full-time job.

I had a very ordinary upbringing, first at St. Mary's for elementary school, and later at St. Pius until college. It was a good childhood. I had strong, loving parents, and although we don't speak as much as I would like, I am still close to my brothers and sisters. By the time I was in high school, I showed some of the aptitude for math and its related fields that my father did, acing my calculus and physics AP exams, so I planned on following in his footsteps.

I first saw Gabriel at one of the student services on Tuesday nights, but I didn't meet him properly until a few weeks later when the Newman Center held its first mixer. It was not a large affair, maybe two dozen of us hanging around the lobby and courtyard, with wine and hors d'oeuvres. All my friends from St. Pius had gone out of state for college, so I was looking to meet people. That was one of the main reasons why I stopped going to Risen Savior Church with my parents, the other being convenience. Back then, Gabriel had long, unkempt hair and more than a bit of stubble. I probably walked up to him because he looked less stiff than the other students, who wore essentially the same clothes they would have worn to church. Which I suppose was true of Gabriel too, but I didn't realize that yet.

I don't remember exactly what we talked about, likely the typical introductory rigmarole: names, majors, etc. What I do remember is that contrary to his appearance, he seemed very serious. Which is not to say that he was sad or angry, just that when religious topics came up, which to me at that time were neither particularly interesting nor particularly consequential, his demeanor changed, and his laughter stopped. Growing up in Catholic schools, you start thinking of these topics less as matters of dire spiritual importance and more like tedious chores. Mass was spiritual laundry, something I did once a week without much thought because it was what all good people did. Gabriel wanted to talk about the week's readings and the sermon, which I doubt I could even remember. Probably because of his appearance, few other students came over to us, so Gabriel and I chatted until it became dark and we both headed home. A friendship of proximity, you might say.

After that, whenever neither of us was running late, we would greet each other in the lobby and sit together during Mass. That first semester I happened to be taking Intro to the Bible, mostly because I had years of religion classes under my belt and thought it would be an easy

A. After I offhandedly mentioned this to Gabriel, every time he saw me, he would ask about the class. What he was interested in was not the context of the readings or the close analysis but what the professor said the readings actually told us to do, which was a really weird way to think about the Bible, or really any college course, as far as I was concerned. Only much later did I come to understand that while at that time I saw the Bible as a historical document to be interpreted, he saw it as a guidebook.

Toward the end of the semester, we were talking about my class and arguing about who knows what, when the Newman Center's office assistant kindly asked us to leave so she could lock up. As we headed back to the dorms, Gabriel asked me about joining a small faith-sharing group.

"Do you already have one?" I asked, assuming no, but with him ... I never felt sure what he had up his sleeve, sometimes literally, given his love for dumb magic tricks.

"No, I'd just like to have more discussions like this," he said. "I don't have anyone else to talk to about our faith." He sounded lonely, but it wasn't like he ever contacted me to meet up outside of church.

"Why don't you take some religion courses next semester?" I said. "Then you can talk all you want, plus get credit."

"You mean like as a second major? I guess I'll try. Music takes up a lot of time...," he said. I had thought what he was proposing was just one of those college larks. You know, a "let's go to Europe this summer" type of thing that you throw out there because it's not going to happen. But of course he was serious. Here I was, trying to enjoy myself for the first time in my life, yet one of my few friends only wanted to talk about God and wouldn't even call me otherwise.

"I don't know, a group sounds so … let's keep things between us," I said, and we split ways for another week. He seemed mollified by this, and I made good on my word. Every week after Mass, we would either walk back to the dorms or eat a meal together and discuss God, the gospels, the sermon, whatever else happened to pique his interest. He was always pleasant and thoughtful, though there was a world of difference between our beliefs. That comes as little surprise to me now, obviously, but at the time, it was frustrating, even mystifying. We'd had the same priests at Risen Savior throughout my entire childhood, and without realizing it, I had internalized their views. Gabriel's ideas, which seemed to come half from his dead grandmother and half from his own head, were incompatible with my version of the religion, but in retrospect that was part of why I enjoyed speaking with him so much. At times, his beliefs seemed as wild as his hair, and being with him made me feel more revolutionary than I ever really was.

Gabriel liked to bring up ideas through "thought experiments." We would talk through the implications as if we were great theologians and not simply students with too much time on our hands. I would usually take the opposing side because I liked to argue, plus this would lead him to strange jumps of logic that kept my interest. Thankfully, I am no longer that way—it would be tiring to go through all of life arguing for the sake of arguing—but at the time, I thought it was fun to play with ideas and see what stuck.

One of these I remember particularly well was the idea of the two holy men. Both men are good Catholics, followers of Jesus Christ who devote their lives to God. They do this completely, body and soul, but their paths are nonetheless different. One joins a holy order. He becomes a monk and spends his days in prayer and absolution. He fasts and says the Liturgy of the Hours daily. He lives a life largely free of sin—for no man, other than Jesus Christ, is without sin entirely—and obeys all of the Bible and the instructions of his superiors without question. When he dies, his brothers say a quiet Mass in his honor.

The second holy man is just as committed to God, but this inspires him not to study but to emulate Christ and the saints. He dedicates his life to the poor, the hungry, the ill, the persecuted. He does not enter into an order and never has time to pray for an entire day because his work is never finished. He is at the food banks, he is canvassing to promote social justice. He is trying to make the Earth into a better, more Godly realm, and while he does it all in the name of our Lord and Savior, he cannot devote every hour of every day to thinking about God. He feels that it is God who imbues his actions, though, and he dies celebrated for what he has accomplished.

"Now which of these two men," Gabriel asked, "is the holier man?"

I let this sit in my head while we walked past students and families relaxing at UNM's duck pond, other students bicycling past us along the sidewalk. I didn't care about the two men, could not force myself to, but it was pleasant to be outside with company. "What do you mean by holier?"

"Good question," said Gabriel. "Let's say more beloved by God. Or closer to God. Or simply less sinful."

"Monks aren't in the Bible," I responded, "but Jesus tells us to be celibate and poor. And to be perfect. If you devote your entire life, every waking moment, to the glory of God, that seems like the holiest of all."

"What about where it says to make disciples of all nations?" he asked.

"What about it?" I answered. "The Bible says a lot of things that aren't literally true, and we all have to figure out what it means for us. For some, the path might be in proselytizing, but for the rest of us, it seems like being conscientious and devoted may be enough. If you were to spend every waking moment considering God's glory, that seems like the holiest way to live your life."

"Maybe you should be a monk then," said Gabriel with a laugh.

I wasn't sure whether to take that as a compliment or an insult.

"Sometimes I think about the saints, though," he continued. "If you were to be the holy monk who devoted himself to God, you could never be a saint, because no one would know who you were. I mean, there must have been thousands of men and women out there in the caves, living for God. But no one has heard of them. No one prays to them for intercession. No one remembers them."

"God does," I said. "And now they're in heaven."

"Yes, of course. But as far as the world is concerned, it makes no difference whether or not they existed," said Gabriel. He raised his voice in exasperation. "Whether or not Saint Francis existed matters. People saw the glory of God move through him and imitated what he did. When he was alive, disciples would walk when he did and speak the way he spoke. They would mimic his coughing, when he stuttered. When he helped the poor, it mattered, and everyone he met remembered him."

"That's a dangerous way of thinking," I insisted. "That's thinking about spiritual matters in terms of results. Effects. You're talking about ends not means. But a prayer exists whether or not anyone hears it, whether or not you speak it out loud."

"I understand what you're saying," said Gabriel. "But I can't help but think of Jesus as someone who was about action. He didn't just pray for the sick, he healed them. He didn't just acknowledge hunger, he made loaves and fish. If God had come down in the form of His only son and stayed in a church praying all day, would we care?"

We arrived at the fork in the path where I would head off to my dorm, alone. We stopped and stood, the sun baking down on us. I wanted to leave, to go inside and shower, but Gabriel wasn't finished.

"So here's my question then," said Gabriel. "Say those two *are* equally holy, or worthy, or whatever you want to call it, but what if the one doing the good works doesn't believe? What if he saves lives through his actions, and aside from his atheism—or maybe agnosticism, it doesn't matter—what if he does the same wonderful things that would be blessed if they were being done by a good Catholic believer? How does he stack up?"

"Not well," I said. "I'm not saying he's going to hell. But as far as I'm concerned, what he's doing is different."

"I guess ... I just don't understand how," Gabriel said. "Does it really matter what your motivations are if you're doing good? What if everyone thought he was Catholic—would that make a difference? Like, what if you were a martyr and you didn't even believe, or didn't even have to die, but you inspired millions?"

"Gabriel, I'm tired," I admitted. "I've got class tomorrow. More importantly, I don't really care. But I do know Christ's commandments. Love the Lord your God with all your heart and with all your soul and with all your mind. That's the first and most important commandment.

To love your neighbor as yourself, that comes second. I'll see you later."

During the last week of class, we talked about plans for the summer. I would be working at an internship my dad helped set up, not at Sandia Labs but at a solar-panel company a friend of his founded. It would end up dull and pointless and begin my process of vocational questioning, but that would come later. At the time, I was optimistic and enthusiastic about my prospects, and that was what I wanted to talk about. Still, as a courtesy, I asked Gabriel about his plans.

"I've been talking to Father Anthony about volunteering for Catholic Charities…," he said, trailing off.

His demeanor seemed so strange that I couldn't help but ask about it. "Why the long face?"

"I didn't want you to think I was, I don't know, showing off or something," he said. "That I was just doing it for, I don't know, myself. Which I'm not."

"Why not?" I asked. "If I did that, you can be sure I'd be showing off."

At this, he gave me a weird look, eyebrows furrowed and nostrils flaring. "Hey, give me a call if you want to do something this summer," he said, then hurried back to his dorm.

I never called him, though, because my friends from St. Pius returned to town, and a summer night spent debating religion with Gabriel never seemed like it would be much fun. He never tried to contact me either.

JOSHUA WHITEHURST

I woke up smothered beneath a white down comforter, sun-yellowed in spots and overflowing onto the wood floor below. Vanilla, mixed with a hint of sour sweat, wafted over from the queen-size bed's now-vacant second pillow, and I took the largest breath of it I could, holding the air until my lungs couldn't take it anymore. The glimmering sound of harpsichord music—eighth notes jangling in perfect counterpoint, accented by the occasional crackle of old, dust-covered vinyl—trickled past the sheets separating Gabriel's room from the rest of the small house. When I finally opened my eyes, I could just make out his shape on the other side of the sheets, head nodding to the metronomically perfect music, a thick book propped up against the kitchen table. As I waited in bed, reluctant to start the day, he fixed himself breakfast, bobbing energetically to the shower, along the way changing the record to Messiaen's nearly discordant *Et exspecto resurrectionem mortuorum* symphony. There was nervous energy in every footstep he took.

That was how I woke up many times during the next three years, though exactly how many, I don't know. Certainly not as many as I wished. Gabriel never let me move in with him, never even made me a copy of his house key, and on more than a handful of occasions seemed to be avoiding my calls. But soon after, we'd be together again, and following a blissful evening I would wake up in his bed, renewing my sense that all was right with the world. He would greet me with a kiss, and as we made and ate lunch together, I felt like this was the life I'd always hoped for, despite that nagging voice at the very back of my head that said I was deceiving myself. But enveloped in his bed's cloud of vanilla, all I could hear was the beauty of those celestial chords.

After freshman year, everything slowed down. We stopped going out nearly as often and toned down the drinking to an almost reasonable level. Parties became the exception rather than the rule. We didn't wait to study until the night before a test, and we kept more or less ordinary hours, even showing up to morning lectures when the mood struck. Our friends' relationships finally stabilized, for the most part, and the novelty of living away from home seemed to have worn off. Some of our freshman group kept up with the craziness of the year before and would do so all through college, but most of those people disappeared from our social circle, slowly fading until they were little more than extras in the background of our lives.

Don't get me wrong, we were definitively not a couple. I can say this for certain because I asked Gabriel about it numerous times, and his varying denials never ceased grating on me. "Let's not try to define things." "Let's just try to have fun." "Why do we have to put a label on what we are?" "Why can't we just be us?" "I don't want to talk to you when you're being like this."

As these fights continued, I began telling him that this was nonnegotiable. This wasn't just some silly little thing I was joking about, I legitimately wanted to tell people that he was my boyfriend. Those words mattered to me, and it hurt that they didn't to him. But Gabriel always knew that I couldn't really set down ultimatums, because I was the pursuer and he was the pursued. Every time I returned to him, apologizing for something I shouldn't have had to apologize for, we would pretend nothing had ever happened. That was how Gabriel preferred things, not to resolve them and move on but to act like all our disagreements were only in my head, that we'd never left Eden in the first place.

So no, we were not a couple, but we were "together," as some of our friends described our relationship. And really, that togetherness was far more important than any definition, even if it was mostly private. We didn't hold hands as we walked around campus, didn't sit in each other's laps while eating lunch at the SUB, but later that night it was still the two of us, plus maybe a bottle of wine and uncontainable hormones. Gabriel's roommates headed out to parties or played Xbox games on the other side of the house, while behind that sheet, we were in our own little world of music and sex. And when he was drunk enough, Gabriel would even kiss me in public, would cling to me the way I wanted him to.

What did we do, then, if we weren't coupling it up all around campus? Like any other pair of best friends, we shared meals, movies, and an incredible number of concerts. Few weeks went by without at least a recital that one of us found noteworthy, and as we began to focus more on academics, attending these performances suddenly seemed to matter. School itself had become, I have to admit, a bit difficult for me. I hadn't done well the previous year, but even without the partying, I wasn't doing much better. Math and science would never be my forte, and my music theory courses turned out to be heavily math-based. I just wanted to sing, preferably solo, so I started drifting away from choral performance, where it's all about blending, to pedagogy. I started thinking that maybe I could be like Mr. Ferris and teach.

Gabriel's enthusiasm for music hardly wavered. Theory and orchestration were no problem for him, and he composed odd, wordless pieces for me to sing, just collections of vowel sounds playfully arranged, and while we performed them a few times, they were really just for us. I could sing one for you—I still remember most of them—but I doubt you'd like it. When asked, Gabriel used to joke that they were about everything: life, death, God, all of existence … and then laugh later when people occasionally took him seriously. Beyond this, he started taking religion classes, but I'll tell you more about that nonsense in a second.

First, there's one more part of our lives that I don't want to ignore. During that summer we'd spent apart, Gabriel seemed to have discovered a latent interest in politics. I, on the other hand, did not. My concerns about defining our relationship weren't political, they were personal. I had no interest in marching against an epidemic of police shootings, or a corrupt governor who sold his policy decisions to the highest bidder, or even for gay marriage. These, I felt, were not my fights. I just wanted to live quietly and enjoy myself. With Gabriel, I was happy, and I wanted to focus on that.

Gabriel disagreed, and he seemed to take injustice personally. He began canvassing for the Democrats and attending political meetings on campus. He was one of the first to show up to any march or demonstration, and if he was going to be there then so, I figured—with no small amount of guilt—should I. It's not like his causes were bad—he wasn't one of those nuts protesting Planned Parenthood. We bought a pile of cheap signposts from a realtor my mom knew, then invited groups over to attach poster boards spouting messages appropriate to whatever the cause of the month might be. I stood in the crowds and shouted the slogans, but Gabriel occasionally took control of the bullhorn. People listened to him, cheered when he said whatever platitude they wanted to hear. He always seemed happiest after a protest, even when it had no effect. In fact, I can't remember a single one that mattered in any real way, changed a policy, shamed someone into giving a damn what a group of unruly students thought, but he never found that discouraging. A few weeks later, there we were again, shivering in the snow as we marched Central's ice-ridden sidewalks.

But these progressive politics seemed at odds with what I mentioned earlier: his increasing obsession with religion. Not religion in general—which I could have understood, like other students' fascination with eighteenth-century poetry or robotics—but *his* religion. Catholicism. Now, I know everyone's significant other has a few blemishes. But Gabriel's Catholicism fundamentally cast me in the role of villain, and even if he seemed eager to ignore that part of his faith, I couldn't. Forgive the hyperbole, but it felt like a time bomb waiting to explode our relationship.

It began that first semester we were together, with an Intro to Religion course. Gabriel always had an active mind, but he dove into that material like nothing else outside of music. He wanted to talk to me about it, and I had to set him straight that I didn't give a crap what the Israelites went through. More than that, it worried me when I saw him signing up for three more religion courses the next semester. "There's so much I didn't know," he told me, as some form of explanation, and I didn't say anything because I figured it was just a phase and that academia would beat his love of it out of him, the way it had started to with music and me.

The Sunday before spring semester junior year, we had our first real fight about religion. I'd stayed over the night before, and I didn't want to leave the bed. I wanted a day of hedonism to make up for the drudgery of classes that awaited us, and since his roommates weren't home, I saw no reason not to take advantage of the situation and have a truly blissful afternoon.

I heard Gabriel's quick steps rushing back toward the bedroom, and as he passed beneath the sheet, he shouted, "You're late!"

"For what?" I said. "I don't have anything today."

"You have Mass!" Gabriel said. "You have to sing." He pulled the covers off me and tossed me the pile of clothes I'd left on the floor.

"Oh, that. I'm not doing that anymore," I said, pulling the covers back up and closing my eyes.

I hoped he would join me in bed but heard no movement. When I looked up again, he was staring at me with a combination of anger and disgust. I knew right then that the relaxing day I'd hoped for was already out of reach.

"It's no big deal, everyone already knows," I said. I'd decided on leaving the choir a while before, but Mr. Ferris had convinced me to keep singing until after Christmas. I told him that I'd miss seeing him and thanked him for all the help he'd given me, but I simply needed the time back. "So now we can sleep in late on Sundays."

"So are you going to go to Mass with me on Tuesday, then?" He still loomed over me, and with an intentionally dramatic sigh, I crawled out of bed and into the freezing reality of the day. His house was poorly insulated, with just an old metal radiator that they usually left off anyway to save money, preferring to use the fireplace and wear jackets inside. Normally I didn't mind, as it gave us an excuse to cuddle up beneath the covers, but now I hated my prickling goose bumps as I hurried to dress. He watched me, waiting for a response. I had, up until that point, done my best to give him the impression that I was as devout a Catholic as he was, just one who didn't like talking about it all that much.

"Well, no," I said. "I don't plan on going to Mass at all."

We stood there staring at each other. He looked ready to yell at me for the first time since I'd met him. Instead, he just glared.

"I don't see why you go," I said. "After all, God hates fags."

I don't know what made me think of that, but there it was. Three simple yet terrifying words.

"What the fuck are you talking about?" he said.

"Remember when we were out there on Central?" I said. "Out by the plaza, past the courthouses? There was that group doing the counterprotest, a dozen or so of those crazy rednecks screaming at us. We weren't even there to support gay marriage, but one of them was holding a sign that said: 'God hates fags.'"

"So what?" Gabriel seethed. "Because a redneck wrote some bullshit on a sign, you're not going to church anymore?"

"I just thought maybe you needed a reminder," I said. "He's not wrong, you know." I don't know whether I believed what I said. But I scrambled for something to pop his bubble of self-righteousness and picked the sharpest thing I could find.

"Of course he's wrong," Gabriel said. "You think Jesus hates us, hates anybody? Listen, if that's all this is, then come with me on Tuesday. Everyone has doubts, but just come, ok?"

"I remember stuff about the meek, right? And the poor and the goddamn peacemakers—all of them were given some sort of amends for their crappy lives. But I don't remember shit about people like us being given anything except fire and brimstone."

With this, I left the room and headed out of the house toward my car. It took him a few seconds to follow me, and I couldn't tell you what he was thinking. By the time he caught up, I already had the engine running, but he banged on the passenger-side window, and I rolled it down.

"Listen," he said, face red from rage or the cold or simply frustration. "That has nothing to do with church. With Jesus."

"It has everything to do with it—you're just not listening. Gabriel, why aren't you out?"

"I don't see how that's any of your business," he said.

"It's my business because I'm your boyfriend. And I think you're afraid of what the church has to say about your 'lifestyle.' I think you're afraid of what the priest would say if he knew you were fucking a man. And I think that telling me to go to church, like it's a sin not to, is the most hypocritical bullshit I've ever heard. I'm tired of this religious garbage. You do what you want, but I'm done with it."

I rolled up the window and drove back to my parents' house, angry with Gabriel, angry with myself, and angry with God.

FR. PATRICK CONKLIN

His fervor was infectious, and over time I grew more interested in our discussions, his little thought experiments and theological digressions. Oh, I primarily disagreed with him, but it was the talk that got my head churning. It was so different from my classes—there were no right or wrong answers in our discussions, and that was what appealed to me. The engineering my father talked about had a creativity to it, but the courses I was taking turned out to be rote. I'm sure that at higher levels, students were designing robots and more, but getting to those courses seemed like a huge waste of time.

By the end of sophomore year, I had changed majors and began focusing on religion and philosophy, where my ability to argue, to articulate my own understanding of the material, was not only accepted but encouraged. Telling my parents about this decision was difficult, and I don't blame them for their muted disapproval. I had always been a good son, the type who stuck to the sidewalks instead of venturing across busy streets, and they had reason to believe I was jeopardizing my future. But I explained to them that while my career prospects were not exactly abundant, I would find employment of some sort. I don't know if they were completely convinced, but they didn't try to stop me.

I tried my hand at dating but with little success, and admittedly a lot of the campus "hookup culture" bothered me. It was completely immoral, and I understand that it has only gotten worse since I graduated, though everyone wants to turn a blind eye to it. Regardless, I wanted to go on actual dates, but asking girls out felt strange, full of pauses and excuses, so after a while I stopped trying. The fairer sex remained a mystery to me, but without this distraction, I was able to keep my nose in the books. Even amongst my Catholic friends, Gabriel was one of very few who also never seemed distracted by women, and I respected him more for it. There were rumors about him, rumors of ... an unsavory sort, but I dismissed them because I heard some of the same rumors spoken about me.

In any case, at the end of Christmas break during our junior year, Gabriel called out of nowhere, his voice cracking as he struggled to maintain composure.

"I need to talk," he said. "Right now. I don't know who else to turn to." He said that things were too important to discuss on the phone, could we meet in person? Immediately? This was a matter of life and death.

It was the middle of the afternoon, and I had nothing else to do, so I said, "Sure."

When I showed up at Winning, he was already huddled over a table near the back. I watched as he took a tiny sip from his mug, put it down, took another sip, put it down again, then repeated this a third time, all in a handful of seconds. I couldn't help but notice the bandages on his hands. I sat, and he asked if I wanted to get anything. I told him no, I was fine, but after he raised an eyebrow, I ordered an herbal tea—I don't really drink caffeine because it upsets my stomach. I waited for him to say something as he stared at the bottom of his now-empty mug. When he didn't, I broke the silence.

"So … hey? What's happening?" I felt too awkward to ask about his hands.

He looked around suspiciously. There was a couple in the shop's other room and a student sitting a few tables away, staring at her laptop, but otherwise it was just the plants hanging near the doorway and abstract paintings of what looked like carpet swatches on the walls.

Fears assuaged, he spoke. "Patrick, I've … I've sinned."

"That's, well, that's bad," I said, unsure what else there was to say. "This isn't something you'd rather talk to a priest about?"

"No, no priest," he said. "I mean yes, maybe later. But I'm not certain it's that easy."

I sipped my tea. "Well, it depends on the sin, doesn't it? If it's just a venial sin, I wouldn't worry about it. Everyone sins. Even the saints."

"But how can you tell?" he asked. "My grandmother, she used to say that the difference between venial and mortal sins was whether you hurt someone or yourself. She used to say that sin is another way of measuring pain. But … Patrick, last night I had a nightmare. I was sitting in a small house, maybe a cabin, and it was cold so I put a couple logs and some newspapers in the stove and started a fire. The logs got hotter and hotter until they lit the stove, the whole room, and soon the house was burning into the floor. Into the ground. As I fell and the room blazed around me, I found myself in … there were no devils, no demons, but we were all in this fire, screaming but unable to hear one another. And then I woke up, and to my side was … well, never mind that, but it was absolutely horrible."

It was obvious he was not telling me the entire story, but we weren't close enough that I felt I could pry. Primarily, I was annoyed with him for acting like this was a big deal. "All this is about a nightmare?"

"It was no nightmare," he insisted. "It was real. I could still smell the sulfur burning when I woke up. It was a vision. All because I sinned, mortally sinned."

"I think you're being melodramatic," I said. "Dreams can come from anything. Indigestion, grades. To me, this sounds like a simple manifestation of your guilt."

"Well yes, I don't want to say I'm not guilty. But this was different." He looked away from me, and his voice became softer. "And, well, I didn't think that what I'd done was so bad it would send me to hell."

"As I said, the thing to do is to go to confession. Clear the air and you'll feel better." I said this knowing that I myself had not gone to confession in more than five years. The last time I had, I'd spent the previous night awake and frightened, and on the way over to church I'd had to ask my mother to pull over so I could throw up. So I gave him my excuse for avoiding confession for so many years. "But of course, if your sin was venial, then you don't even need to do that. If you didn't hurt anyone, maybe you didn't sin at all, or you did but it's not the type of thing that damns you to hell. Really, though, I can't answer that unless you tell me what you did."

"I can't do that." He spoke this forcefully and without hesitation.

"Then I don't know what to say."

"Well..." He paused. "Tell me how you decide for yourself, then."

I didn't know what to say, but I could tell he needed to hear something, so I repeated what I had learned from class. "Thomas Aquinas thought that the difference between venial sin and mortal sin wasn't in what you did, it was in your reason for committing the sin. Any sin committed out of malice is irreparable, but those committed through weakness or ignorance are only venial. So if you sinned in order to hurt someone, or God, then what you did was, well, very bad. But I know you, Gabriel, and I'm sure that whatever it is, it wasn't that."

"Of course not. But…" He paused again. "What if I committed it knowing that what I did was a sin? It hurt no one, not even myself, but I couldn't say I did it out of ignorance, though…"

All I could do was run through a mental list of sins he might not want to confess. Abortion? Surely not. Adultery? That seemed almost as unlikely. Murder? Heresy? Ordinary lying? All of these could be mortal sins but were either so unlikely or so easily confessed that I couldn't understand his pangs of conscience. Maybe he had decided that his little magic tricks were a form of witchcraft? That seemed as far-fetched as my other guesses. Something strange was going on, but it was beyond my detective skills to suss it out.

"The other thing Aquinas said was that penance makes every sin venial. Do a rosary. Do ten rosaries, I don't know. Assuming you didn't kill a man, you'll be fine. You don't have to be perfect to go to heaven."

"Shouldn't we try though?" asked Gabriel, looking straight into my eyes with earnest fervor. "Isn't it a sin not to try?"

"Think about the parable of the two men, remember them?" I asked. "Which one was perfect? Neither, they both had problems. I'm not saying to settle for a life of sinfulness, but you're going to be ok."

"When I was younger, someone would always tell me what to do," Gabriel said. "And when I did it, that made me 'good,' so I liked to obey adults. My mother, my grandmother, my teachers, whoever. But when I was older, I ran into a problem. I'd just come home from the magic store with my mom and had a new card trick I wanted to practice. My grandmother saw me doing it and told me it was wrong, that I was performing sorcery. My mother said it was fine, that these were just little tricks, games that kids played. It was a small thing, but I didn't know what to do. It was the first time I'd had two adults tell me something that conflicted."

"I'm ... not sure what you're getting at," I said.

"Patrick, one of the things I always liked about church was the rules. You could follow them and be a good person. But some of them have contradictions, and some of those contradict what I know in my heart to be true of Jesus and his teachings."

"So what did you do?"

"Well, I ... I mean, either way was wrong, so I did what I wanted. I kept practicing and doing magic. Eventually, my grandmother came around, and it worked out."

"You have to have faith in yourself, maybe that's all it is. It's stupid and it's simple, but I think it's true. The Church changes, it's a living body. But maybe your conscience doesn't. If you know what you're doing is wrong, then stop. But if not, if it feels like a gray area, maybe you trust yourself." Of course, I know much more now than I did that day. I know that these rules do not have gray areas, that the only time we have this sort of internal disagreement, it's because we are lying to ourselves, and to God. But without more information about his particular dilemma, it seemed like good advice.

After that, we said little else, just pleasantries. He asked me how I was doing. I think he wanted to reciprocate, but I didn't have much to tell him, so after a few minutes of awkwardness, watching as a busboy cleared a plate and mug from a vacated table, we said our goodbyes.

He did not show up to Mass for the next couple weeks. I worried about him and what he had been trying to hide. I began thinking that maybe it was drugs or a gang, something of that sort—after all, he was from that kind of neighborhood...

Soon he returned, though, and it was like nothing had happened. I remained curious about the whole affair, and occasionally I would bring it up, but he would quickly change the subject, so I stopped asking. He never really acknowledged our conversation again, and for whatever reason, that felt natural.

During our final year of college, our conversations turned to life after graduation. To be honest, he had more opportunities than I did. One of his professors had spoken to him about pursuing a master's in composition, and I knew he was seriously considering that. I was looking into graduate philosophy programs, even though I had lost some of my passion for the subject.

But then, after Mass one morning, toward the end of the fall semester, Father Anthony asked if we had considered the priesthood as a possible vocation. To be honest, I had already put a little bit of thought into it—not a lot, but the idea had been lingering in the back of my mind. Gabriel, on the other hand, looked completely stunned.

ISABEL ROMERO

They say that nothing prepares you for children, and I'm not saying I disagree. Pero *nothing* prepares you for when those children leave for college. Gabito moving out was a bigger adjustment than when I'd moved out myself. When he still lived at home, I'd grown to love silence, to fantasize about it, luxuriate in it during those brief intervals when I could snatch a few minutes of exquisite stillness. No cello scales seeping from the crack beneath his door, no murmured prayers keeping me up at night when I desperately needed sleep, just me and my thoughts. I missed hearing his footsteps pacing the hallway, picture frames on the walls shaking when he slammed the door to his bedroom, even though I'd told him a million times not to. I started to understand why Mamá always had her television playing, and took up the habit myself. The characters on the screen, always laughing and shouting and running from set to set, made the house feel full.

I stopped going to church entirely. Mamá could no longer make me, and Gabito wasn't around to guilt me about my sinful ways. I would tell him, when he asked at our more or less weekly meals together, that I had gone and the service was lovely, the homily insightful, all that basura. I think he probably knew I was lying, but what difference did it make?

I started looking at other jobs, anything where I could sit down all day in an air-conditioned room. Even when I could get an interview, though, a day or two later I'd hear that the position had gone to someone else. It would be me and a line of younger girls, girls straight out of college wearing short skirts and a pound of makeup, blanquitas with that Valley girl–Heights inflection instead of the quote, unquote "Mexican" accent I had, which anyone who wasn't a gringo knew had nothing to do with Mexico and everything to do with 'Burque bilingualism. It didn't matter that I had excellent references and years of experience. All anyone wanted was a college degree and a pretty face. I couldn't force myself to go back to school, so I shrugged and stayed at Kelly's, smiling at the pinche customers and hoping that if they got drunk enough, they'd leave me a big tip instead of nothing at all. It wasn't a bad job. I liked my boss enough, liked most of my coworkers and the camaraderie that came with long nights rushing from table to table, and gradually I came to accept that it was just what I did for a living.

Even during summers, Gabriel and I didn't see each other as much as I wanted. I usually worked evenings, because I was senior enough to choose my shifts, and the money is a lot better for dinner than lunch. During the day, he was out volunteering, interning, whatever. Something that didn't bring in a lot of money, I know that much. Not that I minded. Maybe it was because he'd grown up poor, but Gabito seemed to find even the idea of money distasteful. He was on a scholarship, and he kept his grades up, and as far as I was concerned, that was his job. Helping Padre Gonzales out at the food banks, that was just a nice hobby. We still ate together whenever we could, sometimes even going to Los Cuates for a nice night out, and went to the movies every couple weeks when we found the time, but it was never the same as before he started college. He didn't like to talk about himself, giving me one- or two-word answers, even when I pushed. More and more, I found myself talking about my own day when really I wanted to hear about his, telling him about some telenovela or screw-up with the cooks, even when I knew my stories weren't interesting. I just wanted to ward off the silence.

I started dating for the first time since Gabriel was born. It filled the time. The men I saw were a kind of low-stakes diversion, and unlike everything else I talked about, Gabriel seemed interested in hearing about them.

By the time he had his breakdown—if that's what you want to call it—he'd already been in college for a few years. He must've been a junior, maybe even a senior, but in any case, it was sudden. I came home late from work, and I could tell he was around because his shoes sat neatly by the front door, which wasn't something I required or even asked for but was his way of being polite. I was exhausted, so I didn't think anything of it. Pero the next day, his bedroom door never opened. Not even to use the bathroom, which I know doesn't seem possible, but I assure you it's what happened. I knocked on it a few times, but no answer came, and the handle remained locked. Every few hours I checked again, knocking and yelling louder with each visit. By the time I needed to head out for work, I was so worried about him that I'd decided to ask someone in the neighborhood for help breaking down the door.

But first, I thought to look through Gabriel's window. I took a folding chair from the garage and stood on it so I could peek in. His blinds were closed, but by pressing my nose against the glass, I could see enough to tell that physically, at least, he was doing more or less alright. Mentally, on the other hand ... well, what I saw did little to reassure me about that.

He was kneeling on the hardwood floor in front of his bed wearing only his underwear. In his right hand was a red lighter, a simple Bic one like you'd buy at a gas station for a buck fifty. I waited for a moment, trying to figure out what he was up to, when his other hand drifted over the small flame. A wisp of black smoke rose up from his hand, then he pulled it away. He cried out, so softly that it was inaudible, even through that thin pane of glass. He waited for maybe thirty seconds, maybe more than a minute. Then he lit the flame again and cupped his hand over it once more.

I pounded at the window, yelled for him to stop. He looked at me with irritation, maybe even anger, but went over to the door and opened it. I came back inside the house and thanked him for finally opening the goddamn door before asking him what the hell was going on.

"I'm just atoning," he said.

"For what?"

"For sins, that's all," he said. He smiled at me, and while it seemed genuine, there was something unsettling about it, an unhinged quality that did nothing to remove my worries. "It's no big deal, really." His hands and arms were sweaty, and there was a terrible burning smell.

"Can I see your hands?" I demanded.

"No."

"Fine then," I said. "But you're coming with me."

I called my boss, told him I'd be in late, then made Gabriel shower and bandage his hands. After he was dressed, I had him come with me to the restaurant and parked him in a corner where I could watch him for the evening. He sat there placidly, staring down at his table as if it had something important written on it. It was all completely inscrutable to me, and after making stupid errors all night, getting one order after another wrong, I left as soon as someone offered to cover for me. After work, I made Gabriel promise not to lock his door again or I'd kick him out of the house, and he cheerfully agreed. But I couldn't forget the weird anger I'd seen through the blinds, anger that he not only refused to explain but refused to even acknowledge.

There are things humans can never know about one another. We can have our guesses, piece each other together like mysteries in a detective novel, but how do we really know what's going on inside someone else's head? How much can we trust that explanations match up with real motivations? I think there's a kind of faith in that, in the idea that who we display to the world is the same as the person in our thoughts. Pero sometimes that faith gets ruptured. I suddenly understood that I didn't really know my Gabito anymore, that maybe I never had.

I can tell you my explanation, but I make no guarantees that I'm correct or even close. I don't think he had a crisis of faith. I don't think he ever disbelieved in Dios or anything like that. Maybe you could say that he had a crisis of faith in himself. I think he felt that he'd done something wrong and needed to atone for it. Maybe he needed to be away from college or whatever had made him sin, so that was why he was back home. More than anything, I think he simply needed some space, some time to figure out his life, and that's one thing college doesn't really let you have.

What I know for sure is that he didn't mention the flame, and I didn't either.

In the end, I don't know that any of that mattered. He went back to school, finished his degree, and bounced back as the same wonderful, happy son he'd always been. At least, that was what I saw, and maybe that was enough. He was the first person in our family to finish college, and I felt so proud of him on graduation day, and just wished Mamá had been there to see it too. He was accepted into the school's graduate program, where he'd write more lovely pieces of music that I wouldn't fully understand. His future seemed set.

He didn't consult me about his sudden change of plans, probably because I would've told him not to do it. I would've told him going to seminary era ridículo. But he didn't ask. Instead, I received a letter from him in the mail, informing me of his decision. After that, I mostly gave up on trying to figure him out, to understand when he was telling the truth about how he felt and when he was just telling me what he knew I wanted to hear. Maybe I should've been madder that he hadn't trusted me enough to say what he really wanted. He was an adult, though, and I trusted him, so I shrugged and made peace with it.

JOSHUA WHITEHURST

The earliest extant composition by Bach is a hymn. "Christ Lay in the Snares of Death" was written for an Easter Mass in 1707, when the composer was only twenty-two and working as a church organist in a small German village, writing music on the side. I couldn't tell you what its lyrics say, I don't speak German, but I do know that both the words and the tune itself aren't original to Bach. They're taken from Martin Luther, who I guess was a musician himself, though no one really talks about that anymore. The cantata concerns Christ's death and resurrection, but you could've probably put that together without my help. More important is that it's absolutely lovely, particularly in its fourth movement where a strong tenor line floats majestically over frilly baroque chords, passion set above a metronome until, all of a sudden, it comes to a jagged break from the expected pattern. A lone voice sustains the German word for death as long as possible before, inevitably, it breaks. The accompaniment returns, a sign of Bach's faith that death itself would inevitably give way to perfected harmony. The hallelujahs at the end of the piece sound flaccid by comparison, but for a moment there, you can feel Bach's dread pulsing between those lines of mathematical precision, and that's the essence of what made him worth listening to.

I did not love Bach before I met Gabriel. I considered him the stodgiest of the stodgy, music's original old graying eminence, complete with robes and wig. To me, his melodies were dusty and dull, each piece indistinguishable from the next. His music sounded like death, funeral dirges all of them, and what I wanted from music was life and pop and fun.

But what Gabriel loved, I came to love too, and in time I came to love Bach, though for the most part it was his secular work I enjoyed. Nearly three-fourths of his existing compositions were written for worship, Mass or sacraments or whatever else God wanted to jump in on, but he was so prolific that this still left me with his cello suite and his concertos and *The Art of Fugue*, works in which his genius for counterpoint, lines of melody heading off on their own yet always commenting on each other, stirred something within me. Almost as much as Britney Spears.

After our fight, or whatever it was, I started to compare our relationship to "Christ Lay in the Snares of Death." I'd thought we were solid, that we'd set our pattern, and like most baroque compositions, I didn't expect more than a few extra arpeggios' worth of variation to keep things interesting. Then came that sudden, unexpected break, and I didn't hear from Gabriel for three weeks. I assumed he had some sort of religious crisis, that I'd finally gotten through to him about the contradictions in his beliefs, though not in quite the way I'd hoped. I'd always thought that his love for me would be more powerful than any religious idea baked into his skull by some long-dead witch of a grandmother. But at the beginning of spring semester, with only my unanswered texts to console me, I returned to my largely abandoned dorm room and wondered what the fuck had happened.

A couple of weeks into the semester, though, he suddenly texted me, asking if I wanted to come over. I did, of course, and we had another glorious evening of wine and music and sex. He acted as if nothing had changed, wandering around the kitchen with a wine bottle in his dirtily bandaged hand, bruising my mouth with the force of his kisses, biting my tongue until I could taste blood. Sure, the wounds on his hands were new, but it was hardly the first time he had unexplained injuries, and I knew better than to ask. I accepted the lack of explanation, the return to normal.

His disappearance was like the break in Bach's first piece: jarring but integral, a poignant note in the lovely composition that was our relationship. I told myself that one day we'd talk about it, and he'd say how silly he'd been, how he regretted never telling me what happened. But right then, I just needed him back, and I wasn't going to say anything that might spook him off again.

I had trouble sleeping that night, as I sometimes do when the mixture of alcohol and adrenaline pumping through my veins won't dissipate. So there I was, sweating slightly, lying still beneath the covers, keeping my breath regular in the hope of letting Gabriel sleep, when I heard a whimper. I thought maybe it was just creaking floorboards or even an animal outside, but it happened again, and I knew it was him. I stayed perfectly still, doing my best to emulate a corpse, listening to his muffled sobs.

This lasted for what felt like ages, but I couldn't move, couldn't make myself console him or even hint that I was awake. He snuck out of bed, and I could hear him crying in the bathroom. I waited. He came back to bed, and I kept my eyes closed, my mouth shut, and tried to figure out what it meant all night long.

After that, everything went back to normal—but not, which I realize is confusing. It was confusing to me too. On a purely physical level, our relationship was exactly as good as before, and I don't just mean sexually. The meals we ate, the concerts we attended, even the conversations we had were the same lustrous, enjoyable affairs as ever. If you were to watch a movie version of us, before and after that evening, you wouldn't be able to spot the difference. We were both so good at acting the parts of a young couple completely devoted to each other, at least in private. But after that, something was never quite right between us.

And the following year, I couldn't ignore his reticence about post-graduation plans. The topic was constantly on my mind, probably because I didn't have much of a clue what I wanted to do next. Gabriel had taken the GRE, I knew that much, and I would have my degree in music education soon enough, though the prospect of actually using it to teach kids was daunting ... or, to be more accurate, depressing. I didn't want to do it, didn't want to teach scales and breathing exercises, didn't want to care whether tones blended, to play shitty piano parts while kids sang off-key, but that was all I could see in front of me, so I was going to apply for teaching positions nonetheless.

But all of that depended on Gabriel. If he traveled, I wanted to go with him, and what would that be like? I tried broaching the subject a few times. "Think you'll want to stay in town?" That sort of thing, but he would smile and say, "I guess." What kind of answer is that? "I guess"? It scared me, because Gabriel had the grades and the aptitude for a real career. I needed some sort of idea where my life was headed, and I was committed to tagging along with him ... I just needed to make sure he felt the same.

I tried to bring it up again one day while we were making dinner. He did the real cooking. The most I could do was chop onions or meat and maybe boil water for pasta. Still, I tried to help, and at the very least offered company in the kitchen by sitting with my laptop at the small table, chatting with him or his roommates. "So are you still headed to grad school next year?"

"Mm-hmm," he said, not turning away from the stove. I don't remember what he was cooking, but I remember he was facing away from me so that I couldn't read his expression.

"What does that mean?"

"Grad school."

"Ok, Mr. Terse. What school? Where? What are you studying?"

"Music, of course. Here, assuming they accept me. I haven't heard yet. Maybe they won't and I'll be one of those sign spinners outside the car wash on Lomas. Good pay, good people. Very good signs."

This relaxed me, like I was silly to even ask. But I was still left wondering why he'd been so secretive. "Why music?" I pushed. "I mean, I'm glad, but I've just been wondering why not some sort of ivory tower religious PhD?"

"Music is religion!" As he said this, he spun around with a flourish and practically leaped across the room to turn up the stereo. One of Bach's cantatas was playing but not one I recognized, so to me it just sounded like orderly chords punctuated by efficacious German singing. "Just listen. Where there's music, God in His grace is always present."

"Don't you mean 'devotional music'?" I asked. This was his favorite quotation by Bach. The composer had written it into his own Bible, and Gabriel once wrote a short faux-baroque cantata that used the original German as its text. The piece had ... not been his best work.

"All of it," he said. "You ever listen to a piece so great that it feels like there's something inhuman about it?"

"Not really? I mean, I hear 'Hey Ya!' at a party, and I think it's a pretty perfect song but not exactly divinely inspired."

"But it is, it really is. There's something about notes coming out right, absolutely right, that I can't explain. No other animal makes music. They make sounds but not with rhythm, not with structure. Whenever someone tells me that there is no God, that humans are just bigger, fancier apes, I think about music, and it all makes sense to me."

"What all makes sense?"

"I don't know, all of it. That's why I don't need to keep studying religion. It's more fun to put a record on and figure things out that way."

"I wish I got that," I said.

"You don't? Not at all?"

"I don't know. Maybe I once did. I just ... now I hear the notes and I hear the melodies and I hear the beat, and it all sounds kind of boring. Unless I've been drinking, then it's fun to dance to, but mostly I'm kind of bored with everything."

"I thought you wanted to teach music?"

"Yeah, because it's a job. And it's good for kids, you know? Maybe some of them will get stuff out of it like you do. I don't know."

"That's it? I thought it was your calling."

I shrugged and smiled.

Gabriel returned to cooking, and while I remember dinner being fantastic, later that evening we had some of the lousiest sex of my life. We couldn't connect, but again, I didn't say anything.

He was accepted into UNM's grad school, and we made plans. A house just for us, maybe a pet—he wanted a dog, but I was sure only a cat would do. We worked on my résumé and did practice interviews in case the school district decided it needed a new music teacher after all.

Another photograph for you to consider: It's Gabriel, me, and three of our closest friends on graduation day. The two of us are in the center, my arm around Gabriel's shoulder. To my right is a friend who would die three years later from a drug overdose, and to our left are Becky and Raymond, who got engaged six months after graduation, now have two kids together, and from what I last saw on Becky's Facebook account, are now headed toward divorce. We're dressed in scarlet-red robes, our eyes heavy, almost shut after two nights of partying, but our mouths are wide open with laughs or smiles. If you stare at it long enough, you might think Gabriel seems a little distant. Is his smile as genuine as mine, or is there something else his eyes hint at? You might think he's pulling away from me a bit. You'd be wrong, though. I can assure you I've stared at that photo longer than you'd think possible and, after taking it all in, there's no hint at his future. It's only after the fact that it's difficult not to assign some fateful meaning to his smile.

That's the last photo I have of us together. Two days later, he disappeared again without saying goodbye, another sudden break in the melody, leaving me to wonder what was next. This time it would be much longer before I saw him again.

MANUEL QUINTANA

Some of us came from cities, near and far. Two from Albuquerque but others from Denver. From Seattle and Portland, San Francisco and San Diego. No more than a handful from any one location, and even those from Oregon were far from their homes.

Some of us came from towns and villages, farms outside of city limits and places so remote that you needed to drive for more than an hour to receive the Eucharist on Sunday. We were more used to the isolation, the quiet of the seminary hilltop, surrounded by copses and framed by a nearby cliff in one direction and a long, dull drive toward society in the other. But even by our standards, Holy Trinity Seminary seemed lonely and sanctified, half a dozen imposing buildings in a sprawling green landscape.

Some of us arrived prepared. With suitcases in hand, we walked off the train or bus, hundreds or thousands of miles across an America whose full scope we'd never witnessed before, whose sheer number of buildings and people and trees and spaces we'd never grasped. We carried with us five sets of black-and-whites, black slacks and white button-down shirts. Five pairs of socks. A razor. A rosary. Our own personal Bible. A cassock, which felt imbued with tradition and belief. We carried with us purpose, ill-defined though it might have been, and a feeling that all we would ever need was inside that suitcase. God would take care of the rest.

Some of us arrived without the suitcase, with only the clothes we wore and a backpack full of all we owned. But no one spoke of this, because within the seminary we were equal, our purpose the same. Those without were provided for, and soon it was impossible to tell who came from money and who didn't. We were all novitiates, all servants of God, though few who entered would eventually choose the priesthood for their vocation and even fewer still would stay with it for a lifetime.

In the morning, we would wake and have half an hour to prepare for the day. Then the morning prayer, "lauds" we called it, from the Liturgy of the Hours. This was followed by Mass and then, finally, breakfast, at which point certain seminarians would be near the point of collapse. But really, seminary was a school like any other, and while we would say more prayers, honor more sacraments later in the day, most of our time was spent studying philosophy and religion and even how to talk. We were here to be told not only what to do but how to think, how to believe. We were here to become orthodox in mind and spirit, to become vessels for the Holy Roman Church. There was some room for individuality, particularly during the evening music rehearsals, but for the most part, we were a fraternity of students still looking to be molded. "Human clay," they called us, and to this we acquiesced, even as we inevitably divided ourselves with cliques and intrigue, factioning even when asked not to. We were not monks, though we seemed to think, particularly at the beginning, that this was what we were being asked to become, and after a few months, our identities were no longer as blurred and undifferentiated as when we first arrived.

Gabriel was one of the first students I noticed, one of the first faces that stood out among the black-and-white monotony. He was also from New Mexico, Albuquerque rather than the north where I came from, but that was still closer than anyone except Patrick. And unlike Patrick, Gabriel was also Hispanic, which I knew shouldn't have mattered, but it did. I never knew quite what to say to Gabriel, but I still felt a kinship with him. He was pleasant, always smiling and joking, messing around with magic tricks until they told him to stop, though he still performed a few when the priests weren't watching, much to our delight. There was no television, so we were always starved for entertainment. He wasn't argumentative, none of us were, at least no one who lasted past the first month. But he was curious and questioning. He accepted his superiors' answers but required them to be good. The rest of us meekly acquiesced.

Gabriel would ask about what obedience meant and whether obedience to the Church was the same as obedience to God. "The Church changes, but God is eternal," he said. One of the priests responded by muttering something about how the Church was the will of God, but I remember thinking that was strangely inadequate. His questioning made me like Gabriel more, though I think for most, the effect was the exact opposite. It made many suspicious of him, and by the end of the first year, he was more than a tad isolated.

Maybe I've always been a little bit strange, but it was questioning that brought me to the seminary in the first place, a search for answers beyond the small town I grew up in. There was a rigorous vetting process before any of us were allowed in. Where once the priesthood's doors stood wide open, now there was a battery of criminal background checks, psychological and physical exams, and extensive personal interviews before any of us made it onto those hallowed grounds. While the Vatican had done its best to hide the rape scandals that plagued its churches worldwide—shuffling priests away in the dead of night, pretending it didn't know about the trail of victims stretching out past the horizon, selling millions of dollars in priceless art and architecture and land in order to hide its monsters from the bright lights of television and court appearances—it had also been thinking toward the future. There would be no more scandals, its bishops claimed. No sex scandals, certainly, but none of any other kind either. God's holy soldiers in the Church's mission against Satan would be a more perfect group, organized and prepared and unified. Those who wore the robes, who offered up the body and blood of Christ, needed to embody His virtues, and any hint of deviation would be shown the door.

What I saw around me at the seminary, though, was not the shining example of Christ or gleaming knights in His army of the righteous. What I saw was dullness. Mediocrity. The men at seminary weren't scholars or great thinkers, nor were they firebrands or holy warriors. Most of us were uncertain and meek. And maybe it wasn't the examinations that did it, the thorough weeding out of anyone who might not fit the particular priestly mold that bishops seemed to have agreed upon. Maybe it was that priests had always been this way. Or maybe it was just the sorry state our religion had slumped into. I couldn't tell you why it happened, only that I saw it around me.

We spoke frequently about how to draw Catholics back to the Church, how to draw new Catholics in. We threw around theories about how we should be more like the evangelists, or the Mormons, or even the Scientologists. How we needed better music or movies. How we should do more outreach to the poor, or to the wealthy. How maybe these things came in cycles, and the best thing for the Church was to keep doing business as usual. The one thing no one seemed to mention was that the Church's spark, long cooling in America, now seemed completely absent. Our rituals were still there, cold and lifeless in museumlike churches, but the rest of it had gone with the spark—as the Church transitioned from the twentieth century to the twenty-first, questions of its relevance seemed to bloom everywhere except inside the seminary's walls. There, all we had were varying forms of denial.

Gabriel referred to me as a friend, but already I was more of a follower. I saw that spark in him, in his questioning and his utmost faith, and that combination was not a contradiction but a sign of the depth of his belief. We came from all over the country to preach the word of Christ, but our belief in Him was far from unified. For some of us, Jesus was like a best friend, always present, always ready to help out so long as we'd be there for Him, and for others He was simply a part of the Masses they'd attended since birth. Most of us were somewhere in between, but for a group of people who were, at least theoretically, devoting their lives to their faith, you'd be surprised how infrequently He came up in conversation. Except with Gabriel.

A common misconception about priests, which you might have dealt with yourself, is that we arrive at seminary with our future already decided. But Major Theologate Seminary is in many respects the same as any other graduate program, and while we were all supposed to have

"heard the call," no one was committed to anything beyond discernment itself—figuring out if this was in fact
the life for us. Few left during the first year, but by the
end of the second, maybe a third of us had departed. We
were a group of men struggling to figure out our role in
God's plan, but we were also struggling to find ourselves,
and often that meant we left. It was understood that at
any time a person could leave, or be asked to leave, and
the constant specter of this haunted the seminary's tall
stone hallways. You would wake up, and the person in the
room next to you would be gone, no explanation forthcoming. Was it his decision? The seminary's? A mutual
agreement? We didn't know, we simply gossiped, making
up stories about students caught drunk on sacramental
wine or masturbating in their rooms, though more than
likely, they'd simply decided that God's plan for them
was an ordinary life with a wife and children. But still,
tales of deviance and even satanic rituals always seeped
into the conversation.

Early on, it was clear that even though Gabriel was
different, spending his time composing or meditating
rather than in classes on ancient Greek, he'd already
discerned. Most of our colleagues wanted to talk about
softball during off hours or to reminisce about their lives
before seminary, but Gabriel only wanted to talk about
faith. There was no assigned activity, from washing dishes
to cutting firewood to studying philosophy, that didn't
inspire him with new questions about God and religion.

"It's tiring," I once heard Father Reynolds, our general
headmaster, tell Father Selman in the dining hall. The
priests ate at their own table, nearest the food, so it was
sometimes possible to eavesdrop—accidentally or not—
when passing by. "The Holy Spirit may be everywhere,

but maybe He's not in the floor when you have to mop it. Maybe you just have to mop the floor."

"Have you considered the theological implications of scratching your ear because it itches?" Father Selman said in his best approximation of Gabriel, which sounded far more like Cheech Marin. "No, Gabriel, I haven't, and neither has anyone else. Now go back to reading your Bible."

The two of them laughed, and I passed without saying anything. What was there to say?

By that second year, there were half a dozen of us who were still friendly with Gabriel. We thought of ourselves as the more serious members of the seminary, and for the most part, we were on very good terms with the faculty. We met once a week, usually late Sunday nights, in Gabriel's room to talk about faith in a more personal, less theoretical way than we did in our classes. No references to texts, even the Bible, just our personal relationship with God. It was almost like an AA circle, each of us sharing stories late into the night until, seemingly at random, Gabriel would end things with a short song or prayer, and we would make our way back to our own rooms and sleep for a few short hours before the next day's studies.

It felt, at times, like an alternate education. I don't know how any of it began, why we all innately knew Gabriel was our leader. He repeatedly stated that he wasn't, that we were all equals. But as soon as he left, the late-night meetings stopped, never to be mentioned again.

It happened sometime in the third year. One morning, I walked past his door, which was usually closed because he was prone to sleeping in, could sleep past half a dozen alarm clocks when he was tired enough, and I noticed it open a crack. I peeked through and saw that his desk was empty, his mattress stripped bare. It was like no one had ever been there.

During breakfast, I asked Father Reynolds. I knew, as I walked up to the priests' table, that everyone's eyes were on me. No one ever asked about those who left. It simply wasn't done. But I needed to know.

"Is Gabriel gone?"

Father Reynolds looked at me with no small amount of amusement. "Yes."

"For good?"

"Yes."

"Well … why?" I had never been certain whether it was against some unspoken rule to ask or if it was just a custom, but I figured that if I was ever going to find out, now was the time.

"He found … we found … there was mutual agreement that he was no longer a good fit for Holy Trinity."

With that, Father Reynolds turned his head back to his plate. I returned to my table and, disappointed, finished my meal and left the room to pray.

Gabriel's departure left no echoes in those eternally still hallways—once he left, it was like he had never been there at all. And though he was perhaps the only real priest I knew during my four years at seminary, even I hardly thought of him until after graduation. The idea that I would see Gabriel again never crossed my mind.

FR. PATRICK CONKLIN

I knew right away that he should not have been there. Oh, I understood why Father Anthony recommended him, and I knew why Gabriel thought it would all work out. I even remember how confident I was, at the time, that he was the pious one, the one more touched by the Holy Spirit. I had my doubts as to what role in God's plan I was supposed to fill. I even felt that perhaps I had been a bad Christian, at least in comparison to someone like Gabriel, who would not let you forget for five minutes just how *good* he thought he was. But it wasn't until we passed through Holy Trinity's hulking brass doors that it became clear to me that this was my home, my world, and it was people like Gabriel who weren't fit for the clergy.

To say that seminary changed me would be an understatement, and as I grew closer to the Church, I also grew to understand how lax and sinful I had been before, not to mention how lax and sinful the society around us had become. Seminary opens your eyes to a different way of seeing the world, but only if you're perceptive to it and willing to listen, and not everyone is.

But seminary is also a place of discipline. You learn when it's appropriate to ask questions and when it's time to listen to your superiors. Gabriel never seemed to understand that balance. He would stay quiet when we discussed Spinoza—probably because he hadn't done the reading—then talk back when asked to take his turn cleaning dishes. We were supposed to be above all of that, to be preparing our souls for a lifetime of service, of meekness and obedience, not shirking our chores in the name of more prayer time.

At first I defended him. We were friends—though our friendship became strained sooner than I anticipated. But I slowly grew tired of making excuses for him, since he made no attempt to change. Even after he was reprimanded in full view of the rest of the other first-year seminarians, he persisted in his negligence. For example, when Father Kennedy asked him to recite a passage from *Beowulf* for our literature course, Gabriel had the gall to ask him why.

"Because I want to hear it spoken," said Father Kennedy. "Old English has its own sound, its own tenor and music, and I want us to remember that as we read through the work. A story like *Beowulf* was meant to be heard and spoken, transmitted not through the page but from person to person."

"Yes," said Gabriel. "That's all very good, a fine lesson. But what does any of this have to do with the Holy Spirit?"

There was a collective in-breath amongst the students, but Father Kennedy only sighed, perhaps rolled his eyes slightly, though I may have added that detail after all these years. Then he asked another student to recite the passage and moved on. I could see how Gabriel's piousness, his focus on faith above all, might seem commendable, and to a certain extent it was. But after months of this, it felt, dare I say it, performative. He needed *us* to know that he put faith before all else.

He was even worse when it came to the priesthood's most sacred vow: celibacy. I don't mean to say that he was out there in the middle of the woods fornicating with whoever came near—of course not—but he was disrespectful, perhaps heretical, when it came to sexuality.

I remember him questioning the doctrine on multiple occasions. He wanted biblical evidence for why we should believe in clerical celibacy, and brought up passages from First Corinthians to support his argument. He was unsatisfied by the history of canon law surrounding the Church's rules, despite the fact that, as you well know, canon law is the fundamental building block of Catholicism.

I remember one particular incident when he absolutely refused to even hear what was being taught, showing a shocking closed-mindedness. We were attending a workshop on sexual ethics, "Freedom and Triumph" I think was the name, in the seldom-used classroom above the dining hall. It was reserved for these special one-off seminars, not only because the room was dusty and old but also because of all the classrooms, it offered the best view. A pair of wide, gaping windows overlooked the lush valley below. Students understandably tended to lose focus in there, staring at deer passing in the nearby meadows and forgetting to keep their minds focused on the texts at hand.

That day's seminar was led by a priest who told us he had been invited by seminaries all around the world to speak on this most uncomfortable of subjects, and we were encouraged to stand up and speak at any time we wished, to ask questions without judgment. I felt this was exactly the type of seminar the Church needed, given the scandals that have damaged our reputation.

He distributed workbooks so that we could follow along, with subjects such as "Masturbation: Who Does This Sin Hurt?" and "Temptress Women and the Devil's Other Ploys." This was important information, straight from the Vatican, time-honored methodologies that priests could use to combat their basest desires. But Gabriel kept laughing, from girlish giggles to full-on guffaws. When asked if he would like to share anything, though, he quieted down quickly enough, staring out the window while more serious students paid attention to the priest's advice. As we brought our particular fears into the room, worries about the souls of masturbators or what to do if a congregant was particularly attractive, it felt like Gabriel was judging us. His face was impassive, but somehow I felt a smirk behind it, as if he were above all of this, all of us.

The session culminated in an unorthodox but fulfilling exercise in which we attempted to reenact the day-in, day-out battle against temptation that happens within all of us. The visiting priest shut the curtains and lit the room with hundreds of small candles. He burned incense, and we watched as he performed a short ritual before producing a set of carefully inscribed name tags, lettered in bloodred, and a set of heavy black cloaks.

I know this sounds a bit ... arcane, but the priest wanted us to embody spiritual abstraction, an uncommon but powerful methodology that I have used with my own parishioners since. Once we donned our cloaks, we were handed the name tags and told to represent the demon listed, from Abaddon and Mammon to Beelzebub and Pazuzu. A volunteer was chosen, and the rest of us circled his desk. Our job was to cajole him to give in to his desires, to masturbate, to watch pornography, to fornicate. We chanted at him. We taunted him, pushed him a bit with our hands. We told him how good those licentious acts would feel, whispered to him that no one would find out. Some priests began speaking in tongues, channeling their specific demons. We offered him deals, from power to the most beautiful and willing wife in the world. We offered him instant exoneration from his sins. We told him everyone else in the Church was doing it, everyone at seminary, that everyone laughed at him behind his back. We whispered that sex could be holy, could be beautiful. Could be godly, if only he would give in and try it. What was the harm in one little taste?

He did not break, and after an hour or so, the visiting priest announced that we were finished. He collected the name tags and cloaks in a large metal wastebasket, then took this outside, soaked it in lighter fluid, and set it aflame, saying prayers to exorcise those demons from the seminary and from us. "Demonic influence is never to be taken lightly," he said.

Gabriel didn't participate, was staring so pointedly out the window that the visiting priest had to pin his name tag to his back, and at some point he must have slipped out.

Although I saw Gabriel in class over the next couple of days, we did not speak about his absence until later. By then we rarely interacted. He had his group of friends, and I had mine, and the two barely mixed. Still, we remained friendly enough, and I still wanted him to succeed, to find his way in the seminary despite, or perhaps because of, all of his issues. As such, I felt I should speak to him about his noncompliance with the visiting priest, the way his disrespect reflected on the entire community. I wanted him to know that what he had done was not befitting of a future priest but that there was no reason he couldn't mend his ways.

What I was not expecting was for Gabriel to come knock on my door early one morning, before my alarm went off. I was groggy when I answered him, and there was something surreal in his appearance that made it seem like I was still dreaming. As I followed him to his bedroom on the other side of the hall, the predawn sky outside was barely graying, and fog was settling across the courtyard. The hallway seemed sapped of color, and it felt as if time had stopped.

Gabriel gestured for me to sit and perched on his unmade bed. Myriad pill bottles, both open and closed, rested on the top shelf. Candles, the tacky kind with images of saints taped to them, rested on almost every surface, though most of them were empty.

"Hey, how are you?" he asked. His voice cracked, at odds with his usual composure.

"Fine, I suppose. How are you?"

"Fine, fine," he said. There was a long pause. "Well, maybe just ok."

I thought of our conversation back in Winning and knew he might need some sort of help again, though what he had been dealing with back then remained a mystery. "What's going on, Gabriel? Why did you need to wake me up?" If he sensed my confusion, he made no sign.

"Do you feel ... I remember when we were first accepted, how excited we were," he said. "We were going to be God's soldiers, holy men righting the wrongs of the world through Christ's grace. We were fired up and ready to make a difference."

"I ... I suppose so." That wasn't how I had felt at all. I had felt unsure, and it was only after I arrived that I began to appreciate the rigor of a life devoted to faith.

"And now that we're here, it's all talk. We're off in the wilderness instead of out there getting our hands dirty."

"Jesus had to go into the wilderness too," I said. Gabriel paused to consider this and seemed to think it was profound. This was an old tactic of mine: when in doubt with Gabriel, mention Jesus, and he would figure out the rest on his own.

"Hmm. Perhaps. But I'm not Jesus, and maybe I can't be," he said. "Patrick, I'm bored. I'm restless. I'm pretty sure none of the priests like me, and I'm not so sure I like any of them. I don't think I belong here."

I knew, intellectually, that he was right. We didn't need some firebrand trying to shake up our spiritual development. One thing I had come to realize was that the Catholic Church was bleeding parishioners because our priests didn't know what they were talking about, and Gabriel's need for constant theological thought-experiment was symptomatic of this. The only way to become the type of priest who could deal with the twenty-first century and all the contradictions inherent in faith was through rigorous seminary training.

But I didn't have the heart to tell him that, since I still saw in him my devoted friend from college. "You're joking, right? Of course you belong."

He stared into my eyes, perhaps wondering if I was being facetious. "Why?"

"Because you're a believer," I said. "And you want to share your faith. That's what really matters. The rest of it is window dressing. So what if Father Kennedy hates that you've never done the reading? Five years from now, do you think that will matter?"

"You're right," he said. "Thanks for taking the time to … well, in any case, thanks."

I didn't know what else to say, and he seemed to want some time to reflect. He stood up, and as I walked to the door, I noticed his "demonic" name tag from the seminar sitting amongst his pills. I considered asking him to burn it like the visiting priest had but decided not to say anything.

Gabriel stayed for another year. For a while, he and some friends held their own private meetings, which I assume was his attempt at transforming seminary into what he wanted it to, be. But in the long run, the mismatch between Gabriel and the seminary proved to be too much. I cannot say that it was directly because of me and what I told him that he stayed for as long as he did, but I did what I felt was right at the time.

I was not sad to see him go, though I never learned the full circumstances of his departure. The student body, which had been fractured while Gabriel was there, seemed to come together afterward, and by the third year, all the less rigorous students had departed. Discernment served its purpose, and those of us who moved forward were the best and the brightest, the ones who understood the real business of being a priest.

ISABEL ROMERO

My friend Alyssa from work used to tell me que su mejor amiga era su hija, Tina. She'd tell me how they went shopping together at T.J. Maxx, modeling all the bargain dresses for each other because the store's curved mirrors made everything look good. She'd tell me how they met for café con leche at the Satellite on Central when her daughter showed her that big diamond ring her fiancé, Ritchie, proposed with, and then again when Ritchie turned out to be another pendejo so she had to leave him. I always figured Alyssa was bragging, that really her relationship with her daughter was the same as the one I had with my son, and she just liked to pretend otherwise. But when I mentioned that she was my mejor amiga and she looked at me with such sad eyes, such disappointment and surprise and judgment all in one dumb look, I knew to add, "Except for Gabito, of course." Maybe she and her daughter were that close after all. Maybe other parents were that close to their adult children too. I didn't have any way of knowing, besides maybe what I saw in telenovelas. I hadn't seen my son in more than a year.

After enough years waitressing, the job becomes a rote dance that you can perform with your brain still asleep. That doesn't mean it becomes any easier: your back still aches, your feet and ankles still feel like you've been hiking up the Sandias even in your most comfortable sneakers, and your desire to tell pinche customers to fuck off only grows. Every catcall reminds you of so many catcalls before. I still wished I could've worked more hours, though, because that would've cut down on the crushing nothingness that awaited me afterward.

I started seeing a man. I won't tell you his name because ... bah, why do I care? His name was Brandon Hewitt, and I met him through an online dating website, which I started messing around with at night so I had something to do during commercial breaks. I liked him mostly because he would call things he liked "lovely," and every time he came to my house he'd take off his boots before coming inside, big black steel-toed things, even though he worked as a paralegal or something. He was thoughtful, and though he wasn't really my type physically, thinning red hair and a long beard combined with enough girth that he looked like an overgrown hobbit, when I first met him he seemed to genuinely care about me. At least, he cared about "bettering me," said I was too smart to die in a dead-end job, and I should go back to college for a real education not just trade school.

"But first," he'd said, voice carefully level, "do you like films?"

His education turned out to be night after night of movies because I'd never seen "the canon." Hitchcock and Godard, Tarkovsky and Ozu, Renoir and a bunch of other fancy European names I could never keep straight, let alone remember why they were all supposed to be so important. When he learned I speak Spanish, he made me watch Luis Buñuel movies, and when I told him I thought they were terrible, stupid stories about dumb situations that could never happen, he said the problem was I needed to learn how to watch them right, so he brought more over. At his house, he had thousands of DVDs, no lie, lining his shelves, in piles beside his television set, even stacked in the kitchen and bathroom, and I quickly realized this was as far as my self-improvement would ever get. Frankly, I felt some relief. It was better than watching TV on my own, and making him happy helped pass the time.

We were watching a movie at my house when Gabito returned, probably something subtitled and boring beyond belief, and I was fiddling with a game on my phone even though it annoyed Brandon. My son walked in and sat down on the couch as if he'd been invited.

"Who's this guy?" he asked.

I was so stunned it took me a second to react, to stand up and hug him and try to answer his question. I didn't want to let go, but eventually he removed himself, so I answered as best I could. "He's my umm, he's my friend..."

"He's your boyfriend," said Gabriel, a statement not a question. "That's fine. What're you watching?"

He acted as if things were normal, so I guess they were. And when Brandon left for the evening—we didn't have to discuss this change of plans—Gabito waved goodbye as if they'd known each other for years.

Gabito told me that he'd left the seminary, though he didn't want to talk about why. I was so happy to have him back that I didn't press, and figured there would be enough time later to learn what happened. I had my angelito home again, and that was more than enough.

I expected Gabito to be happier. He could practice music again, apply for grad school, return to real life. What's more, he could feel like he'd given the whole religious thing a fair shot and learned it just wasn't for him. I felt Mamá and her faith had warped his viewpoint, pero of course the priests wanted him to conform, to stand in line and do what he was told—that's what religion is all about. That he was shocked about it made me feel I hadn't quite done my job as a mother.

I wanted him to know that there was nothing wrong with deciding against the Church, for once in his life. I tried teasing him, calling him "my little heretic," but he just smiled when I said it. I wanted him to react, to tell me off or just do *something*, but even that didn't seem to bother or prod any life into him.

He practiced his music when I reminded him, watched TV with me when I asked him to, but seemed to have little willpower of his own. He never left the house unless I made him. He saw no friends. I'm not even sure what he did when I was at work or seeing Brandon, maybe nothing. He earned no money, but he also ate little, so he was hardly a strain on my wallet.

Weeks passed, and nothing changed. I asked Brandon if he thought my son was suffering from depression, but he was typically noncommittal and mumbled something about "not knowing him well enough to judge," then asked me to be quieter so he could hear Soderbergh's commentary track more clearly.

I left out sheet music from his favorite composers, Bach and Handel and anything else I could find around the house. Five years earlier, these would've been irresistible to him, and even still, I occasionally heard him playing his keyboard in his bedroom, fingers clacking against the plastic keys in a way I associated with a full and cheerful home. I thought maybe he was getting back to normal. But when I crept in after work one day and peeked through the crack in his door, I saw he was playing like a robot, unsmiling and stiff-backed.

Another day, I came home to find him watching television while moving a quarter between his knuckles, the coin bouncing from one to the next and sometimes disappearing momentarily before he made it appear, in the simplest possible illusion, in his other hand. I was glad to see he'd kept up with something, even if sleight of hand was never going to fill grocery bags or pay rent. But I'd never seen him watch TV on his own before. Even when he was little, he'd always been too busy to slow down and watch cartoons. Something about him sitting there, practicing what barely even qualified as a magic trick while listening to mindless celebrity prattle, turned my stomach.

So I tried setting him up with Alyssa's daughter, Tina. I mean, it sounded like a good idea at the time. The way Alyssa tells it, though, the whole thing was stilted and almost surreal. He showed up at her house wearing a blazer and tie, with a small bouquet of white roses. Standing in front of her adobe house with bars across the windows, my '89 Ford Tempo behind him, it was so over-the-top that Tina couldn't stifle her laughter. He drove her to some French restaurant near Old Town, running around the car to open the door for her and taking her arm as if they were going to some aristocratic ball. Once seated, he asked her about her favorite composers, and within a few sentences they'd run out of things to say. It was like he was just going through the motions, pretending he was the leading man in one of the movies Brandon made me sit through.

Tina told Alyssa, who of course told me, that while he seemed nice enough, she'd sooner blow her brains out than go on a second date. When I asked Gabito what he'd thought, he shrugged and said it had gone fine. But that was his answer for almost everything: life was fine, he was fine, the world maybe had a few problems but most people in it were all fine enough for him.

I decided that if there were no other options, I'd try the one thing that might finally work: I brought him back to church. Not that he ever really left—we went to San Ignacio together on Sundays, even if he seemed nearly as unenthusiastic about it as I was. But I'd been listening in on a conversation at Kelly's, a pair of forty-something women discussing how the archbishop of Santa Fe had broken up their church because it was filled with Franciscans. It got me thinking about how different some Catholics are from others. Gabito had clearly gone off to seminary thinking it would be like studying with Padre Gonzales from San Ignacio or maybe a mentorship like he'd had with Mamá. Instead, whatever he'd found there had wounded him. But what if he tried something else? The Franciscans were gone, but they weren't the only game in town. The next weekend, I brought him to Immaculate Conception, an imposing brick-and-concrete square of a building that stood out against a neighborhood of old brown casitas.

During the service, I zoned out and nearly fell asleep, but Gabito seemed to really like it. Afterward, he found the priest and spoke to him, and when we returned the following week, he made arrangements to volunteer with the parish. His volunteering soon became a nearly full-time commitment, and he spent most of his time feeding the homeless or building houses or whatever else they did—I have trouble remembering because I didn't much care. What mattered was that it worked, which I knew because when I arrived home after work and he sat at the keyboard, his chords rang out like bombs. He rocked back and forth on the bench, moving both to the music he played and to rhythms in his head that no one else could hear. When he left again for seminary, this time to a Jesuit one, I still thought he was wasting his talent. But only a terrible parent stands between her child and happiness, so I wished him luck and hugged him for as long as I could before he headed out the door.

JOSHUA WHITEHURST

I saw him only once during that period. I was at the Smith's off Lead Street, the dirty one with the dim lights, grocery shopping with my boyfriend Jonathan, because of course that's how these things go. Gabriel stood, kind of zoned-out-looking, in the checkout line. Seeing him felt like another betrayal. I'd been pushing the cart, and I ran it into a display while I stared at that shithead's lovely face.

"You ok?" Jonathan asked me.

"Yeah, I just thought I saw someone I knew."

"Well, ok, just be more careful. Do you want to go over and say hi?"

"No, I just … it wasn't him…"

"If you're sure…," Jonathan said, clearly not believing me. "I mean, I can wait here if you want to go and check…"

"It's fine. It wasn't him," I said, and with that, we dropped the subject.

If you'd like, I can make up other details. I could tell you what Gabriel was buying, what we were buying, what the cashier looked like. I could tell you what Jonathan and I wore, if we were newly together or if we were about to split up. But I don't remember any of that and don't care enough to pretend. At that point I thought I was over Gabriel, or at least I desperately *wanted* to be over Gabriel. The months I'd spent crying and moping around my parents' house had ended, and I was trying to move on with other men, other possibilities for life.

The main thing I recall is my relief that he hadn't seen me. That he hadn't walked over and greeted me, introduced himself to Jonathan. That he hadn't charmed us both and told me he was back in town and I should call him again to meet up. Instead, I held Jonathan's hand tighter as we left the store.

Two days later, I broke down and called him. I knew it was unhealthy, but I couldn't stop myself. When a teenager answered—someone the phone company had given Gabriel's old number to—I felt so much relief that I broke down in tears.

FR. MICHAEL CARTER

My name is Michael Carter, and I am a Jesuit. I was a founding minister and later the rector in charge of the Jesuit Novitiate of St. José María Rubio in Santa Fe, New Mexico. We usually referred to our small campus—featuring only a dormitory, dining hall, offices, classrooms, and the land between them—as José's Home. The man who founded the seminary, Father Daniel Gallegos, lived for only two years afterward, Christ bless his soul. He envisioned it as a desert oasis, a place where novices' isolation from the outside world would burnish their faiths to such a luster that it would gleam in the world around us. When I was scouting this location with Father Gallegos, I had the one and only vision of my life. For a moment, I saw buildings sprouting from the ground like saplings, and I told him this was the place. A year and a half later, when our first novices arrived, I found myself thinking of my job as a gardener, hoping that their spirits would blossom like the flora that surrounded us, through even the most desolate and parched earth, with a little help from God.

The seminary was purchased from a failed charter school located within the Santa Fe city limits but still far from other buildings, off a road built to allow nuclear waste trucks to bypass the city. I suspect this distance from the city was what made that first school fail, but that made it perfect for our purposes. "Make straight in the desert a highway for our God," as Isaiah wrote. Father Gallegos and I had both spent years teaching in other seminaries and felt that here we could achieve what had proven so difficult elsewhere, creating a true devotional haven free from worldly distraction. We had a rough start, with only three novitiates our first year and four our second, but despite that, and Father Gallegos's passing, despite the lack of air-conditioning in the dorms and the constant need to repair the plumbing, despite a lack of support from our superiors, José's Home thrived.

Gabriel arrived alongside perhaps a dozen other novices. Only half would remain by the end of their two years—no more than half ever made it through. And while I had favorites, predicting who might leave was impossible. But accepting candidates who might not make it through was what made the novitiate matter— our robes and collars weren't participation trophies; they were symbols of our aptitude and training and, above all, our faith. We proselytized for Catholicism, not for the order.

My first real interaction with Gabriel occurred a few days into his studies. I scheduled individual meetings with all our novices, which served the dual purpose of creating an affable relationship and allowing me to size them up. I knew Gabriel's background, that he'd been to seminary before, that he was a classically trained musician. I'd read the statements and recommendations that led him to us, knew his history with the diocesan priests, and had access to his background check, though I never read those. What I didn't know was why he wanted to be a Jesuit. So I asked him.

"To serve Jesus Christ, our Lord and Savior."

This meant nothing. This was the correct answer, but it was pure verbiage. "Yes, of course. We all are. But what else?"

"I don't understand what you mean," Gabriel said.

"What does it mean to serve Jesus Christ?" I asked. "Does that mean helping the helpless? Does that mean praying all day until your knees bleed and your fingers ache from arthritis, developed from moving rosary beads one at a time, hour after hour? Serving Jesus is not one thing; it is different for every individual. If God only wanted one thing from us, he would have made us identical."

This was drawn from a lecture I gave all students, and I could have kept going. As I said, I had been teaching novices for a long time, and although the Lord did not make us identical, he did make us similar. The human experience is both broad and incredibly narrow, and any teacher will notice the patterns.

Gabriel waited for me to say more, but I knew that one of the best teaching tools is silence. Patience. We have a natural need to fill the space of conversations, to remove the discomfort. But this impulse, I have found, results in the saying of many stupid things. I have heard novices describe me as a slow speaker, but I simply think before I talk.

"I ... I'm not sure," Gabriel replied. "I thought maybe you could, the Jesuits could, help with that. Could offer guidance."

"We can," I said. "But that depends on what you need guidance with. Maybe that should be your first goal, to figure out why exactly you *are* here, and whether here is where you need to be."

"I'll pray on it," he said. Then, after waiting to see if I had more to say, he left.

Over the weeks that followed, Gabriel displayed admirable discipline and seriousness, regardless of how menial the tasks he was assigned were. Because of our school's size, basic upkeep was left to the students, from cooking and cleaning to gardening and putting new tar paper on the roof so the old buildings wouldn't start leaking on the rare occasions when it rained for longer than an hour. I considered this as important a part of their education as anything else. Work can be a form of devotion. Labor gives us empathy; it helps us understand those less fortunate, a reminder of our physical selves and the relationships we have with this world. But I should stop lecturing. I know that's not what you're here for. You're here to learn more about my "protégé," as I've heard some call him, though he's no more my protégé than any of my more traditionally faithful pupils. I am not in any way ashamed of him, mind you, I simply wish he wasn't held up as some sort of blemish on my record.

I did not know how Gabriel would handle the "long retreat," especially since he was a talker. The long retreat is the centerpiece of the novitiate, a defining part of the brotherhood since St. Ignatius first crafted it. Ignatius himself helped create abridged versions of the exercise that anyone from laity to monks could participate in— Jesuits have always been realists—but the long retreat is different, and sacred. The exercises are divided into four weeks, so the whole endeavor lasts a month. First novitiates reflect on their past and how they have lived through Christ, or just as often failed to do so. Every sin of their lives should be accounted for, considered. This is the toughest week, the one that sees novitiates either leaving the program or crying for hours as they confront their betrayals and weaknesses.

After this, things get easier. A week is spent learning how to follow Christ as His disciples did, considering His most important lessons and the events of His life: His birth, the sermon on the mount, the resurrection of Lazarus. Then a week is spent on the end of Christ's life, the last supper, the miracle of the Eucharist, His suffering. Finally we meditate on His resurrection, the role of the risen Christ. Through all of this, there is minimal talking between novices and their guides, except for repeated recitation of psalms and prayers. There is no music. No reading, except for prescribed texts. The long retreat is about confronting oneself for thirty days, seeing the ugliness and fear, the hatred and guilt that exists in all of us, seeing when we succumbed to temptation and when Christ reached His hand out to us but we were too prideful to grab it. The long retreat is the largest, most magnified mirror in the world, and our goal as guides is to keep novices from looking away, to help them realize that everything reflected within the mirror, and even the mirror itself, is there only by the grace of God.

Retreats affect everyone differently. For many, like myself, the experience is straightforward, filled with self-reflection that only confirms our conviction to become a Jesuit. Many have a similar experience but with the opposite revelation. That too is expected. But sometimes retreats can be a bit ... strange. Some novices have visions. One saw a vortex from Hell in the center of his bedroom, with great tentacles of fire lashing out to drag him below. Another saw the Virgin Mary weeping at the foot of his bed. Not all these visions have been religious: one novice, who continued his journey as a Jesuit, told me he saw a flying saucer out the window but didn't mind because somehow he knew the aliens were good Christians. You can make of these what you like, but I remain open to the idea that because our retreats are holy, sometimes Christ likes to take a particular interest in them.

At first, Gabriel's retreat seemed ordinary. He cried. He prayed. St. Ignatius wrote about this process as a sort of pendulum, with novices swinging between desolation and consolation. It was during the second week, after he'd passed through the most trying period of the retreat and was now considering Christ's miracles, that Gabriel didn't come to breakfast.

When I went to check on him, I could hear his alarm clock from down the hall, and I found him in bed, despite the sunlight blazing into his room. At first, I worried that he was ill, or worse. After switching off the alarm, I could hear him muttering faintly, the same words or sounds over and over. I approached him, but he didn't wake from whatever dream or trance he was in. I lowered my head to hear what he was saying, but I couldn't make it out.

I touched him on the shoulder, and it was only then that I realized he was hovering above his mattress. While it was no more than a couple of inches, I could have easily slipped my hand beneath him. I waited for a minute, five minutes—it felt endless—increasingly sure of my own eyes and of the spiritual weight of what I was seeing. Nothing changed. I decided to shake him, and it took no small effort to break Gabriel from his mantra. I didn't notice him drop, but he must have, and as he recovered, I asked him if he knew what he'd been doing.

"Do I know?" he muttered, half-asleep. "I'm sorry, Father, I was just dreaming, that's all."

"What was your dream?"

"I saw Him."

"Who? Christ?"

"Yes."

"How could you tell?"

"It wasn't like He introduced Himself, He was just …
He was Jesus."

"What was He like?"

"He was beautiful," said Gabriel. "He was gorgeous.
He was the most perfect man, the most handsome and
lovely human I have ever seen. Not just His face, His
whole body was perfection."

"Can you be more specific?"

"I don't think so."

"Anything else?"

"He was dressed all in white, not exactly a suit, but
not a robe. I don't know how to describe it. I wanted to
stare at Him, in all His glory. I wanted to stay with Him
always, but He said not to. He said I needed to be one
of His shepherds."

"And then what?"

"And then you were here."

I didn't pretend to know what to say. I told him we'd
continue with the exercise later and that, for the time being, he could collect himself. I have heard people dispute
this story, say that a dream hardly constitutes proof of
anything. Of course they are correct. People also accuse
me of lying when I say that he was levitating. I know
no one really believes in modern miracles, though even
before encountering Gabriel, I firmly believed that the
Lord moves not only in mysterious ways but in more obvious ways as well. To the nonbelievers, there's nothing
I can say. I know the truth.

I want to ask skeptics what reason I would have to lie.
Gabriel has only hurt my reputation, irreparably damaged my relationship with my own Jesuit brothers. Why

would I keep this up? What would I have to gain? But then, there will always be skeptics, and this is something I have little time for, especially in my old age. Faith requires skepticism. But it also requires faith.

* * *

From that day on, I took a special interest in Gabriel. I want to make myself clear here: I did not think he was a saint, nor was I convinced he was any "holier" than my other novices. But at the same time, I could not ignore what I had seen. And beyond the miraculous scene in his bedroom, his ideas about the role that Christ's Church should play in the world aligned closely with my own, making him an ideal pupil. Christ was an activist. He didn't accept the status quo. He went out and fed the poor, flipped the moneylenders' tables, brought the dead back to life.

I was too busy to speak with Gabriel terribly often— running an institution, even a small one, meant that most of my time was spent with bureaucratic busywork—but every now and then, we went on long walks together, out past the campus borders. The rest of the seminarians would be relaxing for the evening, usually playing baseball or soccer, enjoying the cool breeze that passed through even during the summer, and while both of us cared little for sports, a few hours away from artificial lighting and old books was too tempting to resist.

It was on these walks that our friendship began, though at the time it was no different from the mentorship I offered any novice looking for support. We spoke about the Church, of course, and Christ. But mostly we spoke about the world outside the seminary. Many students, especially after the long retreat, become cloistered. Such intense inward focus can turn a man away from the world at large, turn him into just another cog in the Church's machine. And yes, the order needs its cogs too, but I'm not going to pretend that those were my favorite students.

A year or so into his novitiate, Gabriel saw me watching a baseball game and asked if I wanted to have "one of our wanders." The sun was setting, but the temperature was perfect, slightly warm but dry and windy. The smattering of clouds above us looked painted.

We walked in silence for a long time. That was something I liked very much about Gabriel. He appreciated companionship, but he was perfectly content when left to his own thoughts, especially after the long retreat. On several occasions, neither of us spoke for the entirety of our walk. This wasn't one of those, though, and eventually, after clearing his throat, Gabriel looked me in the eyes and asked, "Why do we need training at all? Everyone here has read the Bible. Everyone here goes to church on Sunday. Why can't we just head out there and start preaching?"

His eyes were intense. When I first saw them they were brown, but under the right light, they transformed into dark green, as if even his body knew that the best way to get your attention was to challenge your assumptions, your beliefs about what was true. His gaze made me uncomfortable. "If you believe that, why are you here?" I asked him.

"I'm not sure," he said. We walked in silence for a few minutes before he continued. "Maybe there's something to being part of an organization. A brotherhood."

"There are fundamental reasons we don't all worship alone in our own homes," I said. "So yes, I do think there's something to be gained. Christ created a Church and told us to assemble, and there's something different about worshipping at Mass. If nothing else, it lends us legitimacy."

"Legitimacy? Why shouldn't ... I don't see why that should be a concern."

"Really? That's why Christ was crucified," I said. "At least, it's one of the reasons. There are many religions out there, but if you tell someone you spend every Sunday worshipping Zeus in your backyard, people are going to laugh at you. If you tell them you visited the Vatican and went to services with ten thousand other pilgrims and worshippers, they ask how it went, whether it was as moving as they've heard. Perhaps they wonder why they've been skipping Mass lately, whether it might be time to return. If we're interested in spreading the gospel, that's important to remember."

We continued walking until the path ended. The sun plummeted, and the sky dimmed from pink to purple. It would be dark long before we returned, but I wanted to stay there, amid the landscape that others saw as bleak but I had come to think of as blessed. Outside, my sinuses always felt clearer, and the arthritis developing in my knees ached less. It wasn't that I felt younger, more that I felt timeless.

"Is that the only way of creating legitimacy?" asked Gabriel, interrupting my thoughts.

"Well, it's one of them," I said. "The other way is to have proof, of course. Everyone is a doubting Thomas, it's only natural. But once you stick your finger in those wounds, you believe. That's how the first Christians became followers: they were witnesses. But that one's a little bit tougher. We should head back."

I put little stock in that conversation at the time, as it was one of many, and it's even possible that I'm combining a few of our walks, misquoting him, misremembering details. Regardless, it rings in my memory now because of how much he seemed to take what I said to heart. Maybe it was God's will for me to say what I did then. The influence of the divine can be subtle, and wiser men than myself have failed to understand how the Lord makes Himself known.

What made it typical of our conversations, though, was his expression of doubt about Jesuit life. By the time he'd been with us for nearly two years, I wasn't at all surprised to hear that he wouldn't be taking his vows. Once again, he came knocking on my office door. I felt certain I already knew the news by the look on his face, like a dog who knows he's disappointed his master, but I still asked him.

"The process is too long," he said. "Years too long."

"I see," I said. What else was there to say? "I would be sorry to see you leave us. Is there something else? Fifteen years is long, but it's not that long."

He walked over to my desk and placed an envelope on it. I offered him my hand, a small gesture of understanding, and we shook. He had a quarter smile that I couldn't quite read, but it made me think he would be alright.

As soon as he left, I cut the letter open and read it greedily, though it was not as revelatory as I had hoped. I saved it, and I don't think there would be any harm in allowing you to read it.

Dear Father Carter,

Nearly two years ago, on entering the Jesuit novitiate, you asked me why I was here, what it was I wanted to get out of the Jesuit community. After great reflection, I realize that my hope was that life as a Jesuit could make me freer and more available to love and serve God and humanity. But as the time for vows approached, another question developed, whether I would be called to take vows with my novitiate classmates in August or find some other way in which to achieve my goals. I have had to discern this for myself. So now, with a heart full of gratitude toward you and all the instructors at José's Home, I have decided not to take vows, and so to leave the novitiate and the Jesuits.

This was a difficult decision to make and perhaps even more difficult to explain. In all humility, I must confess that I still believe religious ministry is the best way of expressing my modest gifts. Yet when I am most honest with myself, and with God, I realize that vowed life is not the most authentic way for me to live out this path of ministry— that it is not the way in which I am personally called as a disciple of Christ. I believe that the best way of devoting myself to this calling is to join the ministry immediately, regardless of my uncertainty as to what form this will take.

My feeling is that I must make my own ministry, and while my future is unclear, I hope that this next exploration will not be a step away from, but toward, the marginalized and suffering people of God. I believe this not because I have so much to give but because, for now, I think the only real place for me is among the people.

Con todo mi cariño,
Gabriel Romero

It was years before we spoke again.

ISABEL ROMERO

The final time Gabriel moved home was less dramatic. I was in the kitchen making a huge batch of tamales, even though they were out of season. There's something mindless about the process, coating husks with masa over and over again until you lose track of how many you've made, and I had music playing while I worked, the old stuff I grew up with, songs from the seventies and eighties when they really knew how to make hooks. Brandon never took me dancing, like not once, so I had to make do with what I had: my huge mixing bowl full of red chile pork and another full of corn masa, little bits stuck in my hair, but I didn't mind because I was having fun, singing and dancing as I slowly filled the large metal pots in the center of the table.

Anyhow, I was doing my thing when he walked right in and joined me in the kitchen. He gave me a big hug, and without saying anything he twirled me around. As we danced, I was reminded of how much rhythm he had in him, how easily the sounds coming from my pathetic laptop speakers flowed directly into his body. A smile on his face even larger than my own, we bopped through the rest of my playlist, and when it ended, he ran to his room and grabbed an old mix CD so we could dance some more. It felt like our kitchen lights had become disco balls and the colors of my old wallpaper had brightened so that the designs, shapeless and forgettable, danced with us and filled the house with life.

Finally we sat down, breathless but still laughing, sweat occasionally dripping onto the masa. We finished the tamales, putting an olive in each one for good luck like Mamá always did, and while we waited for them to steam, I remembered to call Brandon and cancel our plans. Gabito and I talked for the rest of the evening, and he spoke as if he'd never left home. There was a surety about him bordering on arrogance. He even seemed taller than before, or at least more imposing. My son was still wiry but no longer fragile, and he had a magnetism that made every word he spoke sound like it was profound.

He told me he'd left the Jesuits, but in the same breath he said that he was far from leaving the Church.

"Ok, mijo," I said, because what else can you say about those things? "But what does that mean?"

"It means I need my own church, Mom. A place where I can serve the people, tell them about Jesus without everyone getting in the way."

"Can you ... is that a thing you can do?" I asked. As far as I knew, churches weren't something you founded, they were just there when you arrived, stone edifices that grew out of the ground on their own.

"I don't see why not," said Gabito, and that was the end of that. I could have asked him whether the Church approved or whether it would even be Catholic, but those questions seemed inappropriate, especially given his mood. And really, I already knew the answers—if he'd planned on going through official channels, he wouldn't be telling me about it like this. His high spirits were infectious, and I didn't care that his idea was crazy and impossible.

I was just thrilled to have my son back, to see him happy and healthy and, while maybe un poquito extraño, doing better than ever.

He wasted no time searching for a location. He took buses all over the city, from the Heights to Rio Rancho, both valleys, and all the way out to parts of the city like Taylor Ranch that I had heard of but had never actually visited. I offered to drive when I could or lend him my car, but he said no because he "wanted to spend some time with the people," though later he told me it was more that he didn't want to be rushed. He said he was looking for somewhere both cheap and large, and he wasn't much concerned about the state of the building or the location. "I can pull some favors, I'm sure, and get help fixing the place up, put on a new splash of paint. I just need somewhere that can grow."

The building he found was on Central, east of the fancier Nob Hill and university neighborhoods and across the street from a couple cheap motels and a long-closed Church's Chicken. The marquee of an old movie theater still hung above its doorway, though the building had been closed since before I was born. In fact, nearly every business that shared its old, strip-mall parking lot was also vacant, or at least on the verge of bankruptcy. But the roof was solid, and its owners had removed the asbestos from the walls and replaced the lead pipes, hoping to attract someone to lease or buy it out from them.

We toured the building together, and when the landlord left us alone, I asked Gabriel whether he was sure about the place. The speed of his decisions, from returning home to finding a location for his church, seemed too fast, and I worried about what he would do if things didn't work out again. I worried that maybe the difference between the smiling, overly excited man standing next to me, rubbing his hand against a sagging wall as paint chips flew off, and the one I saw burning himself in his bedroom, was smaller than he let on.

"It's perfect," said Gabriel. "I had a dream, and there was … there was a lot, to be honest, but this was it. This was the place."

I argued that he should start smaller or try another profession, at least briefly, before jumping into this, but that dream became the answer to whatever I said. And yes, I could have said, "It's just a dream, what does any of that matter?" But I saw in his eyes that it did matter, that it mattered so very much. And maybe it was that dream, and all of his dreams, that kept him going.

But the question remained: How was Gabriel supposed to come up with the rent? We went to the bank together, a local one I'd used for decades. While it was easy to set up a meeting to discuss the possibility of a loan, one of the first things they asked was to see his business plan.

"I don't have one," said Gabriel. I'd purchased him a new pair of slacks and a polo shirt for the occasion and dressed up myself too. I'd even gone to the salon with Alyssa to have my hair done. "It's not a business."

The bank clerk tried to stay serious, tried to keep from laughing with that big gringo mouth of his. He tried not to show us his white, dental-insurance-straightened teeth, but I guess he just couldn't help it. He smirked, and it was obvious the only thing holding him back from kicking us out of his office was the amusement we brought him. He started lecturing us about profit margins and how to avoid taxes, upkeep costs and projected tithing rates in the area, when Gabriel interrupted him.

"No, I think you misunderstand," he said. "We will pay back the loan. God will show us a way. I had a dream that we would have this building and—"

"Listen, I don't want to waste your time," the clerk said. "Until you show me a business plan, we're not lending you a cent. I think you can understand."

I did my best not to punch that clerk in his face, but Gabito just shook his hand and said we'd figure it out. His good mood didn't budge an inch.

Now, I know there's been talk out there about Gabriel having raised money through some sort of miraculous means. I know he talked in sermons about how stingy the "moneylenders" are, that banks today are the same as the ones Jesucristo threw out of the Church two thousand years ago. But it wasn't like Dios rained money into Gabriel's bank account like manna from heaven or the Holy Spirit went and changed the landlord's mind about the price. Nothing like that.

I guess you could say I was the means, though that's only partly true. All I knew was that the idea of this church made Gabriel excited when nothing else could, and he had to get the money from somewhere. And if it would keep my Gabito happy and far away from that flame, I was willing to do whatever it took.

I'd raised Gabriel apart from his father's family, and while he received a birthday card from John's mother, Evelyn, every year, I never gave it to him. I wasn't stupid. I took and used whatever I found in the middle of that folded piece of Hallmark dreck, whether money or a check, but I didn't want him thinking about that side of the family. I wanted him to think of them as fictional or nonexistent. To her credit, Gabito's grandmother never forgot, never missed a year, but the cards would either arrive with the prewritten message and her signature or a simple "Happy Birthday!" inside. It seemed clear that she didn't particularly care about him. After all, if she really wanted to see him, she could've easily figured out a way. We lived in the same city, and it wasn't like we'd spent our lives hiding from her.

Without mentioning it to Gabriel, I drove to the far side of town to see if Evelyn still lived in her old house, in the foothills of the Sandias. It had been decades since I'd been there, and the house, always imposing before, seemed less impressive now that its black metal fence was tinged with rust, its yard overgrown with weeds. When she finally came to the door, I almost felt sorry for her. Evelyn sat in an electric wheelchair, an oxygen mask trailing from her face down to a large removable tank attached to the back of the chair.

"Hello, Isabel," she said without a hint of surprise as she answered the door. "Come in, come in. Would you like to have tea?"

I'd known Evelyn as imperious and inflexible. I'd half expected we would fight at the doorway, that she would invoke another round of lawyers because I'd accidentally trampled her favorite blade of grass on my way across her yard. And I could still see hints of that as she made tea, the way she didn't ask me what kind I might like or if I wanted honey or milk or lemon. She just served it the way she liked it. Still, we were talking, making comments about the weather and that sort of thing. Although I still didn't particularly like her, I could see that she was for once trying to treat me with respect, or at least a minimum of condescension, doing her absolute best not to give me an excuse to leave.

When the conversation finally evaporated, she said, "It's been pleasant seeing you, but I'm sure you're not here just to sample my tea or my conversation. And why isn't Gabriel with you?"

I told her Gabito had become a priest and explained his absence with how busy he was.

"That's wonderful," she said. "I'm not religious, of course, but that's a very respectable profession. I'm sure John would've been proud."

"Yes ... I'm sure," I said. It wasn't the time to restart that *guerra*. "But I was just, we were just hoping you might be able to support him in his new work."

Her posture straightened and, though she took a deep breath from the respirator, she seemed to lose a few decades before responding. "What kind of support?"

"It's just, well, he's raising money for his church."

"Why does the church need money?" she asked. "Can't they do a bake sale or whatever they usually do?"

I thought for a moment about how to answer this but decided there was no point in lying. "The thing is, it doesn't exist yet."

"Oh," Evelyn said. "So he's not really a priest, then, is he. Is it a cult? What sort of scam is he involved with?"

"I don't know why I came here," I said, beginning to stand. "This was a terrible idea."

"No no, don't leave. Churches, cults, religions—it's all the same to me. He could be practicing voodoo like your mother, I don't care." Evelyn's eyes looked straight into mine, and for a moment I thought I could see sadness in them. Her voice didn't crack or change, though, as she said, "I just want to see him again."

"I'm sure that if you were to help him with the church's lease, he would be very—"

"And I'm sure you're sure of a lot of things," she said, cutting me off. "But I need more than your assurance. If I were to offer him a generous sum, enough for this lease, we would need to meet. More than once. I would need to get my grandson back."

"I can't promise what he'll do," I said, "but I'll ask him."

"And I can't promise that I'll help out the church either. But you know how to get in touch."

Bringing all this up with Gabriel was … difficult, as you can imagine. Gabito and I had never spoken about his father, let alone Evelyn. But I got through it somehow, and soon we made plans to see her again—and hopefully pick up a check.

"Excellent," said Evelyn later, over the phone. "I'll invite William and Megan over, and we'll have the full family together."

We didn't speak as we walked from our car to the house, dressed in our best clothes. I'm sure the evening was memorable, meeting his grandmother for the first time, passing through a house filled with photographs of the father he'd never known, who I'd spent his entire life pretending never existed. I could see his eyes taking in everything about this strange world, searching for any details in the house that might tell him more about the gringo-landia I'd done my best to keep him from. What he made of any of it—that world of overstuffed furniture and lace doilies, of rooms that smelled of lemon cleaner gone stale—I'm not sure.

Once we were seated at Evelyn's long hardwood table, I thought we were going to get right down to business. Eat our meal, grab the check, head out. But Evelyn made us wait because William, John's younger brother, was late. So we sat there and made small talk, Gabito telling them about his life as if they were people he'd met at a party rather than close relatives. As the minutes ticked by, he chatted with his aunt Megan, a mousy-looking woman wearing an expensive-looking asymmetrical dress and ostentatious gold earrings. He explained some of his plans for the church. He even performed a few magic tricks, producing a deck from his pocket as if that were normal and proceeding to pull Evelyn's card from Megan's wallet, much to his grandmother's delight, though I noticed an eye roll from Megan when she thought no one was looking.

Finally, William arrived, looking a lot like a filled-out, kinder, and more relaxed version of John. He wore a blazer and V-neck T-shirt with jeans.

"Didn't have time to shave?" Evelyn said. "Or buy some decent pants to offset that cheap haircut?"

"No, Mother," William said with a broad smile. "Guess it was a busy week."

"No wonder your wife left you," Evelyn said. "Fine, then, don't just stand there, bring the food in from the kitchen and take your seat."

From there, the meal passed uneventfully. Gabriel was charming, as he always was when he needed to be, and the Fishers hung on every word. The catered food was surprisingly delicious, and I have to admit it ended up a pretty decent evening. My main memory, though, wasn't Gabito's stories or his dumb magic trick, Evelyn's cackling laughter or Megan constantly looking at her watch. It was the sly smile William offered me every time he made a joke and the way he hugged me when the night ended, far too long and tight but not enough so that anyone else would notice.

When we left, Gabito carried a check worth three months' rent for his new church—Our Lady of Guadalupe, named in honor of Mamá, I like to think—plus a pledge that he would see Evelyn again for other family gatherings, coupled with an unspoken understanding that so long as this continued, there would be more checks to come. My presence wasn't mentioned, but I decided to invite myself to these gatherings too, as long as William kept making me feel so welcome.

ANNA FISHEL

When I was really little, maybe like six years old, I used to love horror flicks. My older sister, Danielle, used to rent two or three a week from the Hollywood Video, everything from classics to the latest straight-to-video releases. The bloodier the better, I always thought, and I had a particular thing for serial-killer movies. *The Silence of the Lambs, Se7en, Henry: Portrait of a Serial Killer.* We'd make popcorn in the microwave before running down the stairway to the basement, watching them on an old TV beneath the heavy quilts our great-grandmother made before I was born. We'd move the couch right up to the TV so that if we leaned forward, it was the only thing we could see.

I can't tell you why I liked those movies so much. Maybe it was the certainty, the way you always knew what the threat was. Maybe I liked the way they got my adrenaline up, infecting our house with virtual danger that ended the moment the tape stopped and we hit "Rewind," either to watch it again or to record a copy if it was good enough to add to Danielle's "Collection of the Damned." Most likely, it was just that Danielle liked horror, so I did too. Our mother worked long hours and our father, well, he was a big drinker and ... I'll get to that. But so me and Danielle spent a lot of time together, listening to the same terrible metal bands, arguing about the best way to get out of the house if there were a murderer inside, making plans for what we'd do in the case of ghosts, zombies, or Jason Voorhees. We'd eat sour straws and drink three-liter bottles of store-brand soda until four or five a.m., then pass out until afternoon the next day, ready to do it all again as soon as the sun began to dip beneath the mesa.

Through all of this, we attended church every Sunday morning, ten to eleven o'clock at Annunciation. Both our parents went with us, and I dreaded those hours, sitting restlessly in my seat, Mom pinching me when I began to close my eyes. We had to wear dresses and uncomfortable shoes and pretend to listen to the priest while sitting and standing and kneeling, over and over, chanting and even offering money for the courtesy of this excruciating waste of time. I'm embarrassed to admit it now, but sometimes I'd take the dollar or two Mom would give me, pretend to drop it in the basket, but then actually hide it under my dress. I only got caught once, and though Dad hit me pretty hard, I kept doing it whenever I really wanted the money.

Danielle always warned me not to get on Dad's bad side because you never knew what he might do, especially when he was drinking. And sure, he hit me, sometimes almost playfully but other times hard enough that I had to make excuses to my teacher. He hit Danielle even worse, but at the time I thought she was making too big a thing out of it. That was just what dads did. By the time I was nine or ten, Dad was drinking almost all the time too, so the warning became not so much "avoid Dad when he was drinking" as just "avoid Dad altogether." He liked Budweiser, "not Bud Light and definitely not some godforsaken MGD garbage," he'd say, and would sometimes call it "The King," as in, "Hey, would you grab me The King from the fridge?" Or if he was feeling more playful, "King me," like in checkers. Six or more beers deep, he'd even refer to himself as The King. "The King wants a beer," he'd say, and you knew you'd better get him one or there'd be hell to pay. I have good memories of Dad too, you know, though it might be hard to believe. But mostly I remember him lying on his big leather recliner, an empty can to the side of the chair and another one half-full in his hand. He never missed a day of work, did fine at the auto shop regardless of what he'd hurled at us the night before, but the minute he walked through the doorway, he marched straight to the fridge for one of those cans, bloodred and bone white, like a warning sign to anyone who might want to slow him down. He often passed out in his chair, the TV still on in the background, Danielle washing dishes in the kitchen as quietly as she could so she wouldn't wake him.

If it was just that my dad was an alcoholic, I wouldn't have been any different from every other kid on the block. I heard the same screams coming from our neighbors' houses when they left their windows open, saw my friends get hit with a belt or the back of a hand while playing at their houses, and thought little of it. When Dad was really drinking, I either hid in the basement or closed the door to the room Danielle and I shared, just pretended none of it was happening. I put on headphones and listened to my sister's metal CDs as loudly as I could. Drums banging and electric guitars swirling in my head, I drew in my notebook, comics or storyboards for my own slasher movie.

One of those nights—I'd disappeared hours earlier, drawing until ink coated my hands and I needed more scratch paper to continue the grisly story of The Railroad Murderer that I knew my sister would love—I went to grab another pile of paper from the kitchen, yellow and pink with misprints or printing errors on the backsides that Mom brought home from her office so we wouldn't have to spend a fortune on art supplies. I opened the door to the hallway and heard sounds that … I'm not going to go into detail here. I don't think I have to, or that the specifics are important. Let me just say that I heard my dad forcing Danielle. And like that, it was all over.

Not that I really understood what was happening, just that it was bad. The worst. I couldn't stop thinking about it the morning after, or the morning after that. A couple nights later, after a triple feature, Danielle and I passed out in the basement like normal. At least, I thought we did, but I woke up in the middle of the night to her crying, sobbing into a quilt. I didn't move, did nothing to let her know that I heard her. I was scared in a whole new, terrible way. I'd never seen Danielle like that before, and I didn't want to see her like that ever again. I hoped that if I kept my eyes shut, my head down on the pillow, all of this would disappear, and we would be like before.

I'm not sure, maybe she knew I was awake. We stopped watching horror movies after that. They weren't fun anymore, and to be honest, kids' movies were all I could watch for more than a decade. Danielle suddenly spent a lot less time at home, instead hanging out with kids older than her who owned cars. Dad was too drunk to notice and Mom too passive, or perhaps guilty, I dunno, to say anything. I know now that what I witnessed was probably not a onetime thing. But that day was like a razor slash directly through the middle of my childhood—everything I'd thought was fairly happy and normal got butchered into some seriously dark, David Lynch–type shit.

From then on, church became much more engrossing. Danielle and Dad didn't attend Mass anymore, so it was just me and Mom in our Sunday best, matching periwinkle and white dresses so that I looked like a newer model of her. Like those horror movies I no longer enjoyed, there was a clarity to what our priest said, a definitiveness to his worldview where good and evil were obvious on sight. He was smart, young, and had a way of making the Bible's rules and stories all seem like common sense. More than anything, though, I think what changed my mind about church was what happened when I went to confession a few months after the incident. It was the first time I'd been since my first communion, and the only reason I'd gone then was because you had to. Mom never went, and the idea of Dad or Danielle saying a dozen Hail Marys as penance was laughable. But suddenly I needed someone to talk to, someone to explain the unexplainable, and a priest was literally the only person I could think of who might help me without causing even worse problems. I knew he was supposed to stay silent, because a confession is really between you and God. And I knew from what he'd said during sermons that God would never want to hurt anyone, even the worst sinner. Even me.

So I went into that little wooden closet at the back of the chapel. I expected a screen, like during my first communion, but they'd removed those, so you couldn't ignore the priest's face. That made me even more anxious, so I rambled about nothing in particular, trying to figure out how to make a quick getaway. But he wouldn't let me leave, wouldn't let me tell only part of the story. And as I sat there telling him about what I'd seen, crying, he comforted me. He told me I had committed no sins, that God was watching and would punish the wicked and reward the righteous, both here on Earth and after death. I only needed to be patient and His will would be done. It was what I needed to hear.

By high school, I was one of those church girls. I related the Bible to whatever my teachers assigned, and I insisted on saying grace before any meal, even a few chips between classes. I waited for the priest every week after Mass was done and bombarded him with questions about the Bible. I spent as much time as I could at Annunciation, volunteering three days a week at a musty food bank where I escorted the poor around a sort of simulated grocery store, helping them take cans off shelves and stopping them from snatching more than their fair share. My only friends were a pair of girls who dressed even more conservatively than I did and whose parents refused to let them wear makeup or see PG-13 movies. I didn't really listen to music anymore. Instead I read the Bible, even when it was boring. Reading the Bible was good, spending time at church was good, praying the rosary every day was good, and I latched on to those certainties with everything I had.

Then Danielle dropped out of college and came back to Albuquerque with her head shaved and track marks on her arms. She came by the house to get some stuff but refused to eat dinner with our parents, let alone sleep at home, and rather than talk to her, I prayed for her soul and her safety after she left, secure in my belief that Jesus would protect her. Nothing could puncture my faith, and the priest I so admired, with his nonconfrontational patience and solemn smile, made me feel like this was the way to true holiness. You let time pass and live righteously, and the rest is up to Jesus.

But there he was on the local news one day, his face locked into that smile. The TV was in the kitchen, an old black-and-white model my mom watched while cooking dinner, and as I listened to the newscaster and read the headline—**Local Priest Accused of Molesting Numerous Children**—everything broke again.

I ran into my room and slammed the door, trying to will what I'd seen and heard to be a lie. It was a liberal media hoax. It was a different priest, a different church. A different religion. Or maybe those kids were liars, crying wolf for attention. This was a witch hunt and would destroy the name of a good man. About the time I found myself trying to rationalize—even if he had done it, had been molesting a few prepubescent boys, what was the real harm?—my fury turned to pain. I cried. I ripped my worn leather-bound Bible to shreds. Fuck him and fuck my dad and fuck the Church and fuck everyone and everything, I thought.

I ditched class the next week. By the time my mom found out and made me go back, my hair was dyed black, and I was back into metal in a big way. I spent the rest of high school smoking pot with a few new friends, at first only after school, but by the time I graduated, we'd pack a bowl during lunch and maybe split a blunt during one or two passing periods, because why the hell not? Even as my mom helped me move into the UNM dorms, I'm pretty sure she'd given up on me, which honestly made me happiest. I drank a lot, slept with guys who disappointed me, and still managed to graduate with honors after six years with a Doctor of Pharmacy degree. For some reason, I still wanted a well-paying, stable job.

I've never really thought about it before, I guess because I've never been asked to talk about it all, but local
news has had a huge role in my faith. It's weird, because
I don't normally watch the news, it's just something I put
on in the background, which I must've picked up from my
mom. Anyway, I remember hearing about a miraculous
healing on there one time, and for whatever reason, it got
my attention. Even though that priest I used to trust was
disgraced, I never lost my faith in God. I simply lost my
faith in that particular individual and his idea of God. His
Church. But I knew in my heart that there's more to this
world than what your five senses take in, that all over the
globe, folks have reported miracles since time immemo-
rial. Even when I told my friends I was an atheist, even
when I laughed at how folks "wasted their time" going
to church, I always secretly believed in Jesus.

And then, right there on TV, was a story about a
young priest saving the life of a man on his deathbed.
He was dying of leukemia, they said, showing footage
of his body wasting away, tubes and wires leaking out
of him and into blinking devices. He was bald, and his
voice was strained. The man's clearly once-brown skin
was pale, with veins showing through, his flesh sagging
off features that would've otherwise made him classically
handsome, like someone had starved a telenovela star.

A doctor came on, repeating that the man had been
dying, after first being diagnosed with leukemia years ago.
They'd tried everything, even an experimental treatment
that was, by the doctor's account, worse than going through
chemo. None of it had helped. You could tell that despite
the doctor's affection for the patient, she had given up.

Then his family came on. They talked about how
the man was smart, funny, loved by everyone who knew

him. They talked about how much potential he had, that he was the heart of the family, the golden child. Finally, they explained how they'd decided to bring in a priest, one from their neighborhood, one whose grandmother used to pray for them before. The priest hadn't actually come there to heal anyone, he was just there to offer some peace to the family.

The priest prayed with the man. He anointed him with holy water. He washed his feet and slept at his side in an uncomfortable-looking hospital chair. The next day, a nurse noticed a difference, small but still significant, in his blood work. His white blood cell count had risen, for the first time in forever. Much to everyone's astonishment, the count continued to rise until, two weeks after that first long evening of prayer, it reached the low range of normal.

The doctor said that while she personally didn't believe in miracles, the recovery was, well, miraculous. There was no reason to believe his leukemia might not return, but for the time being, things were good. The segment ended with the patient explaining that the first thing he planned on doing after he left the hospital was visiting this priest's new church, which had replaced an old theater on the east side of Central. The priest himself declined to be interviewed.

If I could have recorded that segment, I would have. I'd love to show you how inspiring it was so you could understand how it made me, and so many others, feel. But really, it made me feel … I dunno, good about the world in a way I hadn't in a very long time, maybe not since those nights with Danielle. This priest seemed different, and I don't just mean with the healing. I decided to visit that church myself the next Sunday, and the service was filled with joy, with music and life and a faith that, for the first time in a long time, I felt like I could trust.

And I wasn't the only one there on account of that TV story. There were dozens of us. We'd all been looking for someone who really cared about folks, someone God seemed to have given some of His own power to. Someone like Father Gabriel.

FR. PATRICK CONKLIN

After finishing my studies at Holy Trinity, I was assigned a small parish in Las Cruces. I'd never been there before, never even traveled south of Albuquerque, aside from a Webelos camping expedition when I was in elementary school, but while I would have preferred an assignment somewhere in the north, this was acceptable. Las Cruces fulfills an outsider's expectations for the entire state: hot, arid, and coated in a sandy-brown, off-putting color scheme, as if buildings were dung piles dropped by giants. The city's primary attraction seems to be its preponderance of strip malls, and during heat waves, you can usually smell the nearby landfills. But the locals greeted me with kindness, and I've grown fond of them as well. It still doesn't feel like home, and frankly, I began thinking about how to move somewhere slightly more ... not wealthy—what's a better way of putting this?—well located, almost immediately. In any case, it's a perfectly decent starting point for my career.

My duties at St. Mary's are simple. Because I'm the junior priest, I officiate only a handful of services a week, otherwise I simply assist the senior priest and facilitate local faith-sharing groups and efforts within the community. This leaves me with a good deal of free time, so I've continued my studies, as any dutiful priest should. My first professional essay was published in a small theological journal during my last year in seminary, and while it has received fewer citations than I might have expected, this early success has spurred me onward. I won't bore you with the specifics—it was an exegesis on the present-day relevance of texts dealing with the church's posthumous treatment of St. Francis—but much of my later research has been in a similar vein, considering the Church's past in order to reinforce the fundamental importance of a more orthodox present. It is not glamorous work. In a way, it's the coal mines, the real drudgery of priesthood that goes unrecorded because it appears so trivial to outsiders. But it is important.

I had not thought of Gabriel since his departure from the seminary. The next time I heard about him was that damned newscast, which I didn't watch myself but heard about incessantly during the weeks and months that followed. "A priest in Albuquerque performed a miracle," my parishioners would say to me. Or, in that heavy Cruces accent, "A real milagro." It fell to me to correct them, which I can tell you I took no joy in, though it was certainly necessary.

Faith healing has always been a part of our religion. Many of Jesus's most famous acts were healing the crippled and the blind, even the dead. All these healings were miraculous, of course, but just as important, they were also historical events. Factual. Objective. Whether or not He is your Messiah is an issue of belief, but whether He healed lepers on His way to Jerusalem or restored sight to Bartimaeus? Any scholar worth his salary will confirm these events, regardless of the debates surrounding their specifics. The Catholic Church has a reputation as this mystical place, a world apart from the concrete one we see in front of us, but it's just the opposite. A miracle is not simply something you believe in, a fortuitous happenstance bestowed on us by the Almighty. It is a carefully and objectively examined phenomenon, requiring experts and a rigorous verification process. Without this, to say that something is "a miracle" is mere exaggeration, hyperbole that serves only to confuse and misinform the general populace.

My hope was that the reporters had simply exaggerated the reality of the situation, blowing events out of proportion as they so often do, and that Gabriel's involvement was mere coincidence. However, I felt a responsibility to discover the truth behind what happened with this so-called miracle, regardless of our relationship. I didn't tell my superior why I needed to visit Albuquerque; I simply requested time off to see my family, which he had no qualms about granting. Once there, I visited the hospital this supposed healing took place in, and after much questioning and, might I add, a fair amount of detective work I'm more than a little proud of, I found the doctor who had worked with the patient in question.

She was middle-aged, dark-complected, speaking with an accent I immediately recognized because it was so similar to Gabriel's. Needless to say, this couldn't help but raise my suspicions. But she was, after all, the expert, and while her opinion alone wouldn't be enough, I was still interested in hearing from her without the spotlights and cameras around. She largely repeated what I had already heard, the fatality rate for leukemia, the patient's history with the illness, etcetera. Eventually, I asked her about the patient's recovery, and it was then that I learned what had so carefully been left out of the news report: the patient had already been in recovery *before* Gabriel spent a day praying over him.

I returned to my parish and my responsibilities, but I couldn't let it go. It took me much longer to track down and convince the patient himself to speak with me, maybe half a year, though I can't be more precise without consulting my notes. Regardless, during the intervening period, it somehow got back to the patient that I'd "grilled" the doctor and "taken what she'd said out of context." Of course this was a misrepresentation. All I did was ask a few simple questions and fact-check the patient's medical records, which were provided for a small fee by a sympathetic nurse. I was in no way aggressive. I was simply interested in getting to the truth of the matter.

We met at his house, a two-bedroom brown stucco in Martineztown that smelled of old cigarettes. After offering me coffee—I declined—the patient repeated his story almost verbatim from the news report, which he'd clearly committed to memory.

Once we'd gotten past this, I decided on a direct approach for my questioning. "But what about your doctor saying that, in contradiction to the news report, your white blood cell levels had risen days before Gabriel first arrived?"

"She said that? That's not how I remember it," he said, careful to stare straight back at me in order to not arouse suspicion. Having sat through many confessions, I knew all the tricks—I'm always surprised by how often people try to lie rather than be absolved by God.

"It's backed up by your records," I said. "Would you like me to show you?" I had brought a copy, because I thought it might be easier to confront him with the evidence rather than get into a he said, she said situation.

I may have misjudged things, though, because he became irrationally angry. "How the hell do you have my records?"

"Let's stick to the facts," I said, trying to keep control of the situation. "I see an upswing in healthy white blood cells beginning two days before Gabriel's visit. Let me show you the chart."

"Maybe," he said, still snarling. "How should I know? I was on my deathbed. I couldn't eat, couldn't drink, couldn't take a dump. And you want me to remember some bullshit like that? You need to leave."

He stood up, and I took his suggestion. But I had to ask him one more thing: Had he known Gabriel Romero before the visit?

"Yeah, 'course," he said. "Everyone knows Padre Gabriel, y su madre y su abuela. What type of dumb-shit question is that?" He slammed the door like we were in a movie—there was no need for that overdramatic rudeness—and I crossed his unkempt yard, filled with dirt and weeds, and left.

That was the only time I was able to speak with him, but it was enough to confirm my theory as to how this so-called miracle was orchestrated. Here is what certainly took place: Gabriel heard about this man's miraculous recovery and wished to capitalize on it. His new church was failing, which comes as no surprise, because it had no institutional support. Frankly, even its claims to Christianity were specious, as far as I'm concerned, since the faith centered more around the cultic worship of a charismatic leader than the veneration of Our Lord and Savior. But in a desperate attempt to save himself from complete financial ruin, Gabriel arranged that charade of a local news story about performing a miracle.

Let me be clear: I never set out to attack Gabriel. I was only ever interested in finding out the truth and making it known. I was as disappointed in my old friend as anyone, though perhaps not completely surprised. I thought of all the time he spent performing little magic tricks at seminary, rather than studying or doing chores, and this so-called miracle was part and parcel of what I had seen there. Regardless of his motivations, this was higher-stakes than some benign sleight of hand. I've heard people describe my work on Gabriel's church as bitter, as angry, but it is not. I simply saw that no one else was going to expose his obvious falsehoods, and I knew it was my duty, as a faithful and devout Catholic, to do so myself.

MANUEL QUINTANA

I heard about Gabriel's first miracle from a parishioner. I was still a part of the Catholic Church then and was fortunate enough to be working at a congregation out on the west side of Albuquerque. I'd been assigned to a newish church, certainly the newest I'd ever seen, with sleek walls, freshly painted white trim, and a fountain in the courtyard that seemed out of place in the desert. Inside, it was less like a gothic cathedral and more like an overly large house, which was a welcome change from seminary—this was supposed to be not only God's home but also a home for the community.

After Mass one morning, a few months into my assignment, a congregant asked what I thought about this miraculous healing she'd seen on the local news. I didn't know what to think, so I muttered the usual "God works in mysterious ways" and made a mental note to look into the matter. The next day, there was a small follow-up piece about it in the *Albuquerque Journal*, identifying the priest in question as Gabriel Romero, my old friend from seminary. I hadn't even known he was back in Albuquerque.

It took a few weeks to get the time off, but as soon as I could, I drove across town to his church for Sunday Mass. From the outside, it looked like a slowly decaying movie theater, and by all accounts, that's what it had been. On the marquee, instead of any "clever" sayings like you'd see outside kitschy Protestant churches, was a list of service times. Inside, the only ornamentation was a single huge crucifix hanging on the far wall, looming above a beaten-up wooden stage with a lectern and altar. The space smelled musty, and every surface showed signs of age, which made me wonder how much of the heavy coating of dust in the poorly ventilated main hall consisted of lead paint. There were seats with armrests between them instead of proper pews, though makeshift padded kneelers had been added in a dark green that clashed with the checkered red and blue pattern on the chairs, many of which were torn or stained. Given the high ceilings and dim lighting, I expected a solemn mood, but instead I saw cheerful greetings, the universal sign of a healthy congregation, and heads occasionally bobbing along with the classical music played by a pianist and half a dozen other musicians.

As the music swelled, Gabriel proceeded to the altar, looking almost self-conscious about the ceremonial aspects of worship. The Mass he performed—because that's really what it was, regardless of what the Church or anyone else may say about it—was simple, unvarnished. Gabriel broke the bread and held up the cup with dignity and elegance, and the effect deemphasized the man making these gestures, putting the spotlight on the worship itself. The beliefs. It was like he was channeling the Holy Spirit directly to the audience, a clear outpouring of God that drew me in, though I can't remember for the life of me what exactly he said.

I'd originally planned on speaking with Gabriel, but after the service I hesitated. I wasn't sure exactly what I'd say to him, for one thing, and for another I wanted to know more about this miracle of his before we talked. I'd been skeptical, had prepared myself for confrontation.

If his church had been the carnivalesque revival house I half expected from how the news covered his faith healing, filled with snake handling or speaking in tongues, I'd have done my duty and spoken to him about whatever blasphemy I found. Instead, I saw a perfect simulacrum of a Catholic service, and the only part at all out of place was Gabriel himself, dressed in a priest's robes without ever having taken holy vows.

After the service, it was easy enough to find Richard Griego, the man who'd been healed. He no longer looked as he had in the newspaper. His hair had grown back a bit, and his skin had regained enough color that you could no longer see his veins. But he still looked fragile, like even a strong gust of wind would've sent him back to the hospital. He was there with what looked like his mother and sister, and all three of them seemed in high spirits.

I introduced myself and mentioned reading about his story in the *Journal*. It was him and his story, I said, that had led me to the church.

He laughed and said, "You and most everyone else."

"Do you have a minute to talk about it?" I asked him.

He said sure and told his family he'd meet them at the car momentarily. We moved away from the crowd to a corner of the foyer, where a ticketing booth still stood in the center and a snack counter served doughnuts, coffee, and, perhaps fittingly, fresh popcorn.

I said that I wanted to know how much of the story I'd read in the *Journal* had been real and how much had been exaggeration. I didn't care either way, I just wanted to hear the truth.

"I don't know," he said. "That's the thing, right? Everyone wants me to talk about it, say it was a miracle, but I just don't know, man. I mean, how can you even say?"

He seemed honest and more than a tad shocked by all the attention he'd received. I asked him to put aside the miracle part. Had the events happened as reported? Had he really been on his deathbed, only to recover after Gabriel prayed over him?

"Here's the thing," he said. "He prayed with me, and I got better. Maybe I would've gotten better if he hadn't. But it was weird. I was kind of half-asleep, half-awake for a lot of that time, and when I looked over in the middle of the night, I swear to you I saw Jesus kneeling next to him. Just like to the side of him, with this sort of glow."

"Why didn't you mention that to the reporters?" I asked.

"I dunno, I thought they wouldn't believe me. And like what if I was just hallucinating? What I know for sure is Padre Gabriel came to the hospital and kneeled next to me and held my hand. He sat there and prayed and said how Christ loved me, even if my suffering made me think otherwise. And you know … I'd been cursing Dios for weeks when my abuela wasn't around to listen. But all that with Padre Gabriel, it made me feel ok again. So I guess I don't know, maybe it was a miracle and maybe it wasn't, but I knew that when I got out of that hospital bed, I should get my sorry ass to church."

I thanked him, and we walked together to the parking lot, which the church shared with a thrift shop and an empty Vietnamese restaurant. I had one more question, unrelated to his healing but still important, perhaps because I'd spent so many years of my life at seminary. Was he aware that, technically speaking, Father Gabriel wasn't a priest?

He shrugged. "You mean like he didn't go to priest school or whatever? Nah, I don't care. Seems like a pretty good priest to me."

Richard and I never became close, but we remained nodding acquaintances, and I still know his family. Like so much of Gabriel's congregation, they came from the poorer, Hispanic areas of the city, and I felt far more comfortable with them than my own wealthy congregation. I came to Gabriel's church expecting some sort of betrayal of the man I'd met in seminary, because I'd never expected to see him offering Mass, but what I found made me feel insecure about both my own path and the services I offered on the other side of town.

I returned to the small apartment provided by the parish, and my day-to-day life continued like before. But any time I had the chance, I drove across the bridge and listened to Gabriel deliver sermons. I subscribed to Our Lady of Guadalupe's newsletter, and after maybe six months, I emailed Gabriel about coordinating an event between our two parishes. I wanted to offer an olive branch from the Catholic Church, to tell him that what he was doing, while maybe not officially sanctioned, seemed to be in line with Christ's teachings.

Gabriel's response was effusive. Of course he'd love a link between our congregations. He was honored by the offer. He also made it clear that, personally, he was happy to hear from me, and I was flattered. In hindsight, this was probably the beginning of my own severing from the Church. I didn't "convert" right then, but I began to doubt.

JOSHUA WHITEHURST

After college, I didn't have any answers. I barely had any questions. For a while, I developed coping techniques that allowed me to live on autopilot. Drinking helped. Smoking helped. Meeting someone at a club or show and fucking him that night without worrying about seeing him again helped. And all these coping mechanisms worked even better in tandem, combining substances and sensations until the blend was thick and delicious. It was never 100 percent effective, but usually it was enough.

I started going to shows three, four, five nights a week. I was a regular at Launchpad, and I was there at Sunshine on the night that bouncer murdered a girl in the bathroom. I kicked it with friends who played in a post-queercore group with regular gigs at Burt's, and made it over to Effex whenever I could after a bartender friend started comping me drinks. When I really needed to bring it down a notch, I'd head upstairs at Anodyne and shoot pool, and when even that was too much, I'd hit up the Copper Kettle, where you could sit in the dark back booths and reach your hand or mouth into someone's pants without anyone giving you a weird look. Life was bright lights and blackout nights and little in between. Sometimes, in the middle of the evening, amphetamine pumping through my veins and tequila sloshing around my gut, I even felt alive.

During the school year, I substitute taught a few times a week, and in the summer I worked at Quarters Discount Liquors, where you'd get to know the local homeless people real well for a few months, until their noses couldn't get any redder and their coughs couldn't get any worse, and then you'd never see them again. I stayed in a house in the Plaza Vieja area west of downtown, spitting distance from the old sawmills where middle-aged white guys would wander home after work with sad looks on their faces and even sadder jumpsuits covering their frumpy bodies. Anywhere from two to four roommates shared rent with me, men and women who found out about vacancies through word of mouth or a permanent Craigslist post. During the years I lived there, I never once met our landlord, just sent checks out that'd get deposited, no questions asked.

When I first moved in, after some time at my parents' house courtesy of my post-Gabriel nervous breakdown, the house intimidated me. It was two stories, with cars parked on its overgrown lawn. A faded red couch sat atop the roof, with a ladder leading up to it. The house's back door lacked a handle, which didn't really matter, since nothing downstairs had any value. The guys living upstairs installed a lock on the door leading to that part of the house, and when one of them moved out, I took over his cramped bedroom and no longer had to worry about my laptop getting filched when I wasn't home.

The guys who lived there when I moved in liked to party, and I guess that's how I got started, or at least it's what gave me an extra nudge down the slope I was already on. One tended a dive bar and the other was in nursing school, and they'd buy a keg or two a week and leave them outside, sitting in an ice-filled trash can for me and anyone else who stopped by to grab a drink. If I wasn't working, I'd hang with them, then bike over to Central and see what was up. I'd get home anywhere from midnight to five a.m. and carry a drink with me to the top of that house. There I could sit and watch whatever stars made it past the city's light pollution until I fell asleep, only to awaken a few hours later with the sun burning my face. Sometimes I'd take guys up there, and even though we were outside and in the center of the city with noise and traffic that never fully quit, it felt as private as my bedroom with the door shut and the blinds down.

One night, I'd been at Burt's for a while, taking swigs from a bottle of Maker's Mark that the band—they were called God's Nipple Clamps—had hidden in a guitar case so the bartender couldn't spot it. The band was notoriously terrible, and drinking heavily was really the only way to make it through their set, but there was still a crowd.

At Burt's, you never could tell who'd show up. On any given night, there could be an unexpected surge of frat boys and their ilk standing around with their crew cuts all in a row like members of the world's douchiest boy band. But I wasn't thinking about the crowd, or the booze, or waking up hungover the next morning to "teach" a high-school music class by hitting "Play" on a DVD. Dissonant chords smashed through the room like a hailstorm, but my attention never left the man in front of me, his hand on my shoulder, his too-loud laughter. I was pretty hammered, and I could barely make out the sound of his voice above the shitty distortion and feedback, so when he told me he was headed to the restroom, I thought he was also telling me to follow him. To be honest, he wasn't even my type, but I figured why the fuck not?

The fuck not was that I'd read his signals wrong, or he chickened out at the last second, or I don't even know. The last thing I remember was him yelling some nasty slurs before punching my head hard enough to knock me out. I woke up to a friend shaking me, asking if I wanted him to call an ambulance. My body ached all over, and I was pretty sure my nose was broken, but I told him I'd be fine. I was still on my parents' insurance, and I definitely didn't want to have to explain any hospital bills to them.

This isn't AA, and that night didn't stop me from drinking. Or doing acid with my roommates on one memorable occasion when we bought a piñata and filled it with those colorful tablets before demolishing it with bats and wrenches down in the basement. Or having one-night stands with random men before telling them to fuck off in a way I'd never gotten to with Gabriel. But I don't want to pretend things were the same after that either. It was a month before I made it back to the scene, and then I didn't go as hard as I used to. I didn't want to black out, to risk doing something stupid and waking up in the hospital, or worse.

After a few more months, I enrolled in my own sort of rehabilitation program: I moved back in with my parents. They were still PB&J, Starbucks Coffee people. They went to work from eight thirty until five every day, read a hard copy of the newspaper in the morning, mowed the lawn on Saturdays, and went to church on Sundays. I could set my watch to my father's bowel movements. And while to the rest of the world I was out and proud, when it came to them, I just couldn't do it. They were content, and I needed their cheerful normalcy to help me through what was still a mess of a time. They encouraged me to start singing again, and I joined a small choir made up mostly of retired women—we were pretty terrible, but that didn't matter, because it was fun. For no particular reason, I decided to take the LSAT and did pretty damn well, which led me to UNM Law School. I don't know, basically it seemed like the easiest path toward the white-collar lifestyle my parents had.

The randomness of my decision hardly stood out among my classmates. A lot of people enrolled for the pot of gold they spied at the end of law school's three-year-long rainbow, but plenty enrolled because they didn't know what else to do. Law school was purgatory, but it was perversely soothing. I thought about Gabriel less, and the white noise of studying and memorization blocked out most negative emotions—most emotions period. While I'd spent most of my undergraduate years avoiding classes and coursework, now I focused on little else.

In one of the required first-year courses, the professor posed a simple question: "What is the law for?" I sat back in my chair, hoping not to be called on because I had no answer. Other students raised their hands and offered pithy responses, gunners hoping to draw approval from the professor.

"Justice," answered one student.

"Protection," said another.

"Keeping order," said a third.

Our professor was an old man, the type of graying white eminence you expect to find mumbling senile lectures, but he gained energy from each rebuke he gave, cataloging ways the law had been used to harm the defenseless, cause disorder, amplify injustice.

"Your failure," he said, pacing at the front of the room and looking smug, "is in imagining that the law is unified. That it's a system designed for a single purpose, or even a dozen purposes." He spoke about how the law had been contrived over decades, centuries, by more people than could be counted. "It helps and harms in equal measure. It's a system with no master, no designer. It's a God that seems to have created itself and carries itself with its own whims."

As the rest of the class sat silently, hoping not to look stupid, I raised my hand.

"Yes," he said. "What is it?"

"If the law is so meaningless, so amorphous, why does it matter what it's for? Saying that it's all of these things … isn't that the same as saying it's for nothing?" I wanted him to tell me that the nihilism I was searching for, that I'd previously found in the scene, could be transposed here.

"It's not meaningless, it's that its meanings are myriad," he said. "One of your chief jobs in law school is to figure out what purpose the law serves in each of your lives. Is it a means to make money, or to change society? To defend the defenseless, or lock criminals behind bars? The important thing is that you make a conscious choice."

I found this inspiring, almost mystical. The idea that your belief in something imbued it with meaning, well, it sounds stupid now, but I latched on to it, used it as a ladder to climb the rest of the way out of the hole I'd been in.

Now don't laugh when I say this, but after all the nothingness of the preceding years, I started thinking about how to grow up and, if you'll excuse the cliché, make a difference. I took every class I could on civil liberties and defense, studied my ass off through The History of

Race and the Law and Advanced Constitutional Rights.
I got in touch with other students interested in legal aide,
wrote papers about the systematic oppression of under-
privileged minorities. The irony of doing so while living
closeted in my parents' home did not escape me, but I
felt that the free room and board was more than worth
it, especially since I spent very little time there. Mostly
I was hunched over in the library, until my third year
when I got an internship with the local ACLU branch.

Here's what I'm particularly embarrassed about: at the
time, after everything I'd experienced, I somehow still
had this idea that good and evil were clear-cut. I'd grown
up with *Star Wars*, with Indiana Jones. With Disney. At a
certain point, I must've internalized those stories, and I
believed that all you had to do was get in with the white
hats and everything would be alright. When I started
with the ACLU, I was under the impression that they
were the good guys, fighting for justice and equality in
a world filled with Nazis and Stormtroopers. Now that
I'm older, I understand that there are often shades of gray.
Martin Luther King Jr. liked to sleep around. Mother
Teresa cared more about fetuses than the people living
in squalor in her missions. Lincoln may have freed the
slaves, but he sure as hell didn't think black people should
have social and political equality. That's not to say that no
one can be fully evil—some motherfuckers are straight
trash—but disappointment with the do-gooders really
upends your worldview.

For three weeks, I believed in the mission. Even as
interns, our caseload was extreme, and I found myself
regularly staying at the office past dinner. I didn't mind.
If protecting people from wrongful arrests or being shot
by the police meant a life of cheap Chinese takeout at my

desk, that was my tiny cross to bear. Our whole office, which including me was only eighteen people, shared this crusading spirit, from the director down to the paralegal. We were understaffed but passionate and had a history of winning big cases by pushing ourselves.

Then in walked Gregory Reynolds, more commonly known as White Power Greg to the online community of white supremacists, his friends, probably even his family. He was tall, maybe six four, wiry and self-assured. His hair was cut short in a way that made the most of his encroaching baldness, and tattoos peeked out from the neckline and sleeves of his polo shirt. This, paired with tan chinos and a pair of Warby Parker glasses, made him look like nothing so much as an accountant who just happened to be racked with fury at Jewish people for being, well, Jewish. I never tried to empathize with him, and maybe that's what set me apart from the rest of the staff, who eventually treated him like he was as deserving of respect as the Cochiti woman whose case I'd worked on, who'd been beaten and arrested by ICE under suspicion of "harboring an immigrant" who turned out to be her very-much-a-citizen son.

White Power Greg barged through our glass front door and marched to the front desk, a half smile on his lips. "I need to speak with the director here, 'cause my rights've been taken away by them folks in city council."

"We don't … do you have an appointment?" I asked. I didn't know who he was then, but I immediately knew I didn't want to.

He stared right into my eyes. "Then tell 'im I'll wait here until he can talk."

I asked my boss what to do, and she shrugged and said we'd wait him out. At the end of the day, he was still there, not reading or doing anything to pass the time, just staring at me and occasionally asking how much longer I thought it might be. When I finally went home, he was still there, and I was glad to think I'd never have to deal with him again. I was very wrong.

The next day, there was an all-hands meeting, and with us in the room was White Power Greg. The director asked us to listen to him, and I stood at the back, too stunned at what I was hearing to say anything. Here's what White Power Greg wanted to do: an anti-Pride protest. He said he'd been wanting to have an official protest for years, he and his local chapter of the White Knights of the Ku Klux Klan, but the city of Albuquerque had been refusing a permit on the spurious-to-them grounds of their being the KKK. Of course I knew about the KKK, at least in a sort of historical, abstract way. I'd seen pictures in my history textbooks. I'd watched *The Birth of a Nation* in a college film class. But they'd always seemed like something the country had shed long ago, like a disgusting snakeskin. Again, I was wrong, and from what White Power Greg said, every year they were stronger, more organized. Those hate-filled men and women had connected with each other across waves and wires, writing on message boards how the mainstream media and public schools whispered lies to their children about equality and acceptance. They filled their tiny brains with Alex Jones, Bill O'Reilly, and Rush Limbaugh until the bile spilled over and washed onto the rest of us. It was time to begin a reckoning, said White Power Greg. It was time for the white man to stand proud once again, as the unquestioned conqueror of history, the ruler of all he surveyed … just as soon as they got that damn permit from the city council.

I spent the rest of the day pretending that meeting hadn't happened. My hope was that the next time White Power Greg showed up, the ACLU would give him the boot—literally, with as large of one as they could find—and tell him to peddle his hateful bullshit elsewhere. More rationally, I expected them to give him a smaller, private meeting and explain why this wasn't a case we'd be taking on. The ACLU had extremely limited funding, and spending its resources to give a hate group the run of the city seemed like the definition of stupidity, especially since this promised to be an expensive case.

Instead, White Power Greg was shown the veritable red-carpet treatment. Aside from a couple pet projects, all work was put on hold so we could help him put on his white-hooded protest and say that people like me could fuck off and die.

I'm making it sound like this all happened during one particularly shitty afternoon, when in reality it took weeks and months of my life. There were meetings to discuss the ethical ramifications of helping White Power Greg and meetings to discuss the ethical ramifications of said meetings. There was a mini protest within the office and a protest against the mini protest. And there were appearances, so many goddamn appearances, of White Power Greg in the office, staring me down and then giving lectures to us, the ACLU, about how free speech was what made America great. The day after I heard the executive director using the exact same arguments as White Power Greg at the annual gala fund-raiser, I finally quit.

It took maybe half an hour for the ACLU to fill my position. Following more than a year of expensive litigation, White Power Greg and a couple dozen of his ilk were allowed their piddling little protest. In the end, I think the only people who actually cared about the damn thing, the only people really affected by it, were White Power Greg and me.

Later, I learned that by some crazy coincidence, the day I quit was the same one that the local news ran its piece on Gabriel's first Big Miracle. Deep in my anger, I hadn't even realized that he was back in town, let alone stirring up religious fervor like an old-timey revival preacher. At that point, I was too self-pitying to really give a damn about the news. As far as I was concerned, the city had betrayed me by allowing the protest, so it could fuck off and look after itself for a while.

What remains when your idealism is gone, when your old nihilism proves the more sensible outlook after all? Embrace the nihilism.

I'll skip the uninteresting period between graduation and passing the bar. The important thing is that this is how I ended up working for Parker & Mullins, ready to do whatever the job required.

ANNA FISHEL

Our Lady of Guadalupe grew fast. Yes, stories of the miracle slipped through the city, but there was also Father Gabriel's magnetism. A current ran through the room when he stood on that stage. But maybe I'm giving the wrong impression—it wasn't like he was theatrical, it was more like watching an acoustic set by your favorite band, stripped down and bare and honest.

Father Gabriel said, "'What Would Jesus Do?' is a cliché and, worse, an impossible question. We are not Jesus. Jesus is God, and His mind is unknowable, His actions unfathomable. Asking what He would or wouldn't do is as pointless as asking how many angels fit on the head of a pin. What we should ask ourselves is what would we do if we saw Jesus here today? If He was feeding the homeless at the Circle K, would you help Him? If He was at the banks of the Rio Grande, would you ask Him to baptize you? How can we fit Jesus into our lives right now? Because God is just as present as He ever was."

And I did want to fit Him into my life, wedge Him back where He'd been before, though what that would mean beyond returning to church once a week, I didn't yet know.

While the number of parishioners grew, it took time for us to become a community. I, for one, had never been good at meeting folks, and while I began to nod at faces I recognized, I had trouble getting any further. Soon, though, I forced myself to speak to anyone who greeted me, from the tall, impeccably dressed black man acting as self-appointed usher to the old woman who struggled with her walker while insisting wheelchairs were for wimps. At that point, I didn't have many other friends, having lost touch with folks from college after they'd moved or had babies. I met Nicole, another new parishioner who shared my sense of humor, and began shopping for church dresses because I wanted to look nice. The newness of everything infused the church with a certain excitement, and I began anticipating my Sundays all week long, planning my life around them. My weeks became gray, out of focus, and almost indistinguishable from each other—it was only at church that life felt worth living.

And while I didn't show up until after the first miracle, as we sometimes called it, for all intents and purposes, I was one of the earliest members of Our Lady of Guadalupe. Not that it's important—we're all equal in Jesus's eyes, of course—I just want to set the record straight.

The first time Father Gabriel introduced himself, I offered him my hand and told him my name.

"That's a strong name," he said. He offered his usual broad smile, natural and unrehearsed. That was one of the things that struck me even then, how regardless of whether he was speaking about God's mercy or worrying about what we could do to help political prisoners on the other side of the planet, he almost always smiled. "Mary's mother was also named Anne."

"Anna," I said. "I didn't know that." I couldn't tell him where it came from, as my parents never talked about that sort of thing.

"Sorry, Anna, I didn't mean ... it's not important," he said. "It's just wonderful to have you as a part of the church."

I thanked him, happy he didn't press me with more small talk. I think he could see my timidity, so instead he left me with that smile and wandered across the lobby to speak with other parishioners.

After that, I hung around every week. It took me a little while to humanize him, to realize that the man who delivered such amazing sermons was almost the same age as me. He was dark and handsome, humble yet confident. But I think what set him apart from the men I'd known, not just in college but all men, everywhere, was that Father Gabriel didn't try to flirt with me. Or anyone. When we spoke, there was no tension, no threat. Maybe that's why the church felt so comfortable, even at the beginning. He felt safe, the way a man of God *should* feel, and that was refreshing.

And he was honest. "Up there," he said to me once, "trying to keep from fumbling my words or tripping on the robes, it can be hard to tell if anyone's listening. Or if what I'm saying makes any sense."

"Everyone is listening," I said. "Of course we are. Why else would we be here?"

"Free wine?" He laughed, then moved on to greet some visitors.

The local news story quickly went viral, so there were always new congregants, new people who wanted to see this miraculous healer. Our Lady of Guadalupe's single Mass on Sundays, with most of the room empty, soon became two Masses on Sunday mornings, plus a Saturday afternoon Mass, and then additional Masses on Tuesday, Wednesday, and Thursday nights. Half of these featured music from Father Gabriel's laptop, plugged into a few donated speakers, but it didn't matter—folks always showed up, and Father Gabriel gave them the best service he could. He put on a show.

I'm pretty sure Father Gabriel hadn't planned this far ahead. Maybe he'd expected the church to fail, or he'd assumed God would provide when the time came. Regardless, it soon became clear that while his sermons were ecstatic, revelatory affairs, his organizational skills were ... less developed. He showed up late to food drives, double-booked appointments. Every week, services came together, altar boy marching with precision to the sound of flawlessly played classical music courtesy of UNM's graduate students, but that was a minor miracle in itself. Late Masses, missing church bulletins, incorrect announcements. None of it stopped the flood of worshippers, but the sloppiness was noticeable. Actually, it was a little embarrassing.

So I decided that's how I would make Jesus a bigger part of my life, and I stepped in. After Mass, I asked Father Gabriel whether he could use some help on the weekends.

"Well yes, that would be wonderful," he said, looking uncomfortable, like I'd caught him in a lie. "But we don't have the money, and I don't like telling people what to do..."

"I'm right here, silly. Why don't I just show up, and we'll go from there?" I insisted, and he shrugged, then headed to speak with other parishioners, incense and vanilla lingering in the stuffy air.

At first I'd bring a thick paperback with me to the back office that served as our administrative base, reading when I wasn't answering the phone. I won't pretend what I did was a massive improvement—there were only two or three calls a day, and I often had to hunt down Father Gabriel for answers—but I think he liked the company. Gradually I took over more responsibilities and had no time for reading.

A church isn't normally a one-man show, even if it seems that way, and from the afternoon naps he took, I could tell he was worn down. He only owned one set of robes, and they were beginning to fray. He seemed to live on a diet of primarily ramen noodles, like he was still a college student. I began to feel like I'd volunteered too late, and not a day went by that I didn't worry about the entire church being one small disaster—say, Father Gabriel getting the flu—away from ending just as rapidly as it had begun.

Father Gabriel basically lived and worked on his sermons in a cramped, monkish cell at the back of the church. It had clearly been a supply closet before, and a hint of bleach, with a strange undercurrent of vanilla, wafted out whenever he opened the door. Inside was a cot and some old wooden furniture salvaged from the street, including a wobbly desk and a bookshelf that looked on the edge of collapse.

When it came to administrative matters, particularly finances, he worked in the main office with me. He wasn't bad at numbers when he put his mind to it, but that wasn't all too often. When I first began, he didn't even use a spreadsheet, just collected receipts haphazardly and put loose collection money into a jar. Checks were deposited into his bank account, which he rationalized by saying that it wasn't like he was collecting any other income, but I put a stop to that immediately because of how it might look.

Aside from the accounting, my main surprise about the church was how correct I'd been in my assessment that Our Lady of Guadalupe was teetering on the edge of disaster. Few members of the congregation tithed, and the majority of what the church made came from one generous donor.

"Who is this?" I asked him at the end of a long afternoon trying to make sense of his records.

"Who's who?"

"This donor, the one keeping the doors open. You just have it marked 'GM' on this page, but it feels like … well, maybe we should do something for them?"

"No no, it's not necessary," Father Gabriel said, seeming a bit irritated. "Leave them be."

"But what if they skip an offering?"

"What if they don't."

I took a deep breath. I've always been nonconfrontational—my way of coping with my dad had been to wait and hope he drank himself to death. But Father Gabriel always stressed the need for brutal honesty and that he valued my opinion, so not saying something felt like a sin of sorts. "Father, we're hanging on by a thread. Either we make absolutely certain that this GM stays happy, or we need to start asking folks to tithe."

He stared back at me and took his time answering, his eyes sad. It made me embarrassed for asking. "I don't want to make them pay to be here," he said. "I don't want a circus. I don't want a Pentecostal revival tent, performing stunts in the hope of a few bucks at the door."

"That's not at all what I'm saying. I'm just saying that if the most you earn on a Sunday is a couple dollars for doughnuts and popcorn in the lobby, there's only so much you can do. What about hiring someone to clean the place every now and then or paying for a permanent administrator one day?"

"I'll think about it," he said. "But let's not worry about that right now. We'll get by."

"I don't want Our Lady of Guadalupe to get a reputation as a grubby, disorganized mess, that's all," I said. "But I'm not here to tell you how to run things. I'll stick with the books."

The next week, his sermon didn't mention tithing. No surprise, things didn't improve. But the week after that, his message changed slightly, and I knew at least he'd been thinking about what I'd said.

"I know that for some people, it's the magic that runs them off from church," he began, walking from the pulpit toward the center of the stage. "They worry that maybe Jesus is a carnival huckster, that the resurrection is a scam to get us to give away money. Could the resurrection be another way of cheating the poor? They see Jesus, and they don't think of the Bible, they think of some televangelist saying, 'Send me a dollar. Give me your credit card number, and I'll heal you. Put a check in your mailbox, and salvation is yours.'"

His voice dropped until he was speaking in almost a whisper.

"But Jesus Christ—I mean the real Jesus Christ, not the one you hear about on the radio, not the one invoked when torturing so-called 'heretics,' but the one who lived and walked on this earth—that Jesus Christ didn't make anyone rich. The Jesus Christ who died and returned to us three days later, His followers were the whores. The homeless. His followers quit their jobs to live out on the streets and have stones thrown at them, have the Romans put them to death. So why, you wonder, did He perform miracles? He performed them because if He didn't, no one would believe Him, even if He was the Almighty.

They were an advertisement for what He had to say, a way of getting people through the door. He performed them because—"

Father Gabriel suddenly stopped. I've heard members of the congregation recount what happened in different ways, but I was right there in the front row. He didn't begin speaking in tongues, like I read in the *Journal*, it was more of a gurgle. I thought he might be having a stroke or an attack of some sort. Internally, I panicked, but like everyone else, for some reason I stayed seated.

Seconds passed. Maybe minutes. Suddenly, as if a video un-paused, I could hear movement behind me. Someone yelled, "Call a doctor," and there was shrieking. But I didn't look back, because I could see his feet rising, first almost imperceptibly but soon enough undeniably. By the time a man jumped up on the stage and touched him, you could've rolled a bowling ball beneath him. As soon as the man's finger made contact with his robe, though, Father Gabriel dropped to the floor, gasping.

After thanking the man, Father Gabriel insisted on completing the Mass. As he blessed the Eucharist, there was tension in the room, like a storm was about to break. I kept waiting for someone to say something about what just happened. Maybe it should've been me. But no one did, and we lined up for the bread and wine like always. I did notice one difference, though. When Gabriel said to me, "Body of Christ," I looked up at his face and noticed that, for once, he wasn't smiling. I may be misremembering, but I recall thinking that he looked old, that his hair was grayer than it had been the day before.

He disappeared after Mass, when usually he would've chatted with me and as many other congregants as he could. I walked to the back of the church and saw that the door to his room was closed. I could've knocked, but I didn't. Instead, I went out and did my best to welcome the visitors myself. I felt this was what Gabriel would've wanted.

The next Saturday, when I arrived around ten to count the previous week's offering and answer phones, Father Gabriel greeted me cheerfully, as if nothing had happened. His youthful energy was in full force as he proposed plans for upcoming church events. I mostly smiled and nodded, not wanting to bring up the fact that in the past, these had always failed because of the organizational issues I've already mentioned.

Once he finished, though, I couldn't help myself. I asked about the attack.

"It was just, you know, one of those things," he said. He didn't seem to mind talking about it.

"What do you ... I mean, I've never had anything like that happen to me," I said. "I don't know if it's just 'one of those things'..."

He gave me an odd look, then shrugged. "Yeah, maybe not. I don't know."

I could've pressed him further, but I was so happy to see him back to normal. I let things be. By the time I started on the spreadsheets, he'd left to work on his sermon. That was probably a good thing, since he might've been appalled by how elated I was with what I found: the week's offering was almost double what we'd seen before. Yes, the usual large donor's check was there, but there were other checks, plus enough loose bills that it looked like a drug dealer had stopped by and unrolled an entire stack into the collection baskets. I may have let out a whoop—not for myself, certainly, but for the church.

When he stopped by later, I mentioned how much there was, and he seemed as unfazed about it as he did his attack.

"This means you can afford those cleaners I'm always bugging you about," I said.

"I have to admit, I don't think I do a very good job of it myself," he said. I hadn't even known that he'd tried, as the place certainly didn't look like anyone picked up after Mass, besides tossing old bulletins into the recycling bins.

I told him I'd call a cleaning company. It was only after that second oversize offering the next week that I started thinking about the possibility of speaking to Father Gabriel about a paid position. Obviously it would mean a pay cut from what I'd been earning as a pharmacist, but I lived alone, had no children to support, and had already paid off my old Volvo. When he agreed, it was maybe the most blessed moment of my life.

ISABEL ROMERO

I don't want this to seem like some endorsement of cheating. I don't want Gabriel to be known as the son of
some puta tramposa, some Malinche moderna. Some
slut. But I'm not afraid to drop a little truth onto those
holier-than-thou church ladies who say a little infidelity
is the end of the world. Here's the secret they—and I suppose you too, Padre—don't know: cheating is exciting.
Invigorating. In some cases, I think it's the best thing you
can do for your health, your happiness.

It's not about the sex, though. At least, it's mostly
not about the sex. It's about the lies. I've never liked the
English word for bending the truth, its slithering *L* and
S, its slipperiness, the way it seems linked with corporations and politicians and gringos. Mentir is rock solid.
Mentir is sensuous but grounded. It's the medicinal dose
that keeps you from going crazy. Mentir is what I lived
by, for a little while at least.

I only saw William once a week in person, at those
dinners with Gabito's grandmother, but I saw him on
television and in movies constantly. He was costarring
with Nicole Kidman, kissing her passionately on the way
to his international spy mission. He was on the back of
Esquire, the front of *GQ*. These men all had the same
jawline, the same skin tone. They walked with the half

strut, half march that William did, different haircuts but the same expensive stylist. Sometimes it felt like when Brandon was watching a Cary Grant movie, or a Brad Pitt movie, or practically any movie really, that he was telling me to pursue William. That Brandon not only tacitly approved of, but maybe even secretly hoped for, an affair, so long as the man I found was all straight lines and cleft chin.

A couple months after that first dinner, Gabito had to leave early, and I expected to head home quickly too. There were dishes to wash, I had a headache, and dinner had been so short that William barely had time to flirt with me. I'd come to look forward to the knowing looks he'd give me after delivering a particularly risqué joke, lightly tapping my foot with his while Gabito and his grandmother nattered on about politics. William loved getting things past his mother even more than he enjoyed riling her up, a quality I found particularly attractive.

So that night, he walked with me outside, past the rusting fence to where our cars were parked, my old Honda and his polished black BMW. There were no streetlights, the neighborhood's wealthy residents more interested in privacy than safety, so I could barely make out his face.

"Do you have a minute?" he asked, his voice playful and confident.

"Sure," I said, and he stepped toward me. I thought I could see the moon reflected in his eyes, even though it was still early and the angle, with him looming over me, would've made that impossible. But still, that's how I remember it. He put his arm against my car, trapping me in place before he leaned in for a kiss. I stopped him after a few seconds and looked shocked. This was how I knew I was supposed to act, how I knew any woman in a steady relationship should act, according to every Hollywood fantasy Brandon had made me watch. I stared at William's face and saw how hungry he was for me and decided I'd made him wait long enough. I kissed him, and he kissed me back; together we were fierce and impatient.

We climbed into the back seat of his car. Through it all, William kept one eye on his mother's house. It was like we were back in high school, middle school even, getting away with something forbidden. I liked that feeling more than I liked him, the way we fumbled in the shadows instead of acting like two responsible people in their forties who had homes with beds. I liked that it was unequivocally wrong, a betrayal, a sin, and that we both knew it.

When I arrived home, Brandon was sitting in the dark, flickering in the light of the fifty-six-inch television he'd lugged from his apartment to my house half a year earlier. I kissed him on the cheek and told him I was going to take a bath before bed. He smiled, then went back to his movie. The sound of clashing samurai warriors filled the house. I almost felt bad for him ... pero I didn't. I hadn't stayed over with William, after all. Era una mentira de omisión: the smallest, and certainly the whitest, of deceptions.

So I slept fine. Life continued. The only difference, if any, was that I felt strong for the first time in years. There is a power to cheating. A power in knowing something that someone else—particularly someone so close that they live with you, eat with you, fall asleep next to you—does not.

It took me a long time to figure out why I did it, continued doing it, but I remember watching some movie with Brandon and thinking how none of the characters in it sat around watching movies themselves. They were all out there: meeting, flirting, dancing, living, and I wanted to be like them. Before, there was only the accumulation of days, weeks, years. There was coming home to the same pinche dinner, a day of work in front of me and another one behind, living in the same pinche town in the same pinche house. I didn't know how I would make it to the next day without chugging a gallon of bleach. And suddenly, there was William, his body pressed against mine, and those thoughts all went away.

The next week, we did it again. We didn't speak about it, didn't even speak during it. Afterward, I didn't want to go home, so instead of following William down Paseo Del Norte toward my house, I sped across Tramway until I found a park I hadn't thought about in years, one that had a rock outcropping overlooking the whole city. I took off my shoes and climbed, gripping the stones with my toes while the breeze tugged at my skirt. At the top, I laid down and looked up.

I wanted to see the stars, pero everything above me was dark. The moon was a tiny crescent, almost blocked by clouds. It was the buildings beneath me that pulsed with light, cars winding down roads and jamming into freeways. It wasn't bad, it just ... it wasn't what I wanted, and for some reason I started to cry. I stayed up there, stones digging into my lower back, wind freezing my hands and legs, until the tears finally stopped.

Brandon was already in bed when I got home, reading on his Kindle. He was shirtless but had tightly tucked the sheets and blankets and pulled them up to his shoulders, swaddling himself like a giant baby. I thought he'd ask where I'd been, and then there'd be shouting, accusations, the throwing of lamps and shoes. The neighbors would complain, and I would be that woman, la perra ruidosa the whole neighborhood talked about.

"Are you ok?" he asked. His voice dropped, and he walked over to hug me. He knew I liked to be held.

I made up an excuse, told him there'd been a fight between me and Evelyn.

"Is there anything I can do?" he asked.

"No, nothing. It was all so horrible," I said. "I don't know if I can go back." I laid down in the bed and curled up beneath the covers. He wrapped himself around me, not so much a big spoon as a big bandage.

I felt guilty. My little mentira blanca had grown into a huge white elephant, invading my house, taking up space until I could barely move, barely breathe. It sat behind the couch while I watched movies, making crude jokes and whispering in my ears. It peeked at us while we made love, asking why Brandon wasn't enough, why I couldn't be happy with the perfectly adequate, perfectly predictable life I'd set up at home.

It didn't matter. The next week I had sex with William again. And the week after that. And the month after that. The worse I felt around Brandon, the better I felt the rest of the time. It may have been illusory, a sleight-of-hand trick, but while it lasted, it was real enough to me. I did, briefly, have it all.

I kept this up for maybe six months. William never hinted at wanting more, and Brandon never hinted at knowing more. If I'd wanted to, I probably could've kept it up forever, and a part of me, a large part, wanted to.

Pero I'd thought my dalliance with William couldn't hurt anyone but myself. I would suffer the consequences, in this life or the next, but that would be on me. When his divorce finalized and William showed off the ring he'd purchased for his new fiancée, I didn't care. And I didn't care when Brandon introduced me to his parents. It almost felt like my life wasn't even mine, that I was watching it play out on a screen in my living room.

But then one day, during the middle of our weekly dinner at Evelyn's, Gabito asked me how Brandon was doing.

"Fine," I said, too fast. I didn't want to talk about him there, to allow the two halves of my reality to intermingle.

"Glad to hear it," Gabriel said. "Sorry I haven't been around much, it's just that we have these plans for a walk against the police, and I'm behind on my sermon like always … but anyhow, tell him hi for me. I always feel like, I don't … he's family, you know."

That word stunned me. Family. And with that, suddenly my little mentira was revealed as a lie after all. If Gabito felt close enough to Brandon to consider him family, I couldn't do it anymore. That elephant I'd kept fenced in my house broke free and stampeded into Evelyn's living room. I made an excuse and left.

The next day, I broke it off with Brandon. I didn't tell him why. So far as I'm aware, he never knew I cheated. I just explained that while I loved him, I wasn't in love with him. The old story, the oldest story, but still true, even if it was far from the whole truth. He was sad, but not as sad as I expected, and ultimately he told me that he agreed. And that was the end of the relationship, though not the end of my guilt. When Brandon walked out the door, packing the last load of DVDs and flannel shirts into his Prius, I had expected the elephant to leave with him.

MANUEL QUINTANA

The original plan had been to meet for lunch. But the day before, he called to say something had come up and asked me to accompany him to a parishioner's house for what he called a "healing." I was curious. I mean, a healing? What did that even look like? What could that possibly entail? I had to find out.

When I arrived at Rosa Rodriguez's house, her son opened the door. A tall man with a grave face, he didn't seem surprised at my presence. Though he asked for no explanation, I said I'd been asked to attend by Father Gabriel, and he led me past a cluttered front room and down a dark hallway with fading photos lining the walls. At the end of it, a sour, mildewy odor seeped out of an open doorway. I had to stop myself from covering my nose as I entered Rosa's bedroom. I would meet Rosa properly weeks later and grow quite fond of her in time, but then she lay propped up on multiple pillows, her eyes shut. I couldn't tell whether the smell came from her or the piles of tissues overwhelming wastebaskets scattered around the room. Votive candles with images of saints lit the room in an otherworldly yellow glow, and I couldn't shake the feeling that I wasn't supposed to be there.

"What does she have?" I whispered to her son.

"Cancer," he said.

"Ah, right … I meant what kind?"

"The liver. And the stomach. And all around here," he said, gesturing at his entire torso.

I stopped myself from asking whether she was in pain, because I knew the answer.

We waited in silence for five minutes, maybe longer. Rosa's son sat in the only chair in the room, and I felt awkward standing against the wall, trying not to be disruptive.

The doorbell rang again, and I told him I would get it. For some reason, I'd expected Gabriel in his cassock, but he showed up in jeans and a T-shirt. He carried a large cloth satchel, almost a purse, which he set down at the end of Rosa's bed. Both he and the satchel smelled not like any specific herb but a mishmash of odd aromas. The room felt even stuffier with him there, so Gabriel had us open the windows, dispelling the cavelike atmosphere with natural light and waking Rosa in the process.

"Padre Gabriel," she said. "You came to help me?"

"Of course I came," he said. "I'll see what I can do, but of course it's all up to God."

"Of course. Mijo, can you hand me my rosary?"

Her son unwrapped it from a bedpost near her head and gingerly placed it in her hand. With large, shapeless turquoise stones and a misshapen cross, the rosary was both ugly and almost mesmerizingly pretty at the same time. Rosa closed her eyes and began whispering prayers, running the beads through her fingers, as Gabriel fished plastic containers of herbs from his bag. He asked the son to bring him hot water, and then he poured a reddish-brown powder into it. After stirring, he interrupted Rosa and had her drink the mixture.

Then he began praying. I heard him say, "Padre nuestro, que estás en el cielo … ," and listened through the Lord's

Prayer and a Hail Mary. He began more specific prayers I didn't recognize, prayers to saints. He took another powder and sprinkled it on Rosa's head. He brought out his own rosary and muttered something while drinking a different concoction himself. He glanced at me, and I wondered if he wanted me to assist him somehow, but just as quickly his focus returned to Rosa. Her body looked like it was collapsing in on itself, frail and shapeless, and I worried that even this much exertion might be too much for her.

Gabriel moved closer to Rosa, almost uncomfortably close, though she didn't react. He carefully lifted the bottom of her shirt and placed his hand on her belly. Now he too seemed to enter into a trance. His dark-green eyes were open but blank, frozen in place. I saw light, faint but undeniable, emanating from where his hand rested. I couldn't help but move closer to the bed, even as Rosa's son glared at me.

The light beneath his hand grew from a wisp, barely indistinguishable from the sunlight, to a sort of aura. Slowly he moved it down her body, pressing but not disturbing her. His movements weren't sexual, but they were sensual. I couldn't help but think of a line from First Corinthians: "Do you not know that your bodies are temples of the Holy Spirit, who is in you, whom you have received from God? You are not your own; you were bought at a price." Rosa's body was a temple, filled with the Holy Spirit, and Gabriel was paying homage to what he found there. What the price might have been, I still can't say.

As he finished, Gabriel's eyes returned to normal, and Rosa gave out a large, almost ecstatic sigh. She looked no different, but she had a slight smile on her face when she said, "Thank you, Padre. May I rest now?"

"Yes, please. Go to sleep," he said.

Rosa's son looked as anxious as I felt. "Is ... is she going to get better?"

"Yes," said Gabriel. "I think so." He offered a half smile to both of us, lines of exhaustion on his face and a shiny coat of sweat on his brow.

As we reached the sidewalk where our cars were parked, I didn't know what to say. But when he seemed to stumble opening the door to his primer-colored Chevy, I caught him and asked, "Are you ok?"

"Yes, yes. I'm fine," he said. "Just a little tired." He smiled again, and wiped sweat off his face with his T-shirt. He looked happy but in an almost delirious way that alarmed me.

"Was that ... was that how it always is?" I asked. "A healing?"

"No, not always." His smile broke for a moment before returning. "Sometimes I can't do anything."

"Well, when you can? Was that normal?"

He seemed unsure. "My grandmother was a healer. She's the one who taught me about herbs and pressure points. All I do is what she taught me, and what her mother taught her."

"What about the light?"

"What light?"

I wanted to race back into Rosa's house and ask her son what he'd seen, verify that I was still in my right mind, but I couldn't let Gabriel leave without asking him more.

"What was it like for you?"

"It was ... after I've prayed for guidance, I feel on a patient's skin for ... it's not exactly warmth, but that's the closest I can come to describing it," he began. "I find that warmth, and I try to displace it, massage it until the body is unified. And sometimes, when there's an inferno blazing, so much heat that I'm unsure if I'll be able to quench the fire and restore the body ... well, it takes a lot out of me."

He gave me a look that said he was finished. But I had one more question: Did he feel the presence of God?

"Yes," he said. "When I first ... when I touch the person, I feel Jesus there with me. My fingertips graze their body, and I feel His strength, His compassion. His love. He's in whoever I treat, and then, for a few fleeting moments, I feel Him in myself. And it's beyond words, beyond my comprehension. But then it's over and, well, here I am again, standing in the heat outside my crappy old car. Now I need to be going. Let's meet again next week and this time actually eat some lunch."

Perhaps this can put some of the rumors of witchcraft and devilry to bed. I witnessed no arcane rituals, no demonic pacts. Prayers and healing, yes, certainly, but all in the name of Christ. Nor was there any publicity, no crowds of admirers or television cameras. Just an old woman, her loving son, and, through sheer happenstance, myself. Healing her gave him no glory, no praise from pundits or acolytes. If all this was just a show, part of some elaborate con artist's attempt to bamboozle the weak-minded, as I've heard more than a few claim, then what would have been the gain?

I drove home, wrestling with the implications of what I'd seen. Before that day I'd still had a few lingering doubts about Father Gabriel, his church, and his mission. But after what I'd witnessed, I couldn't simply continue as usual, writing the same sermons, reciting the same verses. I had seen a miracle, a true act of God, and to ignore it would have been more than foolish, it would have been sacrilege.

For a few days, I hesitated. It took a great deal of effort, but I managed to attend Our Lady of Guadalupe's earlier Sunday Mass that week. There, sitting on a pew in the back, sat Rosa and her son. She didn't look perfect, but she also looked far better than when I'd last seen her. When I spoke with them, her son told me he'd seen the light too. He said that Dios worked in mysterious ways, so who was he to ask questions. "Who indeed," his mother responded as she slowly but steadily walked to their car, and her smile was all the proof I needed.

I couldn't sleep that night, or the next. My appetite disappeared, and while I performed my normal duties, I did them on autopilot. I had devoted my entire adult life to the Catholic Church, had sacrificed everything in order to join the priesthood. When I was ordained, I told the archbishop I would serve obediently for life, una promesa I took seriously because of one I'd broken before it, and up until that week, I planned on following that promesa until I saw firsthand the heavenly kingdom I'd preached about. They say that some of the most stressful events in life are losing your job, separating from your spouse, and moving. For me, this decision meant all three. But I had no choice. Abandoning the Catholic Church was the most difficult decision of my life, yet it was no decision at all.

I met with Gabriel for lunch a couple days later at El Patio. As soon as he sat down, I blurted out my intention of leaving the Church and my hope that he would let me join his.

"Are you sure?" he asked. "I don't want you to make a decision you might regret."

"I just want to help you, to grow your flock."

"If that's the case, I would love to have you by my side," he said, his hazel eyes staring directly into mine.

"I must admit, I'm a bit tired. Doing it all by myself, it makes it difficult to say Mass so often, to come up with new sermons, to balance the budget. Don't get me wrong, I'm happy to do God's work, just sometimes … sometimes I'd like to rest."

"I'm happy to do whatever I can to help," I said. "When would you like me to start?"

"Well, what are you doing later today?"

FR. PATRICK CONKLIN

The Las Cruces diocese is small, but small is a relative term—it still has more than a hundred churches spread out across 350 miles of desert. Rules required each of us to meet with Bishop Diego de la Cruz every five years, and while those of us located nearby tended to see him more frequently—every two to three years—he was still a distant figure. In general, I appreciated his hands-off approach, given the horror stories I had heard during seminary about micromanaging bishops, but this time I thought some form of intervention was warranted. However, I was a junior priest, so junior that I suspected Bishop de la Cruz likely did not know my name, and thus my ability to communicate with him directly was minimal.

Still, I had to try. The quiet life of study and devotion I had hoped for seemed unsustainable as long as Gabriel's blasphemy remained undiscovered. I asked my superior at St. Mary's for assistance, but he said it was none of his concern. So I contacted the bishop myself. I spent a few hours drafting an email outlining the myriad problems with how Gabriel conducted his business in Albuquerque. I detailed the obvious falsehood of his supposed healing, but also the way Gabriel masqueraded as a priest, and I wrote of the irreparable long-term damage to the Church that his antics might cause. The stakes, I explained, were high, not only for New Mexicans but for Catholics worldwide. Gabriel was exactly the sort of false prophet who has always plagued the Church, and I feared he had the capability of becoming the kind of folk idol—leading the people astray, like Jesús Malverde and Santa Muerte—that this region seems particularly susceptible to. But Gabriel might have been even more pernicious: his promises and false piety could be witnessed in the flesh at services where he performed "miracles," and he could be heard on TV speaking about spiritual matters beyond his understanding with increasing regularity. He offered a concrete, worldly alternative to faith, a cheap shortcut to trick any Doubting Thomas into believing in him rather than Christ. This demanded a real response from the Church.

I waited three months for a response. When it finally arrived, I could scarcely believe what it contained. If you don't mind, I would like to read it for the record. "Father Conklin," it began. "Thank you for your correspondence. Communication between the priesthood and the Bishop's Office is important to all of us, and we want you to know that whatever your concerns, we're here to listen." This was all proper and expected. But then: "However, in this particular matter, I am unclear as to why this individual is of any real importance or what reasonable actions you believe the Church should take. This false priest you speak of does not preach within our diocesan jurisdiction, nor does he claim to be Catholic. As such, I feel that you should lay these matters to rest and allow the grace and will of God to guide events as He wishes. Spend no more time thinking about these matters that don't concern you. Focus your time and energy on your own church, your own parishioners. Think what you can do to keep Christ active in their lives. Sincerely, Bishop Diego de la Cruz."

I was furious. I wrote a lengthy response, ripping apart each of his patronizing points, detailing the threat that Gabriel posed, the even greater threat that lay in ignoring him entirely, the futility and stupidity of pretending this was none of our concern. I didn't sleep and hastily crammed for morning Mass minutes before it began, somnambulistically making my way through the service, not that my parishioners noticed or cared. Afterward, I slept until evening, when Father O'Brien woke me for dinner with a women's prayer group. While the women spoke, my mind wandered back to the response I had written and how it might sentence me to a lifetime in this terrible, remote parish, and as I led them in prayer, I ultimately decided not to send it. It was unworthy of my pledge to the bishop and not my place to question him in these matters when my career was on the line. Prayer always guides us in times of difficulty. Let us not forget this.

And so, I willed myself to ignore what I had seen and heard in Albuquerque, did my best to align myself with the bishop's wishes and try, once again, to offer Gabriel the benefit of the doubt. For a few weeks, I refocused my energy back into my research. But little things kept cropping up, whispers that I could not help but hear after Mass or when meeting with parishioners. I heard one woman claim Gabriel could fly and a man reply that no, he simply walked on water. Can you believe the blasphemy? A few days later, an older man mentioned that he had heard of a priest who communed directly with the Lord. A young girl in Sunday school told me that when he walked past you, a sweet fragrance filled the air, and I wanted to chastise her, "No, you idiot child, he just wears perfume like any other streetwalker," but I said nothing. Rarely did a week go by when I did not hear some story about him, even if it came to little more than a sermon he had given that went viral, but I didn't react.

The breaking point came when a parish family asked me to visit their daughter Consuela in the hospital. She lay there, attached to those horrid machines, and they told me about the failures of chemotherapy, of surgery, of radiation. Yet they still had hope for a cure in the north.

That's great, I said. Albuquerque had good hospitals, the best in the area. What had the doctors said?

Doctors? No, they were not planning on visiting any doctors, whose medicines only made Consuela hurt even more. They were headed to "Padre" Gabriel's church, to see if he would bless Consuela and heal her like he had so many others. They wanted him to dab holy water on her hairless head, to kiss her incision scars. They knew he would help, and for the first time in months, they had hope.

I wanted to scream at those people until they understood that they were trusting their daughter, whose blessed soul was as sinless and virginal as the day she was born, to a blasphemer and a charlatan. But I said nothing. I did as the bishop asked and let God's will decide things.

Two weeks later, at Consuela's funeral, I said nothing about their visit to Gabriel. I bit my tongue one final time as they carried her small coffin to the cemetery, did my best to console them, and said that they had done everything they could. I finished my prayers, and they lowered her into the ground.

But in my dreams that evening, I saw Gabriel in a room filled with crying, wailing Consuelas, each an identical version of that innocent eight-year-old girl. Each wore different clothing, and though some were bald, others had long black hair tied in a hundred different styles. I knew they had been sent to Gabriel by their parents, and I watched as he touched each one on her forehead, prayed, then watched her die. He showed no remorse, saying only that it had been God's will.

When I awoke, it was too much for me to cope with. I could no longer rationalize the guilt I felt, no longer pretend my pledge of obedience to the bishop meant accepting the false hope that Gabriel was offering people. And despite what some have said about me, I would have cared even if he hadn't become famous. He had been my friend, but now he claimed to represent the Word of Christ. The falsehood of what he said and carefully left unsaid about these "miracles" was important. But the fact of the matter was that he did become famous, so what bothered me was more than an itch, it was a full-on rash. Lying is a sin, plain and simple. But lying to one person is a different matter than lying to ten, or to a hundred, or to a thousand. The lie's evil multiplies. And to ignore this evil? Why, that would be unconscionable, a complete abdication of my responsibility, not only as a priest but as a good Catholic.

By then, I had formed close relationships with many parishioners and had at times shared my concerns about Gabriel with some. Under my guidance, we formed a study group, soon christened Servants of the Light. We discussed current events and parts of Catholicism that other parishioners, and even many priests, were too squeamish to consider seriously: the evils of apostasy and heresy, the slippery slope toward idolatry that exists within so-called syncretism, the soul-annihilating horrors of "abortion"—a

terrible euphemism for murdering the most innocent—
and the media's outrageous portrayals of the Church as a
haven for pedophiles and corruption. In time, we grew
to several dozen members, enough that we formed multiple smaller groups, though all with the same purpose:
to purify the faith.

Gabriel was a common talking point amongst the
Servants almost from the beginning. He seemed such a
case study in the way a charismatic person could harm
the spiritual development of so many Catholics that I
couldn't help but bring him up nearly every week. Soon,
after a long evening of discussion, we decided that if no
one else was going to, it was up to us to act.

Now, I must withhold a small detail from you here,
and of all people, perhaps you can understand why. What
you might not have heard is that Gabriel's followers were
prone to violence—there's a reason the FBI had them
under surveillance. Certainly, they preached nonvio-
lence, but when push came to shove, they were the ones
pushing and shoving. For the safety of my flock, I and
the rest of the Servants of the Light made an oath not
to reveal the identity of the person who undertook this
particular mission.

By then, another acquaintance of mine from Mount
Angel, Manuel Quintana, had joined Gabriel's "church,"
more evidence of how Gabriel both pretended at
Catholicism and drew followers from our flock. Gabriel
needed someone to say Mass for him—he was busy attending protests, writing editorials for the newspaper, and
generally increasing his fame. He was creating a cult of
personality, and I don't mean that metaphorically. But he
still made a special point of officiating his Sunday morning services, making that the perfect time to catch him

in our snare. He had been known to perform illusions at these services, like a weekly magic show: flying around on wires, healing the "sick," or falling into trances and mumbling gibberish. All the Servant needed to do was demonstrate one example of fakery, and Gabriel's church and its chicanery would disappear, smoke and mirrors dissipated by the clear light of day.

It took several weeks for Gabriel to put on one of his shows. Each Saturday, the Servant drove three hours north and stayed in a cheap motel across the street from Our Lady of Guadalupe. He sat in the front row, ready to pounce, but the first few services were ordinary, with nothing miraculous to disprove. However, we understood that this supposed humbleness was part of the overall deception. Everyone knows that if you perform the same trick every week, people become jaded about even the most stunning illusion. But if you give them only a handful of crumbs at a time, they'll keep coming back for more. He handed them those crumbs, a "healing" here, a vision there, and they ate it up like gluttons.

Finally, it happened. In the middle of his sermon, Gabriel went into a trance. I wasn't there, so I can't tell you exactly what this entailed, can't offer the trustworthy testimony of an impartial eyewitness that I'm sure you would appreciate, but I can tell you what the Servant reported. Gabriel began shaking and stuttering, though he was able to turn away from the audience and hide his face. As he trembled, the room went completely silent. The congregants expected something to happen, something miraculous, something strange. What they did not expect was our Servant to stand up and expose the imposter.

The Servant jumped into action, pulling himself onto the stage. Gabriel didn't react, and neither, given how quickly he moved, did anyone else. Following old Church tradition, the Servant pulled out a long golden pin. His job was simple: he was to stab Gabriel, whose immediate reaction would belie his so-called trance.

The Servant pricked Gabriel, and his eyes opened right up. Our Servant reported that Gabriel winced with pain as a drop of blood trickled from his hand when the Servant pulled the pin out. But here's what we had not anticipated: no one but the Servant could see this reaction. Gabriel closed his eyes and went on with his "trance," and as people chased the Servant out, the test had the opposite effect of what we had intended. *We* knew the Servant had proven beyond a doubt that it was all fakery, but afterward, those in the parish began reporting what happened as more holiness, since to their easily duped eyes it appeared that he had passed the test. He stayed on that stage, still pretending to be entranced while milking that moment for his own glorification.

Fortunately, the Servant who performed this dangerous feat escaped safely and was never identified. The fake mustache and overly large eyebrows we had supplied him with did their job. But from then on, Gabriel became much more difficult to get close to.

I felt even more defeated than before. I continued working with the Servants, and we brainstormed other ways of opening even a few eyes to the lies being told in the north, but little came of it. I realized that I no longer had the resources to fight on my own. I needed to find someone else, someone with a vested interest in putting a stop to these lies, even if that meant going outside the Church.

ISABEL ROMERO

I know some mothers would consider their lives complete if they saw their little boy standing behind an altar, but for me it was, I don't know … muy raro. I mean, think about it for a second. You're in your forties, you spend twenty-four hours a day struggling not to think about what you did to your ex-novio anyhow, and here your little Gabito is going on about temptations of the flesh, and … and, and no.

I did keep going to church, just not Gabriel's. I returned to San Ignacio, walking distance from home. It was an old mission-style church, with a tall blue bell tower looming over emerald-green steps like some Southwestern version of Oz. They still said Mass in Latin once a week, and the church featured the same unpadded wooden pews I grew up with. I liked the familiarity, you know, and that even if I didn't remember someone's name, I still more than likely recognized them from the neighborhood. At the very back of the chapel, a carved Jesucristo hung crucified on the wall. This Jesus didn't stare at you in judgment like the one in Gabito's church, though. He didn't lecture you about sins. He loved you and wanted you to find love in your own heart. Without really thinking about what I was doing, I started lighting velas every week at the little shrine on the side, where a few santos looked back at me and said with their kind eyes that whatever I might have done, I was still a good person.

You couldn't help but notice that attendance was sparse, bordering on embarrassing. A few dozen of us showed up, but it used to be much more crowded, and I don't just mean during Semana Santa. After services one week, Padre Gonzales came up to me as I was leaving. He was still in his white robe, his crown of black hair now a salt-and-pepper gray, but otherwise he looked as strong as ever.

"Isabel, may I speak to you for a moment?"

"Certainly, Padre," I said. I wanted to rush home, back to the telenovelas that could drown out my thoughts, but unless your house is burning, that's the only thing you really can say to a priest.

"I'm glad you're taking la eucaristía again," he said. "Your return to San Ignacio has been a blessing to us and, of course, to you most of all."

"Thank you, Padre."

"But perhaps you've noticed how few others worship alongside us, taking the blessed sacrament as they should."

"I ... I suppose so," I said. "I suppose young folks these days just don't care about church. Millennials, you know?" I was one of the youngest people who'd shown up that morning, excepting a handful of children.

He paused, seeming to consider what he wanted to say, and his cheerful demeanor disappeared. "But that's not my main concern. I wanted to speak to you about your son." Perhaps he saw the anger in my eyes. "It's nothing bad. Your son, he's a very good man. Very good."

"Yes, he is," I said. "A very good man."

"Sí, sí. But well, you see, the problem isn't with him, it's with the community. A church isn't a building, it's the people who worship there. Unfortunately, it seems that a lot of my church hasn't been worshipping here. They've been over at Our Lady of Guadalupe."

"What? How do you know that?"

"It's true," he said. "I don't mean to say he's coming over and poaching them, just that it's hurt our community. This is as much your church as it is mine. You and your son were both baptized here, and so, I've been told, was your mother. We've offered solace and guidance for more than a hundred years. It's such a shame to see all of that tradition disappear so quickly."

"I really don't think … I mean, maybe it's not him." I didn't want to imply anything about Padre Gonzales, but one of the other padres who worked at San Ignacio was a well-known conservative who often clashed with all but the oldest and stodgiest parishioners. He was right, a church was the community, but if the community feels out of touch with the church, the fault rests squarely with the priests.

"But it is," Padre Gonzales insisted. "I don't want to make you angry, but people have told me so. I don't know if you're aware, but your son has been … healing people. They just call him up, and he comes over. He says a prayer or two, sprinkles some holy water on their heads, and they tell me they feel better. They don't tell me at church, though, they tell me when I see them on the street, on their way to their prima's house, and they feel too guilty to lie to me about where they've been for the past two Sundays."

"But weren't they healed?" I asked. "I mean, Gabito just takes after su abuela, that's all. He likes to help people."

"That's not the point. I'm sure the people he 'heals' are fine. Most people feel fine in time. You tell them

Jesucristo requires them to stay in bed for a couple of days and eat nothing but sopa de pollo, and nine out of ten, people get better anyhow. That's not the point. The point is that he's been dismantling our church."

I didn't know what he wanted me to do, exactly, but I was uncomfortable. I told him I'd mention it to Gabriel and made a hasty exit. And I wasn't clueless, I knew about the television appearances, and plenty of vecinos had asked me about Gabito's healing. Maybe they thought if they got in good with his mother, they'd get to cut to the front of the line. I just hadn't thought of it as particularly odd— I guess that's what comes from being the daughter of a curandera. Even Mamá had recognized Gabriel's skillful hands. Some people were born with the gift.

The next time I saw him was at one of our weekly meals. The tenor of those had changed. I wasn't sleeping with William anymore, though I no longer had any reason not to. It just didn't feel right, my breakup turning our nonrelationship from dirty in a good way to just dirty. I could barely look at him. Then Evelyn suffered a stroke. Afterward, she could barely speak, and the left side of her face slumped, had practically melted as if she were some sort of swamp creature. Eating had become a challenge, to say the least, so she preferred thin soups and other easily swallowed foods. With William and me barely speaking and then Evelyn speaking even less, our dinners had become short, unhappy affairs. I probably would've quit going entirely if Gabito visited me more often.

That night, we sat in the dining room as usual. Evelyn's nurse, a short, quiet woman who deserved better treatment than the glares and hissing curses Evelyn threw at her, waited in the nearby kitchen. I'd thought about not bringing up what Padre Gonzales had said, but at least it was a topic of conversation.

"Padre Gonzales, you know him, right?"

"He's wonderful. A good man. A good priest. He gave me my first communion."

"Well, he came to talk to me about you after church last week. He seemed pretty upset, saying you've been driving people out of San Ignacio. That you're healing them and then they start going to Our Lady of Guadalupe. He says it's really hurting the community."

Gabriel paused for a moment. "No offense, Mom, but since when did you care about church?"

"I may not be a priest, but I go to church too." At least, lately. "And I'm not saying I care, I'm just telling you what Padre Gonzales said."

"What do you want me to do, leave them to suffer?" he asked. "I don't tell them to start going to Mass at Our Lady of Guadalupe. I don't tell them to start going to Mass at all. I just answer the phone and try to help. I can't always make it, but I usually help at least one or two people a day, sometimes more."

"I had no idea," I said. "I mean, I guess I had some idea, just not that you did it so much. That's far more than Mamá."

"Grandma had a full-time job. All I have to do is say a few fancy words during Mass."

William coughed loudly, clearly wanting us to change the subject. Gabriel smiled at him and Evelyn. "Sorry if this is boring. Umm, how was your week?" He said this to no one in particular.

I didn't care what either of them thought. They could feel awkward if they wanted to, or they could leave the room. "Are you actually curing them? I just know that ...

well, sometimes I thought Mamá was making it all up as she went along, to be honest."

Gabriel's eyes welled up, but his face was seething with anger, and I couldn't tell if he wanted to cry or reach across the table and hit me. I was reminded of that horrible time when he was in college, when I'd interrupted him burning himself, and I wanted to take it all back. Just like that time, though, he composed himself almost immediately, his face once again a blank and unreadable mask.

"Grandma never lied," he said. "I don't know what … in any case, I do what she did, what she taught me. And we don't heal on our own. It's the power of Christ, the power of the saints. We just channel them. And yes, people do get better."

I should've let things be. I was unhappy with myself, not with him. But for some reason, when he brought up religion, I couldn't help myself. I had to keep prodding. It didn't matter that I knew I'd already gone too far, that I might break something if I kept pushing. I think it was that neutral expression of his, the way he would go blank instead of answering my questions, the way he'd always shut me out from anything truly important in his life. "Well there's someone here with us tonight who could use some healing. Why don't you help *her*?"

The room went so quiet I could hear William's neck crack as he turned to stare at Gabriel. Evelyn's eyes rested on him too, and although her face had barely moved, beneath her respirator her expression changed to one of longing. Her voice came out as a scratchy whisper. "Is there something you can do?"

We waited. Finally Gabriel answered. "This isn't a game, Mom. If I could help, don't you think I would?"

Evelyn made no attempt to hide her disappointment. She suddenly looked so much smaller than she had a month earlier, and I became aware of a mustiness in the room, a hint of urine and decay, unmistakable despite the potpourri festooned in every nook of the house. She started as if she wanted to say something but gave up before her mouth could form the words, huddling her arms closer together as if freezing, even though it felt like eighty degrees in the room.

"I ... I could try?" Gabriel said.

He awkwardly scooted his chair back and walked to Evelyn, taking so long I wondered if he hoped someone might tell him to stop. No one moved. Once at her side, he gently set his right hand on her head and began whispering a prayer I couldn't make out but could tell wasn't the Lord's Prayer or a Hail Mary. The prayer seemed endless, a repetitive chant or mantra, and I thought I saw a haze of white come out of the old woman's scalp, though it could've been dust floating through the dim candlelight. This all seemed appropriate, somehow normal—not like something Mamá would've done but still like Gabito knew what he was doing. Then Evelyn began screaming.

Shrieking is probably more accurate, or maybe wailing. She sounded inhuman, like a car alarm was going off in her mouth. Her body writhed in her wheelchair, and I knew that I should stop Gabriel, say that I'd seen Mamá heal hundreds of people and that it never went anything like this, but I found myself speechless.

When Gabriel lifted his hand, Evelyn collapsed into her chair like a pile of laundry. Her nurse, who'd been watching from the kitchen doorway, came to her side and shooed us out of the room. Evelyn was unconscious, and

Gabriel looked on the verge of tears. William asked us to leave as politely as he could.

Gabriel made a direct line toward his car, but I walked faster and stood in front of him so he couldn't leave yet. "I shouldn't have asked you to do that."

"Why not?" He practically spit the words out. Sweat coated the collar of his shirt and dripped down his neck, as if he'd just run a marathon in his formal clothes.

"Because, well, because of *that*. Will she get better?"

"I don't know. Probably not." After a few seconds, he continued. "Maybe though. I really don't know."

"What happened, exactly?"

"I don't want to talk about it. I just need to lie down, ok, Mom? I'll just … I'll see you in a week or whatever."

I moved aside, wondering how things could have gone so disastrously.

We didn't meet the next week. Or for several after that. Evelyn had suffered another stroke that evening, and when we did see her again, her speech was so difficult to understand that only her nurse could make out what she was saying. Evelyn glared and growled, though the nurse assured us she was still pleased to see us and as insistent as ever that Gabriel keep visiting. William joined his sister, Megan, on the absentee list. I felt so bad about what had happened that I kept going, though I showed up late and left early.

In the meantime, I returned to San Ignacio with one more disaster burdening my conscience. I didn't think I'd done anything wrong, and I certainly didn't think Gabriel had—he'd tried to help. How could he have known? For some reason I couldn't force myself to go to confession, but I thought I could keep lighting las velas and praying to that San Ignacio Christ, so kind to look away from my miserable face, so kind to suffer and ask for nothing more than a pittance of belief in return for ending our suffering.

When Padre Gonzales headed over to speak with me after Mass, though, his purpose clear on his face, I practically sprinted home, blistering the hell out of my feet along the way because I'd worn my nice sandals for church, and they were barely made for standing, let alone a three-block race. After that, I stopped going to San Ignacio.

I never found out whether Gabito's healing really worked for all those other people. But I also never knew if Mamá's did, and there were many in the neighborhood who'd sworn by her herbs and back rubs. One bad experience meant nothing, and the oddness of it all convinced me not so much that Gabriel didn't know what he was doing but that perhaps Evelyn Fisher was the type of person Jesucristo had decided would be better off crippled. The Jesucristo up on the wall in Our Lady of Guadalupe was battered and bloody, but instead of turning away from the suffering, he snarled in retort. Maybe this was the Dios who'd answered her with another stroke.

A few Sundays after I quit going to church, I started using my newfound spare time to clean the entire house, and I'd decided to move on to the backyard. When Mamá was alive, she'd kept a garden overflowing with herbs and plants I never saw anywhere else. When Gabito was a little older, she helped him set up his own garden in my backyard, mostly filled with the same plants, and he maintained it even during college. But after he left for seminary, the heat and wind quickly transformed it to little more than dirt and weeds. I started clearing those away and spent the rest of the day seeing if I could make a functioning garden again, planting some old seeds he'd left behind, more than a little surprised to find a tronadora still growing by the fence, its bright-yellow flowers in full bloom. When I finished, I emailed Gabito, telling him what I'd found and saying that I'd be happy to help with planting anything else that might be useful.

He thanked me and came by the next day to talk about the garden before meeting with a diabetic man living on the other side of the Rio Grande. He couldn't believe how much I'd done already. After that, I took up gardening as my full-time hobby and worked with Gabito to keep his herbs in stock.

I don't know why I'm telling you all this. I guess it's to say that after I stopped going to San Ignacio, I was feeling bad again, but the gardening helped, made me feel like maybe I was doing good through Gabriel. Every hour I spent bent over the dirt was an hour of penance, and at the end of the day, I didn't feel quite as bad as I had when I'd woken up. Maybe he hadn't been able to heal Evelyn, but he had really tried, really given it his best, and that's something. That's at least more than most of you are out there doing, so try and have a little respect. Maybe that's why he worked so hard at his church, miracle or no miracle—he wanted to do a little penance for when things didn't work out, the same as I did, the same as all of us.

ANNA FISHEL

A church isn't a building. That's what Father Gabriel would say when it was just us, or maybe just us and Father Manuel at the office, relaxing at the end of a long day in those uncomfortable thrift-store chairs from a few doors down. He'd be futzing absentmindedly with a deck of cards—he always liked doing little tricks for kids, though he would get embarrassed if you brought it up—humming with his feet up on the desk. A church was people, and the rest was window dressing. The building could crumble to the ground, burn up in a fire, blow away in a tornado—it wouldn't matter. Our Lady of Guadalupe was here to stay. Mass would continue so long as folks showed up and wanted to worship Christ—for where two or three were gathered, that was all it took.

But the definition, he said, was easy. What was harder was his follow-up question, and here he seemed to turn to us for answers: What was the purpose of a church? Or more specifically, what was the purpose of *our* church?

"What is it we can offer that they can't get from the church down the street—from San Ignacio or Hoffmantown? Or from praying at home?"

"You," I said with a smile, only half-joking. After all, he was why I found my way back to Jesus, why Father Manuel suffered his excommunication with a smile on his face and a spring in his step. I liked to think folks stayed around because they saw the truth of what Father Gabriel said, that they didn't just hope for a miracle every week like he was some new form of live entertainment. But regardless of why anyone stayed, he was at least why we all first showed up at that old theater, word made flesh.

I could tell Father Gabriel didn't like my answer, even when I said I was only joking.

"I think we can offer them a little more than that," he said. "At least, I'd like to hope we can. I know we're all tired, but why don't we start brainstorming what else we can do for the community?"

Things began small, with AA meetings in the back room and community meetings at night. We set up weekly volunteer hours at the Roadrunner Food Bank and served meals from our own makeshift kitchen, huge vats of green chile stew and posolé cooked by parishioners. We collected sleeping bags and socks for the homeless and partnered with a nearby women's shelter to help give supplies and even occasional refuge when needed. We began monthly singles nights at O'Niell's and family picnics at a nearby park. No proposal was rejected out of hand. We would just try to expand to keep up, recruiting new volunteers when all of us already had too much going on, trying to keep from dropping the plates we had spinning while adding new ones.

Father Gabriel worked nonstop, really, propelled by an endlessly refilled thermos of coffee, and that made the rest of us work harder. At times I thought the only folks in Albuquerque we weren't helping were ourselves. When I mentioned this, again mostly as a joke, Father Gabriel made me take some vacation time and start training part-time assistants to help me in the office. It all grew so fast, from a seed to a full-fledged tree before we even knew what type of plant we were. Some of our efforts failed, due to mismanagement or a lack of training, but we laughed those problems off. There was an energy, a sense that if we tried hard enough, we really could change the world.

I know this is exactly the type of day-to-day work no one cares about. No one cares how much we raised in our donation drives or how much effort we put into a quinceañera Mass, but that's what Our Lady of Guadalupe was really like. It's always offended me that everyone thinks we were only about protests, or we were out there looking for media coverage. I've heard folks say that the surest way of summoning Father Gabriel wasn't to call the church but to set up a camera, but that's just not true. I dunno, we didn't intend to get involved with protests and politics anyhow— it's more that they got involved with us.

I'm aware Father Gabriel had been a bit of an activist in college, though I don't know much about the specifics. He told me he'd spent time yelling from bullhorns and holding up signs, but since then his interest had faded. Or perhaps it hadn't faded, that might not be the right word … it was put on the back burner. After graduation, he'd focused on the spiritual life instead. "Politics and government—at seminary, they dismissed all of that as background noise, interference between you and Christ." He told me that he would sit in his room, play Bach's motets on his laptop, and meditate. At the time, that had felt like enough. "But what I didn't think about, what no one told me to think about, was how many folks didn't have that luxury. Isaiah wrote, 'Share your bread with the hungry and bring the homeless poor into your house.' If this is truly God's house, it's time we let them inside."

Alex Ramirez came to our first Saturday soup kitchen and kept showing up every week. He looked anywhere from forty to fifty-something years old, with long hair and a curled, slightly matted beard that hid his huge smile and bellowing laugh. Even though it was late summer, he wore a bulging backpack and a winter coat, with brown stains at the bottom of its periwinkle blue lining. He smelled—all of them smelled—but Alex's was musky and not entirely unpleasant.

That first day, there were probably thirty folks who showed up, maybe less. I have to admit, I had difficulty telling them apart ... and I didn't really talk to any of them for months. I knew that giving up a little time to serve soup was no big sacrifice and that helping others was one of the cardinal virtues. Love thy neighbor and all that, so I did my duty. But I didn't really care for the work, or for those indistinguishable piles of clothing, men and a handful of women looking warily around the room, huddled and quietly murmuring while they ate. Oh, they were gracious and polite, but I couldn't help but feel that maybe this was just their lot in life—that folks who looked and acted that way were meant to be homeless. Growing up, when I asked my mom why God let there be homeless folks, why some folks were rich and others so poor, she told me it was all part of God's plan.

I wouldn't have said that out loud, and I'm still ashamed of myself, even though I've confessed and repented for these feelings many times over. But that's what I learned growing up: they were lazy. They were drunks, and junkies, and prostitutes. Don't give them money, 'cause they'll spend it all getting high anyway.

But obviously Father Gabriel wasn't like me. He would spend two hours mingling with our guests, as he took to calling them, even though many wanted nothing to do with him, or the church, aside from the food. That was fine, Father Gabriel would say. That was their decision, and we should pray for them all the same. But Alex was one of the ones he hit it off with immediately.

That grubby-looking man turned out to be a physics grad student. At least, he'd been one years ago, but after disagreeing with his adviser, he'd angrily left the program. A string of fights and accidents, plus bad luck, led him to living on the streets. Alex sometimes talked about himself in third person, even when he was on his own, and this weirded me out. But Father Gabriel said he was smart, a joy to listen to. They'd talk every week, and they both seemed to look forward to it. Father Gabriel hoped to get Alex treatment and maybe convince a parishioner to let him stay with them while he looked for work.

When Alex didn't show up one week, I didn't think much of it. A lot of the folks we fed came sporadically. I told Father Gabriel not to worry. That night, I was on Facebook after dinner, and I learned just how wrong I'd been. Alex had been camping—in a way—near a house in the Sandia foothills, a few miles east of Our Lady of Guadalupe. Someone from the house had called the police. When a pair of officers arrived, they found Alex asleep beneath a blue plastic tarp. Alex was having one of his episodes, though, the type that caused him to fight with his family and his thesis adviser. He asked the officers who they were working for, whether this was one of their raids. During the officers' confusion, he pulled out a small, harmless pocketknife. The officers backed off and called reinforcements. A negotiation began, and the officers said Alex could collect his belongings if he put away the weapon. But once he turned his back on them, an officer yelled, "Bang him." Footage showed a flash-bang device being thrown, then an officer Tasering him. The Taser had no visible effect, so the officers sicced a dog on him. When the dog came near, Alex pulled out his knife again. That's when they shot him.

I called Father Gabriel, and he rushed to Presbyterian Hospital to see if he could do anything to help. He couldn't. Against two dozen bullets, what could?

Over the following months, half a dozen other homeless men, all of them Hispanic or Native American, several with known mental health issues, were executed by the APD. The men who killed Alex went free, their charges of second-degree murder dismissed to a cheering courtroom of police officers. Feeling powerless, we did the only thing we could do, and for the first time since its founding, Our Lady of Guadalupe marched in protest.

One Sunday, more than a hundred of us left the church and walked straight downtown, where we joined a line already forming in front of the courthouse. A cold wind swept through the streets, but we stayed put and yelled. When the cameras arrived, we were still yelling, our throats hoarse and aching but loud enough to make ourselves heard. Less than a week later, the APD announced an internal investigation into the recent shootings, that new training would be given to officers on how to deal with similar situations. It wouldn't bring Alex back. It wasn't even an admission of wrongdoing. But it was something, tangible evidence that we had made a difference. It lit a fire beneath the whole congregation.

So we continued marching for Alex, for a retrial.

We marched for the six other local men killed by cops.

We marched for the men killed elsewhere by police, mostly black and unarmed.

We marched for the rights of disabled folks, after the city council decided it simply didn't have the funding to make needed accessibility improvements in local schools.

We marched against global warming, against climate change, for the protection of the Earth.

We marched against one war and then another. And then another.

We took to marching like there were rocks in our shoes keeping us from standing still. Parishioners brought causes to us, and we mobilized. The church was the people, and our people saw that God's will wasn't being done on Earth. We were there to try and rectify that problem.

Some parishioners got tired of these marches and rallies and left, rejoining their previous churches or removing religion from their lives altogether. And there were other parishioners who criticized our absence at LGBT events, asking why we didn't join in on that fight the way we had so many others. Likewise, there were whispers about Father Gabriel's sexuality, which some folks seemed to think was a big deal, though I never saw why—it's not like they were saying he was a pedophile. But none of this slowed us down. We drew new parishioners from the picket lines. Protests became social events, as much as the picnics or singles mixers. Even with the most solemn of causes, we marched in good spirits. We sang hymns, we laughed and talked, and through it all, we came together. During our first year, Our Lady of Guadalupe Church was known solely for its miracles. During our second year, they knew us for our protests.

In the process, we learned how to make folks actually pay attention—what the media wanted to hear and see. We learned what supplies to bring and what signs and slogans would go viral. How to respond to the police and counterprotesters and when to throw in the towel. I made text chains and Facebook groups that got folks out of bed and onto the streets. I can't definitively say that we made much of a difference, but I can say that we tried. Looking back, all of it felt like training, a warm-up for what came next. It was the end of the beginning, in a way.

FR. MICHAEL CARTER

Time moves slowly in seminary. Mind you, the world and its concerns still exist there. Jesuits are not monks, after all, and in the dining hall, novitiates were probably more likely to complain about the school's lack of internet access than to discuss the Gospel. But we did our best to rearrange priorities, allowing the more transient parts of existence to take a back seat. Once outside of seminary, Jesuits rarely ignore their communities, but they are taught to handle politics with a light touch. We do what we can until our Savior returns, but this tends toward feeding the hungry and sheltering the homeless, not overthrowing regimes. The parts of Catholicism that I am most ashamed of grew out of the idea that we knew best. Jesuits and even popes could be arrogant, could believe they understood the will of God when His unfathomability is one of His most undeniable traits. In order to avoid these pitfalls, our pace was by necessity one of thoughtfulness, of prudence and temperance. But sometimes the world asserted itself, and when it did rupture our little paradise, it practically shook the earth beneath our feet.

That was what happened when a pair of letters arrived on my desk, one day apart. The first was from Gabriel, filled primarily with pleasantries but also the shocking news that he had founded a "small activist church" in

Albuquerque. To say I was taken aback would be a vast understatement, though I should not have been. The last I had heard from him, Gabriel had written of joining "the ministry," and now here he was with his own church, and one actively involved in worldly affairs, which fit the passionate, decidedly anti-Jesuitical side of his personality. I couldn't help but note with relief that at least he had signed his name not with the honorific "Father" but simply "Gabriel."

I needed to pray on this new information, so far had my former charge strayed from the path I had originally foreseen for him. If I had kept up with the news, I would have known more about his work, but the actual business of running the seminary left me sapped at the end of the day, and, as I mentioned, we didn't have reliable internet access. I had also begun to find much of life less interesting than praying and my daily reading of the Bible. As my body has aged, and many of the things I used to find pleasurable gradually became gray and monotonous, prayer and holy scripture have never failed me.

The following day, one of my seminarians dropped the mail onto my desk, this time including a letter from the Archdiocese of Santa Fe. While Jesuits rarely concerned themselves with diocesan matters, because of our seminary's role in the community, the diocese occasionally consulted us about local affairs. This tended to be a formality, and my usual response was to assent to whatever the archbishop thought best. I respected him and his judgment, and felt that the best way to maintain relations was to listen, rather than speak. Besides, except in extraordinary circumstances, I hardly cared. But this letter was the exception, for it concerned the very pupil who had just written to me, whom Archbishop Fausto

Maldonado had heard complaints about from a variety of Albuquerque priests.

The archbishop's letter was long, and it had two main points of contention. The first of these I could hardly fault Gabriel for: it seemed that a diocesan priest had abdicated his vows and joined Gabriel's church. This individual offered Mass exactly as he had before, but he did so with full understanding that he was no longer a priest. I could understand the archbishop's consternation, his feelings of betrayal, but as far as I was concerned, Gabriel had committed no sin through this seemingly inadvertent recruitment. However, this first complaint was closely tied to the archbishop's second, and more important, concern—namely, Gabriel's faux Catholicism.

This claim of fraudulence was far more damning. Defrauding is a mortal sin, and if Gabriel had claimed to head a Catholic church and accepted tithes under that false guise, I would not have been able to defend him. But the evidence was scant, and I wrote back asking the archbishop to investigate these matters further before passing judgment. I also promised him I would ask Gabriel about the matter myself.

Despite what you may have heard, the archbishop did not bring up the charge of heresy until much later. Heresy is a complicated matter, particularly for an individual not affiliated with the Roman Catholic Church. In a literal sense, it means *denial* of the beliefs of the Church, and Gabriel was not technically a member of the Church. But he remained largely faithful to the Church, which is what caused confusion. Could a Protestant commit heresy? I would say no, though I also would never have called Gabriel a Protestant. His church seemed to be singular, and this became even clearer to me in time.

I wrote to Gabriel about the archbishop's charges. One thing I was not concerned about, I must make absolutely clear to you, were the souls of Gabriel's followers. The Church made it explicit during Vatican II that although a Roman Catholic is not supposed to take catechism in any other church, we accept all those who follow Christ as brothers. This was the spirit in which I continued my relationship with Gabriel and that I asked the archbishop to consider as well.

The archbishop wrote back that he believed there was wisdom in my advice, and he thanked me for my "clear-headed insight." Matters seemed resolved, but I carried on my correspondence with Gabriel, though we had little to say to each other. I think the old-fashioned, slower method of communication appealed to him, even though he was so young. After I read about his miracles, I asked him about them, but he would only respond cryptically.

"What do you believe?" he asked me in one letter. "Do you think it's possible I healed that man by invoking Christ and Mary and all the santos?"

I wrote back that if they were truly involved, I was ready to believe almost anything. But I had been wrong in the past and was certain to be wrong again in the future. What was the truth?

"You are the strongest believer of all," he wrote me back. "Many are not so faithful ... You may even be a stronger believer than me. *Mysterium fide.*"

This Latinate phrase is most often translated as, "Let us proclaim the mystery of faith," though more literally, it means simply "the mystery of faith." I interpreted it as an acknowledgment of his own wavering surety, that there were questions about himself and his actions that remained as unresolved to him as they were to me. We take for granted that our senses allow us to understand the world, but one of the marvels of modern science remains the revelation of how much we fail to recognize all around us, the alpha and gamma radiation slipping through pores between our molecules, the dark matter and energy swirling around us and interacting with gravitational waves. It has forced us to reckon with how much faith is required to piece anything into our own version of "reality." I was convinced that Gabriel's levitation had been a miracle, and so I understood how many had judged his other actions similarly. Some disagreed.

Some people, even among the devout, feel threatened by the idea of miracles. Miracles, in their minds, are a relic of the past, something out of stories or myths. I had learned how difficult the concept of a miracle was for your average "believer" long ago with the Eucharist. Transubstantiation, as you're well aware, is not symbolic. True Catholic believers witness a miracle when the bread and wine transform into the body and blood of Jesus Christ, every single week. Yet few are willing to accept this sincerely.

When I receive the host, I relish that moment of change. I close my eyes and think about Christ and his suffering, and I wait for the moment when bread becomes flesh, slowly dissolving first onto my tongue and then into my soul. The wine tastes sweet like grapes but soon grows coppery and thickens until His blood travels down my throat, coating it with His grace. These are miracles I have witnessed firsthand, and they have prepared me to bear witness to other miracles. God's mysteries do not require rational explanations or total understanding.

In one of Gabriel's letters, I learned that a man had pricked him with a needle during the middle of Mass, but he didn't know why. I responded that the needle prick was an old test of sainthood, a way to ascertain whether someone was holy or merely a performer. His response was simple, though a bit concerning: "Did I pass?"

I wrote to the archbishop asking him to condemn the mysterious attack, reminding him that the Church should be above such medieval harassment, but I never received a response. Over time, I sent him a handful of other letters, all regarding Gabriel, all unanswered. In one letter I even asked a question that, among all the discussion of miracles and deception, has not been asked frequently enough: If he were in fact a charlatan, but he was also spreading the word of God, supporting the poor and the disenfranchised, then was he not furthering God's will?

Perhaps I should have known it was professionally unwise to continue sending those letters, but I was and remain a man of principle. Regardless, this is where my reputation as Gabriel's vociferous defender arose.

ANNA FISHEL

I'm sure you know all about the Shell protests, but you might not know the background and why we got involved with that whole mess in the first place.

Father Gabriel had no personal stake in the Española area, but Father Manuel did. He doesn't like to talk about himself, though, so he probably won't tell you all this, which is why I feel like I should. Where Father Gabriel was loquacious and extroverted, Father Manuel was always quiet, reserved. Still, he had as much righteousness in his heart as anyone and couldn't ignore corruption when he saw it in his own backyard.

To the north of Santa Fe sits the Española Valley, a fertile farming area long before the Spanish arrived. The city itself is still surrounded by the largest concentration of pueblos in the state. Shell discovered that land to the southeast of the city was ripe for fracking and bought up every available acre, from the outskirts of the city to the edge of the pueblos. They wanted to start drilling immediately and promised the city more jobs than it could handle. The city council embraced Shell's plans, and anyone who opposed them was shouted down. But the real anger came from the tribes outside the city. They knew that the fracking would destroy their groundwater and cause irrevocable damage, even if it wasn't technically on reservation land. However, the tribes had no say about the city's decisions, even if it affected them—what happened off their land was "of no concern" to them, according to Española's mayor.

Shell claimed that while fracking might have had occasional "issues" in the past, they now knew what they were doing. They'd hired top scientists and engineers to survey every inch of land and sent hard copies of the studies to interested journalists. Trust us, they said.

The tribes knew better—they knew the history of fracking, they knew the history of corporations, and they knew the history of white men who came from afar and promised everything would somehow be fine in the end, if you'd only trust them. The tribes said they wouldn't stop fighting until Shell had left for good.

Father Manuel heard about the protests from a relative's Facebook post, I think. Father Gabriel asked whether he wanted time off to join the protests, but Father Manuel said it was impossible. For reasons he never told me, he said he couldn't go back there. But Our Lady of Guadalupe could.

The following Sunday, Father Gabriel's sermon was about respect for the Earth. He began by reading from Jeremiah 2. He said that Israel was both the land we think of as Israel today and a metaphor for something the Spanish speakers in our parish seemed familiar with: querencia. God had led the Israelites to their homeland, their querencia, but they had polluted it. "And I brought you into a plentiful land to enjoy its fruits and its good things. But when you came in, you defiled my land and made my heritage an abomination." Then he talked about the fracking and the way it would destroy people's querencia to the north. That it threatened not only the tribes but also the Sanctuary at Chimayo—all for a few cheap bucks. He knew how to draw the audience in to these stories, to make hundreds of minds focus together so that they became a group. A church. By the end of his sermon, all of us were livid.

We spent the next week working on logistics. We rented a pair of buses to take parishioners up north, so we had to pay for the rental, the driver. Then there was the question of how we would feed everyone. Where would folks use the restroom? These concerns consumed my life, though of course I couldn't have thought of every-thing, so we would have to improvise constantly once we arrived. Nevertheless, I'm proud of the work I did, and Father Gabriel told me himself that were I not there in the office, from sunrise to sunset day after day, none of it would have happened; the protest would've petered out before it even started.

The following week, we left right after Mass. Parishioners brought their camping supplies: tents and sleeping bags and stoves and as much food and water as we could manage. We loaded up the buses and made our way north.

The actual fracking site wasn't complete yet, but its construction had begun. A chain-link fence surrounded a large, cleared-away square of flattened dirt. There were dozens of trucks and trailers, and in the center a metal tower of beams rose into the air, like a building crane but for the opposite purpose: not to raise into the sky but to reach down into the earth.

The bus dropped us off right in front of the fence. Already there were Native protesters blocking the en-trance so no trucks could enter or leave. They'd erected a shantytown of sorts, and while they looked tired and more than a bit confused about our presence, once Father

Gabriel explained we'd come to join them, they tentatively accepted us. Our groups didn't exactly intermingle, but I figured that there would be time for that later. First we needed to figure out what was even happening and how to help.

Two huge tankers sat on each side of the camp, theoretically ready to move at a moment's notice, though in reality the drivers were fully zoned out, content to sit and watch videos on their phones. Half a dozen police cars were farther back, with officers trying their best to convince the protesters to let the trucks pass. They'd tried threats and distractions, but when all of that failed they'd decided to simply wait things out, so far to no avail, though we soon learned that the threats had been escalating.

So we unpacked our supplies, and soon a few porta-potties arrived courtesy of some favors I'd wrangled before we left Albuquerque. We began notifying every media outlet we could think of and filming the cops around-the-clock so we'd have footage when they inevitably got violent. At that point, we certainly didn't expect to wait for months, though I guess I should've prepared for that possibility. I don't know what I expected to happen when we arrived—a miracle that would change Shell's mind? For God to smite that crane? But nothing happened that day, or the next. Our long wait had only just begun.

JOSHUA WHITEHURST

What no one tells you about working for a large, evil law firm is that it's mostly pretty boring. At least, it is when you're just another grunt working the assembly line. I couldn't tell you what it's like to be a partner, sitting in a plush leather chair with your back to the window as associates struggle to prove they've billed enough weekly hours, but from my desk in the middle of a second-story cubicle cluster, the office looked almost identical in every direction. Our gray-felt labyrinth permitted only the most perfunctory of decorations—family photos, diplomas, press clippings—and did little to alleviate the muted, lifeless air circulating through the building. Think of a casino but without the lights and sounds, just the sense that it could be any time outside, any day, and you would never know it until you exited. Male or female, black or white, we dressed in the same unmemorable attire, automatons-at-law for the sacrosanct partnership of Parker & Mullins. To be honest, sometimes it felt almost liberating ... but it was also boring. Deeply, deeply boring. I began doubling, quadrupling my caffeine load. During the years I worked there, I tried Adderall, speed, cocaine. Anything to force my brain to keep staring at the brief in front of me, to prevent daydreams, or sleep, or tears, or slamming my head against my desk over and over again until at least the room had a little color in it.

I worked in the research department, which probably had something to do with my outlook. Sometimes I learned that whatever odd legal precedent I'd found could help a case, but usually I didn't. Usually I would just email the information to someone else and go on to my next assignment. There was always a next assignment too, so there was never any reason to rush, or try harder, or care at all. I felt like Sisyphus, only my stone was a LexisNexis account, and I had enough coffee pumping through my veins that I couldn't stop rolling even if I wanted to.

In exchange for the boredom, I had money. I purchased a new forest-green BMW 5 Series sedan, and I rented an apartment in the swanky, renovated Albuquerque High lofts, furnishing it with adult furniture made of real leather and wood. After that, I let the deposits slowly add up in my bank account. For some reason, I was convinced that at any moment I might need to run to the bank and liquidate my assets, purchase a new identity, and flee the country. Something about the job made me paranoid. Nothing was ever good enough for my boss, and I always felt on the verge of being fired. I was so miserable there that this shouldn't have terrified me, but it did, so I put in extra hours, and I played nice. The edges I thought I had, they dropped away as I became moldable clay for my boss and firm to form into whatever shape they desired.

So what did I do for fun? Well, I didn't have time for relationships, for dinner and a movie, for days spent in bed appreciating someone's body. Fuck, I barely had time for takeout dinner and a shower. But that's what they made Grindr for, and the app did all the hard work for me. My siren song coasted across the city's windswept sands, luring men back to my apartment with its irresistible melody.

Until now, I've been trying not to inundate you with stories about sex. I've tried to keep this interview PG rated for your precious celibate ears, but at this point, there's no dancing around the topic. I didn't mention it earlier, but when I was with Gabriel, he ... had some interest in BDSM. Kind of. I think he was more scared of kink than I was, but it was pretty clear he wanted to be dominated. One time, he insisted I pour hot candle wax on his back, and I could tell he was into it. I was surprised to learn that I was into it too, causing controlled pain. But I didn't get to explore those feelings, since every time I tried to do it again, Gabriel shut me down. And I don't get off on *that* kind of pain, so I respected his boundaries. Maybe he hadn't liked it as much as I thought, or maybe he was just repressing his real desires. I mean, I know he used to burn himself, so ... I think he had a complicated relationship with pain.

Before Gabriel, I hadn't ever really considered how I felt about kinks, or fetishes, or pain, but looking back, I'd always preferred porn with an edge. One guy I hooked up with in law school asked me if I'd ever used a whip. I told him no, but I was interested. He said he knew a little something about the subject and turned out to know quite a bit. It was a great night, and highly instructive, until things ended a few weeks later for reasons completely un-related to sex and extremely related to him being a racist asshole ... but that's neither here nor there. Suffice it to say, Parker & Mullins left me no time for a relationship, but that didn't quell my desire for sex.

To be honest, it was hardly about the sex either—after a week of close-reading legalese, I just wanted to feel *something*, to be in control of *something*. Everyone at the firm coped differently, and though we all did our best to hide our hobbies, if you stuck around and paid attention in the break room, sooner or later you'd learn all the office secrets. Cocaine by the pound and hookers were common. So were lavish European vacations. One attorney ordered her favorite macarons flown in from Paris every weekend. Another bought mountains of jewelry for his wife and mistress. It was the people who didn't seem to have any of these odd predilections who stood out. My boss was one of those, her and a small but noticeable group whose fundamental humanity I slowly grew to question. What, I used to wonder, was it like in their heads? Did they realize that this was it, their one shot at life, and that *this* was what they'd chosen to do with it? But then, people probably thought the same about me—I didn't talk about domming, the rush of adrenaline and joy and almost ... grace, for lack of a better word, when I felt that power surging through me. Maybe they thought I was another drone too.

Amid the endless months of research and hookups, my sense of time disintegrated. But one side effect of being overworked was that I became an expert in arcane fields of law, mostly related to the energy industry. The altitude and year-round sunshine made New Mexico a perfect place for solar start-ups, and we worked with a lot of those companies to navigate local tax breaks and regulations. We'd strike a progressive pose, affirming their lip service to improving the grid, saving the world. And when oil companies came in the next day, saying they wanted to start drilling in half a dozen spots around the state, we'd tell them their concerns were our number one priority. I sat in on some of those meetings, silently watching while the partners negotiated terms as if the drilling were completely abstract. No one in those boardrooms cared about what actually happened, me included.

Shell was a huge account. They'd heard there might be frack-able land in northern New Mexico, and they'd contacted us because this was exactly the sort of thing we were good at, from setting up arrangements with the local township to dealing with the particularities of oil and gas taxes. We were the local hired guns, and we'd never lost a showdown.

By the time Shell was ready to start drilling, they still retained Parker & Mullins's services as a formality, but they didn't expect any trouble. Once construction on a drill actually begins, that's usually it. No one protests an oil well that already exists, or a factory that's been polluting for the past twenty years, or an interstate exit that went through a housing development two years ago. Except in this particular case.

That's how I first heard Gabriel had reappeared, back with a puff of smoke from wherever it is priests go to be trained in priestliness. Shell told the firm there were complications with protesters and asked us to help deal with the problem. When I saw footage of the protest online, he was one of two people interviewed. He was older, his hair shorter, dark circles under his eyes. He wore a T-shirt with Beethoven's face drawn in the style of *Aladdin Sane* and tight jeans, dust whipping at him from the side while other protesters milled around behind him. I didn't catch much of what he said, though it's easy enough to imagine now. I just stared at his face and thought about how long it had been since I'd last seen it, how much I simultaneously wished I'd never seen it again and wanted to head straight to that protest myself and kiss those perfect lips.

With Shell concerned about the drill's future, the partners called a meeting. I heard people talk about smear campaigns we could run, damages we could sue the protesters for. Some said we should wait and let the thing peter out on its own. Finally, my boss snapped.

"This is ridiculous. We have all the power here. Not just legal statutes and land leases but the physical power to remove them, with force. These people are trespassing, and there are consequences to breaking the law. The easiest solution would be to involve the police."

"What do you mean when you say 'involve'?" a partner asked.

"I mean we call the state law enforcement, ex–law enforcement, anyone who won't get us cited. We tell them we're willing to pay overtime."

I couldn't believe my ears, and one of the partners' faces looked uneasy too. But most everyone else seemed to be on board. Three days later, Shell gave us the go-ahead to unleash the full fury of seventy off-duty, wannabe, or ex-cops on the small encampment of Native people and Gabriel's churchgoers.

In our office, a hundred miles south of the protests, things remained quiet. The air conditioner's hum competed with the fluorescent lights' buzz, and conversations at the coffee machine stayed the same as ever—where were you headed for the weekend? Had you eaten at the new bistro that just opened up downtown?

But up in the north, that's how all hell broke loose.

MANUEL QUINTANA

Sure, I can explain why I couldn't go back to Española with Father Gabriel, though I'm not really sure how relevant it is. And it's a long story. And I know it's a long story because I've been writing about it for the past year, part of a little hobby of sorts, trying to come to terms with my past. I don't know. So I have a draft here, if you insist ... but keep in mind that I was trained as a priest not a storyteller.

The sun was setting slowly in front of me as I walked across the Española plaza, lighting the sky with shades of pinks and purples cribbed from Georgia O'Keeffe's palette. Children in the grass ran toward the same ice-cream truck I used to frequent when I was their age, while a few kids from my high school talked in the central gazebo. I was close enough to listen in on their conversation. I wanted to join them under the stark crimson roof, to bum cigarettes and talk about chemistry class, about the new girl whose family moved back from Santa Fe, about nothing at all. But I couldn't. I skirted the edge of the gazebo and walked along another path, my steps measured. I was in no rush, and the morada was only a few minutes away, no matter how slowly I walked.

I passed houses with views of the hills that lay behind them. The chirping of cicadas filled the air, and I could smell chiles and beans as I passed by open windows. At the end of a street, the morada sat alone in the dirt, a long boxy building with four shuttered windows beside a heavy wooden door. Vigas stuck out from under the roof, the building's only ornamentation. At first glance, it looked like either an unremarkable house or an overly large garage, brown and adobe and cheap. Cracks ran up the walls like fault lines. Like most adobe buildings around town, it resembled an overlarge anthill, slowly disintegrating back into the land.

I dreaded that building but continued toward it. Large wooden crosses jutted from the ground of the campo santo to its left. They ranged from two to more than ten feet tall, some painted white, some unpainted, others long since faded by decades in the sun. Long yellow grass brushed my Levi's as I walked the small path to the morada. I pounded twice on the door, hoping the certainty of my fists would relieve the queasy feeling in my head and stomach.

My uncle Ramón opened the door. "You're late."

"I know—I'm sorry," I said, though I was on time. I wasn't ever late.

"It's ok," he said with a smile that seemed out of place, as if we were simply meeting up for dinner. "But those aren't the words. You remember?"

"*Dios toca en esta misión, las puertas de su clemencia.*"

"Good, good," he said. "*Penitencia, penitencia, si quieres tu salvación.* Now get in here."

I'd been inside the morada before, during Las Tinieblas, but the room looked different now when fully lit, less foreboding. During those evenings the only light inside had come from a candelabra holding seventeen candles in the sanctuary, and the building had been filled with deep baritones singing odd, haunting alabados. Now the morada looked mostly plain. In the central room, more than a dozen hermanos talked and smoked in their work clothes. An occasional retablo, framed by punch-decorated tinwork, decorated the whitewashed walls. The floors *were hard-packed dirt. In one of the far corners sat a woodburning stove, and in another was a small alcove where a figure of Santo Niño de Atocha stood, his tiny eyes staring toward the road ahead. Through an open door to my left I could see the altar and another dozen hermanos kneeling in prayer, rice littering the floor beneath them.*

"You ready?" my uncle asked.

"Yes," I said, because I knew that's what he wanted to hear.

He clapped me on the back. "Manny is here for the entradas," he announced. "We ready to do this?"

The room quieted as everyone turned to look at me. Hermanos by the altar gathered themselves. There was an anticipatory energy as all these field hands and bricklayers came to attention, like I was somehow special, when really I was here to become one more hermano, same as all of them. I didn't know where else to look, so I glanced around the room and was struck by its cleanliness. Despite all the dirt-spattered clothes and mud-encrusted boots, the earthen floor looked immaculate in a way no tile ever could.

The hermano mayor stepped into the doorway. I knew him otherwise as a second cousin on my mother's side who sold and installed car stereos at a store not half a mile away. He gestured for me to walk to the chapel's doorway.

"¿Quién está en esta casa de luz?"

"Jesús," I answered, though my weak accent made this come out strained and awkward.

"¿Quién la llena de alegría?"

"María."

"¿Quién la conserva en la fé?"

"José."

"Now strip," he said. "And come in."

Caught slightly off guard, I began to take off my shirt. My uncle gestured toward the back of the room, and there I found myself next to an old wooden wardrobe. Inside was a pair of white pants, identical to the ones worn by all the hermanos, and I put these on and walked into the chapel.

Here, Jesus on his altar presided over all, but it wasn't the benign Jesus of church, or the friendly child of Atocha, or the colorful and almost plastic Jesus of a children's Bible. This Jesus was gruesome. Bloodred paint splattered His naked body, especially His hands and feet and head. He wore only a torn and dirty loincloth and a crown of thorns, blood dripping from each tiny piercing. His long, stringy hair looked like it might be human, and He was carved into a position on the cross that looked particularly uncomfortable, like the stress positions used by the military for interrogations. His ribs stuck out, giving the impression that even before He was crucified, He'd already begun taking our sins onto Him. Here was a man who had suffered.

I knelt on the rice, jagged little grains stabbing into my skin, and swore myself to the Hermandad, to the rules they'd told me to memorize, and, most importantly, to Jesus. I felt the hermanos staring at me, perhaps remembering their own initiations, their own oaths. The maestro de novicios, a sometimes substitute teacher, sometimes handyman my mom said drank too much to keep a real job, asked if I'd been told what came next. If I was prepared.

"Yes," I said. He'd been the one who'd told me what to say, so he already knew the answer, but all of this was performative anyway.

An hermano I didn't know came behind me and asked me to look down. In his hand he held a pedernal made of sharpened obsidian, and he cut three gashes into my back, shallow enough to avoid slicing muscles but deep enough that I felt, for a few seconds, like it was going to stick straight through my back and into my heart.

Without time to recover, the maestro said, "Sing." So I sang, the alabado he'd taught me, asking for forgiveness. Hermanos brought rags and tubs of soapy water for me to wash their feet.

It was all a bit forced, and I couldn't concentrate because of the blood dripping down my back, soaking into my waistband.

"Now what do you want?" asked the maestro when I finished the song.

"Por el amor de Dios, las tres meditaciones de la Pasión de Nuestro Señor."

There was a tiny bit of applause at this, words of approval.

Then the man who'd cut into my back struck me three times with a disciplina made of yucca. Tears welled in my eyes, and I couldn't catch my breath. The disciplina normally wasn't supposed to be too bad, but the pain of those fresh gashes overwhelmed me.

I tried to return to my body. During the time it took me to recover, I thought I was done. This had all been a mistake. Then I somehow found myself saying, "Por el amor de Dios, las cinco heridas de Cristo."

Perhaps he saw in my eyes or my shuddering that I was weak, that I couldn't take much more, but the man with the whip was gentler on me the next time. Even so, the pain was incredible, immeasurable. I heard my uncle say quietly, "Look to Jesus. Look at His suffering," and I did. I stared up at that wooden carving, and somehow my back hurt less. Somehow I was no longer doing this for my mother or my uncle or anyone else. I understood. This was for Him. This was all por el amor de Dios—those weren't just words, they were an ethos, a way of life. My pain was only a trifle compared to His.

"Por el amor de Dios, las siete últimas palabras."

Crack, crack, crack. The disciplina landed seven more times, and my blood was now everywhere, like Christ's on the bulto. The entire room smelled like me, my blood and sweat. I collapsed on the floor, whimpering. Seconds dragged into minutes, and the hermanos all waited silently. No one spoke or moved from their seats. Finally, I pushed myself up and whispered the final words. "Por el amor de Dios … los cuarenta días en el desierto."

And the lash rained endlessly on my back, again and again and again and again. I lost consciousness. While I was out, I had a vision of Jesus walking off that cross, laying His hand on me and healing me like He did so many others. He didn't look like He was in pain, just sad. He sat with me for a few minutes and told me it would all be ok. Then He walked out of the room, and I found myself disturbed by His absence. Jesus wasn't supposed to leave—not then, not ever. And though my back no longer hurt, somehow I was far more frightened by His absence than I had ever been for my body.

When I awoke, I was laying on my chest, and an hermano was treating my wounds with ointment and herbs. The lashes still stung like a swarm of wasps had attacked my back for the last hour, though.

"You alright?" asked my uncle.

"I guess? I mean no, not really."

He laughed. "You're alright," he said. "I told the sangrador not to take it easy on you, and I guess he took it a little too much to heart. But you're alright. And after all, it's por el amor de Dios."

He patted me on the head and left. I started to stand up, but when I flexed my back, I almost collapsed again from the pain.

★ ★ ★

"Mrs. Surkowski asked about you in chemistry. I told her you were sick," Marianna said. "I told her it was pretty bad, so you might not be back for a while."

"Good."

"Do you think it'll be that long?"

"I don't know," I said. "I don't really think about that sort of thing."

She asked if I wanted to come back to her house, but I knew I'd feel cornered there, unable to make a quick exit. Her mother wouldn't be home until after five, so we had hours and could've hung out in her bedroom, but that was even more frightening. I'd never been there, and I didn't want today to be the day that changed. I had too much to process already.

"I just want to go for a walk. And then maybe lie down for a while. I feel tired."

"Mind if I come?"

I shrugged, and we set off on a circular route through side streets away from my house. It was early spring, and trees were still in their awkward in-between phase, not quite barren but not yet recovered from what had been a particularly harsh winter. Marianna put her hand out, and I grasped it with a half smile. We wandered like that for more than a mile, past innumerable brown adobe buildings and pickup trucks. I didn't want it to end, but I also didn't want to say anything, so I just enjoyed the small pleasure of her skin against mine. Her soft hands felt so small and fragile they almost seemed fake.

"So was it ok?" she finally asked.

"Was what ok?"

"You know what."

"Oh," I said. "Yeah."

"You don't have to talk about it if you don't want, I guess."

I didn't say anything and hoped she understood that was my answer.

"But if you do," she said, "you can talk to me."

"I'm ok. Just a little tired, like I said. And maybe a little sore."

She took her hand back. "Wow, I guess my boyfriend was beaten and whipped all night by a bunch of weird old men, but he's still good. Just a little tired, and maybe a little sore."

"They didn't beat me."

"Ok, sure. I mean, I guess it's kinda funny. Like, you're all supposed to be these super Christians, and Jesus is the prince of peace or whatever, but as soon as no one's looking it's like, let's see how many times we can whip someone before he passes out."

"How did you know I passed out?" I felt ambushed and suddenly wanted to cry again.

She stopped walking. "Wait, shit, you passed out? Like, they really … is that supposed to happen? God, I'm sorry, that's just … God, that's fucked up."

"I don't know. I guess I could ask my uncle."

I changed our route, heading back toward my house. I wanted to lie down, take a bath. Eat ice cream until I couldn't force any more down, even though it was Lent and I'd sworn not to eat any sweets.

"You know I think the whole thing is fucked up," said Marianna.

"I know. You told me yesterday. You told me two days ago. You tell me every day."

"Yeah, well, because it's true. I mean, I've been there for Tinieblas, and I've seen the procession, and it's not like this super-secret awesome thing. It's dumb. It's just like Mexican fight club but even stupider because guys like you and my brother act like it's this big sacred deal."

"I don't know, it makes my mom happy."

"It makes your mom happy to see you pass out because some old dudes wail on you? Chinga tu madre, you're being a fucking idiot."

We reached my house. I wanted to run inside and hide under the covers for a week. Instead, I hugged Marianna as hard as I could and was grateful when she gingerly patted my shoulders, avoiding my burning back. She kissed me on the mouth, a quick peck, but I liked it more than when we'd made out the previous Saturday. The intimate thoughtlessness of it, the way it almost felt like nothing at all.

* * *

The bathwater was as warm as I could take it. I could hear my mother's radio playing rancheras and corridos from the other room, punctuated by the sound of her knife against the cutting board as she prepared dinner. When I got out of the bath, we'd eat enchiladas, because they were my favorite, and she was spoiling me. I pictured her swift motions as she effortlessly minced onion, saw it coming to pieces from a million small cuts. I forced myself to stop thinking about it, because it made my back hurt, and I was trying to think of anything else. The maestro said that if you thought about Jesus, the pain would diminish, that He was like Advil cranked up to eleven, but I couldn't concentrate on that because when I did, my mother's voice would come through, singing along with the radio, and I'd get distracted.

It was my mother's voice that made me join the Hermandad in the first place, her voice that spoke up for a child who was too young to know any better. My older brother, Joaquín, had just enlisted in the army. He hadn't made the cut for the marines, but he wanted to enlist anyhow. "I just want to know what I'm made of," he'd told us. "I want to see what else is out there."

"You can do that from college," my mother had said. "Or working with your tío building houses."

He'd smiled at us, a big ugly grin, and I was too young to know he was mocking her. I still thought we were all happy then, maybe because my mother was too scared to say anything harsher, in case her criticism was the last thing he ever heard from her.

Months later, a letter came from Joaquín saying he'd finished basic training and was headed to Iraq. Mom cried then as if he'd already died, but she didn't give up hope. That night she prayed, and made me pray too.

She made a promesa that if Jesus Christ would return Joaquín to her, whole and healthy, I would join the Hermandad. I didn't know what joining the brotherhood meant—I already had a brother—and she didn't explain. Only years later did I learn that usually it was the firstborn son who became an hermano, and that by joining the army instead, Joaquín had skipped out on this birthright. I was only five or maybe six—none of my memories from back then are too clear—but I said what she told me to and made that promise.

When Joaquín returned, two years later, he joined the hermanos after all. But they kicked him out less than a year after his induction, for problems related to drinking that no one would ever fully explain. Soon afterward, he moved out. He lived on the other side of town, but I hadn't seen him in more than a year, and the last time I had, he and a couple army buddies had tried to get me drunk on a forty of Labatt and some Jägermeister. The night ended with both of us throwing up. When Mom forbade me from seeing him anymore, I hadn't fought.

Mom's voice rose in the other room as she tried to harmonize, and she warbled in time with the music. "Five more minutes."

"Ok," I said, though I made no move to get out of the tub. One of the last things my father did before he passed was redo the bathroom. As a gift to my mother, who'd always complained about the old tub, he'd installed the largest one he could fit. It and the kitchen were new, with tiles and fixtures he'd installed after long days putting together houses for other families. The rest of the house was old, constructed by my great-grandfather and poorly insulated, despite all the work Dad put into its upkeep. I had no memories of him, only photos and stories, but Mom said that he'd been a wonderful hermano, that the brotherhood had meant a lot to him.

Before I joined, Ramón told me that my father had been an hermano mayor for a few years, though positions changed annually. Ramón had been one too, as had other Quintanas in the past. Ramón didn't need to recruit me, I'd already been promised, but he still seemed to feel the need to talk it up. "Marianna's brother is a fine member," he'd said. "Strong man. Serious and holy man. Pay attention to him, alright."

"Marianna says he's stupid," I'd said. "She thinks he wastes his time and hurts himself and that he'd be twice the mover he is now if he stopped. Says he'll be crippled by the time he's thirty-five."

My uncle looked so disappointed with me that I apologized and said what do girls know anyway, the Hermandad was sacred. I understood that.

I heard the doorknob turning but didn't have time to yell for my mother to stop. The bathroom's lock had broken years ago, during a fight between her and Joaquín.

"Dinner, mijo. Or did you forget?"

"It smells delicious. Thanks."

She handed me a towel, and I barely even registered embarrassment at my nakedness. I just saw how proud she was, that she looked at me with a certain glow I would do anything to keep alive. So I ate dinner, made small talk. Cleaned the dishes. Then I headed back to the morada.

* * *

"It's not torture, it's respect," Ramón said.

We stood outside the morada, waiting for others to arrive while Ramón smoked. He said it wasn't allowed in the morada, because that was a sacred space, so I waited with him, feeling chilly as the sun began to dip beneath the hills.

"I didn't say it was torture," I said. "I was just asking why."

"You don't get it. You act like it's masochism. Like we're trying to hurt ourselves. But it's not about that at all, it's about obedience. And customs. And the past."

"But then ... I mean, if it's about obedience, why can't we do something else? The army's all about obedience too, and they don't do this."

"The army? Shit," Ramón said. "Your brother did just fine in the army. Could've made sergeant or whatever, no sweat. He had no problem stamping around that field, pointing his gun at who they told him to. Pulling the trigger. But that obedience is here, in the flesh." He grabbed at the flabby brown skin of his love handles and laughed. "That's bullshit obedience, that's what it is."

"People die for the army."

"Fuck, people die crossing the street to buy toilet paper. An hermano knows real obedience, real sacrifice. To be an hermano is about total surrender, mind, body, and soul. You know they say living with pain is worse than dying, right? You obey God even when it hurts, even when doing so flays the skin off your back. That's being an hermano. But the maestro can tell you about that shit better than I can."

I didn't want to argue, though I didn't think he made much sense. He threw his cigarette butt to the ground, pulled a pack from his pants, and offered me one. I declined. He shrugged and lit up another.

"How old is the morada anyhow?"

"I don't know. I probably should. Maybe a hundred years? Two hundred? Something like that."

"Is this all it's about though?"

"What do you mean?"

"I don't know."

"Well alright, we used to do more," said Ramón. "When I was a kid, there were the food drives and charities. We'd pay for burials or just do it all ourselves in the camposanto. Prayer vigils for the sick. Help people get jobs. I don't know. Caridad."

"Charity?"

"Yeah. That's what it's all supposed to be about, living the good life, the holy life."

"Well, why don't we do that stuff now?"

"People are poor and tired. And alright, I guess after Easter, some of us just want a break."

"So that's it?"

"No. I mean if someone asked, I guess we'd probably do some shit. But no one asks."

"Like for help?"

"Yeah. I mean, we help each other. Hermanos, you know? But like, I get what you're saying."

"I'm not saying anything."

"Yeah you are. I can tell—you just don't want to say it out loud, but that's fine. And that's the thing, once you're a full Hermano de Luz, you can make the morada into something else. Most of us are old. When I joined, they initiated half a dozen. Last night it was only you."

"I'm jealous. Being alone was … not great."

"I don't know what I'm even saying. I see Martin coming."

He threw his cigarette on the ground, and we went inside the morada and changed clothes. We had a long night ahead, discussing plans for Friday's crucifixion.

* * *

It was overcast the next day when I met Marianna at the edge of the high school parking lot. Her hair was down, jet-black curls cascading all the way down her back. At one point she'd told me that her father cried when her older sister had cut her hair a year earlier.

"Hey," I said.

"I told Mrs. Surkowski you might have meningitis, but it's too early to tell," she said.

"You even know what meningitis is?"

"Does anyone?"

I certainly didn't, so I shut up.

Marianna looked at my face for a moment, I guess searching for something, then she started walking toward her house, so I followed.

"You don't look so bad," she said. "They drown you last night instead?"

"Nah, we just talked. And prayed. I don't know."

She took my hand, and soon it started to sprinkle. When we reached her house, she asked if I wanted to come inside. When I said yes, she was surprised.

"You never want to," she said.

I shrugged and tried to look mysterious. If she knew that my thought process mostly boiled down to her delicious smell, like fresh pan dulce, and that the rain was kicking up in intensity, she might've rescinded the offer.

No one was home. We wiped our shoes on the front mat, then went to her bedroom and closed the door. Like the rest of the house, it was small, filled with an oversize dresser, a child's desk, her bed, and a fair number of stuffed animals, mostly bunnies and cats. But my overwhelming impression was that a tornado of paper had blown through—drawings covered every flat surface, from pencil doodles to fully inked still lifes that must've taken weeks to complete.

"I … didn't think you'd actually want to hang out," she said, slamming her closet shut before I could see inside. "I would've cleaned."

"I like it better this way," I said. I knew that she drew, that she always had a pad of paper with her, but her room made me realize it meant more to her than the "little hobby" she played it off as. She leafed through a black leather binder of CDs and put on a mix I'd sent her, one of more than a dozen—I rarely knew what to say to her, what words could match my feelings, but some of the people I listened to seemed to get pretty close. Tom Waits began singing, and without either of us speaking, I closed the curtains, took off my shoes, and lay down with Marianna on her midnight-blue quilt.

We kissed. Gently at first, then passionately. Then almost painfully. I tasted blood and didn't know whose it was. Our legs and arms intertwined as we rubbed against each other. Her fingers pressed into my back, and it stung, in a good way, but I didn't want her to see those marks, to realize how deep they really went. So our clothes stayed on, a thin cotton barrier between us. Maybe she could sense my reluctance, because when "Slum Beautiful" started playing, she took my hand and guided it down the front of her pants.

I had never felt so connected to anyone as I did with her right then, and I had never felt as alien. I closed my eyes, and my hand crept tentatively around until I thought I'd found what she liked. She began unbuttoning and then unzipping her pants, then unbuttoning mine, and suddenly an alarm of some sort triggered in my brain, one I hadn't known existed. "Stop," I said softly. "Really, stop." So we did.

In a movie, I imagine this would be where the scene ended. But life doesn't cut, and we had to figure out what to do next. We lay against each other while the CD continued, our bodies still close but no longer touching. I felt awkward, and I'm sure she did too, but I liked her breath up against my ear, didn't want to leave the sweet and flowery scent of her hair on the pillow.

"Is it because of the Hermandad?" she asked when the music stopped.

"No. Something else. I don't really know."

"Your brothers get to see you naked, but I don't?"

"They're not my brothers."

"Oh right, they're your 'hermanos,' sorry."

"My brother's a piece of shit."

"You waiting for marriage or something?"

"No, nothing's changed. I just ... I don't want to screw this up." She bought that, or at least seemed to, but

I remember wondering whether she was right. Whether I would've slept with her a week earlier. I didn't feel different, didn't love her any less. Didn't want her any less. But here we were.

"Don't you have to go?" she asked.

"I guess. Maybe I should just skip tonight."

She knew I wasn't serious and sat up. "I don't think my brother's gonna be able to go through with it."

"He seems strong," I said. "He volunteered, you know."

"He has a bad back. He volunteered because he cheated on my sister-in-law. That's what Mom says."

"I don't think the hermanos know."

"Which part?"

"Either, I guess. No one mentioned anything in the morada. I think ... I think they figured if someone wants to do it, that's better than asking someone who doesn't. Are you going to watch?"

"I've seen it before, it's disgusting. My brother's coming back here tonight because his wife kicked him out. Mom says she won't take him back for doing some stupid Jesus thing anyhow, so it's all a waste. I don't know when the house will be empty again."

"He'll be fine," I said. "He seemed pretty confident. They all agree he's strong." I kissed her, a chaste goodbye kiss, then headed home for a quick dinner before another night in the morada.

★ ★ ★

"Who decides the roles?" I asked the maestro. We stood in the corner of the main room, near the inactive fireplace and a portrait of Doña Sebastiana, which I found off-putting but still preferable to all the mutilated Christs adorning other parts of the building. The rest of the hermanos were praying in the chapel as preparation for the evening's smaller, more intimate procession in honor of Maundy Thursday.

"The hermano mayor."

"And that's it?"

"That's it. But I mean, we're a democracy, so he listens. We're all hermanos, and you have to remember it's an honor not a punishment."

"Has anyone ever been really hurt?"

"Of course not. Well, rarely. You have to remember, we reenact the Crucifixion as a form of prayer. Our pain and suffering honor Dios as much as the words you say in church."

I thought about passing out a couple nights earlier, the way they'd told me afterward that it was rare, unexpected. "Ramón said it wasn't about that. It was about obedience. Or charity."

He shrugged. "It's about a lot of things. It's different to everyone. I don't pretend to know why everyone here does it. Maybe it's just something that has to be done."

★ ★ ★

That night, I dreamed about Marianna. The two of us were in the morada, me in a tuxedo, her in the red dress she'd worn to prom the year before. All the santos looked down on us from the walls, from the corners, from the altar where candles lit the room with a flickering, twisting light. We made love on the hard floor beneath their eyes, and though I knew they judged me, condemned me, I didn't care.

In the morning, Marianna told me I looked distracted.

"It's a big day," I said.

"You know you can tell me whatever," she said. "You know that, right?"

"It's a big day. I don't want to screw up."

"How would you screw up? Accidentally whip someone else? You'll be fine."

I thought about telling her that her brother would be fine. I thought about telling her about my dream, that maybe I was ready now, that I'd had cold feet, but we could put on another CD and remove every thread of clothing and spend the whole weekend in bed together.

"I'll see you on Monday," I said.

"I'll tell Mrs. Surkowski you seem to be doing better after surgery, but it's too early to say—you might need bed rest for a month."

"Thanks."

★ ★ ★

We walked out of the morada shirtless, wearing stark white pants and black hoods to keep us humble, to keep us from indulging in these ceremonies in order to be seen. But being seen is the point of any procession, and we walked upright and proud, with our braided disciplinas and la Muerte in su carreta, a wooden effigy of Death herself carrying a bow and staring out toward the horizon with her empty eye sockets, pulled by Ramón and another hermano by a rope digging into their naked shoulders. As a child, I'd loved the spectacle of the penitentes, the clothing, the blood. The resolve. We always came out to watch them march up the hill they called el Calvario, almost two miles from the morada, and even now that I was with them, walking barefoot into those rocky hills, whipping my back with the disciplina's harsh sting, I felt like a spectator, watching it happen to someone else.

Maybe that was because of the pain. You had to think about something else while marching, find a way to escape your body as it trudged step after step through misery. You saw yourself not so much as an individual but as a part of a sacramental whole, performing these rites to quiet the parts of yourself that protested, that had any doubts whatsoever. Those could wait until later, until showers and antibiotics and lotions, until evening prayers with family and Sunday services and the miracle of Easter rebirth. Our procession had no time for any of that. You stepped forward and you flogged yourself and you imagined Jesus Christ watching from on high, witnessing your suffering with a certain divine approval. He understood the sacrifice you were making, and that made it all worth it, even if occasionally you snapped back into your body and couldn't quite figure out why you didn't simply drop your disciplina and run back to Marianna's arms, never to set foot in the morada again.

At the back of the procession walked Marianna's brother, who seemed thinner than he had in the flickering candlelight of the chapel just the night before. He was dirty, his hair muddy and unwashed, his beard a scraggly mess. He carried an enormous cross over his right shoulder, a dozen feet of pine he struggled to drag behind him. The blood on his face browned in the sun, a result of the crown of thorns on his head. Occasionally, new trickles made their scarlet presence known. Still, for the first mile he seemed more or less ok. His determination and dedication to the sanctified role saw him through the beginning of the arduous journey, the same way it did me, the same way it did all of us. We grimly ignored the punishment our bodies were taking and made our slow, methodical way up to el Calvario, flanked by a few dozen women, children, and even the occasional gringo who'd come for the spectacle.

In the middle of the second mile, I heard our Jesus crying out to God, asking why he'd forsaken him, using colorful language that never appeared in the Bible. I couldn't tell whether it was an act, another part of the ceremony, or a real curse. Then he fell. I was at the back, walking near the hermano mayor, and the two of us were supposed to whip him with the disciplinas—not hard but enough to get him going, like he was a pack animal. I could see the deep furrow his cross had dug, snaking all the way back to the morada. We hit Marianna's brother as prescribed, nothing more than light taps, and it did get him moving. After another hundred feet, though, he fell again, and this time no amount of whipping helped, so instead the three of us shouldered that hulking madero and continued onward. Despite these difficulties, there was still a festive, if solemn, air to the day. The sound of our alabados, accompanied by flutes and matracas, covered our footsteps. Those watching beside us talked loudly and ate. I could hear Marianna's brother sobbing faintly.

When we reached the top of el Calvario, it was impossible to ignore his wailing. This wasn't supposed to be how it happened, how I'd seen it happen every time my mother had taken me growing up: our stand-in savior was supposed to be strong, dignified. He would feel pain, would curse and struggle and suffer, that was undeniable, but he was supposed to take it all with a manly sigh. Perhaps even enjoy it. Marianna's brother looked old and pathetic. He wasn't even thirty-three, but you could tell that he smoked. His skin sagged, even though he was skinny, and as a pair of hermanos began tying him to that cross, a block of wood below his feet to prevent him from dislocating his shoulders, he looked on the verge of collapse. Here we were supposed to be offering ourselves up, but he looked not like a sacrifice, the best we had to offer, but like a victim.

We began praying. I watched him like everyone else. Minutes passed, and the spectacle grew sadder. The hermanos had talked this up as a moment of glory, when the whole community came together in faith, celebrating the resurrection by recognizing the violence that made it a necessity. But instead of feeling fulfilled, I felt guilty, or at least complicit in this man's misery. The wife he'd hoped to impress wasn't even here—it was just a sad man roiling pointlessly in his own pain, and I couldn't cope with it any longer. I couldn't understand how Christ's love and this man's pain could have any relationship with each other.

"How long?" I asked the hermano mayor.

"How long what?"

"How long until we take him down? He looks like shit."

"He's fine. It's just for a little while."

So we waited. But a little while came and went. And he was still up there. In agony.

"We have to take him down," I said.

The hermano mayor said, "Patience."

I was out of patience. I grabbed the knife another hermano had left sitting at the base of the cross and held it above my head to begin cutting him free.

A couple of hermanos stepped forward, half-heartedly attempting to stop me. One had his hand on my shoulder, telling me that if it were truly that serious, he'd ask to be taken down himself, and then of course we'd do so. But I didn't stop.

"Let him," said the hermano mayor. "Maybe he's right. Either way, the penance will be his to suffer afterward."

Two hermanos stepped forward to help Marianna's brother down off the cross, and once on the ground he collapsed like his bones and muscles had dissolved into jelly. I wondered how he would feel the next day. The next month. And with that thought, I had the opposite of an epiphany. I felt complete and total despair. I realized I couldn't do this any longer, no matter what promises my mother and I had made, no matter that my family had been members of the Hermanos de la Fraternidad Piadosa de Nuestro Padre Jesús Nazareno for more than a hundred years, fathers and sons going back in a line to long before they added the "New" to Mexico. This didn't feel like my religion, the version of Christ that I'd grown up with or that the priest spoke about on Sundays. So I walked.

I heard voices behind me, but I ignored them. I walked down from el Calvario and back to Española proper. I entered the morada, put on my T-shirt, and exchanged my bloodstained white pants for the jeans I'd worn when I arrived that morning. Then I walked some more. I couldn't head home—my mother hadn't been able to get the day off work, but as soon as she came home, she'd find out what I'd done, the way I'd disgraced myself. So instead I took Paseo de Oñate until it became Santa Cruz Road, and I kept walking east.

* * *

I could claim I didn't know where I was headed, that I drifted aimlessly for the next four hours, but that wouldn't be true. I had a destination in mind, I just didn't know why it seemed so important. El Santuario de Chimayo was a pair of churches a dozen miles from Española, a stream passing by one side with only a few sprawling ranch houses nearby. I'd visited the Santuario many times during the Fiesta or to watch people dancing la Azteca or las Matachines. When my mother was younger, we'd walked las Posadas there, and we'd ended those nights with midnight Mass, followed by hot chocolate and doughnuts. I don't know that I ever felt the site was holy, exactly, but it felt different from everywhere else.

I wasn't the only one walking that route. There were other pilgrims, both large families talking loudly and individuals lost in their own thoughts. More disconcertingly, I passed by other groups of hermanos, carrying crosses or altars as they headed toward the Santuario. Some dressed normally or even wore collared shirts as they marched, while others seemed closer to my own morada. I did my best to ignore all of them.

When I finally reached the Santuario, there were hundreds of people milling around the dirt parking lot, and the mood was social and festive. Crosses were everywhere, hundreds of large discarded wooden ones laying up against a nearby wall, thousands of miniature ones laced into the chain-link fences leading up the path inside, even stone ones made out of bricks mortared together and signed by congregants. I made my way to the Santuario proper and waited in line for almost an hour to get in. People prayed in the pews, sitting tightly together in the small chapel, elaborate bultos and retablos of Christ and various santos gazing down at us from the walls, their colors slowly fading from the sunlight peeking in through tall windows. An old woman stood up, and I took her place in the pew, staring forward at the main shrine, the reason for this church, Nuestro Señor de Esquipulas.

When I was younger, my grandfather had told me how this black Christ came to be in a Hispanic church in the middle of nowhere. There had been a local friar, doing penance not far down the Santa Cruz River, who saw a strange light in the sky. He followed it and found that the light was coming from a crucifix, its black Jesus bloody and perhaps already unconscious, His head slumping down onto His shoulder. The friar took it back to Española, but it disappeared, only to be found back in its original spot. After this happened again several times, they built a church around that location, and the hole, one room over, was the very same hole He'd been discovered in.

Only later did my mother tell me this was all una tontería—an hermano had made the crucifix, and it had never been removed or miraculously teleported. The hermano simply liked that original spot and thought it'd be nice to have a church there.

Somehow, I kept these accounts of the story in my head and considered them both true, the miraculous and the mundane. Why did I have to pick just one?

I stood up and made my way to El Pocito. It was a small room, more of a closet really, lit only by candles and a tiny window. In the middle of the hard dirt floor was a hole, where a priest with a trowel gave each person a small bit of dirt to take with them. When I had been there before, my mother always had us bring empty jam jars, but obviously this time I hadn't come prepared. Still, I held out my hands, and the priest poured a shovelful into them. I placed the dirt in my mouth, swallowed, and hoped this would somehow help.

Even my mother agreed that El Pocito was holy. Magical. When sick, she'd put a bit of the tierra bendita into her tea. My grandfather used to dab it on himself at each of the spots where Christ had been wounded, perhaps remembering when he'd been the Cristo himself, like Marianna's brother. The dirt tasted like ordinary dirt, except it was smooth and almost sweet.

On my way out of the chapel, I walked through a dimly lit room lined with hundreds of crutches and prayer notes posted with pictures of loved ones. The crutches were left by people who, after eating the dirt, had been healed. Every other week, the church donated them to the local hospital, but today there were so many, a pile had been stacked outside the door.

I made my way past more visitors until I came to the other church. The shrine to Santo Niño was newer and better kept. A stone statue of the little Lord sat above the doorway, and elaborate carvings and stained glass windows made for a welcoming entrance. Though the church was just as busy as the rest of the Santuario, the building still felt airy. Carved trees flanked the front altar, a pastel-colored scene decorated with dolls and children's shoes. Even the pews were ornamented. I waited in a long line that led to the left of the altar into the shrine itself, a small room where the Christ child presided over more tiny shoes than I could possibly count and an infinity of photographed loved ones on the walls.

Eventually, the people kneeling in prayer left, and I took my place. I prayed for what to do next. I prayed for direction, and for how to make things up to my mother. I prayed and prayed and prayed, and there, amid the whispers of other visitors, I received my answer. Santo Niño didn't come alive, didn't speak to me, but I heard a voice in my head, the angelic voice of a child who told me what to do.

People leave their shoes for Santo Nino because they say He wanders, bringing food for the hungry, clothes for the homeless, money for the poor. Not literally the statue, no one believes that, but baby Jesus himself, who somehow wanders the rocky hills nearby and tends the faithful at night. The proof was that the shoes left at the statue wore out, so He constantly needed new ones to continue His wanderings. I never believed that story, but I do think it was Him who came to me and spoke: *Wander, like I do. It's time to leave this place. Wander like me until you find your new home.*

* * *

I walked back to Española. The sun had set hours earlier, but I couldn't return home. If I saw my mother, I would want to stay, no matter how angry she was, no matter how disappointed. Instead, I knocked on Marianna's window and climbed inside when she opened it.

"I can't believe you," she said. She wore a light-blue nightgown, sheer but not enough for me to see anything.

"Yeah," I said.

"Thanks, I guess. For helping my brother."

The day had been so long, I'd almost forgotten about him. "Sure."

"You shouldn't have, you know. He would've been fine."

"I did it for you," I said, though that wasn't true. "I thought you'd be happy."

"I don't know how to feel."

I had no words to respond. Eventually I smiled at her, then began taking off my clothes.

"We can't," she said.

"I know. But I can't sleep in my clothes. I've never been able to."

"Ok, but let me put a towel down on the bed so you don't get blood on it. You really could use a shower."

"I know. I'm sorry," I said, and lay down beneath her covers. She curled up close to me, and we held each other. I stroked the ringlets of her hair, wondering how anything could be so beautiful.

"Thanks," she said.

"For what?"

"Just thanks."

We didn't do anything that evening, but I fell asleep to the sound of her breathing, and that was enough. To be honest, I try not to think about her, because the pain of leaving her behind stung far more than those lashes against my back.

When I kissed Marianna the next morning, I think she knew it was goodbye. "I'll tell Mrs. Surkowski you died during surgery," she said, and we both smiled, but we didn't laugh.

I ate a small breakfast at McDonald's, then hitch-hiked to Santa Fe, where a friend who'd graduated the year before was attending community college. I slept on his couch for a few months and made enough to eat by washing dishes. The next semester, I enrolled at the college too. After graduating, I went straight to seminary, strange as that may seem.

★ ★ ★

So that's why I couldn't go north with Gabriel. I told you it was a long story. It probably sounds to you like I punished myself more than the hermanos ever would have, by running away and staying gone so long. And you're probably right, though it didn't feel like running away at the time. But the longer I was gone, the more impossible it became to return.

So when the Shell protests started, I stayed behind, tending the members of our flock who couldn't travel, watching the events unfold on TV and across social media as days and weeks turned into months.

FR. PATRICK CONKLIN

I heard about the fracking and the protests. About Gabriel fraternizing with shamans and their followers, wowing them with his card tricks and slick promises, dancing with them like some insensitive actor in an old western. I heard about the state troopers and their high-powered hoses, their rubber bullets and body armor, the Humvees and tanks and blockades. Frankly, I felt sorry for him, though I felt much worse for the people he was with. Your average parish is not prepared for that sort of assault, believe me. A local parish is more about potlucks and picnics, perhaps figuring out how to fight back against the hedonism you see in Hollywood, not wholesale guerrilla warfare. I have no firsthand experience, but what I saw on TV was pretty ugly, and yes, I prayed for their safety.

It was with those people in mind that I knew, once again, I needed to act. If Gabriel wanted to feel the force of a riot stick against his face, that was his business, but there were innocents caught in the middle of his little attempt at media martyrdom, and they needed help.

In one of those fortuitous coincidences that allows us to see the ever-present guiding hand of the Lord, my older brother, Caleb, happened to be married to an FBI agent. I had always found her a bit brusque, a bit … mannish, in all honesty, but I respected her, and if that's who the Lord saw fit to match Caleb with, then who was I to judge. And so I made arrangements for dinner with them, and I asked her, politely, how one might go about reporting a terrorist.

"Patrick, what are you … are you serious?" she asked.

"Of course," I said. "I would never joke about such a thing."

"I'm just not sure how you came into any information…" She paused. "Is this about drugs in Cruces? Human trafficking? Are you sure this isn't something to report to the local police? The DEA?"

"It's not about drugs or anything like that," I assured her. "It's about a priest who, it would seem, is trying to radicalize his followers and destabilize the state. If that isn't a matter for the FBI, I don't know what is." I explained everything I knew about Gabriel and why the FBI needed to open a file on him.

Caleb still claims that, at first, she was simply placating me, but the fact of the matter is that she arranged a more formal meeting with another agent—why not Caleb's wife, I can't say, I'm not privy to FBI protocol. We met in a large tan building in Albuquerque, just off I-25, that looked more like an expensive school than a headquarters for federal law enforcement. After waiting in the lobby, I was taken to a small room on the second floor, where I met with a woman who introduced herself as Agent Cook.

I'm not sure how much of our meeting I'm at liberty to discuss, legally speaking, but what transpired was not terribly interesting in any case. I talked, and she took detailed notes but asked few questions. Then I felt the need to ask some questions of my own.

"I have to assume this meeting means you're serious about Gabriel Romero, right? That you will be moving forward with some sort of operation to stop him."

"I can neither confirm nor deny any sort of 'operation,'" she said.

"But the fact that I'm here has some significance. Presumably you'll do something? For instance, these notes you're taking. You're serious, or else you wouldn't be taking them."

"Sir, with all due respect, not necessarily."

I stood up to leave, feeling defeated yet again. But as I left, she told me one final thing.

"I will say that Mr. Romero is someone the Bureau has been following for some time, and the information you've provided has been helpful. Please keep in touch if you learn anything else that might be relevant."

With that, I headed back home to Cruces, feeling that finally, I might have put an end to Gabriel's sway over the good Catholics of Albuquerque.

FR. MICHAEL CARTER

As I said earlier, I do not stay abreast of the news. My information about the fracking protest near Española was minimal and largely dependent on what Gabriel told me. The first time he mentioned Shell, it was just one in a long list of battles. He never had any shortage of injustices to fight, a trait I found both honorable and, to be frank, a bit tiring. A month or so later, he wrote that most of his time was spent preparing for a protest, though I did not realize the size and scope he had in mind. His next letter was postmarked from San Ildefonso Pueblo and included concrete information about the protest: how many parishioners had traveled with him, how many Native Americans were already there doing their best to protect their land from pollution. Later, I noticed a subtext running through his letter, hinting at uneasiness between him and the tribal leadership, but his enthusiasm gave an initial impression of grassroots support and unified resolve. I didn't learn about the brutality occurring there until much later, when we arrived in person. He neglected to mention that even once. All his letters boiled down to the same thing: he wanted me to join him. And he was certainly smart enough to realize that beatings from law enforcement are rarely an incentive.

The pressure increased every month. "It would be a pleasure to see you again soon" became "I'm sure your leadership here would make an enormous difference" became "There's a warm campsite I have set aside for you whenever you're able to break away and visit." While I could have become offended by his presumptuousness, I sensed a creeping desperation. Gabriel did not seem like the type of man who relished asking for favors. He wanted to be seen as self-sufficient and self-made, an individual who had performed the impossible task of pulling himself up by his own bootstraps, even though we both knew that sort of sociological levitation was even more difficult to achieve than his physical one.

At first it was easy to beg off his pleas. I had obligations. In a way, my life itself was an obligation. Service was my calling, and I rarely left the seminary. The idea of visiting Gabriel at the protests seemed antithetical to my aims as an educator and adviser to the next generation of Jesuits. But as the letters continued, I meditated and prayed, and my feelings changed, particularly when I reflected on what he wrote in the only long letter that arrived during his stay up there, a request that drifted into personal feelings. I cannot recall all of it, but one passage has stayed with me.

"Prayer isn't just something you say out loud, the whispers or thoughts running through your mind while kneeling in church. Prayer can also be an act, or even a performance, so long as it's done for the glory of God. Prayer can mean asking what Jesus really would do to help those in need and going out there and doing it in His place. I want to make my church a place where this type of prayer is offered up as readily as any other, a place where we pray not only with our mouths but also with our bodies, our souls."

What touched me so much was not simply the sentiment but the way I could tell he had adapted lessons learned with us at José's Home. I cannot tell you whether any of this was conscious or not, if this was a manipulative, albeit clever, way of convincing me to visit or if these words were really the ethos he hoped to live by. Regardless, they touched me deeply.

Twice a month, the seminary held an administrative meeting. Because there were only five of us who taught there, these tended to be somewhat informal, a place for us to discuss student development without being overheard in the dining hall. Financial and organizational disputes occasionally arose, but I tended to leave the instructors alone and they, in turn, were more or less content with how the institution was run. Because of our collegial working relationship, I expected little pushback when I brought up the idea of taking the entire seminary, or at least everyone interested, north for the protests.

"No," said Father Amalio. "I don't know where you came up with this crazy idea, but no."

"Let's not be so hasty," said Father William, stroking his beard. "Perhaps there's more to it than he's said so far."

"The interruption to my classes would be unconscionable," said Father Renaldo. "Think of the students' development."

"Time is the most limited of all resources," said Father Amalio. "And time spent outside the seminary is time that can never be recovered."

"I would like to say yes, my friend," said Father Patrice. "But I don't think now is the right time. Maybe in a few years, when we've more fully considered the ramifications. But let's slow down before jumping into politics like this."

Our discussion went on for quite a while. I didn't try to defend the idea. It seemed clear to me almost immediately that doing so would be pointless. Instead, I invoked the privilege I had as seminary rector, a privilege I had scarcely used during all my years in charge, and said, "This is not up for discussion. We will adjust schedules and make allowances for students who are interested. No one in this room will be forced to attend, but students will be granted the option. This is final." With that, I ended the meeting— in retrospect, perhaps more abruptly than I should have, but I felt strongly that my decision was righteous and that dragging things out would only cause more discontent.

In the end, the only other priest who went with us was Father Patrice, but I was accompanied by every student in the seminary save a pair whose health would not permit camping during frigid winter nights. We would leave the day after the Feast of the Holy Innocents and planned on staying only until after Epiphany, little more than a week later. It would be a brief interlude, an extended field trip, really, and the novices would return with experience about the world under their belts and a better understanding of the relationship between faith and praxis. While the other priests grumbled all the way through our preparations, I felt confident that in time they would come to see why this was so important, or at the very least would hold no grudge about the matter. Some have observed that I am, on occasion, a poor judge of character.

During the weeks leading up to our trip, I sensed a change in our novices, an extra skip in their step and fervor in their prayers. I cautioned everyone not to become too excited, but seminary life was so simple and repetitive that any alteration was greeted like a new friend. When asked by some novices what I thought would happen, I told them not much. We would perhaps shout slogans, put our bodies directly in the way of something evil, but it would not be dangerous. I should have paid much more attention to the news reports about the size of the protests, as I arrived completely unprepared for what awaited us.

JOSHUA WHITEHURST

My boss swore I would lose my job if the Shell arrangement fell apart. I'm not saying that means I'm not complicit, I'm just saying that I was under the gun the entire time I was there. Particularly frustrating was that one of the reasons I'd gone into research had been to avoid any sort of guilt about what I was up to, hoping the distance between my efforts and Parker & Mullins's actions could keep me from caring what I was involved with. I was there to pay off my student loans, drive a nice car, and buy some tailored suits for when I went out, not to attack a bunch of Native Americans trying to defend their land. I don't want to pretend I was unaware of what we were doing, that I didn't take part in meetings where we brainstormed ways to crush the protesters. I arrived at work each morning filled with anxiety and frustration, hoping I might be moved onto something else or that Shell might end our contract altogether. But I have to admit, I did still come in on time every day, doing my job whether I found it distasteful or not.

At first, Gabriel's involvement made it easier. A little bit of me still wanted to punish him for leaving me how he did, and when I had no more will to keep working, I imagined every one of those protesters as him, hundreds of Gabriels who needed to face some consequences. But those little rushes of motivation only did so much, and when I watched videos and saw the real faces of those miserable men and women still standing, month after month, in protest, I felt terrible. My anger toward Gabriel ran out of fuel, and the campaign against them just wouldn't end.

Shell was asking us for something far grander than what was spelled out in their official contract: they wanted us to bend the law, and really the world itself, to their will. Our goal was to win, and to achieve this aim, we had to be willing to do whatever it took, with no time spent on ethical considerations. Any corporate attorney worth their salary knows that the law isn't a set of statutes decided on by Congress, it's what you can get away with. My boss wanted me on the case because I'd already proven myself a master of loopholes, and over and over, it was up to me to identify how to go one step further than we had before.

I was on the committee who chose the "security firm" Shell went with, a paramilitary group known as Crimson Scorpion composed primarily of ex–police officers and dishonorably discharged military veterans who couldn't find other work. When they asked about using high–powered water cannons on the protesters, I was the one who had to assure them of the legality. Trained dogs to bite the protesters standing in the way of our trucks? Precedent showed there was no way they'd be prosecuted, for pepper spray or stun guns, rubber bullets or riot sticks. It was *my* job to let them know that, short of outright murder, no amount of violence would result in prosecution. And even murder wasn't a sure thing.

Then there was the "legitimate" law enforcement. I read up on strike-breaking tactics, and our team used my findings to write and send guides to the local police departments. Soon, the sheriff was arresting and strip-searching as many protesters as he could, leaving them naked and shivering in cold jail cells. The goal—straight out of our playbook—was to humiliate them, to demoralize the cause.

On social media, we employed Russian trolls to question the protesters' every word and action, turning the slightest gaffe into a scandal. I had to spearhead a more localized smear campaign, leaking dirt on prominent protesters—including Gabriel—to the press. By this point, my generalized anxiety about my role meant racing through Xanax and Klonopin prescriptions just to get through the day, but I never had the nerve to suggest changing tactics. I also never outed Gabriel, since that would have been going above and beyond my professional duties in an especially gross way, even though at times, particularly at the beginning, I was sorely tempted. Who knows, it probably would've been self-sabotage as much as anything.

In any case, the press ate it all up, loved changing the story from "do-gooders fight against big corporation" to "criminal protesters think they're so much better than us." We knew there was no way to make Shell look good, so instead, we tried to make both sides look equally bad. After all, if the protesters were a bunch of rabid hippy communists, then who could say who the real villain was?

FR. MICHAEL CARTER

The most important area of the protest was a Maginot Line at the rig itself, maybe fifty or so people standing proudly in the way of tanker trucks parked outside the compound's razor-wire fences. There around the clock, they wore coats and woolen hats, heavy boots and scarfs, as if headed for a day of skiing on the nearby slopes. The cold up there felt worse than the thermometer implied because of the inactivity, hours spent shivering in place.

The camp itself was roughly a mile farther and much larger, a patchwork of colorful tents located outside the San Ildefonso Pueblo. Sitting atop the snow-sprinkled plain were teepees and trailers and portable toilets, cars parked in every direction, horses milling about the des-iccated grass. Driving behind us on the dirt road to the clearing was a pair of pickup trucks loaded down with palettes of water and food.

"It's Standing Rock all over again," one of the novices observed, and at first I was inclined to agree. Of course, I had never been there in person, but I had seen news cover-age of that ultimately unsuccessful campaign. But before we had even stepped out of the van, I realized there was a crucial difference. The muddy road we'd driven in on literally split the camp into two factions, with hundreds of tents on either side.

It did not take long to find Gabriel. A novice asked one of the people who greeted us, and she pointed us toward a small navy-blue tent bordering that odd road. Someone, perhaps Gabriel, had taped a small white cross above its entrance. Not fifty feet away was a much larger tent—the type that might be used for an outdoor wedding—with a ten-foot wooden cross standing on one side and a lectern and makeshift altar on the other. Gabriel stood next to the lectern, talking to two men. When he saw us, he broke away.

"You made it," he said. "I know you said you'd come, but I didn't really believe it. Seeing you here, it's surreal."

"I have always been a man of my word," I said.

"You have, you have," he said. "I just can't believe it, is all."

He seemed a little delirious to me, but of course I had not seen him in a long time. I introduced my novices and asked where we might set down our tents.

"Oh, anywhere," he said. "Anywhere that doesn't seem like it's in the way and that's on this side of the road."

"Yes, the road. I was wondering about that. Is there—"

"Don't worry about the road," he interrupted. "It'll all be sorted soon. Just get yourselves set up, and we'll talk later."

We pitched our tents and lugged supplies to the commissary. There were two commissaries, two restrooms areas, in fact two of most everything the camp might need, the halves obstinately mirroring each other. I began asking around.

One of the cooks, a young man from Albuquerque named Henry, told me his version.

"It's about Gabriel," he said. "Well sort of."

"The road?"

"All of it. The road, the two camps. The whole thing."

"I see," I said, though I did not. "So he has proven a divisive leader?"

"Well, that's the problem, right? I mean, the tribal leadership says he shouldn't be a leader at all, and they've got a point. But like, I heard about this whole thing 'cause of him, and so did a lotta folks. He's on the news like every day, talking about the cause, fund-raising for supplies. He's really trying."

By the time we finished setting up, the sun had almost departed, and it had started snowing. My old legs ached with the cold as I made my way to Gabriel's tent, feeling newly uncertain why I'd come. Though I was barely past my sixtieth birthday, I felt old, exhausted. Gabriel's letters had assured me of a cooperative atmosphere. He had made it sound like a utopia, where people shared work and supplies to support a well-intentioned cause. Walking the grounds and speaking with people, I had found frustration and exasperation. Relations between the two halves of the camp had deteriorated to the point of almost non-existence. One side was largely Native American, with groups from all eight of the northern pueblos, plus Apache, Zuni, Navajo, Comanche, and others from around the state and beyond. The opposite side was largely Hispanic and Anglo, members of Gabriel's church or people who had come because of what he'd said on television, on the radio, and on the internet.

We sat on a tarp, eating a simple meal of beans and tortillas. It was just the two of us, and Gabriel seemed in high spirits, his sweet, almost perfumed smell contrasting with the dirt and grime all around us. He was more interested in asking about the seminary and me than about the present situation. When I finally pressed him about the split camps, he said, "Well it wasn't my idea, if that's what you've heard. It was the Church."

"Your church? I don't understand."

"No, yours. The Catholic Church. I guess they're jealous or some nonsense. Someone over there seems to carry a real grudge."

It took me a few seconds to gather myself for a response. "I'm ... unfamiliar with the situation."

"The Church told the tribes that I'm some dangerous heretic trying to ruin their plans."

"How do you know this?"

"Oh, no one will say it, but it's happening. They're good people, and most are good believers, so if the Church tells them something they'll listen, even if it's crazy. Even if it makes no sense."

"Why? I don't understand the logic," I said.

"Exactly! They never leave me alone. I thought maybe I'd get a break from it up here, but it's worse than before."

"I heard there were some ... disputes over leadership," I said, trying to calm him down and broach the subject from another angle.

"And who do you think started those rumors? When I first arrived, the Native protesters were grateful for the help. Then, overnight, it was like someone poisoned their minds. I heard priests from nearby were telling them I should return to Albuquerque, I'd 'done enough damage,' as if I were trying to sabotage their efforts. Not that you see those priests at the drill. No, they just come here, say a few prayers, then go back to their cozy churches."

"So the Native Americans, they've asked you to leave?"

"Not officially. Some members of the tribal council have spoken with me. Some have asked me to stay and some have ... had less kind words. But with you here, maybe that nonsense will dry up."

"What difference do we make? We come here in no official capacity."

"But you're still Jesuits. You're still a priest, and everyone who sees you knows that. This makes the Church's actions against me much more difficult."

"I see." Unable to think of anything else to say, I made an excuse to leave.

I felt disappointed: in him, for using me in these internecine politics, and with myself, for being so easily duped. I spent the next day wandering the other side of the camp. People did seem surprised by my presence, and there was some genuine religious discord between the groups. But this played only a small part. Something about the way Gabriel had arrived, ready to "save" the locals, sat wrong with many of the Native people I spoke with. They felt he had done little to integrate with them, had maintained an outsider's viewpoint by trying to take charge, whereas they were developing a less centralized, more egalitarian approach.

The novices and I spent most of our days protesting at the drill, which left us a lot of time to talk. I learned about the people who had been imprisoned, that Gabriel himself had been arrested, though due to his notoriety, he had been released after only two weeks. The police and state troopers threatened us, and I did my best to shield myself when they attacked us with dogs. One of the novices required stitches, and a few asked, and were of course allowed, to return to the seminary. I did my best to make it through the icy water they sprayed at us on freezing mornings and warmed myself by the campfire later. I was only bruised, but several protesters caught pneumonia.

Through it all, the internal division remained—and if I could see it, then I was certain the police could as well. It seemed more likely that the police had manipulated local priests into speaking against Gabriel, rather than shadowy figures in the archbishop's office. Where Gabriel saw conspiracies, I saw law enforcement. The problem was that while creating division is easy, unifying people is difficult, sometimes impossible.

I told Gabriel my thoughts, as clearly and bluntly as I could, hoping he would humble himself before the tribal council instead of allowing the police to continue sowing discord.

"You're right, you're right," he said. "But it'll be better soon. I think everyone needs a bit of a break. Stay for Epiphany and you'll see."

"I don't think you can wait," I told him.

"I'm not waiting," he said. "It's just that these things have to be done right, at the right time."

I seemed to be the last one in camp to hear about it: on the day of Epiphany, there was going to be a dance. A troupe from Taos or thereabouts was going to perform. Everyone gathered around a dirt stage in the center of the camp. There were a few hundred of us, though of course some needed to stay at the drill, so despite the notoriety that came later, there were not as many witnesses as you might have expected. Nevertheless, there was a carnivalesque atmosphere. Members of Gabriel's church brought truckloads of food from Albuquerque. I stood with Father Patrice near the front.

Around noon, storm clouds started forming in the distance, and the dance began. A man in a wide-brimmed hat held aloft a statue of Christ, one of the crude wooden types the locals call bultos, and walked with it in front of two lines of colorfully dressed dancers. Each one wore a miterlike headdress, ornately designed in red, black, white, and turquoise. Ribbons streamed down the back, and black fringe and large kerchiefs obscured the front, so you couldn't see any of the dancers' faces. They each carried a rattle in one hand and, in the other, a three-pronged trident, shaking both in rhythm to a guitar and violin, the same short melody over and over again as they slowly made their way to the makeshift stage. At the back of the procession walked a young girl dressed in a white dress and puffy coat, a man wearing a crown, a bull or buffalo creature walking with a pair of huge canes, and two hideous figures wearing repurposed Frankenstein and Medusa masks and holding whips. I struggled to grasp this arcane symbolism.

"Have you ever seen something like this before?" I asked Father Patrice.

"Matachines," he said, as if this were explanation enough.

I spotted Gabriel on the other side of the road, watching the performance as if there would be a test on it later. As the dancers weaved in distinctive patterns, one of the masked figures broke away to taunt the audience and the other dancers. I couldn't understand what they said, but one of them lewdly bared his backside, and the other stole a boy's shoes and threw them into the audience. Yet some of the main dancers wore capes with the image of the Virgin of Guadalupe and other saints.

"I don't understand," I said to Father Patrice. "Is this a Christian dance, or is this pagan?"

He shrugged.

"And are the dancers Native American or Hispanic?"

"I don't know," said Father Patrice. "Both, probably. Genízaro. Just enjoy the show."

So I did. And I must admit, as the dancers' capes spun in the air behind them, I lost myself in the movements. When they formed into a cross, I felt touched by this display of devotion. But soon afterward, I was shocked by the dancer in the Medusa mask performing a ritualized castration of the bull character, complete with fake testicles.

All of this seemed to be building toward a marriage of sorts, between the man in the crown and the little girl. She danced toward him, then they made some elaborate movements I could not decipher. When she took and then returned his trident and rattle, the man in the Frankenstein mask yelled, "Engáñalo, mi'jita."

"Who are they," I asked Father Patrice, "and what is he saying?"

"She's Malinche, and the Virgin Mary. He's Montezuma, and the man is yelling 'deceive him' or 'cheat him,' something like that."

"I see," I said, though I didn't, not at all. The rest of the audience seemed to be having fun. They broke out in cheers and applause. I watched both sides of the camp intermingle as they enjoyed the same spectacle. As the music crescendoed, the dancers bowed, and the one in the Frankenstein mask took it off, revealing ... Gabriel himself. The audience broke out in another hearty round of applause.

By then the entire sky was gray. Small hailstones and cold rain began sprinkling the camp. With all eyes on him, Gabriel pointed to the northeast, toward the oil rig. We all turned, and a moment later, a colossal bolt of lightning struck right where he had pointed.

There was a long, strange pause.

Then, thunder shook the ground, and the drill exploded, igniting the hilltop.

Cheers erupted across the campsite.

And with a naturalness that made it seem planned, contemporary dance music began playing beneath the church tent. Though wet and muddy, campers celebrated well into the night. Of course, the seminarians and I did not dance, but we were nonetheless elated. The divided camp suddenly seemed unified. We spoke with protesters and watched the dancing until late into the night, and when we departed the next day, I left with the conviction that I'd fulfilled God's purpose for our trip: to bear witness to that night. Was it a miracle we witnessed? Well, Gabriel invoked lightning, and the bolt arrived as called, to smite his enemies. Make of that what you will.

ANNA FISHEL

Lightning didn't strike the fracking drill. Trust me, I was there, standing in plain sight of that ugly tower. I volunteered to stay there during the dancing and festivities, to be part of the skeleton crew of protesters needed to continue blocking the trucks. Storm clouds filled the horizon in every direction, but no one expected things to go nuts like they did.

And no, I didn't say there was no lightning, just that it didn't strike the drill, which is how so many who weren't actually there told things later, even after I corrected them. A horrible boom, like a thousand gunshots, pierced the air, and a white light arced down from the heavens into a nearby storage tank bigger than an SUV. The tank launched into the air toward the center of the drill. When it smashed into those thick metal bars, the tank exploded in a blaze of blue-white flames, launching burning shrapnel in every direction. This ignited a dozen other parts of the rig, while the drill itself began to topple backwards, thankfully away from us. Just like that, that terrible machine we'd spent so long crusading against was destroyed.

The surreal nature of the catastrophe made it feel almost destined or somehow planned. I still have nightmares about that evening, the screeching of the tower's legs giving way, the chain of small explosions that made me worry the next one would take us out too. But no one was killed, and injuries were minor—somehow all the workers inside had been gone. It was like God's hand protected us.

When I arrived at the main camp, the party had already started. I practically cried when I saw so many folks dancing together, eating together, laughing together. That probably sounds melodramatic, but after what I'd just witnessed, and the months of divisiveness that had come before, it was almost too much to handle. The festivities continued late into the night, but I returned to my tent and collapsed.

Folks talk about the miracle of the lightning and say that, just like that, we won. Again, I want to put those rumors to rest. The very next day, after most of the camp had recovered from the night before, I sat with Father Gabriel in his tent, watching streaming video of firefighters sifting through the ashes and mangled metal of the drill site. I asked him what he thought, and he said, "It's nice, but it's not over."

"What do you mean?"

"They'll build another drill and be back at it in six months And if we blow it up again, they'll build another one."

"God will show us a way," I said. "He sent the lightning."

"Yes. Maybe."

I was tired. My enthusiasm for the protest had been running on fumes. I wanted to return home, to my cozy office with the coffeepot always twenty feet away. I couldn't do another six months of porta-potties and leaky tents and a stinky old sleeping bag. I think Father Gabriel saw it in my face.

"Maybe it's time we try something different," he said. "I spent the evening talking to the council, and they have new ideas that might be worth trying. Ideas that don't involve waiting in the cold."

Father Gabriel and I spent the next few days in discussion with the tribal council. The idea that eventually bore fruit came from a Cochiti Pueblo lawyer who'd watched a similar fight play out in Mora, a small town farther north. He realized that while Española proper had agreed to the fracking, the actual hilltop the drill had been built on was not within the city's boundaries—technically, it belonged to the more liberal and sympathetic Santa Fe County. So he proposed repetitioning at the county level. The council also decided that while Father Gabriel would continue fund-raising and might speak to the media for that purpose, from then on the council would be the ones making all the decisions. Father Gabriel seemed as happy about this as anyone.

It was no longer necessary to keep bodies between oil tankers and the drill, and the campsite disbanded by the end of the week. I hung around with Father Gabriel until nearly everyone else had disappeared, cleaning and listening to grumbling arguments about who should be responsible for restoring the land that the camp had basically demolished, but soon I was back home in Albuquerque.

Suddenly my tiny house, with its cramped kitchen I'd always hated, felt like a palatial estate. But any sudden noise, from the floorboards creaking to the radiator banging, made me jump, though generally the house felt too quiet. I started leaving the television on in the background. I considered adopting a pet but worried about what I'd do if another long campaign started and decided I'd better not. Father Gabriel told me to take some time off, but I found myself bored. I headed back to Our Lady of Guadalupe after a few days, to try and catch up on the mountain of accounting and logistical issues I'd let slide.

For a couple of weeks, things seemed normal, the church returning to its old rhythms, along with the small pleasures and irritations of work I'd missed so very much. It wasn't perfect, but I think I would've been happy for years of that.

Father Gabriel, on the other hand, seemed a bit off. Sunday Mass had always been the "prime-time show," as he'd jokingly referred to it. Before Española, he appeared effortless during his sermons, though I knew how hard he worked on them, the stress he felt about getting things just right. Back then, we'd had a routine. He'd pace around the office and adjoining hallways, murmuring the words of his upcoming sermon, reading them off freshly printed pages, crossing things out and revising as he walked. I'd be at the front desk drinking coffee and speaking with any parishioners who came by, letting them know he was too busy to see them until after Mass.

Once we got back from the protest, he still delivered excellent sermons, but they didn't seem to keep his interest. He began dropping vague hints about the future, "big changes" coming for the church and his hopes that "we'd be up for it." I worried another campaign like the Shell protest might be on the horizon. I wish I'd been right.

ADRIANA COOK

I am here in my official capacity as an agent of the Federal Bureau of Investigation. As such, I hope you don't expect me to release any information that might be classified. However, I have been told to coopcrate, within reason, with your own investigation into Mr. Gabriel Romero, and I will do my best to remain forthcoming about anything I deem relevant. Please tell me if you need further clarification about anything I say.

My background is certainly unclassified, but I have no desire to go into great detail. Suffice it to say, I majored in criminal justice in college, then worked as a municipal police officer for seven years, after which I attended Quantico. At the time I was assigned to gather information on Mr. Romero, I had been working at the Bureau for five years.

I understand there are certain conspiracy theories surrounding the Bureau's investigation into Mr. Romero's activities. Trust me, we pay attention to all corners of the internet, from 4chan to the Daily Stormer, and are fully aware of what's said. I feel it's only responsible for me to refute the idea that we became interested in him due to internal church politics. We take careful note of all prominent individuals involved in antigovernmental activities, including, but not limited to, Antifa, certain neo-Nazi cells, Black Lives Matter, Al-Qaeda, ISIS, Juggalos, and many others. This is standard operating procedure that predates the Cold War. Due to past criticism of the Bureau for overreaching its jurisdictional bounds, in the vast majority of cases, we only monitor activity. When we do need to act, we try to use a light touch. Our resources are limited, and we need to prioritize high-risk and combative individuals. I can neither confirm nor deny that Mr. Romero was such an individual.

One thing I can say is that the easiest way for a person on our radar to come under active investigation is the purchase of a large amount of explosives or material that could be converted into explosives. We treat the threat of domestic terrorism very seriously, and the handling of such materials, regardless of intent, is a red flag. While the mixing of binary explosive components for personal, nonbusiness use is legal, the federal explosive laws, as amended by the Safe Explosives Act, prohibit anyone other than an ATF licensee from knowingly transporting, shipping, causing to be transported, or receiving explosive materials. Persons not holding a current ATF explosives license may not transport or ship explosive materials, even within their state of residence. This can be an extremely difficult law to enforce, but an investigation into such an offense can be used to obtain warrants.

While I am prohibited from fully disclosing details about the incident that occurred at the Shell fracking site, I can say that chemical analysis of the area found trace residue of a military-grade explosive compound called cyclotrimethylenetrinitramine, or RDX, in the remains of a disused water canister. This in no way changes the fact that investigators also found localized damage that included melting and deformation indicative of a lightning strike. Due to the complexity of the fire, with multiple accelerants present at the fracking site, a definitive cause for the fire could not be determined.

Another thing I am permitted to say is that Mr. Romero and his known associates remained persons of interest following this incident. However, due to circumstances I'm sure you're familiar with, we had difficulty keeping close surveillance on him in the following years. Consequently, much of our information about this period is apocryphal.

ISABEL ROMERO

I never went to his protests, either in town or up north. I didn't want to encourage him. Everyone knows la policia will kill you for looking at them the wrong way, let alone standing in the way of gringos stealing oil. I guess Mamá was looking down on him from on high, acting as his guardian angel, because no one shot him. And while I read that he was arrested, and it worried me sick, soon enough he was back out and talking to Action Seven News like nothing happened.

I like to think maybe my prayers helped a little too. Every day he was up there I said un rosario. When the weather was nice, I would say it outside, sitting on a plastic lawn chair in the garden. I kept tending those plants for whenever Gabito might return, and when it was too cold, I said my rosario inside by the stove. I don't know why I did it, but it calmed me. I started looking forward to passing those beads through my fingers, the way the words lost meaning, then gained an almost transcendent meaning, and then lost it again over the course of those repetitions. When I was little, I only ever said el rosario como castigo, when the priest or Mamá made me and I was too afraid not to. The last time I'd said one before Gabito left town, I was thirteen, right before realizing that no one, not Mamá or the priest or anyone else, could tell whether I'd said a word of it or not. Then suddenly I understood that you could lie not just to people, but to Dios, and never be punished. Your hair wouldn't fall out and your forehead wouldn't grow horns, your clothes wouldn't suddenly get itchy or stop fitting. Nothing would change. So I figured, why not lie?

But while Gabito was gone, I said my rosarios. I said them in English and in Spanish, and I didn't lie to Dios anymore. I couldn't, even if I wasn't sure I believed in Him. And my son did come back, and that was good enough for me.

I saw him just a few times, at awkward dinners with Evelyn where we did our best to pretend her stroke never happened. Gabriel seemed withdrawn and disinterested. I asked if he was excited to be back in Albuquerque, and he said, "Sure. I guess." He didn't even look up from his food. We mostly made small talk, but even this was a strain.

I still felt awkward in his church, but I wanted to see him. We'd grown so distant that I didn't know how to talk to him anymore, but at least I could watch him from the sidelines. I sat in the back pews, leaving early so as not to run into him in the lobby. He ecstatically bounced around the stage, giving parishioners a full-on show like no priest I'd ever seen before. He said he was so glad to be back home in Albuquerque, in his querencia, where faith wasn't just a relic of the past, it was alive. You could see smiles all around the church, the room filled with goodwill and approval. A few days later, I'd see him again at dinner and his eyes would be dead and vacant. He'd hunch over his meal with the weariness of a seventy-year-old man.

I should've reached out to him, but I just didn't know how, so instead I kept watching and wondering, thinking maybe he needed Prozac or a therapist or something. A few days off, maybe. But I never said anything. After all, he seemed so strong in church, in the interviews he gave online, in the news—so what if I was wrong? I guess I was afraid that if I tried to really talk to him, I'd push him away even more, and now that it was just me, with no other family or boyfriend and not even much contact with my friends anymore, losing him was what I feared the most.

One day I got home from work and it was still light out. I went to the backyard to water the garden before heating up dinner, and I saw it had been ransacked. At least, that's what I thought at first. Pero, what really happened was that it had been harvested, leaves and petals and stamens all plucked and removed. Back in the house, I found a small note on the kitchen table saying, "Thanks, Mom," and nothing else.

When I went to Mass at Our Lady of Guadalupe the next day and saw Padre Quintana was officiating, rather than Gabito, I didn't need to be told the rest. Soon it was all anyone could talk about: Gabriel had disappeared.

ANNA FISHEL

A few months after the protest, I was working on a Saturday morning and still trying to put the church's accounts back in order. The phone rang, and on the other end was what sounded like a woman's voice, asking for Father Gabriel. I rarely connected people with him directly, particularly on Saturdays when he was busy getting his Sunday sermon ready, so I asked the caller what I could help her with.

"Then can you be sure to deliver this message to him?" she said.

"Sure. Who may I ask is calling?"

"Please tell Gabriel that his absence from *any* LGBTQIA+ events in town has been noted by many, and the fact that his supposedly 'progressive' church has completely ignored any event focused on the rights of our community has made many activists unhappy."

"Who is this?"

"Please also tell Gabriel that we find his refusal to come out of the closet, or even acknowledge us publicly, particularly ironic given his past relationship with a man in college, a quite public relationship that lasted for years. We find it galling that he's become complicit in the oppression of his own people."

"Excuse me, but who are you and—"

"And finally, please tell Gabriel that we want to see him—and your church—next Wednesday at the anti-LGBTQIA+ adoption policy protest, and that if he isn't there, we will be forced to take action. Outing a closeted person against their will isn't something we want to do, nor is it something we take lightly, but he and your church have been silent for so long that this is our only option. Thank you and goodbye." With that, she hung up.

I'd heard rumors about Gabriel's past. How could I not? I was around the church all the time, and if anyone likes gossiping, it's church folks. I never really thought too much of it, though, both because they were rumors and because if they were true ... then so what? I guess it would've been a little weird if Father Gabriel hadn't had some sort of relationship before becoming a priest, not that that was any of my business. But I could see how *some* people might have strong opinions about it, so I went to tell Gabriel right away.

"I see," he said. He looked concerned, though not entirely surprised.

"So what're you going to do?" I asked him. "It's too late to put the event in this week's bulletin, but you can mention it at the end of Mass. Or, I don't know, do you want to talk about this?"

"No, I just ... I'll have to think about it."

"You know, everyone here will support you," I said. I didn't want to influence his decision, because it seemed so personal, but I wanted to at least say that much.

"Thanks for that," he said, though he seemed distracted. "It means a lot. Now I need to get back to preparing my sermon for tomorrow."

That was the conversation I kept replaying in my head over the next few years. I knew I should've said more, should've told him that any parishioners who didn't accept him weren't worth having around anyhow. But he never did like to explain himself. Father Manuel said I shouldn't blame myself, that everyone has their own journey, their own path to God, and it's foolishness to try and dwell on something that's in the past. But still, I couldn't help but wonder if there was something I could've done to change the way things turned out.

The next morning, he wasn't in the office when I got there a couple hours before Mass. He wasn't anywhere in the building. After thirty minutes, I went to the parking lot and saw his car was missing, at which point I started to panic, my stomach dropping like when you're on a roller coaster. I unlocked the door to his room with the building's master key and peered inside. For a moment it felt invasive, but once I saw the stripped room, I stopped worrying about that. His sheets had been taken off the bed and neatly folded, papers on his desk stacked to one side. Not a speck of dust was visible, and I knew how bad Gabriel usually was about cleaning. I felt an intense sadness well up in me, the type that makes you nearly throw up. I lay down on his mattress for a few minutes. I didn't really have the time to spare, but I couldn't bring myself to get back up.

Once I could move again, I found an envelope on his dresser with my name on it. I grabbed it, then called Father Manuel and told him everything. Mass was in thirty minutes, and he'd have to figure something out.

Yes, I saved my letter. This has kind of opened up old wounds, though, and well, I ... here, why don't you just read it yourself.

Dear Anna,

First, I would like to remove any possible suspense and tell you that it's with the utmost regret that I'm leaving Our Lady of Guadalupe Church. Even before we returned to Albuquerque, I'd been questioning my path. I've never quite known what to make of priesthood, which is probably why I've never quite been a priest. Time and again, I find I'm either in the wrong or simply uncomfortable when I take on the mantle of leadership. I'm not even certain what's best for myself.

I hope you understand that none of this is because of you. Like Peter was to Jesus, you have been the rock I've built my church upon, and all the success Our Lady of Guadalupe has seen is due more to your effort than anyone else's. My hope is that you and Manny continue growing this wonderful community I've been blessed to be a part of.

Christ's grace and mercy be upon us both,
—Gabriel Romero

We carried on without him, but there was a wound within the church, a feeling of betrayal that lingered for a very long time. Even I felt betrayed. But then, I still had my job, and Father Manuel still gave Mass every week, and life moved on. No one ever called again or tried to out him to the media or anything like that. Maybe they would've if he'd stayed, maybe they felt too ashamed once they heard he'd left, but then again … who knows.

Our Lady of Guadalupe lost its magic, and while I didn't lose my faith, it sort of went on the back burner. I adopted a pit bull from the pound, and giving him the attention he deserved took up a lot of my time. I don't really know what else to say about that period. I don't like thinking about it. Though I dunno, talking to you about all this, how much I missed him then, how much more I miss him now … I think I'll need a minute before we continue.

JOSHUA WHITEHURST

Here's what no one remembers about the protest: until its spectacular conclusion, our campaign worked. Now people celebrate it as one of the most successful protests in recent history, but that only happened in retrospect. At the time, they'd begun infighting, dividing themselves between Gabriel's group and the Native protesters in a series of events even Parker & Mullins couldn't have foreseen. New protesters were no longer coming in to replace those worn out from months of abuse, and the movement was almost out of money after donations began drying up due to our "news" stories. But then Gabriel blew the whole fucking thing up.

The entire office was in an uproar, scrambling to try and salvage a win for our client. I was both horrified and, strangely, kind of exhilarated. I was pretty sure I was going to lose my job, but I'd stopped really caring about that. I guess I'd realized my soul—and I know, you must think it's ironic I'd use that word—was worth more to me than the security of a cushy paycheck or my fascist boss's approval. Shell retained our services for a few more weeks, looked into fighting Santa Fe County's fracking ban, but at a certain point, they decided that would just be throwing good money after bad. Even for Parker & Mullins, this was the loss of a huge client. My boss was true to her word, and I was one of the first people they laid off.

Suddenly I had a lot of free time on my hands. I found myself spending far more hours than I probably should've looking into that lightning strike. I read about the chances of lightning striking a person, a building, an oil rig, and found that in all these cases, they were not small … but they were also far from large. The chance of it happening at an exactly predicted time and place was essentially zero, even in a storm. I watched all the crappy cell phone footage I could find, analyzing every angle, and that led me to Reddit threads about the event, which led me to more general Reddit threads about Gabriel. Soon enough, I found myself on other websites and conspiracy pages that tried to make sense of his miracles. I kept thinking of all the magic tricks he used to do during college. He'd been good, but not that good. I started to think that there had to be something more to all of this, particularly that lightning strike, which seemed inexplicable.

Even Shell's insurance claim officially listed the ultimate cause of destruction as an "act of God." We use that phrase every day, even in the law, but mostly we don't believe in any of it. I know it sounds strange, but if I hadn't had a previous relationship with Gabriel, I probably wouldn't have believed any of it either. I never really had before. But it was Gabriel, and … I won't pretend I found faith just then, but I did find something: questions that I didn't have answers for—and that no one else seemed to have answers for either.

* * *

It was late afternoon on a Saturday when I saw him again. I heard knocking on my apartment door and opened it to find Gabriel staring at me, concern and maybe even panic written all over his face. I think I did a double take, because I'd been reading about him just hours earlier, and the chances of him appearing at my door like that seemed roughly on par with the chances of that lightning strike.

"Hey Josh, how've you been?" he said. "I know this is weird and all, but I just thought 'who do I know who lives around here?' and, hey, I've never come to visit you, even though we both live in town, and so I thought I'd say hey."

"Uhh, hi," I said. "It's, well, it's nice to see you. Do you want to come inside?" I hadn't known, until he was literally standing in front of me, exactly how I would feel if I saw him. Whether there might be some lingering anger I wouldn't be able to repress, whether I would surprise even myself and greet him with a punch. Instead, what I felt was relief. It was good to see him again. It was natural. Life might somehow be getting back on track.

"Thanks so much. I really appreciate you inviting me in, really."

As he walked inside, I noticed a bandage on his hand, like he'd had during our fight in college. I offered him a drink and a seat, but he could hardly sit still while I made G&Ts in the kitchen.

"So, well, what are you doing here?" I asked, joining him on the couch. "I mean, what's crazy about you showing up like this is … I was just reading about you. Well, not exactly about you but about the lightning strike up at the drill. I have to say, I've been wondering about it for weeks. Like, how did you pull that off?"

"Why does everyone keep asking me things," he snapped, "as if I know all the answers?" After that flash of anger, though, he stopped himself and took a breath.

"I'm sorry, I just ... I'm sorry. I guess I just needed to talk to you. Somebody who really knows me. Somebody who wouldn't ... judge."

"That's ok, don't worry about it," I said. "I was just saying, because of what I'd read, that I've been wondering if it was real. Was it, like, a miracle the way people are saying? I read that Tesla knew a way to call down lightning, and I guess he was in that movie with magicians and—"

"Josh, can we just talk for real for a second here?" Gabriel's mood changed, and he seemed less panicked, more sad. "I just want to talk like friends, without all these questions. Everyone's always asking things of me these days, persecuting me. After everything I've done."

"Sure, I guess. I'm sorry. What do you mean about people persecuting you?"

"Activists, or so they say. I'm complicit, apparently, just because I'm trying to run a church."

"I don't ... I don't quite follow you," I said. "Maybe you can slow down a bit. Catch me up on your life."

"I just can't believe it. I've been fighting injustice since the day I first started preaching, but because I won't stand up for one thing I'm 'complicit.'"

"Complicit?"

"I spend all my time fighting the system from the best vantage point I can, setting up a place where I can help as many people as possible, and yeah, sometimes that means picking fights to stay out of."

"Fights to ... wait, is this because...?" It suddenly dawned on me what he wasn't saying. "Is this because you're gay?"

"Josh, I'm not gay."

"Of course you are."

"I'm not. I'm not saying I'm straight either. I'm a priest. That's my sexuality, if you have to say that I have one. I'm celibate and sworn to God."

"I can't believe what I'm hearing. You came all the way over to my apartment, after years of silence, just to lie to me in the weirdest, most roundabout way I've ever heard. Just be honest with everyone, Gabriel. You're a gay priest."

He stared down into his lap. "I just … I've been trying to figure out where I am in all of this, and I realized long ago that what I love most of all is God. And spreading the word of God. And His love. And … you can't do that as a priest and be gay. I'm not saying I wouldn't like to, but no one would listen to me. No one would respect me." He took a deep breath. "I haven't been gay since we broke up. I've sworn myself to the Lord."

"You're married to the Lord now?" It was all so ridiculous, I couldn't help myself. "Is that like being a male nun? Is that like an exclusive thing or is it poly because there're three of Him?"

"Be serious for a moment. Be an adult. That's what being an adult is about, making hard choices, sacrifices. Leaving you behind … it was the hardest choice of all. But it was the one I made. If I were gay, no one would come to Mass. No one would listen to me. It wouldn't matter if I raised Lazarus from the dead—they wouldn't want me."

"That's not true of all Christians," I said. "Maybe the shitty ones, but fuck them anyhow. It's your church, do with it what you want."

"You don't know Christians like I do. You can tell them to kill in God's name, and they won't think twice. But talk about men having sex with men, and that's it.

That's the end. I have to preach about love every week, every day, because that's what's hard for these people. Hating is so easy. It's too easy. But you have to fight for love every step of the way."

"Does that matter? You know you're a hypocrite, right? I mean, doesn't living life honestly matter more?"

"If it means I have to be lonely to help everyone else live a better life, that's a small sacrifice. I'm hurting no one but myself."

I wanted to tell him that this wasn't true, because it meant I was lonely too, that I'd been lonely for years, but I couldn't make myself say the words. We sat in silence, listening as the loud clanging of the building's radiator kicked on. There didn't seem to be any point in talking. Then I felt his head rest against my shoulder.

"Is it all true?" I asked as quietly as I could.

"Is what true?"

"The miracles. The healings, the flying, the predictions. Did you cause that lightning at the Shell rig? Is any of it true, or is it all just a big trick? A way of convincing them to stay around and listen to you talk about love?"

I could hear his breath next to mine. He still smelled like vanilla, and I couldn't help but picture him beneath his heavy down comforter all those years ago. The weight of his body pressing against me still felt right, still felt both cozy and sexy at the same time.

"Yes," he whispered with not a hint of irony or deceit. "It's true. All of it. I don't understand it. I don't understand why. But it's true."

After a few minutes, he stood up and said he had to leave.

"Will you come back?" I asked.

"To see you?"

"Yes."

"I don't know. Maybe? I don't know."

I stood, thinking that was it, but then he hugged me. The hug lingered, our bodies pushing against each other almost of their own accord, and I thought how strange it was that he still felt the same, even as we'd aged, even after a decade apart. We were still the same two men who'd stayed in bed all day listening to Brahms, skipping class just to spend another hour together. Then I felt the soft touch of his lips on my neck for just a moment. I would replay that in my mind a thousand times before seeing him again.

★ ★ ★

I could think of little else after he left. Just two days later, I tried calling him at his church. The woman who answered asked who I was, and I said I was an old friend who'd seen him on the news and wanted to reconnect. She apologized and said that he'd just disappeared, with no explanation and no way to reach him. Of course he did, I thought. Of course.

The first time Gabriel disappeared, I'd sunk into despair and more or less given up. I never tried looking for him, and it took me forever to move on. This time, I decided I would at least try to find him, even if that proved futile. I went into every online forum that seemed even vaguely interested in him, from the conspiracy nuts to the religious zealots, and began asking people to report anything they could about his whereabouts, no matter how inconsequential.

A week later, I began working at a new law firm, Palmers & Murphy, two blocks from my old office, distinguishable only if you were absolutely committed to finding the differences. But I no longer felt depressed at work, because when I wasn't there, I had a new hobby: collecting stories about my missing ex-boyfriend, trying to piece together his life on the road.

THE DESERT

FIRSTHAND ACCOUNTS OF GABRIEL ROMERO'S FOUR-
YEAR DISAPPEARANCE
[SUPPLEMENTED BY FURTHER INTERVIEWS AND SOLICITED
TESTIMONY]
[Reddit post—/r/Christian - Author: JReilly89]

That day, the sun was burning a hole in the sky. Arizona was always worst in the afternoon, dry and barren even in the city, a parched landscape of endless buildings. As I made my way across a small patch of dirt and dead grass we liked to call a park, all I wanted was an escape from the heat. I briefly sat on a bench beneath the waving branches of a willow tree, but its shade barely helped. Soon, I was desperate enough to go into the cathedral nearby.

It had always been there, or seemed to have, cool stones indifferent to the heat, indifferent to most everything. The area was poor, but the church suggested that perhaps it hadn't always been. I felt drawn to it like light into a black hole, its coolness something I could only dream about given the swirling drama and emotions of the last few years of my life. I remembered going to church when I was young—not this church, another one in another city—and remembered finding solace there.

At first, I was alone in the pew. I listened to the silence, the contrast it offered to the rush of modern life outside. I looked at the statues and the stained glass, images of saints I'd learned as a child but had long since forgotten, scenes and symbols representing a faith that, at that moment, I wished I had. I tried to think of what prayer I might say but could come up with nothing.

I heard quiet footsteps. In the room's meditative stillness, I might not have registered his presence if he hadn't sat down next to me. I turned to look at him, and he was so close I could make out the pores on his face, his stubble turning from black to gray, the wrinkles around his tired eyes.

"May I wash your feet?" He whispered these words so quietly I thought I must have misheard.

I didn't respond, and we sat in silence for a few minutes. Eventually, he repeated it, and this time there was no chance of mishearing: "May I wash your feet?"

I mumbled no and tried with my posture to communicate my discomfort and desire to be left alone.

Slightly louder again, though still barely above a whisper, "May I wash your feet?"

This time he looked at me, stared straight into my eyes, into my soul, his soft brown irises pleading with me to let him do this small, simple act. We were in a church, after all.

"Alright," I said, though I still don't fully know why.

I waited for something to happen. He made no move. Finally, he asked, "Would you mind taking off your socks and shoes?" I looked at him for signs of instability, insanity, but he was calm. Sad, perhaps, but calm and perfectly lucid. Whatever it was that made him ask, he was certain about it, as certain as I was that the cathedral's stones would stay in place rather than rain down on our heads and crush us.

He knelt on the floor next to me, water bottle in hand. I couldn't look at him. I felt shame and revulsion, not for him but for myself. I realized how sweaty and smelly my feet were. I'd stood on them for hours beneath the punishing Arizona sun. I had to close my eyes and pretend I was somewhere else, that I was alone.

The water felt cool on my toes, though he poured only a bit, and his hands caressed my feet in an almost intimate way. At the end, he bent down and kissed them. It felt like a blessing somehow.

He stood up and thanked me. Without looking him in the eyes, I murmured some half-formed response. He left the church as silently as he'd arrived. I stayed seated for ten, fifteen minutes. Longer. I couldn't face the world outside that church, so I stared at the crucifix directly in front of me, hanging heavy on the wall. I thought of how cool my feet felt, except for where his lips had touched. There I felt an oval of heat, a warmth that showed no mark

but has stayed with me ever since. Without knowing why, I found myself crying, and walked home
barefoot.

★ ★ ★

He wrote to me after he left his church, though I could
no longer write back to him, as he never included a return
address, and the postmarks were from all over the country.
There was seemingly little logic to his travels, with letters
appearing from the same location for months, then suddenly
jumping states and arriving from hundreds of miles away,
then back again. However, rarely did the letters feel frantic;
if anything, they seemed more carefully thought over and
crafted than the ones he had sent before. He seemed, for
a period at least, to be at peace, and given the difficulties
I was going through, it was nice to hear from him.

He revisited the protest, defending his tactics while
apologizing for bringing me under "false pretenses."
As I've told you, I had already forgiven him for that,
but it demonstrated one of the ways he seemed to have
changed. Gabriel had always been contrite in what I
would describe as theologically sound ways. He understood that we are all sinners, and he had a desire to
do penance. But his letters showed a willingness to
acknowledge more specific grievances, and that is something I have seen even the most devout men struggle
with. To admit to having done wrong in the abstract
is far easier than admitting to specific wrongdoing, let
alone atoning for it.

★ ★ ★

[Transcription from *Holy or Hoax?:* A History Channel Production]

Well [expletive] yeah I recognized him. My grandma liked to put on the news before dinner, and he was on there like all the time, and he would talk about what the [expletive] pigs were up to and it was like, "Man, that guy's a church dude but he's like talkin back to the Man and stuff." I know my grandma thought he was cute or something and that was way weird, but it was like, who cares because dude is like yelling at the cops. I could get behind that, I mean I *got* that.

So yeah when he was just like walking down the street and I was like, [expletive] man what you doing in Belleville? And he was like, I don't know, what are you doing? And I was like, Ok right, fair 'nough.

So right but the even weirder thing was, like, he looked all dirty and like maybe he was homeless or something, and like he smelled. Real [expletive] bad. But then later I'm eatin' dinner with my grandma, and she's just like askin' what I did that day and I'm tellin' her who I saw, how it was that priest dude and he was like smelly and all, but then like right there behind us on the TV is that same guy at some protest clear across the country. But there on TV he was clean-shaven, wearing a nice suit, and I'm like ok, so what the [expletive] is goin' on?

And my grandma tells me that I'm just dumb, that I'm always makin' stuff up and my brain is all messed up from weed I buy from my boy Derek—oh [expletive], sorry Derek—and I'm like no Grandma, it was him. And she don't believe me but whatever.

So the next day I'm like out with my boys and I see him on the street and I ask him, dead-on, if he's that famous priest guy that was clear across the country last night? And he laughs and I'm like, Dude, are you? Then he says to me, Go in the name of Christ, and I'm like, For real man? And he's like, Oh yeah, so I'm like, Ok, but I didn't tell Grandma nothin' 'cause she'd've just told me I was stupid and [expletive] again.

★ ★ ★

Mostly, he wrote about others. He never told me how he got around, hitchhiking or bus passes or simply walking from town to town, but he largely slept in the houses of generous strangers. Sometimes they were Catholics he met locally, but just as often they were not. Many were lapsed or Jewish or atheist. Some were Muslim, and those he described as being more generous than anyone else when it came to food and accommodations. The only people who tried to convert him or even cared what religion he practiced were the Protestants.

★ ★ ★

Gabito called me on the phone maybe a year after he disappeared. I was so happy to hear from him, I started crying. "Mijo," I said. "It's you. I can't believe it's you."

"It's me, Mom," he said, waiting for me to compose myself. "How have you been?"

"I've been praying for you daily," I said, "like Mamá would've wanted me to. And I've been going to Our Lady of Guadalupe every week. We miss you there."

"Ha-ha, that's great."

"I'm thinking of leaving Kelly's."

"You always say that."

"Yeah, I guess I do," I said. "But maybe I will this time."

"That's great. Hey Mom, I just wanted to say thanks for keeping the garden for me. I'm sorry I didn't say goodbye."

"Oh mijo, of course I kept your garden. And thanks for calling. You're not in some sort of trouble, are you?" Suddenly this call from my self-sufficient little boy seemed strange. Why now?

"No," he said. "I just wanted to call. Make amends a little. You know."

"Where are you?" I asked.

"I'm in San Francisco."

"What are you doing there? Do you need money?"

"I'm doing fine. I'm staying with a man I met on the road. He gave me a ride. I'm just crashing on his couch for a few more days."

"Oh?"

"Yeah. Then up to Portland. A guy here invited me to work on his farm."

"You're going to go work on a farm?"

"It's not like bad farm work. It's a collective. You grow what you eat. It sounds fantastic."

It didn't, but I didn't want to say anything that might annoy him. "You be safe, mijo. Just watch your back while you're up there."

"I'll be perfectly safe. They're great people, I'm sure."

"Why don't you call me when you get up there, just so I know."

"Ha-ha, sure, Mom. Ok I gotta go, my host got a text and I should let him use his phone again."

"Thanks for calling. I love you and miss you. Please tell me when you're safely in Portland," I said. He hung up.

I waited a week, then another. I made sure my phone was always charged, and answered every call even when it looked like a scam. He didn't call, though, and by the end of the month, I stopped waiting. I don't think he meant anything by it, that he was trying to hurt me or was angry. I think he just forgot.

* * *

[Revivalizer: A Forum for Concerned Christians—User Name: Clarence]

I know this must sound weird, but I didn't know he was Catholic. Don't know many of us did, maybe none of us. I certainly wouldn't have shown up if I'd known. But anyhow he was with those revival tent folks. We don't get that many of those things coming around, and so me and my wife Clarice, we went down to see what they had to say. Big white tent, just like they had in the old days, and half a dozen preachers ready to get the crowd all riled up, evangelizing and so forth, which was all good and proper. I didn't like that there was so many folks from the other side of town, but I guess it was ok if they were good, churchgoing folks, as long as they went back when things were done. Clarice, well she was just taken with the Holy Spirit that day and I don't think she even noticed, what with so many Amens and so forth.

I think he came on in the middle. Introduced himself real good, just saying he was Reverend Romero, and I remember thinking he looked real young but he talked on that pulpit like he'd been doing it for years. And then he was telling us how he'd sinned, had done some real big sins for a long time but then he came to the Lord. And there weren't anything flashy to it, just a solid sermon, good message, and so forth. And I don't know if there was supposed to be some sort of business with snakes or healings like people like to talk about, but it was just preaching, and it all seemed pretty proper to me.

It was Clarice who got to talking to him afterwards, hearing how he had been Catholic and so forth. I guess she asked him how he could do it, believe in all those pagan saints and so forth when everyone else out there was just good Christians, and I guess he told her, "It's all the same God." Clarice told me she liked that very much, and so she asked him how he'd come to be with these folks, and he said he wasn't really no Catholic no more, but he wasn't really no Protestant either. "I just like telling people about Christ," he said, and Clarice liked that real good too.

So I guess nobody with the tent really knew who he was or how he got on the program that day, he just kinda snuck on and spoke and they didn't figure it out till later. He didn't seem to have nothing but the shirt on his back, so Clarice asked me if he could stay at our house, you know, just for a couple days. But our house is small and there ain't enough room for Clarice and me, let alone some Catholic bum from out of town.

Can't say I know what he did instead, but I figure somebody put him up and so forth, and anyhow it weren't our concern. I saw this here post about him and thought I should make an account to say what I remembered, though I know it ain't much.

★ ★ ★

He spent a few weeks picking fruit in California and said he had never been so tired in his life. Too tired even to pray.

★ ★ ★

I had no particular methodology, I just put out feelers everywhere I could think of online. Google Alerts tended to come in bursts, attached to a teacher's union protest in Missouri or a coal miner's strike in West Virginia. Then, after a couple weeks or even days, the media would die down again as people lost interest, and I'd lose track of him for a while. Sometimes a very long while.

The disparity of locations was fascinating to observe, especially when stories from far-flung locations arrived back-to-back or even simultaneously. One instance in particular seemed impossible, when he was supposed to have been spotted at a protest in Georgia within a few hours of giving a guest lecture at Yale Divinity School. There were photos from both appearances, and while theoretically he might have been able to make it to both if he had a private jet handy, that didn't seem particularly likely. A few other explanations were floated online, but none of them really made sense. The most obvious one, the one Occam's razor suggests, was that he was at both, though, as I said, that seems impossible.

So I read the stories and I bookmarked them, and sometimes I almost considered flying out to meet him, but I always stopped myself. Chances were that as soon as I arrived, he'd be gone again.

One time, a man I was hooking up with saw the Google Alert and asked me about it. He was the type of guy who always had to know what you were up to the moment you weren't actively paying attention to him, so I told him Gabriel had been my college boyfriend.

"Be serious," he said.

"I am," I said.

"No really," he said.

I told him about Gabriel, and I still think about the face he made, the distaste and disbelief. The unvoiced insinuation that I was a desperate groupie, a bizarre liar. His face spoke volumes, negating years of my life. I didn't know what else to say. You might not be surprised to hear that we broke up soon after.

* * *

A letter from North Dakota said the Holy Spirit had visited him in a dream. "Before, I almost always thought of the Father or the Son," he wrote. "I could see the face of Jesus, imagine His skin, His eyes, His sweat. I could see the power of the Father, the world He'd created around us, the sun up above and the earth down below. But the Holy Spirit always felt distant." Then the letter stopped. I waited for an explanation, how that aspect of God appeared to him, in the next letter. Instead, he related the birth of a calf in Arkansas.

★ ★ ★

I'll tell you, Father, I've never liked confession. Does anybody? Probably some people do. Some people are much better Catholics than I am. In any case, I've always found it an awkward, difficult experience. But my husband was converting to Catholicism before our wedding, which meant he had to do it. Hearing him talk about everything, asking me questions about how judgmental the priest would be and all that, made me feel guilty for skipping it myself for so many years, so I decided I'd go to confession too. In solidarity.

So I went into that little wooden booth, like a closet but somehow more claustrophobic, and the sliding window made its disconcerting *whoosh*, and suddenly I was staring at that brown mesh screen telling the priest on the other side about … things. I'd like to keep my private affairs private, but I will say it was an emotional experience. The priest was patient, but he kept asking questions, prying at me to say more, and eventually I broke down. I hadn't realized just how wicked I'd been, how many things I'd been hiding, even from myself.

He assigned me penance, though much less than I expected, and I stepped out. I needed to compose myself before I left the church, so I waited in one of the pews. I'm not sure how long it was, but at some point the priest's shift ended, and I watched as he exited the little booth.

In confession, you're not supposed to know which priest it is, though I guess you would if you went regularly, like you're supposed to. But I still went to Mass, and it took me a few seconds to realize the priest who'd just exited the confessional wasn't one I knew but some other, youngish priest I vaguely recognized but couldn't quite place.

The other thing I noticed about him was a tiny trickle of blood coming from each of his palms. Not enough to make a mess or even really noticeable if you were to just glance at him, but I guess because of my surprise I'd been staring.

I did something then—I guess it's not exactly forbidden—I snuck into his side of the confessional. I don't know why or what I expected to find, but I felt compelled. Mostly it was just like the one I'd kneeled in, only with a cushioned seat, and you could see through the screen a bit. Then I noticed two tiny red stains on the green seat cushion, small but unmistakable. The scent that lingered there was something else entirely, something sweet like vanilla.

I told my husband about all this when I got home, but I'm not sure if he registered what I said. He was stressed about his own confession, and wedding plans, and a promotion. I didn't think about it again until recently.

I'd never heard of Father Gabriel, though I guess he was a bit of a sensation in the southwest. But then I saw all the recent coverage on TV, and I knew immediately he'd been that strange priest who'd taken my confession. About the rest, I can't say for sure. It was a long time ago, so feel free to chalk it all up to an overactive imagination. But it was definitely him. What he was doing in Cleveland, I haven't the foggiest idea.

★ ★ ★

He performed a baptism for a couple living on a farm near Portland. He said they didn't believe, "But they wanted to be sure in case they were wrong."

Afterward, he offered the couple communion and was surprised to learn one had been raised Catholic, the other Baptist. "They declined," he said. "I asked why, if they wanted to be sure about the baptism. What would be the harm? They told me they wanted to be sure for their daughter but were willing to take the chance for themselves."

★ ★ ★

[Reddit post—/r/GabeWatch—Author: LeBronLeBoi321]

> I saw him sitting with Will and Jada at a Lakers game. I know, sounds crazy, but you can pull up the tapes and see for yourself. The camera zooms in on Will and Jada, and he's there, cheering with them and Jaden and Tiffany Haddish. The announcer doesn't say anything, probably didn't know who he was, but I swear to God it's him. I don't know if that means they were friends, or he just lucked into some really sweet courtside seats, or what, but I swear to God I'm not making this up.

★ ★ ★

I gave it a couple weeks, hoping that Anna was wrong, but when it became clear I was on my own for the foreseeable future, I cut back on the number of Masses. It helped that Our Lady of Guadalupe's attendance shrank precipitously, but I was still overworked for a long time. That was one of the issues with having no larger network of support from the Church—we couldn't have a priest from across town help out if I got sick and lost my voice. On those weeks, we just had to make do with my half-whispered prayers and cut out the sermon entirely.

A year or so after Gabriel's disappearance, Anna got a call at the church from my uncle Ramón. It sounded like my mother had had a cancer scare, and she wanted me to come back to Española to see her before it was too late. Unlike the protest, this I couldn't ignore, so I took a few days off and went back home for the first time in more than a decade. The plaza had changed, with new sidewalks and a more suburban, manicured look that contrasted with the run-down, disreputable feeling it had when I was growing up. There were still kids in the gazebo, but they seemed different, with their collared shirts and skinny jeans. No one wore work overalls or a wife beater. No one smoked.

I knew from Ramón that my mother had moved years ago, but I still wanted to see our old house, the one my great-grandfather had built. It too had transformed in my absence. The brown stucco walls had been replaced by a two-story home, all white, with a pitched tile roof like you'd find in New England. Disappointed, I headed to Ramón's. I wasn't ready to see Mom yet. I wanted to prepare myself in case things were really bad.

When he answered the door, he looked as strong as ever, but he leaned against a cane and had three or four days' worth of a graying mustache and beard. His hair was long and messy, unceremoniously falling onto his red flannel shirt. Ramón had always been dapper, which is difficult to achieve when you work on cars all day, so this was as depressing as the destruction of my childhood home.

"Took you long enough," he said. "Well don't just stand there letting the heat out. Come inside."

He made us cafés con leche, then sat in a large recliner opposite an old tube television and a fireplace where a few logs slowly burned to ash. I took a seat on an old faux-leather chair that smelled faintly of cat pee.

As soon as it wasn't rude, I asked him about Mom, how she was holding up.

He shrugged and said she was doing alright. "Guess the cancer wasn't so bad."

"What do you mean?"

"I guess … I guess it turned out to be benign. They took the lump out anyway, just to be safe, but it was no big deal. She's doing fine."

"I can't believe … but she still asked for me?"

"Well no, not exactly…"

"What do you mean?"

"I admit, that was all me. I wanted to see you. Talk to you. It's been too long."

"You could've just called."

"Would you have come?"

I thought about it. "No."

"Then you know why I did it. Anyhow, you're here now, so be angry with me later, but for now try and just be family."

I took a moment to calm myself and realized he was right. There was no point in leaving in a huff. I asked about the family. He told me that most everyone was doing fine, but my brother, Joaquín, was in jail for sticking up a convenience store with a friend.

"How did Mom take it?"

"Not well, as you can imagine. Her health is fine, but she's ... not a happy person these days. You know a couple years back, in the middle of those protests, Padre Gabriel came by looking for her."

"He never told me."

He shrugged. "In any case, they talked. He told her you'd become a priest like him. Said you were doing well."

"What'd she say?"

"I don't know exactly. She's still angry."

"About me?"

"You. Your brother. Your dad. All the men in the world. She's doing fine, just don't talk to her about men or you'll get an earful."

"What about you? You're not mad at me anymore."

"Manny, I was never mad at you. Disappointed, maybe. Confused, certainly. I couldn't understand why you didn't like the hermanos. What you had against us."

"I'm not sure I ever knew. I think I was just ... trying to do my own thing. Find my way to Jesus without all that violence. I didn't understand it then. And I didn't think I'd fuck it all up as badly as I did."

"Well, but you're a priest now, right? I don't think Padre Gabriel's visit did your mother any good, but my worries weren't about the hermanos, they were about Jesus. And knowing you'd become a priest, well, I figured maybe you were doing ok."

"I was just too young then."

He looked straight into my eyes, perhaps trying to appraise me. Eventually he said, "You'd make a fine hermano. Do your dad proud. But I don't think I could convince the rest to forgive you."

"Makes sense."

"Doesn't mean you're done. You still have your promesa."

"What do you mean?"

"I mean just 'cause you're in Albuquerque doesn't mean you can't worship like your familia."

"How's Marianna?"

"Don't change the subject. What do you say?"

"Say about what?"

"About starting a morada in Albuquerque."

"I ... I have a church now," I said. The notion was so strange. "What about Marianna?"

"She's fine. Married a gringo, had a couple kids, moved to Santa Fe, and works for the museum, I think. I see her around sometimes during the holidays."

"Oh." I didn't know what I'd hoped to hear.

"Why, you gonna go visit her too?"

"'Course not. Bet she'd want to see me as much as Mom does."

"You know just 'cause she's angry doesn't mean you shouldn't see her," said Ramón.

"I ... you're probably right."

"I always am. I've probably kept you here too long—go over and say hi to her."

So I drove across town to her house, a small adobe building with a well-kept, xeriscaped yard in the front. A glass hummingbird stuck out of a flower pot, and a hummingbird feeder full of nectar hung from a pine tree. I could see light and movement past the curtains of her windows, enough to tell she was home. After half an hour, the sun was nearly down, and I forced myself out of the car.

I trudged to the front door, though my feet felt weighted down with sandbags. The door was painted a darker shade of brown than the rest of the house and had a peephole in its center. I knocked. From the open windows, I could hear the faint sound of movement within the house. I waited. The door stayed shut.

I knocked again and said loudly, "Mom, it's me. It's Manny." No answer. I put my hand on the knob and twisted a little. It was locked. It would've been so easy for me to climb through the open windows, past the billowing red curtains, and be inside. I could've told her I loved her. That I missed her. That I was sorry for what I'd done all those years ago and had devoted my life to Jesus.

I walked back to my car and drove home to Albuquerque. To the church.

That talk with Ramón stuck with me, though. I'd never heard of a morada in Albuquerque. Maybe there was one somewhere. Maybe in Bernalillo, maybe way out past the Valley in Bosque Farms or Los Lunas. But just as likely, there wasn't, or hadn't been for fifty, a hundred years.

I thought about it for a long time. After another year, while I still wasn't convinced about starting one, out of curiosity I asked Anna whether we had enough money in the budget to purchase a small shack on the outskirts of town, somewhere near enough to a mountain or hill. She told me it shouldn't be a problem, but it might take some time to loosen up the funds and do our research. A little more than a year after that, Our Lady of Guadalupe officially purchased a disused auto shop between the South Valley and I-25.

* * *

He built houses in Pittsburgh while staying in a hostel. He wrote that the priest there gave the "loveliest" Masses, and it made him feel bad for no longer offering his own. But he said he liked watching them more. "I'd forgotten what it was like to be on the other side of things. To listen and stay quiet. To follow in worship, not to lead."

* * *

My brother. Not me. But my brother doesn't like to talk about it. Says maybe things will go back if he does. Likes to pretend he could always see. Likes to be normal now, like me and Mom. I don't blame him. I don't like to talk about it either. But you're a priest, so it's probably ok. Mom says you can trust priests. Except the bad ones. You're not a bad one, are you? The man who helped David was a priest too, so it's probably ok, right?

I don't know how Mom met him. Maybe it was at church. Maybe it was at the bus stop. He stayed with us for a weekend. He slept on the couch. Mom offered him her bed. He said no. He said he was fine with the couch. He looked tired, but so do most adults. He said I was cute but didn't play with me. Most adults don't want to play.

Mom walked in with David. The priest went to him. The priest put his hand on David's head. The priest smiled. I don't know what he said to Mom. I know he unpacked his bag. I know he pulled out dried leaves. I know the dried leaves smelled real strong. Not bad. Strong. He put them into water. Heated the water. David drank the water. The priest put his hands over David's eyes. He held them there. Held them there a long time.

The priest said an Our Father, like Mom makes us say before we go to bed. The priest said it again. And again.

And again. I got bored and played with Legos. I built a helicopter. No one else moved. The priest kept saying the Our Fathers, and I hoped he would leave. But it was good he didn't. He took his hands off David's eyes, and David started crying.

Mom started crying.

I asked what was going on.

David said it was too much.

I asked what was too much.

He said the colors.

I asked what colors.

He said all of them. And the shapes.

I asked what he meant and flew my helicopter over to him. It might have been a plane.

He said he could see it.

I started crying too.

The priest didn't say anything for a while. The rest of us hugged. Mom made spaghetti, and afterward the priest went to sleep.

He stayed for another day. It was weird. Mom had to work. David played with me on the rug. He liked looking at the Legos. Then we went outside and walked around the block. We went real slow, so I was bored.

When we got back, the priest was kneeling. He chanted words. Weird words. I don't think they were English. Maybe he made them up. I told him to stop and make us lunch. He made sandwiches but left the crust on, so I didn't like it. Then he kneeled until Mom came home.

The priest left the next morning. Mom said he had other people to help. I asked how David could see. Mom said he just could. Mom said Jesus came down and helped him.

I said I didn't see Jesus. I just saw the priest.

She said Jesus sent the priest.

I asked how.

She said she didn't know.

I asked the priest's name.

Last week, I saw the listing in the church bulletin with his picture—I can read now, and I read it all by myself. Mom said not to talk to strangers. Mom said strangers could be mean to girls. But I thought the church bulletin was ok. But if David can't see anymore, you have to come help.

* * *

In one of the more cryptic letters, he wrote, "I know that pain is a blessing. I know I'm lucky to have these aches, daily reminders that I am God's creation, and mortal, and fallen. I know that pain focuses the mind too. But I must be honest, sometimes I wish I were a little less blessed."

* * *

One of the few things I can confirm during that period is that Mr. Romero consorted with other known persons of interest. This included politically minded groups that I mentioned earlier, as well as others with a more violent bent, and he is alleged to have been involved in more radical forms of domestic terrorism than the peaceful methods he espoused while working within the apparatus of his church.

However, most of our surveillance methods rely on electronic networks. Mr. Romero largely circumvented these networks, avoiding air travel, credit cards, even logging in to his personal online accounts. When he reappeared on our radar, it would be under such impossible circumstances that many within the Bureau suspect he was aware of our surveillance and was attempting to deliberately obfuscate. For instance, when he would occasionally log in to his bank account, it would happen from multiple locations—often hundreds of miles apart—at the same, or nearly the same, time, and subsequent investigations found no other trace of him in either area.

I know that some of Mr. Romero's followers like to invoke the religious concept of bilocation to explain some of the rumors arising from this period. Clearly, though, he was working in concert with one or multiple associates.

In any case, the vagabonds and agitators, dissidents and rabble-rousers he met on the road seemed to only further his alienation from mainstream American values. When he left the church, he was an organizer, but when he returned, he was a radical—antigovernment and antiestablishment. Above all, dangerous.

* * *

His next letter was from Philadelphia. "I broke bread and gave thanks on the ground floor of an abandoned building. There were maybe thirty of us, and it was wonderful. I've never felt so connected to anyone. For music, someone brought out their laptop and we sang along. Afterward, we danced and drank until the morning, and I would love to stay with these lovely people forever."

* * *

[Transcription from *Holy or Hoax?*: A History Channel Production]

I know this guy Reuben who lives out in the North Valley, maybe like half a mile from the Trader Joe's,

and he's got this big ranch-style house he inherit-
ed from his parents. He's kind of a jackass, one of
those guys with too much money and not enough
responsibility. Tell you the truth, he's not really my
friend, but he was dating Rachel then, and Rachel
is stupid about guys but absolutely the best when
it comes to anything else. Anyhow, Reuben had
some absolutely top-notch shrooms and he wanted Rachel to come over and do some with him, and
Rachel won't do shrooms without me because of
this one time when she was on her own and she
ate too much of a cap and went somewhere really
[expletive] dark. Rachel knows I have her back, and
Reuben ... well, nobody trusts Reuben. Not really.

So we're hanging around his living room, listening to music on these old leather couches
and recliners his parents must've bought back in
the nineties. The room smells a bit like dog piss
because of this yappy little mutt he has running
around. Rueben pulls out a shoebox filled with pills
and powders, all meticulously arranged, and takes
out a Ziploc with three shrooms inside. He hands
me the baggie and asks me to rip off how much
each of us should take, "Since you're the expert."
He's a condescending jackass, but whatever, he's
the one giving us all this for free, so I ignore it.

Reuben puts on the TV, and we're watching
some dumb animated show on Netflix, which looks
like crap but has a lot of dirty jokes, so it's still pretty good. Reuben goes to the fridge and pulls out a
thirty-rack of High Life, and we kill a few cans while
waiting for the shrooms to kick in. After a couple
episodes, things start getting kinda squiggly. So I

tell them to get ready, and a few minutes later it's almost like we're inside the show, not animated or anything but just like there with them on the sets. I mean, they *are* animated, just we're not, if that makes any sense, and it's not just me having this trip, it's all three of us.

Right, so we're wandering around these sets, and I guess we must've walked off them because while we're still in this kind of shoddily animated wonderland, suddenly we enter a chapel. Not quite a normal chapel, 'cause it's all colorful. Almost psychedelic, but like pastel? It's still animated, but somehow more lifelike than the rest. None of this seems weird in the moment, and so we wander down the aisle. There's classical music playing in the background and incense, but incense that smells all good and sweet. At the far side of the chapel is this Mexican-looking dude, and he's smiling. He starts praying at us. I can't remember what he said, just a lot of Christs and Gods and peace and all. It was kinda nice, and Rachel and Reuben told me afterward they liked it too.

So yeah, that's where I saw him.

I mean, it's possible I'd seen him on TV before, sure, but really that wasn't the weirdness. The weirdness was that we all saw him, all three of us, and I've never had a trip like that, before or since. Yesterday I emailed Rachel with a picture of him you guys'd sent me and asked her if he was the same dude from our trip. She told me definitely, same dude.

I don't go to church, and I've never really believed in the whole God and Heaven thing. But it's freaky, you know? Like I think about how peaceful I felt in that tripped-out chapel, and it feels like a *sign*. Maybe all that magical religious stuff is real after all. I dunno.

★ ★ ★

He wrote from Florida that he was nearly run off the road by "some lunatic with a pickup truck suspended so high you needed a ladder to get in." In the same letter, he said that while walking through some nature reserve, he watched a humongous, dinosaurlike alligator consume a normal-size alligator like it was a cheeseburger. He crisscrossed many cities and states repeatedly, but that was the only time he ever wrote me from Florida.

★ ★ ★

[Reddit post—/r/GabeWatch—Author: GraebleJ]

It's nothing exciting, but I did see him buying groceries at the Publix a few blocks from my house. No miracles, no prayers. Just groceries. Everyone's gotta eat.

★ ★ ★

At one point, there was a long gap when I did not hear from him at all. However, given that this was during the period when I was relocating, I thought little of it and figured Father Patrice would send along his letters as soon as time permitted. Months later, though, I received a postcard from

Quito, Ecuador, saying he had been having a fantastic time there and in Bolivia, attending protests and demonstrations, that he had hitchhiked the whole way down.

* * *

[Huffington Post blog entry—"A Life's Worth"—
Author: Anon.]

What is the worth of a life? Of a person? I'm not asking in some allegorical sense but in a literal one. A fiscal one. I'm talking about how much money a company should spend in order to save one person's life. I'm talking about how we should enter this data into a spreadsheet so that it comes out in a way that makes sense to shareholders or members of the board. Can you give me a ballpark, even? Is it a hundred thousand dollars? A million? And let's not waste time with the simplistic, juvenile notion that human life is priceless—the whole of human history vehemently disagrees.

I can speak accurately about shareholders and meetings because I was the chair of a large, well-known pharmaceutical company whose name I can't mention due to certain nondisclosure agreements that are in my best interest not to break. Our newest drug, a more aggressive form of Rogaine, if you can believe it, was nearly ready for market, with ad spots already booked. Then one of our trial subjects dropped dead.

It turned out that our drug could be fatal given a specific set of circumstances, which our researchers estimated would occur every one in 1,000,000 users. Given those odds, I knew we could likely have the product out for years before any public fatalities arose, let alone any that were plausibly traceable to our drug. It seemed reasonable to release the product as planned, sans further warnings or testing. I made the decision.

When I arrived home, the house was quiet. My wife had put the kids to bed and was reading in our bedroom. After undressing, I fell asleep fast, as I usually did, exhausted from a long day at the office. I don't usually dream, but that night I had a particularly vivid one.

I was sitting behind the large oak desk in my office. Without warning, a priest appeared in front of me with an old brass and turquoise rosary around his neck, telling me not to release the drug. "It will crush your soul," he said. Of course I now know who he is, but at the time he seemed like any other priest, with his collar and superior disposition. I don't like being told what to do, even by people I trust, so I refused.

He told me to warn people about the side effects, to let them make their own choice about the risk.

Again, I refused.

That's when he asked the question I posed earlier: "What is the worth of a life? Of a person?"

I threatened to call security, but he left my office with a sad sigh. Suddenly, the building began falling, dropping down, down, down. Soon I was in the Earth's core. I opened the office door and there, on the other side, was incredible heat, flames, and screams of pain.

I awoke, startled but largely unfazed. After all, it was only a dream. But the next evening I had almost the same dream. Me in my office, the priest pleading for me to do something about the drug, a sad look on his face. This time, though, after he sighed and began to leave, I asked him to stay. Somehow, I thought this might prevent the rest of the dream from recurring.

"I'm sorry," he said. "But I can't." He closed the door, and once again my office fell and fell. I refused to open the door this time, but it began creaking open all on its own. I smelled sulfur, then a wave of heat hit me at my desk. I heard terrible, terrible laughter. I didn't wake up for a long time...

The story of how I added that tiny label to our product, so small you'd have to squint, and soon afterward was forced out of the company, is long and not worth telling. Did warning people about a side effect save even one life? Probably not. But I stopped having those dreams.

Maybe a year later, my wife dragged me with her to the Episcopalian church she sometimes went to. I found it terribly dull at first, as I find all religious services, but then *he* took the lectern to preach. The priest from my dream. I couldn't believe it, but I knew I had to talk to him.

"Do I know you from somewhere?" he asked.

"This is going to sound crazy," I told him. "But you were in my dreams."

He stared at me for a long time, then said, "Ah, yes. Of course."

And then someone interrupted us.

I would claim that I never saw him again, but no one remembers all of their dreams, so I can't be certain.

* * *

"Let me ask you a hypothetical question," one letter began. "Suppose Jesus Christ was not God. Don't stop reading, please, Father. Just suppose he was simply a well-meaning man who inspired untold millions of people with his good works and sacrifice. He brought peace to those who needed it, but the whole walking-on-water bit, and the part with Lazarus, not to mention the resurrection itself, those were all made up. Doesn't matter if he was playing everyone or if the gospel's authors decided to take some liberties or whatever. Would that mean that every priest in the world is a liar? Would it mean all of us are perpetuating this same lie? Or would it make us artists of a kind, like Picasso, taking those lies and sculpting them into something true and real for the people we speak to? Would that mean everything we preach is true, after all?"

* * *

I felt vindicated when Gabriel left. After all, the most likely reason for his disappearance was guilt. I knew from counseling parishioners that when a person feels guilty and cannot face up to it, the natural inclination is to run. It takes a mature person, a mature Christian, to want to confess.

335

The first question you have to ask is what he was running from. What sin had he committed in New Mexico that meant abandoning his flock, such as it was? Often, as you know, there is a direct correlation between the magnitude of a sin and the lengths taken to run from it. Perhaps, then, Gabriel finally felt guilty about all the lying and misleading he had wrought, particularly with regard to his church. He wanted to escape the "miracles" he had performed, and that left him with two options: either admit his lies to the entire community or leave. He took the easier path.

While he was gone, I heard that attendance at his church fell precipitously, and while I felt bad for Manuel for having been taken in like that, he should have known better. He and that church remained in a purgatorial state, apart from both God's one true Church as well as its own founder, though still busy enough to keep its doors open. I felt a bit of schadenfreude about the entire state of affairs, though I made myself do penance for those feelings.

Still, I became disconcerted about the stories I heard, the endless online rumors passing through our gullible parish. He had delivered a baby in El Paso, and bullets bounced off him in Juárez. He had spoken with the president of Mexico and attended a procession in honor of Santa Muerte in Chihuahua. One parishioner said that while visiting family in Pittsburgh, she had seen him begging for change outside a CVS. Some stories were miraculous, others were not, but it was their proliferation that worried me. Even the Servants of the Light seemed to enjoy trading tales of his exploits.

For a long time, I wondered why anyone in Las Cruces cared about Gabriel anymore. He had abdicated any claim he might have once had at spiritual authority. Why did the Servants share accounts of him they were almost certain contained lies and falsehoods? And why, despite myself, could I not get enough of them?

* * *

In a letter from Las Vegas, he said he had been arrested again. I never found out why, he just wrote that he had "tried to follow Jesus's example with the moneylenders but was thrown out of the temple. And into jail." In a later letter, he explained, "I wasn't visiting the city to rail against its greed and corruption. Las Vegas isn't even the most capitalistic place in America. I went because someone in Nebraska told me David Copperfield still performs there almost every night. He does, and he's better than ever. Can you believe that!"

* * *

I have to admit, my life was a lot easier after Father Gabriel left. I missed the fire of his sermons, the passion of his causes, the mystery of his miracles. But there was something nice about routine. Father Manuel and I learned to work together with such clockwork precision that weeks flew by, and I never came into work wondering about what new demonstration I'd have to organize or TV interview we'd need to contort our schedule to fit in. Our Lady of Guadalupe became a conventional church, and that was nice.

But still, I began doing something a little bit ... un-orthodox. I started praying to Father Gabriel. At first I was a little ashamed about it—after all, who prays to a priest? So I didn't tell anyone, and I only did it when I felt particularly lonely or desperate.

It started when my dog, Duke, went missing. I was leaving for work, and he followed me out the door. He did that sometimes, and it wasn't usually a big deal, but then there was a loud noise in the neighborhood, a car backfiring or maybe kids with fireworks. Duke jolted and sprinted down the street. I tried following him, but he was too fast, and I had to slow down and catch my breath. I spent the next hour looking for him, shouting his name, but he'd completely disappeared.

At work, I was so worried I didn't get anything done. I started praying and found myself praying not to Saint Anthony but to Father Gabriel. When I arrived home, Duke was waiting for me at the front door. I know it wasn't a miracle—Duke was always a good boy—but I don't know, it felt like those prayers helped. After that, I added a short prayer to Father Gabriel to my nightly routine, and I felt that maybe wherever he was, he might hear my message and, I don't know, somehow know that back in Albuquerque, we still missed him.

* * *

"Another hypothetical for you: What if Christ had been born today? Or maybe thirty years ago, but in any case, what if He was here preaching his gospel of love and forgiveness? How many followers do you think He'd convince, even with Twitter and Facebook at His disposal? The Bible gives us a hint: no more than a dozen, and even those dozen disciples would be full of doubts and treachery and, frankly, stupidity. Would it take hundreds of years for anyone to care what He had to say, or would He and his dozen followers be forgotten no matter what He did? Would the Son of God even get a Wikipedia page?"

★ ★ ★

[Revivalizer: A Forum for Concerned Christians, user name: Jimmy McNab]

He seemed like a homosexual to me, and I knew he was Mexican. He preached at our church once, had been spending some time in the area, from what I heard. When I told the other deacons what I suspected, they agreed we didn't need some illegal sissy corrupting God's word. So I called up Bill, our preacher, and I told him what we thought about having somebody like that up there talking to us.

Bill sent him packing. Told him to get right out of our church and go back to wherever it was he came from. After that he stayed out of Fayetteville. Knew we were onto him.

★ ★ ★

"This one's not so hypothetical. I stayed with a good couple in Dearborn, Michigan. When I say good, I mean it—love for their neighbor, love for each other, love of nature, hatred of injustice. One was a social worker, the other a teacher, and both volunteered at the SPCA. They donated their extra money to worthy causes and were raising their three-year-old to be a model person herself. They might have been the two sweetest individuals I met during all my travels, a pair who lived Jesus's teachings with every breath they took. Here's the thing: they're Muslim.

"So are they going to Hell? I understand how the Church views the Fate of the Unlearned, that they may be permitted salvation because they would have sought Christ if they'd known ... but that's not what I'm talking about here. This couple wasn't unlearned. Of course they'd heard of Christ. They just didn't believe.

"I have known Christian rapists, Christian child abusers, Christians who crush the lives of the poor and cause wars all around the world. But they believe in Christ. Will they be in Heaven while this sweet couple gets sent to Hell?"

* * *

[Columbus Parenting Forum, Birthday Party Rec's thread, Author: JennyK]

There was this tiny magic and joke shop, and I don't know how they stayed in business. Trick decks of cards, whoopee cushions, floating balls. Even some kind of creepy ventriloquist dolls that I am just sooo thankful my son never got into that stuff, because it would've completely given me nightmares lol. We went there sometimes because my son just LOOOVES magic, ever since his dad, MAJOR moron, bought him that kit when he was in second grade. They have this bulletin board by the front, and I just picked a card off at random for his birthday and called it up.

He didn't ask for much and said he'd perform for up to 45 minutes, which is actually a REALLY long time with kids. Really it was more like two 20 minute sets with a little break, but that was OK because the kids needed to run around. He just put on his laptop, with some old-timey harpsichord or something, and then did all the usual stuff, scarves and cards and making a wand disappear. To be honest, it was a totally fine show but didn't blow me away. Then again, he only charged like, I dunno, $70 or something, so it was also like, "Ok, I'd recommend him."

I asked him, after the show, if he was the same Gabriel Romero from you know, like everything, and he said, "What do you think?" I said I think yes, and he said, "You got me," but then he winked like it was a joke, so I guess I'm not so sure? I don't know, what do you guys think? A lot of people asked me, did he do anything religious? And the answer is NO. So no need to worry about that if you want to book him.

* * *

[Transcription from *Holy or Hoax?*: A History Channel Production]

My kids would tell you a completely different story, but I'm a psychologist, and I'm well aware of how our memories operate. We conflate events and combine them. Erase and embellish. The past happened, and it's real, but what we make of it later is essentially fiction. Almost instantaneously, our memories transform the random events of life into stories, chains of causal events with a beginning, middle, and end, when in reality life is random, unstructured, and fundamentally plot-less.

The actual events, at least as I recall them, were straightforward. I was driving down I-75 with my wife and our three children. We were headed to Atlanta to visit my family for Thanksgiving, and I saw a man with his thumb out on the side of the road. After a quick argument with my wife, we decided to pick him up, in the spirit of the holiday. He asked if we could drop him off in Atlanta. I asked him where, and he said it didn't matter, which was obviously more than a little odd.

Soon, my wife recognized him. She works for a nonprofit and is involved with activist groups all around Nashville, and he was apparently fairly well known in those circles. They spoke about politics, and he asked her about her work—they got along very well. At a certain point, the conversation died down, so he tried to entertain the kids. He did a few magic tricks that were fairly impressive, and he told stories to make the time pass. Finally we reached the city, and he asked me to drop him off "any old where," which is the only thing I remember him saying verbatim. He didn't have a suitcase, just a small backpack and sleeping bag. He seemed surprisingly clean for being on the road. And he had an easy laugh. Afterward, Angie told me she'd assumed he would be more formal and imposing, based on some fiery speeches she remembered from videos on Facebook and Twitter, but she was much happier with the man who'd actually ridden with us.

Now my kids, they remember things a little differently. They say he cured Jordan of a terrible fever, which certainly never happened, because if he'd had a temperature, we wouldn't have made that long drive. They say that among his magic tricks, he shot sparks out of his hands like a Roman candle and that he cut my tie in two before bringing it back. I'm positive I wasn't wearing a tie, because I only wear them to work. They say his deck of cards glowed in the dark, but it was daylight throughout the drive. They also claim he insisted we play heavy metal music for the whole drive and was an absolute expert on the subject.

None of these assertions are correct, obviously. Kids will be kids, as they say, and they like to make up stories. Adults do too, of course, but I doubt they would be as fanciful as the ones my children tell. Now, that isn't to say that my memory is perfect either—this was a small blip in our lives, and I was sitting at the wheel the whole time trying not to crash. Nonetheless, I feel fairly confident about my version, though if you'd like, you can interview the kids as well.

* * *

The last letter I received during his wanderings was particularly haunting, and not just in retrospect: "What if Jesus hadn't died? Or rather, what if Jesus hadn't been killed? He was God, regardless, after all. What I'm wondering is whether anyone would've remembered him or his teachings? Say he continued preaching and offering miracles for the next thirty years, then passed away from cancer. Would Christianity exist? If so, then why is his martyrdom so important? Why is the image we wear around our necks not a symbol of healing but an instrument of torture?" Why, when we think of life everlasting, do we have to picture pain and humiliation offered in its place?"

ANNA FISHEL

I arrived at my office a little before nine a.m. like usual. I unlocked the doors, put a pot of coffee on, and began checking my email. Since Father Gabriel left, they'd slowed to a trickle, and I often found myself with time to kill. Fewer parishioners meant fewer lunches and community picnics to organize, fewer weddings and baptisms to schedule. I'd adjusted to the wide-open hours, reading romance novels or working my way through Sudoku books. I was on Facebook and Twitter a lot and played more games on my phone than I like to admit.

Then Father Gabriel walked down the hallway, asking me if there was any news, anything important for him to get to before working on his sermon. It'd been almost four years, but he spoke like he used to, pleasantly authoritative, though with a new nonchalance to his tone. He had an overgrown beard, with new hints of premature gray creeping in, and wore jeans and a T-shirt so faded that I couldn't make out its image. What made everything feel ok, almost normal even, was when he smiled, the same mischievous smile in the framed picture on my desk.

I did my best to compose myself, though I was more in shock than when he'd disappeared. "Nothing. No news. You're going to, uhh, work on your sermon? For Sunday Mass?"

"Yes, for tomorrow. I'm sure Manny has some nice remarks prepared for today, and I wouldn't want to get in his way. I'll be working in my room if you need me."

And just like that, he'd returned. Maybe I should've followed after him, asked some questions, said literally *anything* about how weird this all was ... but instead both Father Manuel and I pretended like he had never left, that the church had been trapped in amber for the past few years, waiting for Father Gabriel to dig us out again. After all, that seemed to be what he wanted.

I sat in the front row on Sunday morning, like I always used to. It had been too long since I'd heard one of his sermons. Father Manuel was an eloquent, intelligent man, but he lacked fire. I didn't blame the church's slow disintegration on him, but it was impossible not to notice his growing hesitance from the pulpit. Father Gabriel was blessed with a silver tongue, even when thrown off. I could sense his disappointment at the lone pianist, his dismay as he looked from face to face across the small crowd, clearly wishing it was larger. But his sermon was excellent, and I remember some of it still. "Christ means love, but love cannot come without sacrifice," he said. "Love is active, and sometimes it hurts. Sometimes it means doing what's difficult for us, forgiving the unforgivable, even within ourselves. But that's what Christ asks of us. That's what love asks of us." He even wept for a moment. Were they tears of happiness? Tears of sadness? I don't think any of us could really say.

After Mass, he spent forever talking to all the parishioners, greeting them like old friends—even the handful he'd never met before. He made small jokes to dodge their questions about where he'd been, and no one pried too much. But I wanted to talk about it—I'd spent all the previous night thinking about what to say. I knew I couldn't bring up the phone call that seemed to trigger his departure, but I needed to know what he'd been doing, if not why he left. Something more definite than the rumors and stories that occasionally breezed through the pews and the internet.

When everyone else had left, I stopped him on the way back to his room.

"Hey," he said. "What's up?"

"Do you have a few minutes to talk?"

"Not really," he said. "I need to work on the next sermon. I'm already behind, and I feel completely exhausted. Are there usually this few people?"

"What about tomorrow?"

"Tomorrow? No, I'll be with one of the small faith-sharing groups."

"What about dinner?"

"I'm meeting with an activist group at the Peace and Justice Center."

"Later in the week, then?"

"I'll give you my schedule. Just figure out when and we'll do it."

`He already had so many plans, for both himself and the church. I had no idea how he'd found the time or energy to make them. So we were back on the old treadmill, but it felt more frantic than before, less coherent or thought out. He wasn't free until Thursday, and even then he was late because of another meeting.

We met at a small Italian place that I liked and rarely had an excuse to go to, since I didn't like eating alone. In all the years I'd known him, that was the first time we went out together, just the two of us.

He arrived fifteen minutes late. "Central used to have two lanes," he said. "I keep forgetting how slow it is now."

I didn't mention that the restaurant was still only five minutes from the church. Once we'd ordered, I noticed him shifting in his chair awkwardly, tapping his silverware. I will say I was a bit aggravated by this point, but I still dreaded bringing up what I'd asked him there to talk about. So at first I rambled, about Duke and the local elections, and he seemed keen to do the same. Finally I found enough courage to bring up his absence. "So did you find it?"

"Find what?"

"Whatever you were looking for out there."

"I don't know. I didn't even know I was looking for something," he said with a grin.

I sighed. "Fine. I guess that was the wrong question. I just want ... we didn't know if you were ever coming back."

"I didn't know either, Anna. You know, I've never really liked the phrase *God's plan*. It assumes God doesn't want people to just ... be. Maybe God's more of a listener than a talker these days."

I sighed. "What does that even mean?"

"When I left, after you ... got that phone call ... I was already worried that maybe I was screwing everything up. The church, the protests, just ... everything. It got worse after we all got back from Española. I couldn't stop thinking that maybe I wasn't meant to be Christ's messenger."

"And then what, you realized you were wrong?"

"Yes," he said, his voice firm again, like during his sermons. "I was wrong."

MANUEL QUINTANA

I sat on a concrete bench behind Our Lady of Guadalupe, staring at a beautiful hunk of cottonwood. I could see the shape inside, what it should be, but I was scared to start, scared to mar the wood. Resting against the wall behind me were a few of my most presentable carving attempts, all of them terrible, but perhaps not so terrible as the dozens I'd used as firewood. I knew I'd been improving, and I didn't want to tarnish our church's namesake with my inexpert hands. But she was the only image I could see in the wood, eyes closed, hands together in prayer beneath that starry turquoise shawl. I opened my eyes and began chiseling away, hoping at least to approximate the vision in my head.

The church's metal door creaked behind me. It was Father Gabriel, freshly showered and shaved, drinking from a thermos of coffee.

"Morning prayers?" he asked.

"No, I…"

"I'm only joking. I just came to chat. I wanted to talk to you about demonstrating again. Getting out there and fighting injustice. Hitting the streets like we used to."

I laughed. "Gabriel, there aren't enough people left in the church for anyone to care if we're protesting or not. The momentum has shifted."

"It can shift back."

"Maybe. But since you left, no one has been clamoring for a big demonstration. Trust me, I talk to the parishioners. Everyone just wants to go to Mass and receive the Eucharist and then go home. Maybe eat a doughnut and talk to a few friends for five minutes afterward, but that's it. Even those who *are* more devoted, I don't know … maybe I've been a bad priest. I haven't been trying to rile them up. I've just been trying to keep the lights on."

"You're a great priest. The best." He sat down next to me on the bench, and I felt a little awkward about the wood chips littering the ground.

"Ha-ha, sure."

"I mean it. You believe, you're unwavering in your faith. And you use that faith to instruct our flock in how to love Christ and each other. That's all anyone can do."

We sat in silence. He picked up the aspen and rotated it, moved his hands over it like he was caressing something alive. He held it inches from his face, breathed in deeply, then put it back on the concrete in front of us.

"The thing is," I said, "I'm not kidding when I say that the church has quieted down. Politics have quieted down. We've kind of settled. It isn't as exciting, but people seem to like it."

"There's still a fascist in the White House—how have politics quieted down?"

"Isn't there always? I don't know, it just feels like … like I said, people want to go to Mass and then go home. They don't want to change the world. There's a certain momentum that these things have, and when it dies down, it's just that. Dead."

He put his arm on my shoulder. "If there's one thing Christ is good at, it's defeating death. All we have to do is find a way to make them listen again, and soon we'll be an even bigger church with bigger demonstrations than ever. No one will be able to ignore us, not the governor, not the president, no one."

"Fine," I said. "You do something to bring the crowds back, bring the media back, and we'll talk about demonstrations. But for now, I don't know, let's slow down a little and take stock of what we do have. Build from there."

His voice changed a little. No longer strident, he sounded ... not sad, exactly, but something else. Maybe depressed. "I take your point. I guess I'm still adjusting. I didn't expect everything to be exactly the same as when I left ... but maybe I did. How do you create something that lasts? How many miracles does it take to stay trending on Twitter longer than a panda petting a puppy at the zoo? I know I shouldn't be, but I'm frustrated because I want to do something *now*."

"You can't rush things. It's like with carving. It takes a lot of little cuts—if you try to do it all at once, you only make a big, ugly mess." I pointed to the disappointments behind me, my own personal wall of shame.

He stood up and took a closer look, examining my poor depictions of Peter and Daniel, Francis and Theresa, more than a handful of ill-executed Christs. He picked up my carving of St. Stephen, the first martyr. The parts I'd intended to represent stones on his shoulders and head looked more like humongous tumors. It was a bit embarrassing.

"Don't be down on yourself," he said. "These are all good, you should paint them."

"Maybe one day. When I'm a little better."

"At least paint la Virgen when you finish with her. She won't look right in the morada without it."

He left, the door clanging shut behind him. I looked back at the block of wood, wondering how he'd seen her too, or whether he simply knew me well enough to guess what I would carve. It was impossible to say. And I hadn't told *anyone* about my intentions for the morada. I was half-convinced it was a stupid plan … but maybe it wasn't.

JOSHUA WHITEHURST

Sure, I'd been in a few churches since college. There'd been Grace's wedding, to a man named Reggie who I couldn't stand, and the weddings of various other relatives, friends, and coworkers, though to be honest, only a handful of those actually involved a church. Once I even went to Christmas Mass with a boyfriend, though that was at a Unitarian church, so it hardly counts. It wasn't like I boycotted them, I'd just grown to associate them with the type of socially acceptable homophobia that infected my life enough as it was. So Our Lady of Guadalupe's was the first real service I'd attended since singing at the Newman Center in college.

I'd driven past it a thousand times since finding out it was Gabriel's church, but until he returned, there'd never seemed to be any point to going in. The Sunday after I read he was back in town, I showed up bright and early. I wanted to find out if he still performed miracles during Mass, wanted to witness one myself. Instead, I was initially surprised to find a typical, boring Catholic Mass, made even more awkward because there were only a few dozen people in the large auditorium. However, Gabriel's sermon was an absolutely gorgeous take on that famous passage in First Corinthians describing love. I suddenly understood how he'd been once able to draw all those followers. He talked about the role love should play in all our lives, and I felt myself swoon a little. But there were no miracles. I admit to a little bit of disappointment.

Afterward, I was nervous. I'd decided I was going to actually talk to him. For the first time in years. For the first time in forever.

While I was waiting in the foyer for the congregation to clear out, I witnessed the only nontraditional part of Gabriel's church that I would ever see. An old woman came up and asked for help with a terrible cough. He prayed for her, placed his hand on her forehead, then brewed her some kind of herbal tea. More than a handful of people were watching him closely—I stood back so he wouldn't see me—and immediately after drinking the tea, the woman swore she felt better. I didn't find that particularly odd, since Gabriel had told me when we lived together how much he'd learned from his grandmother about herbal remedies and whatnot. Here I was expecting miracles, magic and pageantry, but all I saw was an old Hispanic folk remedy. Again, it was a bit of a letdown.

After the last worshippers trickled out, I walked over to him. I saw immediate recognition in his face, a shadow of deep emotion impossible to read. Love? Fear? Something else entirely? He composed himself and walked toward me with a big smile. "Josh? Is that really you?"

"It's great to see you."

"It's wonderful to see you, an absolute pleasure."

A woman walked up to us from the back of the building, asking if Gabriel had a minute to talk about accounting issues.

"Later, later," he said. "Anna, this is, I mean I want to introduce you to, I mean … wow, I'm just all tongue-tied, aren't I. This is one of my oldest friends, Joshua Whitehurst."

"Hello," I said, offering her my hand.

"Oh, hi. I've never met one of Father Gabriel's friends before. I mean, besides Father Manuel."

"Ha-ha, well yes ... we haven't spoken in years," Gabriel replied awkwardly.

She seemed to catch the hint and retreated with a curious smile on her face. Gabriel led me over to a bench, covered in a faded cushion that looked like it hadn't been replaced since the building was converted.

"I can't believe you're here," he said. "I simply can't believe it. It's too much."

"I feel the same way," I said. I moved to sit closer to him, so that our legs pressed up against each other. He didn't move away.

"I have to ask, though, why are you here?" he said. "I mean, I would like to think it's because of Christ, but..."

"It is and it isn't," I lied. "I mean, it's not entirely. I wanted to see you. See how you do ... all of this. See how you're doing. You know."

"Ha-ha, I'm doing well. The church is ... ok. Maybe it's not doing quite as well as I'd hoped, but we're getting by. How about you?"

"Can't complain. But I mean, you're back."

He laughed again. "Yes, I'm back."

"So does that mean ... are you staying for good? For a while? The last time you left was just after we talked. Does this mean you figured things out?"

"I'm here right now," he said. "That's all I can say for sure. But I guess ... yes, I came to an understanding. It took a lot, but..."

"So you're out?"

"Yes," he said, then took in a large breath. "I'm out. I don't know how that really changes anything. I don't have any plans to start dating or anything like that. Celibacy is still a part of the priesthood, but I can say it now: I'm gay."

"Feels good, doesn't it?"

"Yeah," said Gabriel. "I guess it does."

I wondered what to say. I didn't want to push him, but internally, I was already celebrating.

"So I don't know ... I'm sure you have other stuff to do today, but do you want to grab lunch this week?"

"Yes. There are a thousand things to do around here," he said, standing up. "I should get back to it. I don't have a cell phone or anything, and my schedule is kind of a mess, but call the church and we'll make plans."

We hugged, a long hug, though not inappropriately so. Not a romantic one, but longer, I would think, than what he gave ordinary members of his parish.

A few days later, we had lunch, an epic lunch with two hours of flirting. It was still chaste, but I felt something between us, some of the old electricity. We made plans for another lunch.

And the next Sunday, I went to Mass again. I wouldn't say I'd become a believer, at least not in God, not then. But I did believe in Gabriel, in his strong chin and piercing eyes, his large hands and incredible ass. Even in his miracles.

FR. PATRICK CONKLIN

Now to turn from the question of why Gabriel left to the equally damning question of why he returned. Certainly, I'm no psychologist, and I can claim no certification when it comes to diagnosing pathological behavior. However, I am well acquainted with Gabriel and familiar with the circumstances of his life, so I do believe I can offer a reasonable opinion about what his thought process must have been like. And despite claims that his departure and return were caused by angels whispering to him in his sleep and affirming his ministry, the reason is far more simple and concrete: he missed the crowds.

The fact of the matter is that for Gabriel, creating a church was never about God. It was about the cult, the adoration. If you're looking to interpret his adult life, you have to understand it was about the love of strangers. Not *for,* but *of.* Even when we were younger, when we were friends, this desire to be liked, to be admired, was obvious, and he always had the charisma to achieve it too. In retrospect, there was something ... alarming about this desire. If pressed, I would say he exhibited signs of narcissistic personality disorder. Not only because of the grandiosity of his expectations but also because he exploited and lied to those around him. Narcissists need to be loved, and when they are not, it can slowly gnaw away at them, causing antisocial and ultimately destructive behavior.

The issue for Gabriel, though, was that what he found upon returning was a far smaller, shabbier church than the one he remembered. Narcissists thinks of themselves as special, as exempt from the rules that bind the rest of us, and it seems quite likely that he expected his cult to grow in his absence. But tending a parish is like tending a garden, requiring constant labor and support. Once the smoke and mirrors were gone, what reason was there for people to keep worshipping there? The faithful never went to his church in the first place, while those looking for an entertaining show each Sunday morning scattered like so many rats out of a burning building the moment he left. Even after he returned, the parish's size and fervor remained low, no matter what he did. And I think it was making him desperate.

A couple of months later, I began to hear whispers about something big planned at "that wandering priest's church" up in Albuquerque, as my bumpkin flock had taken to calling it. No one I questioned knew anything specific. Just that it would be momentous. Needless to say, this was extremely alarming. The last time he'd done something "momentous," there'd been a literal explosion. People had nearly lost their lives.

Some might claim my worry was needless, that Gabriel had never shown any propensity toward violence, but people can be naive. What alarmed me most was my knowledge of how these fringe religious movements function. I'd been studying them in far more detail over the previous few years, due in no small part to the cult of personality that had deepened around Gabriel during his "wanderings."

Think of the Branch Davidians. Jonestown. Think of the punch they drank at Heaven's Gate or the killing shacks of the Matamoros. Think of the trillion-year contracts of Scientology, their hotboxes and indentured servitude. The pattern isn't difficult to discern.

Given what I knew, I contacted the FBI again and told them my suspicions. But before you try to lay the blame on me, keep in mind that what happened happened because of Gabriel. I was merely a passive observer, interfering only when I felt the safety of others might be at stake.

JOSHUA WHITEHURST

Her name was Agent Cook. I don't know her first name. I don't think she ever told me. I have difficulty imagining she even had one—it's easier to picture her as being born straight out of Quantico, with a badge and attitude rolled off the assembly line. Her brown hair was short, maybe an inch or so longer than mine is now, and she gave off an air of someone used to being in charge.

After knocking at my front door and introducing herself, Agent Cook asked if I had a moment to talk. It probably would've been smarter for me to make up some excuse and say no. To say I would only speak with a lawyer present, despite the fact that I was a lawyer. But I knew the FBI wasn't particularly keen on wasting its time, so if they're on your doorstep, your best bet is usually to hear them out.

Anyhow, despite my reservations, I invited her inside. I asked if she wanted anything to drink and went to get her a glass of water. She sat on my leather couch. She took a perfunctory sip from the glass and then never touched it again.

I sat opposite her on a matching recliner and took a long drink of beer from a stein Grace had given me as a birthday present years earlier. I didn't have Saturdays off very often, so I wasn't going to let Agent Cook throw off my plans, which included my favorite bathrobe, the beer, and *Jesus Christ Superstar* on full blast.

"What can I help you with?" I asked as casually as I could.

"Can you confirm that you have been attending Mass at Our Lady of Guadalupe Church for the past six weeks?"

"Sure, I guess." Maybe I imagined it, but I thought I saw her glare at me, just a little bit, just a small thinning of her eyes. "I mean yes. If that's all this is, it might have been easier just to call me. Or send me an email. I don't think there's anything wrong with going to Mass."

"Of course not, Mr. Whitehurst. I just want to make sure we're on the same page. So you've been attending, and while there, have you heard anything about future plans for the church?"

"Slow down, Ms. Cook. What's all this about? If you're wondering about their plans, maybe you should try contacting them? I'm sure they'd be happy to speak with you. Now is that all?"

The second time, I definitely wasn't imagining things. She offered me a glare that could cut through steel. Agent Cook clearly didn't like me, even though we'd never met before. I have to admit, I didn't much like her either.

"For various reasons, Mr. Romero has become a person of interest to us."

"What does person of interest mean?"

"He's seen by certain people as possibly dangerous. Some of the views he's espoused in the past have been seen as anti-American, and given the large amount of influence he has had in the community—"

"Dangerous? Maybe you ought to go listen to his sermons. They're all about peace and love and forgiveness, hippie nonsense. Seriously, anyone who thinks he's dangerous is deranged."

"Others view things differently. And some of his past causes have shown distinctly anticorporate and anti-American slants that have led to the loss of property and life."

"You can't be serious," I said. No one died at Gabriel's protests. The idea was ridiculous. I thought of saying so, but what would've been the point? "So let me get this straight. The United States Federal Bureau of Investigation thinks that Gabriel Romero has hatched some big plan to overthrow capitalism from his tiny little church that's falling apart, along with its, like, sixty congregants? Don't you have neo-Nazis and arms traffickers and, I don't know, real problems to deal with?"

I could practically see the gears of her brain turning as she decided to try a different tactic. Her voice changed, becoming more human, very faux-empathetic. "No one is happier to hear about Gabriel remaining peaceful and stable than I am. You have to believe me. I'm not here to try and entrap him. He's not a criminal. We simply want to keep closer tabs on him as a precaution."

"What do you mean, 'closer tabs'?"

"Doing this, essentially. Finding out more about him, preferably from congregants."

"I've told you everything I know. He's a nice guy. Talks about God a lot. Talks about love a lot. It's really not worth your time. And I have to ask, why are you coming to me?"

"Frankly, given your history with Parker and Mullins, and given Mr. Romero's role in the Shell drilling incident, we assumed you would be more amenable to our proposal. It seems we were wrong."

"You've been spying on me too?"

"That is immaterial. Listen, I'm not here to attack Mr. Romero. I'm here to listen to what you have to say about him, his church, his plans. That's all. We'd like to get an inside perspective. We'd pay you as well, of course."

"I'm not a narc."

"Everyone says that. But the fact of the matter is that if you say no, someone else will say yes. And if you say no, we would have to place you, and your illegal solicitation of prostitutes, under closer scrutiny as well. I'm sure the State Bar of New Mexico would be interested in hearing from us."

"What the fuck? I do not solicit." I didn't. Never have. Not that I have anything against sex work, I've just never had the need. I shouldn't have been surprised by the cheap homophobic tactic—it was the FBI, after all—but I admit it threw me off.

"Do as you see fit, Mr. Whitehurst. I'll see myself out."

She placed a business card on my coffee table and left. As I carried her full glass to the dishwasher, I found myself thinking about her so-called offer but not in the way she'd intended. If I were her contact, that meant I could feed her whatever information I wanted, protecting Gabriel from further harassment. You may not believe me now, but I swear that was the extent of my thought process—my decision to stay in contact with Agent Cook had nothing to do with saving my own skin from some phony charge. It was all about keeping control of the situation.

The next day, I called Agent Cook and told her I would cooperate, that I would tell her whatever I could. She didn't ask why I'd had the change of heart. I assumed she probably didn't care. She told me to email her biweekly with summaries of what went on in the church, taking particular note of changes in Gabriel's "messaging." These informal reports weren't expected to be long or terribly detailed, just, as she repeated, "keeping tabs."

Then I called up Gabriel and told him the FBI had contacted me and that they were watching him. Closely. I told him I would do what I could to help him but that he needed to watch himself. He assured me that the surveillance was no big deal, and not to panic. He said to provide the FBI with whatever information they wanted—he had nothing to hide. "It's no coincidence that they chose you, Joshua," he said. "It's all part of God's plan."

"Do you really believe that?" I asked. "That God made an FBI agent come to my apartment and bother me? Really?"

"Why not?"

FR. MICHAEL CARTER

When his next letter arrived, I was no longer in Santa Fe. I had been stripped of my position at José's Home and transferred to another Jesuit training center near Kansas City, Missouri. The process had been painful and surprisingly public. There had been an airing of grievances by the other priests, largely stemming from the Shell protest but also bringing to light other disputes I had assumed were largely forgotten. Priests have long memories, and even Father Patrice, who I considered almost a brother, voted for me to be let go. Transferred. They pretended it was simply that I was old, that the needs of Jesuits today were not the same as when we founded the seminary, but I could see these for the flimsy excuses they were. In the end, I left without putting up much of a fight—if everyone wished me removed, it would only be foolishness to stay.

An air of disgrace trailed me to Missouri, whispers behind my back that occasionally grew to more than whispers, but eventually it all died down. Then I was left with something even worse: isolation. I had thought solitude was what I wanted, spending hours contemplating Christ, but confronted with the reality ... I must admit, it was difficult.

The break between letters was long enough that I assumed either the post office had decided to stop forwarding my mail, or perhaps the seminary was keeping them from me.

Nevertheless, the possibility that he was dead or otherwise imperiled never entered my mind. I had heard some describe his actions as madness, but what I saw was a man touched by Christ. Flawed, yes, as we all are—even the saints, lest you forget, are not without sin. But the idea that a person listening directly to Christ should act "normal" would be preposterous. God's will is ineffable, so why should the acts He commands His servants to carry out be any clearer, any more rational to mortal minds? I never understood Gabriel's journey, but I also never tried to. I was his friend not his analyst. Not even his confessor.

When a new letter from him finally arrived, it had a return address: Our Lady of Guadalupe Church in Albuquerque. Hungry for news, hungry for any human connection, I savored that letter, carefully opening its envelope and taking my time with its contents.

Dear Father Carter,

I've returned to Albuquerque, my home, mi querencia. Coming back has been odd, like waking from a dream. Our Lady of Guadalupe changed while I was asleep. Manny changed. Even my rock, Anna, changed, though perhaps less than anyone else. I'm not sure why I expected things to remain the same or if I would even want them to, but I can't help but feel some regret. No one falls asleep and hopes the furniture will be rearranged when they wake up, that their lamp will no longer be in the right place and their books will be thrown haphazardly on the floor. I can't help but wonder what would have happened if I'd stayed—would Our Lady of Guadalupe be bigger than before? Would we have grown into the force for good I've always desired? Everyone knows that only a fool deals in hypotheticals, but sometimes it's impossible not to.

Christ never told me why I needed to leave. That's not His way, I suppose, and what I'd hoped to find while wandering this country, listening carefully to every scream and song and cry I came across, may have only ever been a dream. I walked past endless tracts of livestock in the middle of the country, cows destined for slaughter as far as the eye could see, and swam through poisonous rivers downstream from factories. I saw good too, I swear it. I saw beauty and joy, cookouts and birthday parties, simple evenings of families watching TV reruns together and laughing because it felt good. But when you wake up, the nightmares are the only parts you remember in any detail. The only parts you have trouble forgetting.

Now that I'm awake again, I find myself worrying about what's next. I know that those we fed are hungry once more. The laws that we kept from passing years ago have returned for another round of votes. Shell has rebuilt its plant and begun stealing oil from the ground we fought so hard to defend. And beyond this, there's the inescapable chaos of modern life. Two weeks ago, a Planned Parenthood was bombed in Phoenix, a few hours' drive from here. Here in Albuquerque, the police killed another homeless man last week. He literally begged for his life as the first bullets shredded through his skin. If we stand for righteousness, what does it matter? I've been praying for God to offer me guidance, to show me how to make a real difference. Something that might last longer than another night of restless dreaming.

Beyond this, I also fear that once again the Catholic Church has placed a target on my back. I'm not sure what I did. What I wish the archbishop would understand is that

I love the Church, was raised in it, and only broke away due to slight philosophical differences—my understanding of Christ's message of love is not limited by the same rules as his. I've tried communicating this to him, and to others within the Church, but it's been useless. For now, I plan on disengaging and hoping that as time passes, they'll begin to reassess. I'm not asking for your help with this, just stating the facts as I'm aware of them.

In any case, I hope you've been doing well. If you have the time, I would love to see you again. I promise you I have no further agenda. We could meet in Albuquerque or at the seminary, whatever's easiest for you.

With sincerest affection,
—Gabriel Romero

For once, I was able to write him back, though it felt a bit odd. His earlier letters had allowed me the voyeuristic thrill of observing him without the duty of responding, and in a way, this was the role I had become happiest with. After being pushed out of the seminary, I found myself wary of offering advice, particularly when it came to spiritual matters. I considered myself a failure in that arena.

Still, I felt that perhaps in his journeying, Gabriel might have become as lonely as I had, that he may have been searching for companionship. So I responded, though my ineloquent words said little of any value. Nevertheless, I kept a copy, though why, I can't say.

Dear Gabriel,
It is good to hear from you, as ever. I am glad to learn that you have returned to Albuquerque, and although you may not have found what you were looking for, it is in the

journey itself that they say wisdom lies, not simply in the outcome. I cannot say for certain whether this is true, but perhaps it can offer you some small solace when considering what you have discovered.

I find that, unfortunately, I have little advice to offer. I am no great activist, as you are well aware. I have always been more concerned with saving a few souls than changing the world, but this may be a matter of temperament, and yours is turned toward greater things. I have never been much of a classicist either, but it might be worth considering those who have come before—not rulers or politicians but holy individuals with similar pursuits. The saints are honored for various reasons, and though they may not have rid the world of evils, perhaps they persuaded a few to turn their eyes toward God.

As for meeting, I must tell you that this would be difficult to arrange. Likewise, if you are able to mend your relationship with the Catholic Church, it would not be due to my assistance. You may notice the postmark on my envelope is from Kansas City, Missouri. Shortly after you left, priests in the seminary saw fit to report me to superiors within the order. There were claims that my actions "against" the archbishop threatened the Jesuits' relationship with the diocese and that I flaunted my disobedience. Of course, the archbishop had no jurisdiction over me, nor had he communicated any wish for me to stay away from you or the Shell protests—but this was found immaterial. After a great deal of dramatic unrest in the seminary, I was stripped of my position and have been given a perfunctory role here, instructing the occasional student in only the most basic tenets of Ignatian spirituality. While my health has seen somewhat better days, I am nevertheless doing fine.

Despite the punitive measures against me, I would not worry a great deal about the Church and think your approach is probably best. They're unable to move you across the country and unlikely to do more than grumble a bit to themselves. While it is the true Church of Christ, it is also a bureaucratic goliath. There is no point trying to second-guess yourself and try to make them happy—do right today, in all things, and you will be doing the work of the Lord here on Earth.

The blessings of Christ be with you always,
—Father Michael Carter

I sent this letter the next day, well aware that continuing my correspondence with Gabriel was unwise from a career standpoint, but my career was essentially finished. My faith remained untarnished, and if the Jesuits thought I should be sentenced to sitting by the fire, reading and tending to my thoughts, a worthless shell of a man no longer fit for real work, then so be it. More and more often, I found myself drifting off while reading or even while lecturing students, so perhaps the order was correct after all. Hearing from Gabriel again cheered me greatly, and I began anticipating another letter. It was probably best for my own morale that I didn't know how soon our correspondence would end.

ADRIANA COOK

Mr. Whitehurst was indeed one of our paid informants. I visited his apartment to speak with him about the possibility of monitoring Mr. Romero's activities at Our Lady of Guadalupe Church. During our search for possible informants, we placed a particular emphasis on new parishioners like Mr. Whitehurst, who began attending as soon as Mr. Romero reappeared. He was a corporate lawyer with a clean record who had formerly been involved with the Española Shell legal team, making him a particularly viable candidate.

Since returning to Albuquerque, Mr. Romero had rekindled ties with other local radical elements, including Black Lives Matter and the Peace & Justice Center. He'd been noted speaking with community leaders within the Progressive Democrats, the Green Party, and the Libertarians, a sign that he was returning to his old patterns. The last time he mobilized a large group, the resulting destruction of corporate property had been immense, measuring in the millions of dollars. Had Mr. Romero cut his ties with these questionable elements, we would not have continued pursuing him as a person of interest. But he decided to continue in this vein, and that kept him on our radar. Decisions have consequences.

We only asked Mr. Whitehurst to watch Mr. Romero and report what he saw. I explicitly warned him not to draw attention to himself, to avoid any form of observation that would be out of the ordinary. We never wished to interfere with genuine religious worship. I am fully aware of the rumors about our involvement, but let me assure you, this is conspiracy mongering and nothing more. The Bureau has always been subject to such speculation. And yes, I am also aware of our alleged involvement when it comes to assassinations. I know what they say about JFK and RFK, Fred Hampton and Mark Clark, Martin Luther King Jr. and Malcolm X. Let me assure you that despite what social-justice activists on Twitter tell you, the days of COINTELPRO are long past. The Bureau today remains strictly within the constitutional limits of the law.

I see you don't believe me. And you don't have to. I know that certain events of the last decade have permanently undermined the trust Americans put in their government. But when it comes to Mr. Romero, I am not lying. Let me repeat, we simply asked Mr. Whitehurst to watch and report. To watch what Mr. Romero said and did and report this back to us. Watch and report and leave anything more important to us. That's all. We were not responsible.

Although our materials about Mr. Romero remain classified for what I assure you are important, constitutionally sound reasons, those who say we had anything else to do with what happened are consciously spreading misinformation, presumably for their own malicious purposes.

JOSHUA WHITEHURST

As our relationship began anew, Gabriel and I didn't suddenly become lovers again, but we did become more than friends. We started meeting up several times a week, not just for meals but also for movies or concerts. We never seemed to run out of things to talk about, and I don't just mean God and theology but also books, ethics, politics, even the law—whatever happened to come to mind. And even though we weren't going any further than kissing, there was a freedom to being with him in public that I hadn't felt even during college. No, we never quite became a real couple, but we did occasionally hold hands. We made out during the boring parts of *Phantom of the Opera*. We giggled and flirted and disappeared into a world of just the two of us, a world I never wanted to leave.

And every week, I returned to Our Lady of Guadalupe. The congregation grew—not exponentially but by adding a new family this week, a couple curious individuals the next. Gabriel spoke with them all personally after Mass. He had a skill for reading them, could tell instantly whether new parishioners wanted a few jokes to feel comfortable, or needed solemn words of wisdom, or if they'd shown up in the hope he could heal a family member. Whatever they desired from a priest, from a church, he did his best to provide. He was amorphous, and I couldn't help but question some of my own memories of him. What had he been thinking when we lay in bed together so many years earlier? What had he been thinking, almost four years ago, when he showed up on my doorstep? What had he been thinking a month ago during that long hug? And what did he think when offering me the Eucharist, placing the body of Christ directly onto my tongue with the utmost delicacy?

After the FBI's visit, I would meet with Gabriel for lunch every week and we'd decide what I would tell them, though ultimately there didn't seem to be anything to tell. He and the community at Our Lady of Guadalupe were passionate but otherwise ordinary. Maybe even dull. I was always one of the last people in the lobby after Mass, and I'd met a few other parishioners over doughnuts and coffee. I liked more than a few of them, enjoyed our meaningless chats about the news or the weather or the sermon we'd just heard. Some even knew I was gay—as I said, I was long past hiding it—and they didn't give a shit. Maybe that meant Gabriel's peace-and-love rhetoric was working, or maybe he naturally attracted a better crowd of church folks, who can say, but I did feel surprisingly comfortable there. Not so comfortable that I would've continued going if Gabriel took another hiatus, but enough that seeing him wasn't the only reason I enjoyed visiting Our Lady of Guadalupe every Sunday morning.

We'd been seeing each other for a few months when he invited me back to his room after a show one evening. This felt intimate, and my heart quickened when he locked the door behind him. His room was cluttered but otherwise simple, a monk's cell—maybe a monk who didn't think that cleanliness was next to godliness. He brought a chair over from his desk for me, and he plunked down on his cot a couple of feet away, facing me.

"I have something to ask you," he said, leaning forward. "Something serious."

"Um, alright," I said, caught off guard by his tone. It was conspiratorial rather than romantic. His foot tapped restlessly on the floor.

"This isn't...," he began. "I want you to understand, you can say no to me. To this. I'll understand."

"Ok, but you're starting to freak me out. What's going on?"

He looked down at the floor, not meeting my eyes. "I need you to stab me."

I didn't know what to say. I'm sure he could read the confusion and dismay on my face, and I wondered if he'd misinterpreted what I meant when I mentioned the other day that I'd taken to domming men. I was prepared for a lot. A hot love tryst. A casual conversation. I'd rehearsed this moment in my head countless times, but as usual, Gabriel threw a curveball with such a weird spin that I couldn't even begin to figure out where it was going.

"I ... what?" I finally sputtered. "I mean, I ... fuck, Gabriel, what the fuck?"

"It's not what you think," he said. "I don't mean for you to hurt me. Not really. I just had this vision, this really important vision, and the vision had you in it. I've had them before, though never quite like this, and ... I don't know if I can explain it, but they're always true. They always happen. I know it sounds completely ridiculous. I'm sorry."

There was a strange contrast between the harsh minimalism of his room—all wood and rough, almost militaristic bedding—and the mystical nature of what he was saying. Here we were, just two guys calmly chatting, not tripping on acid or even a bit tipsy, and he's talking about visions and prognostication.

"What do you mean when you say they always come true?" I asked. "Like ... these visions. You have them a lot? Is that how you knew about the lightning strike?"

He seemed uncomfortable, his foot-tapping now so spasmodic it was like the thumping of hail on a car roof. "I've had them from time to time. And yeah, they've never been wrong. Never. Even when they've seemed crazy. Even when I didn't understand them. Like ... yes, up there by Española at the Shell protest. I knew the lightning would hit the drill because I'd seen it happen. I'd seen it in a vision every night for a week. And sometimes when I heal someone, I close my eyes and I see this light guiding me to the right herb, to the right spot on their bodies, and it works. I don't understand it. I just know to listen."

"That's just ... that's ... wow, Gabriel. I mean, I knew you managed to do *something* at that drill, but ... why didn't you tell me about all this earlier? And, wait. So you've had plenty of visions before, but you said you hadn't had any like this. This is ... I mean, stabbing? What exactly was in this vision that I'm supposed to play so central a part in? Beyond the stabbing, I mean."

"In my vision, I'm preaching Sunday Mass. It's toward the end, and I walk down into the congregation, and you stab me in front of everyone. Only nothing really happens. I bleed briefly, very briefly, but that's it."

"You mean ... just a small cut? A graze?"

"Not at all. You stab me straight through. You don't hold back. And for a moment, I can feel the life draining out of me. But then Christ heals me, the way He's helped me heal so many others. In the vision, I saw His divine light on my chest, then the feeling of warm blood was replaced by a comforting feeling of … I can't explain it, but it felt cool and soft. It felt right. And that's it."

"That's it?"

"That's it. The wound is gone. The congregation is in an uproar, but I stand up, and they fall silent, confronted with the miraculous healing power of our Lord."

I didn't know what to say. I waited to hear if there was more, but apparently there wasn't.

Finally, I found words. "This vision … why would God … ? I mean, what possible reason would He have for any of this? I understand why God or whatever would want you to heal people, but…"

"I don't pretend to understand the mind of God," he said, "but I think it's to bring the church together, to make it grow and gain notoriety, so we can continue doing good. So Our Lady of Guadalupe can have a *real* impact in this terrible, terrible world. And with all that goodwill, I can finally come out publicly, without the risk of losing it all."

"That doesn't really … I used to be your lover," I said. "I'm your … more than friend now. And I'm not even sure I believe in God, your God. Not fully. Wouldn't having me do it just make everyone *more* antigay, *more* bigoted? Not that I'm saying you should actually act on any of this, but wouldn't it make more sense if Father Quintana were to do it? I think you'd need a true believer."

"I'm not explaining this well at all, Josh, I apologize. In the vision, after I stand up, I explain to everyone that you're my … lover. That you were chosen by God to execute this test of faith, like Abraham with Isaac. That *we*, you and I together, are a living sign of God's blessing on queer couples. I guess maybe I'll ask Manny if you won't help me. And I don't want you to feel forced. I just ... for some reason, I thought you'd be the one who'd understand me if I explained it all."

"Jesus, Gabriel. That's ... well that's beautiful. I mean, what you're describing is terrifying, but that's beautiful."

Gabriel didn't begin crying exactly, but he didn't stay straight-faced either. I moved to join him on the bed. I put my arm around his shoulder and pulled him toward me. He pushed his face into my arm, and I could feel his tears soaking into my sleeve. We stayed that way for several minutes, but finally I had to ask.

"How can you know this is from God? Those other visions, they came true, so maybe they were, but ... this one is so violent. And so fantastical. Happily-ever-after. What if it's from somewhere else, somewhere bad? Or what if ... what if it's wish fulfillment? What if you've been under so much pressure and your brain finally, well, snapped? I don't mean snapped, I'm sorry, I just mean what if it's *you*, and you only think it's God? You'll end up dead."

"I know, it sounds crazy. Don't think I haven't considered the alternatives—I'm the one who's been having visions for years, after all. But I know. I know what having my wishes fulfilled looks like and it's ... it's not this. This performance is not what I want, I just want what comes after. I'm not going into this blindly, and I don't want you to either. My God *is* a God of violence, you know. Look at the Old Testament. Abraham and Isaac, as I mentioned. Job. A million other examples. Hell, look at the lightning strike—people still have PTSD about it, for all it was a miracle. But no one died then, by the grace of God, and this is no different."

"But then what if I'm arrested? Or everyone there tries to jump me?" I asked.

"They don't," he said. "I'm there, so they can't. But you have to have faith." He pulled his head back, and we stared into each other's eyes. His were brown, like rich soil, and wet, a pair of deep springs welling up from the ground that I could feel myself soaking in, splashing in. Drowning in.

"I want to. Believe me, I do. But I don't know if I can. And last time I trusted you, it didn't exactly work out. I need to think about all this."

Gabriel took my hand and brought it to his cheek. His skin was perfectly smooth, not a hint of stubble, though I knew he could grow a full beard in just a couple weeks. He kissed my hand, so softly it was like the caress of a butterfly's wings. He pulled my face to his lips and then, and then...

Look, I've tried to be honest with you, to be straight-forward and clear. I've tried not to whitewash my past, even when it leaves me looking like shit. So be it. But I'm going to leave out the details of that afternoon, of who did what to who and how. I'm not going to tell you which opera he played on his computer's diminutive speakers or what cologne I wore. Gabriel wanted his bedroom door locked that day, and despite everything that happened later, I'm going to honor that and remain silent.

Three days later, we were in his room again after a lovely dinner together. The door was locked, and it was late. We'd been lying in bed, not sleeping but not talking either. Just being.

At some point, Gabriel sat up and said, "I don't mean to ... but, well, I have to know. Will you do it?"

I'd had a lot of time, during those intervening three days, to search my soul for what I really believed. And what I'd come to realize was that I did believe in him, had faith in him, and if Gabriel told me that God had sent him this vision … well, he was special to me, so why couldn't he also be special to God?

"Of course I will," I said.

"So you believe me?"

"Yes."

He took a deep breath. "Ok. So you promise? Next week?"

"I promise. I'm scared, but I'll do it."

"Thank you," he said.

I'd always thought of myself as skeptical. Rational. As a person who thinks about things with a clear mind. But now that I've had so much time to think about it, I see that I've never really been a logical person at all. There's a word for why I believed in Gabriel, despite my lifelong rejection of anything mystical or magical or spiritual, and that word is love. Which is another way of saying faith.

ANNA FISHEL

Father Gabriel was already filling his thermos at the coffee maker when I arrived. He looked like he hadn't slept well, though he had even more anxious, nervous energy than usual. I asked him if everything was alright.

"I've had a lot of visions this past week." He sighed. "Some almost contradictory. They were confusing and disturbing … I don't know. I'm ok, though. It may be difficult, but I think we'll all be alright."

He smiled, but it was strained, obviously put on for my benefit. I told him to sit down and asked if he could tell me about these visions. I wondered whether this was a prelude to another desertion—the prospect filled me with dread. But maybe this time I could help.

"They were bloody," he said. "They were violent. There was pain, and I just…"

"Take a deep breath, Father, then start at the beginning."

"The first thing I saw … remember how law enforcement had been watching us up in Española? I found out it's happening again, the FBI this time. Watching the whole church but me in particular. They don't like me pointing out how hateful and racist and corrupt the government is, how bad capitalism is. They don't like me saying how Christ really feels about the situation. And they've had enough of it."

"What do you mean?"

"God has revealed to me that they plan ... they have violent designs. They've decided to do whatever it takes to stop me, and there's going to be an assassination attempt."

I was in shock and couldn't really process what he was saying. "Are you sure? I don't mean to question a holy vision, but could you be misinterpreting it? I just ... the FBI planning an assassination? That's almost unbelievable. Maybe the vision was metaphorical?"

"My visions are never metaphorical," he responded. "That's not how God talks to me. And the FBI's been involved in plenty of political coups, plenty of murders. Just they usually manage to pin the blame on someone else."

"Ok, so it's not metaphorical. Oh my God," I said, hyperventilating slightly. "Do you ... did you see when this was supposed to happen? Is it soon?"

"It'll happen this Sunday. That was perfectly clear."

"Then take a break for the week! Let Father Manuel take over on Sunday, maybe longer, and we can figure out things from there."

He paused for a long moment, staring down at the floor. "I can't do that. It's only after they strike me down that God shows us all He's more powerful than this hate, than any hate. He heals my meager human wound, and I stand up. And this miracle unites our church, brings us together, allows us to spread His message of love, of real acceptance and unity, throughout the world. It's the next step, Anna. I just have to—we all have to—be like Abraham and put our utmost trust in Him."

This wasn't the first time Father Gabriel had told me to prepare for something miraculous, and in the past, he'd always delivered. So like, I'd come to trust his visions, really, even if they sometimes needed a little help, some extra preparation from the church or something. So I said the only thing I could say. "What can I do to help your—I mean God's—plan come to pass?"

"Thank you for your trust, Anna. And your faith."

"Of course."

"We need to make sure that God's message of love goes out to as many people as possible, that as many people as possible witness this miracle and hear what I have to say. All of us at Our Lady of Guadalupe need to get the word out about a very special Mass this Sunday. And we need to have faith."

We kneeled, right there in the hallway, and spent the next hour in deep prayer. It was the closest I ever felt to Father Gabriel, both of us whispering words of praise and supplication. In his left hand, he clutched the old brass and turquoise rosary he always kept around his neck. I don't know what he prayed for, but I prayed for his safety and that this miracle would lead the church into a new age.

When we finished, Father Gabriel left to speak with Father Manuel, and I returned to my desk and began calling every individual who'd ever been a member of Our Lady of Guadalupe, everyone I knew on Facebook, even distant friends I hadn't seen since college. I told them they needed to be there the following Sunday, that we all needed to attend because something big, a miracle like they'd never seen before, was going to happen. You can ask anyone, they all knew before showing up that this wouldn't be just an ordinary Mass—they all knew that Father Gabriel's visions were real, that God saw fit to offer him a tiny bit of His divine plan. Folks showed up in droves, because they *believed*.

Thinking about it now, it's impossible not to wonder whether Father Gabriel misunderstood the vision, or whether something went wrong, or a thousand other questions. But the one I ask myself most is whether Father Gabriel knew, or guessed, but kept the full truth from me and Father Manuel. Whether he knew we would have stopped him from offering up that Mass, the most important one of his life, if we'd known. Whether that was more important to him than telling us the whole story. But it's not my place to question God, or Father Gabriel.

ISABEL ROMERO

I knew as soon as he returned to town. I just had a feeling one evening, a small tickle at the back of my neck that told me my little boy was nearby again. Mamá had the same gift and so did Gabito. She used to tell me to listen to it, to those little premonitions and feelings you have, because those were los santos whispering in your ears, telling you secrets nonbelievers were too stupid to pay attention to. I used to tell her she was mistaking shivers for an angel's muttering, that we just needed a new furnace, but at a certain point ... I don't know. I guess I started thinking maybe she made some sense after all, even if I couldn't explain it. The very next evening, there he was at my home, snacking on chips and salsa like he was still fifteen, casual as could be.

Evelyn died while he was gone, so Gabito was under no more obligation to see her. I'd somehow convinced William to keep Gabriel's inheritance funneled toward Our Lady of Guadalupe, and there were several years of funds still left. So other than filling him in on all that business, there wasn't too much news. I had a few more gray hairs maybe, a few more aches in my knees and ankles, but that was it. Instead of having some sort of heart-to-heart, we watched TV together. Even with the suddenness of his return, it was casual. Familial. Before he left, he asked for my work schedule, so he'd know when I'd be around, and after that he popped by every week or so, pretty much at random. We'd watch something, and while we never talked much, it was still the best part of my week. The house felt full again, with food and noise and purpose, and that was all I really wanted anyhow, my son coming by without needing some favor.

We were almost like a pair of old friends. There was no pressure. He didn't have to perform, didn't have to be a perfect Christian role model, didn't have to heal my sinus infection or set my broken bones with the power of Christ. He could relax, take off his shoes, ask me who the guests were on *The Tonight Show*. It was so ordinary, and I loved every minute. Sometimes I'd come home and he'd already be in the garden, digging into my compost of old newspapers and mierda de pollos.

He knew I went to his church, and sometimes we even saw each other there. But I didn't go to his Masses. I stayed with Padre Quintana. I just felt, for whatever reason, that it would be harder for us to stay so casual if I saw him at that altar. I'd want to say something, and he'd have to respond, and pretty soon it would be a whole thing. It's like, what if you were Bob Dylan's mom, you know? You wouldn't go to all his shows. I felt the same way, like I'd make his Masses more awkward. I liked hearing about them, and I asked about them when the opportunity came up, just not when Gabito was around. Did he heal someone? Did he speak in tongues? Was it just a really great sermon? I wanted to know every little detail, but I knew not to watch, even from the back like I used to. He'd know I was there, the same way I'd known he was in town. Sangre de familia: you can't hide the scent, no matter how hard you try.

Those last few months ... they were some of the happiest of my life. Kelly's hired a dumb new manager I hated, but with Gabito back and doing so well, I felt almost, I don't know, content. Maybe I just remember things as so happy because of what happened later, but I really believe that time was special.

Then, on the Wednesday night before his ... ok, this is even harder than I thought. I can't, I'm sorry ..., It's just, this is really difficult. Give me a minute, please.

★ ★ ★

Right. Really, I'm alright, I just need to get through this. Maybe a glass of water will help.

Ok, enough stalling. I'll tell you what happened, and then maybe I'll never have to tell it again. I don't know exactly how to start, but I'll try. I'll try.

On the Wednesday night. Before. He came over. I'd started cooking for two on the nights I was home, because there was a good chance he'd stop by, pero if not, at least I'd have lunch made for the next day. When he arrived, I already had rellenos in the oven. We watched some local news while waiting for dinner to finish, and I let off a little steam about work during the commercials. I served dinner on the coffee table in front of the television, volume low enough for us to talk over. Gabriel gave me a weird look and said, "Mom, do you think you could come to church this Sunday?"

"Sure," I said, wondering what was up. I thought maybe he was sick—he looked like he hadn't slept much lately or maybe had some indigestion. Maybe he was anxious about me seeing him, so I should make things as easy as possible. "I'll be there. Eleven o'clock, right?"

"This is really important," he said. "I need you there. I can't explain, it's just … I need it."

"Of course, mijo. Whatever you need. I'll get Rita to cover my shift, it's no problem. Can you tell me what's wrong?"

His relleno sat in front of him, untouched. He looked at it, then said, so quietly I could barely hear it, "No."

"It's ok," I assured him. "I'll pray to Mamá tonight, ask her to watch over you with San Cristóbal. I know he kept a close watch on you for a while, what's another couple days?"

Gabito looked at me. "I'm not a child anymore, Mom. He watches after children."

"You'll always be my child, mijo. Now eat your dinner before it gets cold. I'll see you on Sunday, and then we can go out and get cinnamon buns and orange juice at the Frontier like we used to when you were little."

After he left, I started planning what to wear. Hearing my son offer Mass for the first time in forever, and by invitation for a change—it was like going to his first communion again but even better. He'd be giving me communion. I wanted to look nice but not too nice. Vanity would be unbecoming of a priest's mother. But still, I wanted to stand out, if just a little bit, so I splurged on a new dress and a pair of heels to match it.

I prayed to Mamáy los santos that evening, asked San Cristóbal to make my son less nervous on Sunday, but I didn't ask any of them to protect him. The idea that he might need it never even crossed my mind.

I can't say if Our Lady of Guadalupe was full that day, but there sure were a lot of people. More than a few hundred, maybe more than a thousand. It seemed more like Easter Mass than a random Sunday. I sat toward the front, close enough that I'd get a good view of Gabito without having to put on my glasses. There was a different feeling to the room than during the small Saturday afternoon Masses with Padre Quintana. I couldn't tell you whether this was typical, but it was loud and lively, filled with gossip and expectations. It felt almost like a show, especially when the musicians, more than a dozen of them, began to play one of Gabito's favorites: Bach's *Mass in B Minor.* The audience grew silent, and for the next ten minutes, we listened while a singer and a flute traded lines, the other instruments drifting in and out behind them. Both melodies were lovely on their own, but there was something in the arrangement that meant these two melodies and the harmonies behind them sounded more complete when mixed.

After that, the Mass began as normal, but there was a certain grandness about so many voices greeting one another, reciting the Apostles' Creed together. The sounds of prayers echoed off the tall roof, bouncing around so they never seemed to begin or end. It looked to me like Gabriel loved this effect, rejoiced in it. He smiled broadly as he made his way across the sanctuary, leading us in prayer. He burned incense, but instead of the usual sharp mixture, it smelled strangely sweet, like the vanilla he'd worn for years. As he moved through the aisles, the smoke began to coat the room.

I don't remember the readings. Something from Matthew, I think, and something from Acts of the Apostles. What I do remember is the sermon. I think everyone who was there remembers it, or at least parts of it. Gabriel walked to the altar, and though he didn't have a microphone, his voice filled the hall.

"I want to remind everyone of a sermon that Christ our Lord and Savior once told us, one I feel goes forgotten far too often. In our world, Christ is invoked constantly—by politicians pandering to their base, by sheriffs hunting down men like they're animals, by corporations that would rather let people die than insure everyone. That's not the Christ I know. The Christ I know looks to help the weak, to end injustice. The Christ I know said blessed are the meek, for they shall inherit the earth. Blessed are those who hunger, for they shall be filled. Blessed are the poor, for theirs is the kingdom of God. The Christ I know is the Prince of Peace. He doesn't support the NRA; He asks us to turn our swords into plowshares.

"So who now, I ask, are those who Christ supports? Who are the meek, the hungry, the poor? Who are the pure in heart and the ones who mourn? I tell you they are the same now as they were two thousand years ago, and that God has not lost sight of them, no matter how much the rest of us have. God tells us this: blessed are the immigrants, for they shall find comfort in the land of God. Can I hear an amen?"

"Amen." Our voices came as one, forceful and confident.

"Blessed are the homeless, for they shall find shelter."

"Amen," we said, even louder.

"Blessed are the addicts, for they shall find relief."

"Amen." Louder still.

"Blessed are those who suffer from racist oppression, for they shall find justice."

"Amen!"

"Blessed are those who find themselves with child and choose not to carry to term, for they shall find compassion."

"Amen!"

"Blessed are those whose lands have been stolen and colonized, for they shall own their own destinies."

"Amen!"

"Blessed are the prisoners and the unjustly convicted, for they will find freedom."

"Amen!"

"And blessed are those shunned because of their gender or sexuality, for they shall find love."

"Amen!" This last one crashed over us like a shock wave, prayers louder than bombs. Everyone was standing, and an energy pulsed beneath our feet, ready to explode, to lead us to glory.

I was close enough to see that as he began listing these beatitudes, he also began crying. Small, almost invisible tears, but tears nonetheless. I wanted to hug him, to tell him everything would be ok, that surely Dios was on his side and yes, yes, yes! The kingdom of Heaven must be like he'd said. He was my baby boy, and I was so proud of him, and I felt, briefly, like this was why he'd wanted me to come. It was the sermon he'd been building to his whole life, the one that explained why he'd needed to found his own church and how he understood Christ's message. If it had ended there, it would've been perfect, beyond my wildest hopes for what he could be as a priest and as a person.

It didn't end.

He began walking forward, off the stage and among the pews. He walked along an aisle, saying, "But not everyone understands that God's love is a love of joy and acceptance. An unconditional love. Not everyone believes. Some want proof. And sometimes, we believers are tested, tested so that we can display our faith, and the weak faith of others will no longer make excuses and falter."

He stopped. Next to him was a man—I won't say his name, I wish I'd never heard it—who was about his age with short blond hair, wearing a well-tailored suit. He looked very serious. He looked very nervous. I could see sweat beading on his forehead.

My son looked this man straight in the eyes and said, with the utmost calm in his voice, "Do what you have come here to do."

The man raised a long, wicked-looking knife. His hand was shaking. He stepped forward and stabbed it through my son's chest. Gabito grabbed the hilt with both hands and tried to remove the blade. I saw him pulling at it, desperately, but the man jerked it up, and the knife cut deeper...

¡Ay Dios! I think I need another moment...

But there isn't much more to say, so I'll just try and finish. I'll try.

Chaos erupted. People grabbed that man, wrestled the knife from him, and pinned him to the ground. Others tried to staunch the blood draining from my son's chest. I ran forward as fast as I could, yelling like everyone else. Over all of this, I still heard my son's last words, words that showed my Gabito didn't simply preach peace, he lived it. "Forgive him," he said. Just those two simple words: "Forgive him."

That's it. That's all of it, all of that horrible day that mattered anyway. The rest was the hospital and the police, and then all the goddamn reporters, and I'm too tired to talk about it, too tired and too ... I mean, what's even the point? I have more to say about Gabito, about Gabriel, but I ... I need to stop now. I'm too tired. Too sad.

No, I'm glad you came, Padre. It's important to set the record straight, I know that. It's just ... it doesn't get any easier. It doesn't hurt any less. Maybe we can talk more tomorrow or the next day. But right now I need a little break. I need to rest. Maybe you can say some prayers for him, Padre. I think he'd like that. I think maybe that would help.

JOSHUA WHITEHURST

"Forgive me." Those were the last words he spoke. "Forgive me." You can make of them what you will, but they weren't an abstract proclamation or some pseudo-last-rites buzzer-beater penitence. Those words were directed at me. He knew that what he'd told me, the miracle of his healing, wasn't going to happen. Maybe he knew before that moment, or maybe he figured it out right then. I can't say. But I do know that what he said was perfectly clear, perfectly straightforward. Whether or not anyone else believes me doesn't change what happened that day—all it changes is what happens now, and that's largely out of my hands.

What you have to understand is that I didn't even want to go through with it. Of course I wanted to help Gabriel, believed in what he told me, but that didn't make it easy. I hadn't slept in days, had no appetite, couldn't concentrate at work. Through it all, though, I knew that his miracle, the one that would stand as incontrovertible proof to everyone, was important enough that I needed to be a good soldier and do what I was told. When we talked about it over dinner a couple days earlier, he explained my role as almost like a magician's assistant, as blasphemous as that might sound, a sort of human prop to help him illustrate God's power. His power. It wasn't supposed to be a big deal—he was going to be the center of attention, the one who held the secret. And while I dreaded using that knife, I also fantasized about what came afterward. He would claim his sexuality, make it clear that I was his lover. I was ready for him to show me, show all of us, how the power of Christ could work wonders and bring about justice and equality, even in today's horrendous world. It would've been one hell of a miracle.

All of this is in the public record, no different from my testimony elsewhere. But what I want you to understand, Father, is that it's not just words I'm throwing around for my defense. This is what I really believed.

And when it came down to it, I didn't even truly have it in me. Not really. The irony is, I barely cut him. It was a graze, a scratch. I knew he wanted me to thrust deep, to slice him open like a butcher so the crowd would have something to see, a Grand Guignol–style climax to make the miracle undeniable. "It can't be subtle," he'd said. But as much as I've enjoyed inflicting pain, I never wanted to legitimately hurt someone. Especially not Gabriel.

The real damage was self-inflicted. He grabbed hold of the knife and forced it deeper, yanked it up. He pushed it into himself with so much strength, I couldn't do anything to stop him. For the thousandth time, I confess that I stabbed him, but he did the real work himself. The knife went up, into his heart, because *he* moved it there. That's the truth. I know what the coroner said, that there's no way for a person who's been stabbed like that to exert the sort of force that could drive a knife into their own heart. I know that the coroner said the angle was all wrong, that the blade would need to be longer, sharper. But Father, you of all people should know a miracle when you hear one, so you might be able to understand how, somehow, despite all these factors, he still managed to puncture his heart. The coroner wasn't accounting for a miracle, after all. She didn't understand whose corpse she was examining.

Immediately afterward, I was slammed into the back of a police car and whisked off to jail. I was in shock, but once that wore off I was crazy fucking angry with him. For weeks, I was convinced that I'd been Gabriel's dupe, that I'd just been an integral part of a strange suicide. That he'd been insane, and I'd been collateral damage. But as I told you before, I've had a lot of time to think since then.

If Gabriel had only wanted to kill himself, he'd have needed no one's help. Whatever it was, this was no straightforward suicide. What he did, he did with conviction. And he did it in good faith. I believe that. I have to believe that.

So what if Gabriel was right all along, his vision proceeding exactly as planned ... until God pulled the rug out at the last second? Changed the stage directions, decided Gabriel would be more useful to Him as a martyr than a living priest? That's not the God Gabriel told me about or talked about in church, not the one who spared Isaac at the last second, just as Abraham was primed to do the deed.

Or, what if Gabriel hadn't told me—hadn't told anyone—his real vision? What if all he told me was what I needed to hear in order to fulfill the prophecy? In those last moments, what I saw on his face wasn't terror but grim acceptance, the look of a man doing what he needed to, even though it was difficult. I guess you could call that the very model of a self-fulfilling prophecy. And I'm not sure I like that scenario any better...

So do I know what actually happened, what Gabriel actually thought, what he actually heard from God? Of course not. I can't tell you why what happened happened.

When it comes to the thoughts of the dead, only God has answers, and I suspect that even you, with all of your Vatican finery, might have some difficulty getting a straight answer out of Him.

And yet. The fact that you're here talking to me right now, Father, tells me that something about Gabriel's vision worked out just fine. From what I've heard, he's already a martyr to many, and that number is only growing. He's bringing more followers to the Lord in death than he ever managed in life. A folk saint, I've heard him called.

ADRIANA COOK

My research into Mr. Whitehurst was standard. I looked into his occupation, education, family history, religion, political alliances. What I failed to research was his personal history, his suspicious lack of a social media footprint beyond his Grindr profile. If I had done a more thorough job, I might have discovered Mr. Whitehurst's prior sexual relationship with Mr. Romero, but I believe few agents would have acted differently.

We only discovered Mr. Whitehurst's obsession with Mr. Romero after conducting a routine search of his computer following his apprehension. He had a folder of bookmarks filled with hundreds of articles and forum posts that made mention of Mr. Romero. In addition, we discovered a physical file in his desk containing hard copies of many of these. Nothing within them indicated any inherent malice or ill intent toward Mr. Romero, but I can tell you from professional experience that such obsession is … not normal, or healthy.

Had I known about the romantic past between these two men or about Mr. Whitehurst's continued infatuation—or at least fascination—with Mr. Romero, I would never have proposed him as a possible informant. Had he mentioned this past to me, either in person or through later email communications, I would have severed our relationship and moved on to other methods of monitoring Mr. Romero. Up until that day, I would have characterized him as an ideal informant, rational and critical and extremely observant.

What I need to stress is that despite the rumors and news coverage that followed, Mr. Whitehurst was in no way whatsoever acting on the behalf of the FBI when he attacked Mr. Romero. He had a relationship with us, but hopefully by now, the extremely limited nature of that relationship has been made clear to you. Our desire to make the media circus around this supposed "brutal FBI murder" die down is in fact why I was permitted to speak with you today. There was no cover-up, no black ops. Just a tragedy we unfortunately failed to foresee.

Mr. Whitehurst stabbed Mr. Romero because his obsession went sour. These things happen. Usually it doesn't concern as high-profile a member of the community as Mr. Romero, but then sometimes it does.

I am fully aware of Mr. Whitehurst's insistence that Mr. Romero orchestrated his own death as some sort of elaborate murder-suicide ritual, but there is nothing to indicate such a pact in any of the communications Mr. Whitehurst sent me. The FBI plans on cooperating fully with the district attorney's office in its case against Mr. Whitehurst, though I understand that a plea bargain is still on the table. In any case, feel free to contact me with any other questions you may have about Mr. Romero, Mr. Whitehurst, or our involvement with them, but I can make no guarantees as to what information I will be able to divulge. I'll see myself out.

MANUEL QUINTANA

I was watching from the back of the chapel when Father Gabriel was stabbed, standing in my favorite pew, way off to the side where it was easy to hear and difficult to be seen. I rarely missed one of his Masses, and I certainly wasn't going to miss that one. I knew about the prophecy, and while I was afraid for him, I did as he asked and stood by as everything that he said would happen did ... up until the end. While everyone else panicked—rushing to staunch the bleeding and grab the assailant, which wasn't difficult because he made no attempt to run or resist—I called for an ambulance and tried to clear a path from the entrance of the church to where Father Gabriel lay. Someone had to tell the cops and paramedics what the hell happened, and I was the only priest we had left.

Mass had begun at eleven a.m., but it was past midnight by the time the cops finally departed. They'd taped up the doors to the chapel, blaring yellow warnings only hinting at the day's violence, but it was my church—my *home*—so I didn't care. I slipped past those strips of plastic and went back in, hoping to see ... I'm not sure what. Maybe something that could make meaning out of what I'd witnessed. The room felt too large, too empty, I walked down the worn aisle and past our makeshift pews. I walked slowly, looking for signs of the earlier

399

commotion, but aside from maybe a few hymnals on the floor, there was none.

The exception was the pew he'd been stabbed at. There was blood everywhere. I expected to see some sort of police markers there, little yellow numbers and a chalk outline like on *CSI*, but instead there was just the blood. It coated the carpet, seeped into the chairs, ran all across the kneelers. Most of it had already turned brown, but its smell was still overpowering and made me gag. I left the chapel, practically ran back to my small room, hoping the smell wouldn't follow me. I never entered the sanctuary again.

I canceled Mass for the next day and the next. The cops probably would've wrapped up their investigation and let us use the chapel again if I'd pressed them, but I didn't. What would've been the point? The tape remained at Our Lady of Guadalupe longer than I did.

The last Mass I offered was his funeral service the following Sunday. Anna helped me make arrangements at Santa Barbara Park in Martineztown, a few blocks from his mother's house and across the street from the cemetery he'd be buried in. The turnout was immense. Thousands of spectators covered the grass, the nearby basketball courts, and the playground. A string quartet from UNM began the ceremony with Bach's "Contrapunctus XIV," a heartbreaking piece I'd never heard before. It stopped abruptly, midmeasure—Anna said Gabriel had always liked it. I'm sure plenty of the people had never been to Our Lady of Guadalupe, but Gabriel wouldn't have minded. The words I said in his honor were few and unworthy, but people seemed to like them, and maybe they were enough. I don't know. I try not to think about that period very much.

I felt torn about Our Lady of Guadalupe. Father Gabriel would've wanted it to carry on as a place of worship. He'd seemed happy that I kept it going while he was gone. But this time we knew he wouldn't ever return, and every time I walked past the sanctuary, I smelled blood. I spoke with Anna, and we agreed to let the lease end. I moved into her spare room and did my best to stay out of her way while I tried to figure out what I would do next.

We transferred the auto-shop title to my name, and I spent a lot of my free time fixing it up. It wasn't a real morada, didn't have any history to it, didn't have any hermanos, at least not then, but it felt right to me. I liked that we were reusing the space, giving it some purpose when otherwise it would've just fallen into further decay. I'm not sure exactly what changed in me, but maybe it came from watching Gabriel. I saw how self-sacrifice could be a form of worship beyond language, beyond rationality—your body itself transformed into a prayer. I wanted to participate in that, to show others, to try and start una hermandad in Albuquerque.

I returned to the Catholic Church proper—no longer a priest but as a member of the laity like everyone else. This felt right too—I'd never been a good preacher, just a good believer. A former parishioner got me work doing landscaping for his uncle, and I found a place of my own near Atrisco on the other side of the river. I still thought of Gabriel often, prayed for him, but what more was there to do?

A little more than a year later, I was celebrating Viernes Santo with my hermanos. There weren't many of us, about a dozen, but no one who'd joined had left, and I rarely went more than a few weeks without someone else inquiring about initiation. Two of our three novitiates that year were women, and while that might've shocked me as a child, now it only seemed natural. The hermanos weren't about gender or sexuality, they were about devotion, and as hermano mayor, I felt free to change the traditions that had outlived their usefulness. I think Gabriel would've approved.

Our Calvario was a hill far up University Boulevard, near an almost-vacant area called Mesa Del Sol. The distance from the morada was shorter than in Española but no less grueling. There were few trees along the path, and the ground was rocky and barren. I liked it because our route barely passed through the city—there was no one to watch, no parading past tourists or gawkers, no invasive photographers. Just us and the hill, with no pretensions toward glamour, only piety and penitence. When prospective initiates asked me what they would get out of una hermandad, whether it was tradition or discipline or religious ecstasy, I would tell them one word—nothing. When pressed, I explained what my family never did: that there would be pain and suffering, hardship and humiliation, and that was it. That was the reward. Some understood and stayed, some didn't and left.

The weather that day was terrible. Water crashed down on our heads, coating the black hoods we wore and causing each of us to fall at least once, our white pants stained brown with mud. We heard thunder from all sides, lightning crashing down and igniting the cloud-darkened sky. Juan dragged the cross, carving a dike along the ground behind him. From the front, I set our pace, slightly worried about someone catching pneumonia if we stayed out too long.

Halfway to the top of el Calvario, I looked behind me to take stock of the hermanos. A few of them sang alabados you could barely make out over the storm, but most struggled to just keep up. Rather than the eleven hermanos I expected, though, I counted twelve. But I couldn't be sure whether I'd simply miscounted. Beneath that pouring rain, the hoods blended together. As we struggled up the path, I fell back and recounted, this time as carefully as I could. Still, twelve.

We reached the peak of el Calvario and began tying Juan to the cross.

"Stop being so lazy and help me with this knot," said a voice I thought I'd never hear again.

"Gabriel?" I shouted, though it was mostly lost in the storm.

"Quiet," he said. "This isn't about me, it's about Christ. And He's up there." He pointed at Juan up above us, who laughed and sobbed, tears joining the rain trailing down his face.

After what felt like ages, I asked Juan if he needed to come down, but he told us to keep him up. He was trembling as the elements battered his poor body, and I was tempted to take him down regardless, to make the choice I had in Española, to say that it was too much. But Gabriel put an arm on my shoulder and whispered, "Let him choose. It's only flesh."

When Juan was finally ready, we brought him down and went back along the same path, half sliding down the hill in our hurry. The storm had only gotten worse, but we felt triumphant and sang loudly over the wind and rain. I was bursting to ask Gabriel more, but while I did my best to keep an eye on him, at some point I lost track of which hermano he was beneath the black hoods. When we arrived back at the morada, it was only the other eleven hermanos and me—Gabriel had disappeared.

That was the last time I saw him in person, in the flesh. Because of his visitation, I decided to carve a permanent place for him in our morada, a santo to bless us on all our future crucifixions. It rests in one of the corners, not on the main altar but near Tomás, the doubter, and Esteban, the first martyr, ready whenever he wants to join us again.

FR. MICHAEL CARTER

His death was in all the newspapers. A prominent priest and activist murdered in front of hundreds? Rumors of FBI involvement? Rumors of the supernatural? A possible scandal with an ex-lover? A possible scandal with the Catholic Church? I couldn't blame reporters for using sensationalistic terms—even as a friend of Gabriel's, I was caught off guard by the strange circumstances surrounding his death. There was a sense of the surreal about all of it, a sense that his death occurred less in reality and more in the heightened drama of television and tabloids.

As time passed, the truth of what actually happened only became murkier, despite, or perhaps because of, the presence of so many witnesses. Their accounts varied wildly. One person said that Joshua, the confused-seeming man who killed him, had been wheeled in for healing but then drew a knife. Someone said Gabriel had been shot by a sniper and not stabbed at all. Several witnesses, or supposed witnesses, claimed to have seen a dim white light ascend from where Gabriel's body lay, though one claimed that a demonic black aura seeped into the ground. There were also quite a few sightings after he died: around the church, around the city, around other cities. I read one account of a nun in the Philippines who said his face appeared to her on a tree trunk in a convent garden, and it so surprised her that she accidentally broke her vow of silence.

One might think I would have tried to get to the bottom of this, to understand what truly happened to my devout but idiosyncratic friend. I did not. Rather, I followed the evolving story, watching as certain narratives emerged and became accepted as "facts." They told me little about Gabriel himself and much about the world at large. He became a cipher onto which people could project their faith or paranoia or outrage, developing whatever version of him they needed most.

Three weeks passed before I received his final letter. The address was in his handwriting. As for the delay, although I enjoy the pleasures of pulp novels as much as the next person, I have no reason to believe that the FBI or some similar organization tampered with it. Likely it was due to either post-office incompetence or seminary pettiness.

> *Dear Father Carter,*
>
> *I'm heartbroken about the impossibility of seeing you, but due to circumstances outside of my control, a trip to Kansas City isn't something I can make until at least the end of the year, if not much later. Our Lady of Guadalupe is very busy these days, and I recently had a series of visions, dreams at least, in which the Spirit revealed to me images of the future that leave me worried. Very worried, if I'm being completely honest, though I suppose only for selfish reasons. In any case, I fear to say much more about it, in case I might be misinterpreting them—God works in mysterious ways, and what's more mysterious than the future?*
>
> *But let's forget that doom and gloom. If we can't meet in person, we can still maintain a correspondence. I miss*

your guidance and wisdom, and know that due to my travels, our communication has become unfortunately one-sided. With that in mind, I thought I'd ask you for help in a spiritual matter I'm struggling with. A parishioner recently asked me about the Gospel of Thomas, which I must admit I'd only heard of in passing before. I was aware of the existence of other, apocryphal accounts of Christ's life, but I hadn't read them, or even thought about them, since college. The parishioner wanted to know whether this Gospel told the truth or not, and I had to answer that I didn't know—not only because I hadn't read it but also because even if I had, how could I tell?

I'm not sure what to make of these texts. I've now read a few, which kind souls have published online, including a Gnostic one that was particularly interesting. In any case, thinking about them has done more than a little to make me reconsider parts of my faith—not the core elements, of course, but certain philosophical tenets I'd thought little about before. I'm aware of the inconsistencies between the canonical Gospels, of course. Even the synoptics agree less about basic details than two drunk men arguing in a bar, but at some point, I must have internalized the idea that multiple versions could be right, or at least that none of them are wrong. Perhaps we've been limiting ourselves. Have you read any of these texts, and if so, could you tell me which are worth the time and which you think are filled with wholesale fabrication? I'm Catholic—regardless of what some within the church claim, we both know this to be true—but the Church is fallible, because all of us are fallible, and I can't help but think that there are elements of Christianity that I haven't fully considered.

With sincerest affection,
—Gabriel Romero

I assume that the visions he mentioned did, in fact, come to pass, and that these were the same visions Manuel Quintana and Anna Fishel shared with officials. I have little else to say about this part of the letter. What interests me is the rest. Had Gabriel known for certain what his visions meant, I do not believe he would have devoted so much of the letter to a scholarly subject about which I'm far from an authority. These were the words of a man convinced he had more time, eager to spend it enhancing his spiritual understanding. It was a letter full of curiosity, which is the opposite of morbidity.

In any case, Father, I hope this information has been helpful to you during the compilation of your positio. My own opinion is that Gabriel Romero was certainly a servant of God—whether or not the Church wishes to recognize that is, I suppose, up to you, but I do think it's worth considering that even to the end, he identified as Catholic. I hope you keep this in mind when deciding on the story of his life you wish to tell.

Now I hate to admit it, but I'm growing tired. I find even the simple act of remembering to be exhausting these days. If you have any more need of me, I will be here at the seminary, doing my best not to get in the way of the next generation of Jesuits. It might not be how I planned on spending my old age, but it leaves a lot of time for prayer, so I suppose I should be thankful. May the Grace of God be with you.

FR. PATRICK CONKLIN

It's getting late, Father—would you like a nightcap before finishing? Some wine? Or scotch? Nothing too fancy, but it is single malt—Macallan 18. No need to be shy. I don't drink much, of course, and never to excess, but when I do, I prefer to drink something worthwhile. Discussing Gabriel often makes me want a drink, no matter the time of day. I suppose we could drink to his memory, though that might be in poor taste.

Still, that would be fitting in a way, as I believe the only thing left for us to discuss is the end of his life, and my knowledge about these things comes largely second- or even third-hand. I did not see him again, did not visit his church or even attend his funeral. And while we may have had extreme theological disagreements, I was still saddened to hear of his passing. My hope had been that he would close his blasphemous church and return to Catholicism. We can only hope that God's mercy extended even unto him, at the last.

So what of his final days? It's certainly telling that of all Gabriel's preaching, the main thing that people remember is his final sermon. I understand why—it was recorded, it was dramatic, its form cribbed from the greatest sermon ever given—but the fact of the matter is that it also pinpoints the key heresies that separated his church from ours. While we Catholics try to respect and alleviate the pain and suffering of all humans, we do so from a Biblical standpoint. After all, it is the Word of God, and we respect it regardless of what may be politically correct.

Gabriel's words advocated a heretical relativism, a misdirected empathy that fuels the victimization complex held by today's youth. On the surface, it might seem the same as Christ's radical empathy, but in actuality it is firmly directed at overthrowing the Church and thereby antithetical to the beliefs of any real Catholic. This is the language of revolution, not resolution.

But I want to note that the real heresy here, the words that go fundamentally against everything the Church stands for, is what he said about abortion, which was so controversial that I'm certain many are unaware that he even said it. The transcribed version of his sermon that circulated most widely online—posted ad nauseam on Twitter and Facebook and chain emails—omitted that part entirely. Members of my own parish initially shared a version and discussed how much his sermon espoused Christ's views in the twenty-first century, completely unaware that abortion was ever mentioned. When I asked them to listen to the unedited audio, they found themselves horrified at what he said.

Let's put things as simply as possible: murder is a sin. To kill your own flesh and blood is even worse, and to murder your own defenseless child is truly beyond comparison. Don't get me wrong, the Lord can forgive this sin, as he can forgive all sins. But by placing it in his list of phony beatitudes, Gabriel gave it a kind of equivocation, not simply hiding the sin but assigning these murderers a place of honor. This is the danger of unorthodoxy. This is what happens when a silver-tongued trickster takes hold of the Good News and distorts its meaning into something absolutely against God's laws. The Church's hierarchical system may have its drawbacks, but it is set up in order to protect us from exactly this type of personality cult.

But let's look beyond that one misbegotten sermon and take final stock of Gabriel Romero and what he achieved on this earthly plane. As for his so-called miracles, in Matthew, Jesus warned us about false prophets who dissemble with signs and wonders. I do not believe Gabriel did half the things his followers claim he did, and most even sound like the urban legends they so assuredly are. And yet I hear that many have already folk-canonized him as a martyr. There seems to be a complete misunderstanding about what martyrdom entails—it is not just dying for your beliefs, as you well know, Father. It's dying for your belief *in Christ*. In what way was Gabriel murdered for defending his faith? Perhaps he was killed by the FBI, as some claim, or more likely by his spurned homosexual lover, which—given the content of that final sermon—seems far more likely to me. But what does any of this have to do with faith?

So where does that leave us? He has a small cult in Albuquerque and a few other places, particularly within the Hispanic community. Even in Las Cruces, though I'm ashamed to say it. Truly, though, he seems more popular with the secular than he ever was with the faithful, and it seems likely he'll become a folk-narco saint, the next Jesús Malverde or Juan Soldado. But none of this is important. Holiness is measured in how well we live by God's rules, His commandments, and here is where Gabriel utterly failed.

Thank you for your time, Father. I appreciate the effort put into this investigation, and I trust you will understand that everything I have said to you has been motivated not out of malice but simply out of concern for the continued sanctity and orthodoxy of the Church. Perhaps, before you leave tomorrow, I can interest you in taking a look at my most recent essay, which concerns one of Paul's more pertinent epistles—Second Thessalonians—and if you like it, you might send some good words up the line? I've always hoped to one day visit the Vatican, and even if no one around here appreciates scholarly work, I've always felt that perhaps God has greater things in mind for me. In fact, I'm certain of it.

ANNA FISHEL

We knew that there were folks who hated him. There was the man who stabbed him, obviously. He'd been close with Father Gabriel, and I'd seen them talking frequently after Mass. I think they even went to lunch together sometimes. I'd been glad he finally had a friend. But then this Josh turned out to work for the FBI. But there were others too. Those folks who picketed the Planned Parenthood and then picketed *us* after he spoke against them. A group of white supremacists who made threats toward him and other members of the parish but never actually did anything. Even folks in the Catholic Church seemed to have it out for him, particularly Archbishop Maldonado, who had a serious ax to grind when it came to Father Gabriel. Then there was a smattering of local politicians, union busters, NRA nutbags, and probably loads of other crazies who cropped up every now and then. You get a lot of hate for spreading a message of love. You get a lot of hate for acting out the words of Christ, who wasn't particularly popular in His day either.

But I didn't worry until he told me the prophecies, and even then he assured me there was no real risk. Knowing the government was watching Father Gabriel only made me prouder to be working with him—the FBI has attacked some of the greatest leaders in this country's history. Even when he was away, I didn't truly worry about Father Gabriel's safety. He'd always seemed, in some sense, untouchable. Even when we were out there protesting, he never seemed to have dirt on his shoes or wrinkles in his shirts or robes. Once he returned from his wanderings, I'd had this feeling ... I guess it was more a fantasy than a feeling, but anyway, I had this idea in my head that we'd be there together, in Our Lady of Guadalupe, until we were both old and gray. Maybe we'd move, get the money to build a new church, a real church made of stone and mortar that had never been used for anything but worship and that would last for decades or even centuries to come. We'd still drink coffee together every morning, maybe one day have the money to switch to something better than Folgers, and we'd chat before he left to work on his sermons. It's silly, I know ... but that's how I saw it happening.

Afterward, Father Manuel and I decided to close the church. We barely needed to discuss it—it had been Father Gabriel's church, and without him, it would always be an empty shell. So it was an easy decision, but it was still sad. Our Lady of Guadalupe had been my second home since I first walked through its doors. Now the building still sits vacant. My hope is that it gets demolished, every wall torn down, since nothing could ever replace Our Lady of Guadalupe in my heart.

Father Manuel and I both took it all pretty hard, as you might imagine. He stayed in my house for a while, sleeping on a foldout couch in the spare room I thought of as Duke's. He helped around the house, cooking and cleaning and watching TV with me. He took Duke for morning walks, and the two of them really got along. But without Father Gabriel around, there wasn't much for us to talk about. You might've thought we'd spend a lot of time praying, or reading the Bible, or something. Discussing Christ and Heaven and all that. I did grief counseling, and most of them told me how much that stuff helps. But anytime even a faintly religious subject peeked its way into our conversations, I put a stop to it. At that point, anything religious set me off. Just seeing a Bible, or a cross, or hearing Father Manuel whisper a Hail Mary before he went to bed. So instead, we both read a lot. He spent time carving in the backyard and did handyman work around the neighborhood, while I trudged off to the library for another pile of books, then brought them home and napped. All of a sudden, six months had passed, and he was moving out, while my savings had completely disappeared.

I kept in touch with some of the parishioners. That had always been my role at Our Lady of Guadalupe, and even after we closed the church, I sent out a weekly community email and kept our Facebook page active. At some point, I guess I mentioned kind of offhand that I was looking for a job, and someone on there told me they were hiring at the Walgreens not far from my house. At first it was weird to return to pharmacy work, but it's perfectly fine and pays the bills, and right now, where I am in life, that's all I'm really looking for.

The best part about it is that at five o'clock the day is done, so it never interferes with the real work I do, my passion project: a foundation in Father Gabriel's memory. We funneled the church's leftover money into it, which ended up being more than $100,000 after some generous souls felt particularly charitable during his funeral—I suppose it was a little tacky to pass the hat there, but it would've felt like a missed opportunity if we hadn't, and

I don't think anyone really minded. Our primary goal is to help local charities: the Roadrunner Food Bank, Catholic Charities of Central New Mexico, the ACLU. Our secondary purpose, at least as I see it—and as foundation director, I was able to write it into our bylaws—is to protect Father Gabriel's legacy.

This has been a bigger time sink than I would've initially thought. For one thing, the man who murdered Father Gabriel claimed to have had a longtime relationship with him. I'd seen him with Gabriel, as I said—he'd even introduced us—and I knew that Father Gabriel may have had relationships with men when he was younger. But that was before he'd become a priest, and what I knew for sure was that Father Gabriel would *not* have broken his holy vows. I know Father Gabriel was all about acceptance, but now it's up to me to preserve his legacy. And now this man is spreading lies about some sort of elaborate murder-suicide, which is just so ridiculous I shouldn't even have to debunk it, but I guess I do. Trust me, I knew Father Gabriel better than anyone. He was devoted, heart and soul, to God, and all these conspiracy theories about a hidden lover and nutso plots to get himself killed are evil, pure and simple.

The media wants a scandal, and that's particularly true when it comes to religious figures. The idea that someone could be a true believer and, even more than that, the idea that God might have singled him out for His blessing, is something the media can't understand. What *I* can't understand is why they're so focused on him, instead of all the horrible things the "real" Catholic priests have been doing in the shadows. That should be keeping them plenty busy, but it hasn't, so I, and the Father Gabriel Romero Foundation, have done our best to combat the hearsay, slander, and libel that have been committed against him. Shutting down scandalmongers is thankless but important work, and I'm glad to be able to serve Father Gabriel in this small way after all he did for us.

So between the foundation and my job, I'm as busy as ever, Father. But I have found time for one more thing. I've begun going to church again—though at an Episcopal place, St. Chad's, because I've had so many … experiences with the Catholics. No offense, Father. And I don't know, Chad's isn't like Our Lady of Guadalupe, not really, but the people there have welcomed me, and, I don't know, it's starting to feel a little bit like home. Just a little bit.

ISABEL ROMERO

I don't have many photos of my Gabito. It sounds weird to say it—there are photographs of him everywhere, after all. The ones I have, here in the house, are almost all from formal occasions. I have his first communion, where he wore a cute little suit with a red clip-on bow tie Mamá picked out for him. There's his high school graduation, where he tried to look adult and serious but just ended up looking goofy in a shiny green gown and cap. And of course there's his college graduation, wearing a red gown among an endless line of other red gowns, hunched over and nervous looking. None of them are terribly special. None of them have much to say about him. They're just pictures.

I have his old yearbooks stored in a box under his bed. I left his bedroom the way it was when he moved out, but after he passed, I went through it all, looking for traces of him, both the Gabito I knew and the one I never really understood, the one who burned his hands so many years ago without ever telling me why. None of his high school yearbooks have many signatures. The messages are all just "Have a great summer" or "Stay in touch," nothing worth reading. But the photos are pretty good. He's always smiling in them, an honest smile that makes you want to trust him. They're good pictures, but there aren't many of them, just four head shots and the orchestra group photos. Maybe I should've taken us to one of those fancy studios, but I just never wanted to. Even when Gabito was traveling and not calling me, I never felt the need to look at his photos. It's only now that he's gone, gone for good, that I wish I had more from when he was little, more ways to hold on to the memories.

Usually when I want to see him, I go online. There's a famous one of Gabito standing in the background while the president talks. It's always the same photo, though sometimes the lighting is much darker or lighter, I don't know why. My son looks stern, almost harsh in a way that's barely recognizable to me. It reminds me of how unhappy my boy could be, how much he took this broken world to heart. There's another photo of him in full priestly regalia, pointing at something we can't see, bright lights below and behind him. He looks fervent, like some firebrand ready to throw Satan out of the church by his horns. But my favorite one is from one of the protests. He's with two other people—a woman and a man I don't recognize and who I've never seen identified—and they're all standing off to the side, laughing. Behind them, you can see trucks and tents. I always preferred the candid photos, and this one seems to capture the son I actually knew. It's the one I look at to feel happy. The others just make me ... not sad exactly. Maybe depressed. Or lonely. I like them, because they're my son, and I miss him, but after I see them, I have to go lie down. They wipe me out.

The thing about all those pictures, even the ones I like, is how little they say about him. Like, photographs only capture a moment, and that moment doesn't tell us much. They say a picture's worth a thousand words, pero a thousand words are worthless when it comes to a human life. A thousand words couldn't describe the thoughts going through your head this minute, this second—not really. Whenever I look at a photograph of my son, my little Gabito who grew up to stand so tall and mean so much to so many people that thousands came to his funeral and thousands more wrote online about how big a loss his death was, how he was Christianity's shining star, lighting the way for Catholics in the twenty-first century with compassion and activism ... I just think of how meaningless those photos really are.

So usually I close my eyes and imagine him. I imagine him at whatever age I want, young or even old, the version of Gabito I'll never get to see, and even older—the version no mother gets to see. In my head, he is complete. Whole. His full personality, his memories, his history. He's not a two-dimensional image you can fold up and discard. I'm not interested in reducing him to a symbol, even if it felt like sometimes that was what he really wanted. I want to keep him human, unable to be contained by a thousand words or a million, and I want that to be the person you take away from me, from all of this.

When Gabriel was still a little Gabito, sometimes Mamá would read to him from the *Lives of the Saints*. It was an old leather volume, its golden edges long since faded to a sort of dirty brown. On the inside covers were two full-color stained glass re-creations—of which santos, I could never tell—and then a saint for every day. For every occasion. For every need or woe a person might have. There was even an index filled with hundreds more saints they'd left out. Sometimes I'd listen in on those stories, and I was struck by how much magic and mysticism and strangeness they contained and how utterly *boring* they were. Every last one of them. They felt two-dimensional, symbolic and phony.

I asked Mamá whether any of them ever existed, and she told me, "Of course they did. All of them."

"I doubt it," I said. "At least, if they did, they were nothing like in those stories."

"What do you mean? Of course they were," she said. "Didn't you pay any attention?"

"No one is like the people in those stories, Mamá. No one. Doesn't matter if they're a santo, those people sound like robots, doing good even when it makes no sense. When it's absolutely insane."

"That's what made them santos, mija."

"That's how I know they didn't exist."

She looked exasperated. "Sometimes the edges get sanded off a little bit. Maybe. They call them hagiographies because they're not exactly true. But they're not exactly false either. They happened."

There was no point in fighting with her. She was going to believe in her santos regardless of what I said. Pero still, that's been my worry for Gabriel, now that he's gone and there's no one to protect his memory. People on those TV news shows like saints, and they like sinners. They like categories, not real people. I worry that somehow the more images and quotes that all the jóvenes share on their phones, the less of him that exists. My Gabito, I mean, the one who actually lived, the one people who really knew him still remember.

But they'll do what they want with him, as will you, Padre, I suppose. All I can do is say my prayers every night, for his and Mamá's souls. I like to think they're up there in Heaven together, finally reunited, finally at peace. They always understood each other far more than I could.

Padre Quintana brought me a carving of Gabito, un santo he called it, though it seems … off to have one for your son, you know. Still, I appreciated the gesture, and it sits out in my garden, watching over the herbs he loved so much. Since he died, I stopped tending it, and I thought it would be overgrown without my help, but of course this is Albuquerque, so it's just a lot of dirt back there, dirt and a handful of weeds and my old tools slowly growing rusty.

In any case, Padre, I'm glad you came by. I'm always happy to talk about Gabito, so long as people are willing to really listen. Me? Well, that's kind of you to ask. I'm not ashamed to say I'm seeing a new man. His name is Andrés, and he works at the Bank of America over on Lomas. We don't see each other much, but that's good— he's younger than I am, and I worry if he saw me more, he'd get bored. This way I keep a little mystery in the relationship. Oh, and I'm thinking about finally leaving Kelly's if they don't give me a raise or promote me to manager. I know I told Gabriel that for years, but this time I'm serious. Maybe I'll do like they say online and pray to Gabito for his help. I mean, it can't hurt, right, and who knows? If he's really able to intercede and work all these milagros like everyone says, you'd think he'd at least spare a little bit of magic for his mother. But who can say, Padre, who can ever really say.

JOSHUA WHITEHURST

My lawyer told me not to talk to you, Father. And he's probably right. No good can come from my speaking with pretty much anyone, but especially a priest who's trying to put who knows what sort of spin on Gabriel's life. And if the media hears about your visit, I'm sure they'll make it look like you're only here so I can make confession. Or perhaps they'll fan the conspiratorial flames and say we were secretly colluding all along. Maybe both.

But I couldn't help myself. It gets lonely here, and I like your company. I like talking about Gabriel. My lawyer said that getting involved with your investigation, or whatever you call this, is ludicrous, but he's not a religious man, and he didn't know Gabriel. And I don't think he cares about anything other than getting me out. Which is good. That's what I pay him for, but I'm pretty sure he doesn't get what else is at stake here. I mean yes, there's the matter of the first-degree-murder charge, but he's assured me that won't stand, and who am I to doubt him?

What I have had reason to doubt was that any of this—the real Gabriel, his mission, his faith—would ever become known. Or worse, that it would be known but only in some twisted way, published online and in full-color tabloids, memorialized in sordid headlines and overcooked prose.

So that's why I'm talking to you. To tell you the truth, even if I don't expect you to believe much of what I've said. People choose to believe lies every day, after all. Evidence fails. Truth fails. It's what we believe that matters.

And beliefs change—I'm proof of that. I know I'm the Judas of this story—I've seen it in the papers, and it's even become my nickname in here, perverse as that sounds. At first I was horrified. But are you familiar with the Gospel of Judas, Father? You might not be, since the Catholic Church has tried to suppress this so-called heresy for centuries, but the Gnostics revered Judas. They believed that, rather than the ultimate betrayer, he was the one true believer, willing to follow his Savior in whatever He commanded, even into Hell itself. They believed Judas was reminded of how he was the "beloved disciple" of God, of Christ Himself. Hell, some even believed they were lovers. But, as I said, beliefs change. Your Church made sure of that.

Still, if you take away just one thing from all my stories, let it be this: I did what I did out of love. Gabriel used to say that Christ's one commandment, His only commandment, was to love Him, and I finally understand why. To love is to believe, unquestioningly, unreservedly. It's as simple as that. If I hadn't loved Gabriel, I never would have believed him. But I did love him. And so I was willing to believe in his visions, his miracles, maybe even his entire cosmology. I was willing to believe in him, even unto death, when it came down to it. I did what I did out of love, and while it's still a tragedy, that doesn't mean it wasn't everything Gabriel hoped.

ACKNOWLEDGMENTS

Thank you an infinite amount to Heather, as without your help and your refusal to let me give up, this book never would've been finished.

Jason Kirk, your excitement and faith (yes, I think that's the right word here) in me and this book can't be understated, and knowing this kept me going. It's such a privilege to work with an editor whose enthusiasm for a topic possibly even exceeds your own, and I'm truly thankful to have somehow found you as a partner in this crime.

Thanks again to Jesseca Salky for seeing a glimmer of a book and helping turn it into a reality.

Joe and June, thanks for the endless amounts of encouragement and patience. Not just while writing this book but always.

Thank you to Sue, Pat, and Miguel; without your help, this would've been a drastically worse book.

Matthew, I hope this book isn't too weird for you, and Daniel, I hope you're not too offended by it—feel free to skip this book and (God willing) read the next one instead.

Thanks to Nicholas Collura and Phillip Medrano for speaking with me about your experiences in seminary, I'm sure that everything I wrote is nevertheless wildly off base, but I think that's ok.

Thanks to Pete Schreffler for your support and flexibility.

Many thanks to Blake Foley and Charlie Lupica for endless distractions that kept me sane. Thanks to Ben Willow, Noah Gelb, Dailey Jackson, Alex Kolberg, and Sam Coulter. Thanks to everyone in the now-quite-large LAB, given all the kids you've had in just the last couple years. Thanks to Katherinna Mar, Jim Joyce, Sarah Kovach, David Prichard, and Chloe Stricklin.

And thanks, of course, to Tib, Lavender, Midnight, Skittles, and Tinka. Writing can be lonely work, but having you as goofy, fluffy companions has meant it doesn't have to be.

ABOUT THE AUTHOR

Sean Gandert is the author of the novel Lost in Arcadia. Born and raised in Albuquerque, New Mexico, he has an MFA in creative writing from Bennington College. A freelance writer and college-English instructor, he currently lives in Florida with his wife and an increasingly large pride of cats. For more information, visit www.seangandert.com.